MUSIC LOVER'S GUIDE TO
GREAT BRITAIN
& IRELAND

Guide to the Best Musical Venues, Festivals & Events

GW00507184

Anne Bianchi • Adrie..... ⌐.......

Printed on recyclable paper

PASSPORT BOOKS
a division of *NTC Publishing Group*
Lincolnwood, Illinois USA

Library of Congress Cataloging-in-Publication Data

Bianchi, Anne, 1948–
    Music lover's guide to Great Britain & Ireland: guide to the best musical venues,
festivals & events/Anne Bianchi, Adrienne Gusoff.
        p. cm.
    Includes index.
    ISBN 0-8442-9006-8
    1. Musical landmarks—Great Britain—Guidebooks. 2. Musical landmarks—
Ireland—Guidebooks. 3. Music festivals—Great Britain—Guidebooks. 4. Music
festivals—Ireland—Guidebooks. 5. Concerts—Great Britain—Guidebooks.
6. Concerts—Ireland—Guidebooks. 7. Opera—Great Britain—Guidebooks.
8. Opera—Ireland—Guidebooks. 9. Great Britain—Guidebooks. 10. Ireland—
Guidebooks. I. Gusoff, Adrienne. II. Title.
ML21.G7B5 1995   95-38535
780.78'41—dc20   CIP
                                                                             MN

PHOTOGRAPHIC CREDITS

Michael Goldfried Front cover: top left, center, lower right; spine, 1, 21, 30, 66, 72,
75, 121, 123, 144, 219, 232, 247, 258, 285, 289, 305; **British Travel Association**
Front cover: top right, 10, 48, 103, 187, 191; **Black Cat Rythmn Band** 33; **Virgin
Records/David Schienmann** 43; **Hannibal Records/Paul Slattery** 53; **EMI
Records** 86, 131, 240; **Atlantic Records** 99; **Temple Records** 135; **Gavin Evans** 151;
Steorra 182; **Nancy Carlin Associates** 209; **Timothy Phillips** 216; **Tara Records**
281, 286, 301; **Gift Horse** 245; **Telarc** 237; **Windham Hill** 262; **Vanguard
Recording Society** 270; **Island Records** 308

TEXT CREDIT

Material from *The Commitments*, pp. 249–253, used courtesy of
Beacon Communications

Cover design by Nick Panos
Interior design by Ellen Pettengell

Published by Passport Books, a division of NTC Publishing Group,
4255 West Touhy Avenue, Lincolnwood (Chicago), Illinois 60646-1975
©1996 Anne Bianchi, Adrienne Gusoff

5 6 7 8 9 VP 0 9 8 7 6 5 4 3 2 1

Contents

Northern Ireland

Northern Ireland — 305

Acknowledgments

Many, many thanks to all who helped us with their time and recollections, especially Nicki Perry, New York's "unofficial British Ambassador" and owner of the city's premier British expatriot and Anglophile hang-out, Tea & Sympathy, who seems to know *Everyone* in the music biz. Special thanks to Suzy Sureck (Wales) and Beth Seriff (Ireland), who generously took time from their vacations to do some fact gathering for us. To Ned Sherrin of London for generously giving his time. To the folks at Tardis Sound in Edinburgh, everyone at the High St. Hostel in Edinburgh, Steven in Dublin, Steven in Glasgow, Petie in Doolin, John and John in Liverpool and the Carboni family in London.

And last, but far from least, a resounding "Ya done good!" to Michael Goldfried, our assistant, researcher, photographer and man-on-the-scene, who provided so much texture, humor and detail to this book. A million thanks! We couldn't have done it without you!

To the best of our knowledge, all information in this book was correct at the time of writing. If you find that some of these venues have closed their doors, or if you come upon interesting new places to hear music or discover a wonderful performer or group, we would love to hear about them, so that we may update future editions.

Anne Bianchi
Adrienne E. Gusoff

ENGLAND

London and Environs

It is difficult to imagine, when visiting the country today, that England was long considered a "land without music." With the exception of Henry Purcell (1563–1626), Britain had few native-born composers who contributed significantly to Western classical music from the seventeenth through the eighteenth centuries. England, however, attracted foreign-born composers of great stature. Handel considered the country his home after 1713, and the British certainly take him for their own. J. C. Bach, who also lived in England during the latter part of the same century, was known as "The English Bach." Mozart's first symphony was composed on a visit to Chelsea as a child. By the late nineteenth century, with the well-loved comic operas of native sons Gilbert and Sullivan being performed worldwide, Britain could finally claim to be a major musical force.

Although England can't boast the sheer number of early classical masters as can, for example, Austria, Germany or Russia, the English are without doubt some of the most well-trained and appreciative connoisseurs of classical music, including early music played on original instruments, in the world today. London concert halls are among the best in the world, and the classical recording companies in the United Kingdom have taken on some very impressive projects such as Hyperion recording of Leslie Howard's performances of the complete works of Franz Liszt. The BBC Proms concerts, famous the world over, are broadcast as far away as China.

The 1960s produced a whole new breed of British musicians, who absorbed the American rock and roll of Elvis Presley, Chuck Berry and Buddy Holly and the blues of Robert Johnson, Otis Redding and

Ray Charles, to name just a few, and made them their own. Exported to the United States, the music became "The British Invasion," giving the world a generation of immortal musicians—the Beatles, the Rolling Stones, Eric Clapton and many others. Since then, British rock has pretty much ruled the world, bringing to the vernacular "punk rock," "glam" and "rave."

While the United Kingdom made it through America's "Jazz Age" without showing much interest in the form, musicians and listeners have started making up for this lapse with a vengeance during the past fifteen years or so. Jazz festivals now proliferate throughout Great Britain. The prestigious Blue Note label recently signed its first British musician, vibraphonist Orphy Robinson.

As long as we've mentioned festivals: Britain has more music and arts festivals than there are tea leaves in Harrod's. It seems as if every town, no matter how small, has at least one such celebration during the year, and the big festivals, Glastonbury and Reading are two, are a true English phenomenon. Usually held over a weekend, tens of thousands of people gather to hear hundreds of performers on dozens of stages and in scores of tents. The primarily young audience generally stays for the duration, pitching tents in makeshift campgrounds. Imagine Woodstock, five times a year! Of course, there are plenty of sedate—even elegant—classical festivals as well with performances held in ancient castles and Victorian and Georgian theaters.

From British folk to world, from hard-driving house to dignified chamber recitals, from angelic church choirs to relaxing, almost-formless ambient music, truly, for the music lover, Great Britain has something for every taste.

Londoners are some of the most sophisticated consumers of music in the world. Is it any wonder the world's largest record megastores were born here? Appreciation of music cuts across all age and socioeconomic classes—just witness the crowds at the Henry Wood Promenade Concerts—"The Proms." London concert halls are among the finest on the planet, hosting both internationally renowned stars as well as talented new performers. Many of the world's finest orchestras call London home including Michael Tilson Thomas's London Symphony Orchestra, Klaus Tennstedt's London Philharmonic, Neville Mariner's Academy of St. Martin-in-the-Fields, Giuseppe Sinopili's Philharmonia Orchestra, Vladimir Ashkenazy's Royal Philharmonic Orchestra and the BBC Symphony Orchestra.

And there are probably more rock venues in London than in the whole of several other countries combined. Jazz clubs are popping up everywhere and world music has found an appreciative audience among young and old alike. To find out what's going on musically while you're in the city and who's playing where at what time, pick up a copy of *Time Out* or *What's On,* both of which have detailed entertainment listings.

⚙ Test Your Musical I.Q.

They were born with these names, but they're better known as...

1. Peter Noone
2. Gordon Sumner
3. David Robert Jones
4. Marie McDonald McLaughlin Lawrie
5. Barry Moore
6. Frederick Bulsara
7. John Beverley
8. Harry Roger Webb
9. Folosade Adu
10. John Lydon
11. Declan Patrick MacManus
12. Clementina Dinah Campbell
13. Stuart Goddard
14. George O'Dowd
15. Reginald Kenneth Dwight

(Answers on page 34.)

CONCERT HALLS
Classical and Opera

London has scores of concert halls, some dedicated exclusively to classical music. This listing is just a sample of some of the major classical venues. Look at a copy of *Time Out* or another local periodical for a comprehensive directory.

Royal Albert Hall (Kensington Gore, SW7, info: 071/589-8212, tickets: 071/923-9998; South Kensington tube). Open daily 9 a.m.–9 p.m. Tickets are also available from Ticketmaster: 071/379-4444.
Royal Festival Hall (South Bank Arts Centre, info 071/928-3002, box

office 071/928-8800; Waterloo or Embankment tube, across Hungerford footbridge). Home of the London Philharmonic and the Philharmonia Orchestra, the spectacular Royal Festival Hall is reputed by classical music lovers everywhere to have the best acoustics of any recital hall in the world. Built in 1951 for the Festival of Britain Exhibition, it, along with **Queen Elizabeth Hall** and the **Purcell Room** (same phone numbers as listed earlier), comprise the **South Bank Arts Complex.** The season is year-round, so you're likely to find a concert at one of the halls in the Complex on any given night. There are also frequent free lunchtime concerts in the foyer, from jazz to jump-jive, from classical to flamenco. Tickets range from £3–£25. Student standby tickets go on sale two hours before concert time and are available at the lowest price for that performance.

WHERE IT'S AT | **ROYAL ALBERT HALL**

Built in 1871, this magnificent concert hall was the dream of Prince Albert, Queen Victoria's royal Consort, a man devoted to education and public affairs, who envisaged it as a forum for the advancement of both the arts and sciences. Unfortunately, Albert died before construction actually began, but his vision was kept alive by Henry Cole, the prince's scientific and artistic advisor. The building was finally completed ten years later. At that time, it boasted the world's largest dome. It also housed the world's biggest organ, which is still considered one of the finest ever built.

The original Charter, by Queen Victoria in 1866 and amended several times since by Acts of Parliament, designated specific activities for which Albert Hall was to provide a home, including both national and international congresses for arts and sciences, conferences of arts and science societies, and national and international exhibitions. Also featured on the list were performances of music, especially the organ.

Over the years, the acoustics and lighting have been modified and improved to near technical and acoustic perfection. "Spaceship" discs installed on the ceiling in the late 1960s eliminated an annoying echo. Technical improvements, which reduced lighting changes from the previous twelve hours to a mere two, have drastically

improved turnaround time for performances. Despite these technical changes, the interior appearance of the hall remains virtually
unchanged.

This elegant hall accommodates an audience of thirty thousand
and is used for a wide variety of performances including musical
(from rock to classical concerts), sporting events (basketball to sumo
wrestling, tennis to a marathon), ice shows, charity events, fashion
and awards shows. (During a 1967 visit to the Albert Hall by the late
rock legend Frank Zappa and his Mothers of Invention, the keyboard
player climbed up to what Zappa called "the mighty Albert Hall
organ" and belted out that old audience favorite, "Louie, Louie.")

The Albert Hall is probably most famous for the BBC Henry
Wood Promenade Concerts, commonly called "The Proms," held
here each summer from July to September since 1941, when the
Proms's former home, Queen's Hall, was destroyed by German
bombs. Tickets start at £2, making the music of some of the world's
most illustrious performers affordable to the general population.
Long ticket lines encourage instant friendship, and this sense of easy
camaraderie and festiveness permeates the entire Prom season.

Closing night at the Proms is the main event of the season.
Exuberant attendees are chosen by lottery, and only those who've
been to at least five other Prom concerts are eligible for the drawing.
The last-night audience, with faces traditionally painted like the
Union Jack, raise their voices in a moving version of "Land of Hope
and Glory," closing with a rousing chorus of "Jerusalem."
Outrageous dress and behavior are the norm, and even the performers join the festivities. In 1985 Sarah Walker dramatically unfurled a
British flag hidden in her dress. Kiwi diva Dame Kiri Te Kanawa
pulled a similar stunt by whipping out a New Zealand flag. And in
1993 Della Jones's outfit included a Welsh dragon.

The Wigmore Hall (36 Wigmore St., W1, 071/935-2141; Bond St.
or Oxford Circus tube) is a smaller, more-intimate setting offering
top-notch solo performances and chamber groups. Many music
lovers prefer the churchlike, almost reverent atmosphere of

Wigmore to the grandness of the bigger halls. Tickets range from £5–£15 or, for lowest prices, go standby one hour before performances. Another mostly classical hall is **Barbican Centre** (Silk St., EC2, 071/638-4141; Barbican/Moorgate tube) with a varied program ranging from Bach to contemporary composers conducting their own works. Tickets are £5 to about £50, depending upon the performance.

SPOTLIGHT ON   THE BACH CHOIR

The Bach Choir was founded in 1876, conducted by Otto Goldschmidt, husband of Jenny Lind, "The Swedish Nightingale." Their first complete performance was Bach's *B Minor Mass*, the first time it was performed in England. In their more than a century, they've only had a handful of musical directors including Sir Adrian Boult, Ralph Vaughn Williams and Walford Davies.

The choir comprises more than 250 singing members, all of them amateurs, from every walk of life. Each must undergo a rigorous audition and be reauditioned every three years (no cheating up there in the back).

In addition to having an impressive catalog of recordings including Mathias's *Lux Aeterna, O Come All Ye Faithful,* a collection of Bach Choir family carols, and Vaughn Williams's *Sancta Civitas,* the choir has also sung backup for Mick Jagger. They perform regularly at most of the major concert halls in London and the U. K., and put in appearances across the globe. The choir is funded by donations and benefactors, both corporate and private. If you'd like to become a Friend of the Choir (with all accompanying special privileges), write to The Bach Choir Friends, 2 Little Cloister, Westminster Abbey, London SW1P 3PL, England.

For opera lovers, there's the elegant **Royal Opera House** (Bow St., WC2, 071/240-1066; Covent Garden tube), which is home to both the Royal Opera and the Royal Ballet. This is the place to hear international stars of the opera world. Seats go for as little as £1 up to £25. For advance purchases, visit the box office at 48 Floral St., from

10 a.m.–8 p.m. **English National Opera** (London Coliseum, St. Martin's Lane, WC2, 071/836-3161 for reservations or 071/240-5258 for bookings by credit card; Charing Cross or Leicester Sq. tube) is a government-supported company that performs in English. Ticket prices start at £8.50.

SPOTLIGHT ON   PROMS HIGHLIGHTS OVER THE YEARS

1885   The original Proms concerts are almost stalled due to financial problems. Saving the day is Dr. George Cathcart, a Harley Street throat specialist, whose friend, Scots baritone W. A. Peterkin, was a voice student of opera conductor Henry Wood. Cathcart agrees to underwrite the concerts at Queen's Hall, but only if Henry Wood conducts Wagner. At the time, it was unheard of for an Englishman to conduct the German composer, but conduct Wagner he does. Thus begin the traditional Monday night performances of Wagner, amounting to nearly five thousand performances to date.

1895   The first concerts cost a shilling (5p). Back then, the shilling was worth the equivalent of today's £22! By comparison, concerts are considerably cheaper today at only £3.

1896   Tchaikovsky's *Nutcracker Suite* is heard for the first time in Britain during extra Saturday night Proms.

1911   Henry Wood becomes Sir Henry Wood.

1913   Wood opens orchestra positions to women.

1914   First appearance by Solomon, an eleven-year-old pianist who "appealed tremendously to the audience with his winning, soulful eyes, his little silk shirt and short knickers."

1926   Robert Newman, manager of Queen's Hall since its opening in 1893, originator of the Proms, and the man who chose the then-twenty-six-year-old Henry Wood as conductor, dies.

1930   The BBC Orchestra takes over the Proms from the Queen's Hall Orchestra, which abandons the concert series due to financial problems. Also, the first complete performance of Beethoven's Ninth Symphony with the chorus is heard. Until then, lack of funds had precluded the additional personnel.

1935 Sir Henry Wood appoints the Proms's first female orchestra leader, Marie Wilson.

1939 World War II interrupts the Proms when the BBC Symphony Orchestra is moved to Bristol, then Bedford, for security purposes.

1941 In May, German bombs destroy Queen's Hall. Concerts are moved to the Albert Hall. For reasons of security, the BBC declines to sponsor the Proms during these war years and Wood forms a temporary partnership with a private promoter, Keith Douglas.

1942 The BBC picks up the reins of the Proms once again.

1944 Wood, now seventy-five, is made Companion of Honour. Illness had prevented him from summoning the energy needed to lead an orchestra for several years, but on July 28 he finds the strength to conduct his final concert of Beethoven's Seventh Symphony. Sir Adrian Boult says it sounds like "the work of some brilliant young conductor in his early 40s." Wood dies on August 19.

1945 The Proms are officially renamed "The Henry Wood Promenade Concerts."

1947 Because there are over 10,000 hopefuls for the 6,800 seats, large, revolving "sweepstakes" drums are used to distribute tickets for the first and final nights.

1953 "Sea Songs," which have been a staple since 1905, are removed from the program but the public protests in the form of banners, defaced posters, and shouts from the audience. Finally, the songs are restored as an encore and continue to be a favorite fixture.

1964 The first appearance of television cameras causes quite a disturbance in the orchestra pit, as musicians change seats for every piece, striving to be seen on the small screen.

1966 The first opera to fill an entire evening's program is performed, as the Glyndebourne Festival introduces its production of *Don Giovanni*. The opera has been a tradition ever since.

1966   The first foreign orchestra—The Moscow Radio Symphony—visits the Proms and paves the way for others, changing the Proms forever from exclusively British to international.

1974   During a performance of Orff's *Carmina Burana,* one of the singers faints. Fortunately, a student named Patrick McCarthy knows the score and comes to the rescue by finishing the part.

1985   A broken piano lift delays Bartok's *Second Piano Concerto,* eventually played by Peter Donohoe, by nearly forty-five minutes, while the BBC continues to broadcast live. In the interim, radio announcer John Holmstrom carries on like a trouper, filling in the time creatively with the latest sports scores, readings and so on.

1993   A heavy downpour combines with a hole in the roof to make a soggy mess of the stalls and the arena. Londoners, however, are used to unexpected showers, and soon the hall fills with a colorful explosion of umbrellas.

1994   The Proms celebrate their one hundredth season.

Last night of the Proms—the Albert Hall

CLUBS AND DISCOS
Rock

As anywhere, different clubs attract different types of crowds, so, depending upon whom you ask, the same club might get a rave review from one music lover and a pan from another. Also, just as in any big city, what's hot one month, is outré the next, so it's best to ask around among those who seem mostly likely to share your tastes.

Most clubs offer "one-nighters," with the type of music, the crowd and the dress code changing drastically from night to night. A recent scan of the schedule for one club showed a '60s psychedelic music fest on Thursday, a jazz dance party on Friday and blues and zydeco on Sunday. It's best to check the schedules in *Time Out* or *What's On* before deciding where you want to party. *Take note:* public transportation shuts down long before most clubs start to cook and taxis aren't always easy to find, so plan ahead, transportationwise, by carrying with you the phone numbers of some of the radio-dispatched cab companies.

FOCUS ON   ROCK

A glossary of (mostly) rock terms (thanks to Jay Stiler, New York City musician/producer, for assistance with musical genres)

ambient   light, listenable, evocative music with a vague structure and unimposing sound; meant to be atmosphere rather than foreground. Brian Eno is a major influence, from Roxy Music to *Music for Airports* to his production work with U2.

British invasion   used to describe the dominance of English bands on the American music charts in the mid-1960s. After years of U. S. dominance in rock and roll with the do-wop, girl groups, rockabilly and R&B hits of the late '50s and early '60s, suddenly fans were screaming and girls were fainting for the Beatles, the Rolling Stones, the Kinks, the Animals, the Yardbirds, Herman's Hermits and the Dave Clark Five.

buskers   street musicians.

glam   a style of dress, very effeminate and flashy, perhaps including for example three-inch platform shoes and tight satin clothing, adopted for the most part by hard rock and pop bands. Marc Bolan was an early influence.

gothic   gloom and doom. An update of punk attitude with a gothic (think Morticia Addams) look and feel, exemplified by Sisters of Mercy.

house   originally an American inner-city dance club mix including '60s and '70s R&B, funk and hip hop beats and featuring relentless drums. Usually present is a steady, pounding 4/4 beat with a kick on every beat.

industrial   a reflection of chaos and despair over postindustrial greed and corruption in modern society. This most recent update of punk attitude relies on sophisticated equipment and programming and screamed vocals; typically noisy and distorted over complex and harsh technoid tracks. Representative groups: Cabaret/Voltair, Nitzer Ebb.

Mersey Beat or **beat music**   the rock sound that came out of Liverpool in the mid-'60s, so named because the Mersey River flows through that city. The hallmarks of the Mersey Beat are a very listenable quality with tuneful melodies, vocal harmonies, and easy to understand lyrics mostly about teenage love. Mersey Beat exemplars were the Beatles, Herman's Hermits and Gerry and the Pacemakers ("Ferry Across the Mersey").

punk   a reaction to the bloated corporate rock scene in the late '70s; meant to shock and insult playfully. The look—short, spiked hair and outrageous fashions—had as much or more impact than the music, best illustrated by the Sex Pistols and the Clash.

rave music   music usually played at a rave. May be techno, house, even orchestral records speeded up by the DJ to 130–270 beats per minute. Includes a heavy emphasis on psychedelia, hallucinogens being a big influence.

skiffle   the equivalent of the American jug band with washboards, tub basses and other such "instruments," playing mostly American country and folk music; popular in the mid-'50s.

techno   evolved out of house; employs harsh, noise-oriented, discordant keyboard sounds. Originally meant to shock and convolute.

trad session   traditional folk pick-up session, usually held in a pub.

trance dance   more natural and orchestral sounds and world music beats. Repetitive motifs are intended to produce alpha waves in the brain and coax the body into a relaxed and meditative state.

For the biggest names in popular music check out these clubs: **The Grand** (St. John's Hill, Clapham Junction, SW11, 071/738-9000; Clapham Jct. British Rail station [BR]) offers a wide variety of popular music nearly every night, such as Lonnie Liston Smith, Herbie Hancock, The Verve, Brazil's Joyce, and John Hiatt. Tickets range from £7 to about £15. Credit card bookings can be made by calling 071/284-2200 or through ticket agencies around town. After the live show on Friday nights it's Disgraceland and on Saturdays it's Club Night at the Grand. Voted "Venue of the Year 1993," the **Forum** (9–7 Highgate Rd., NW5, 071/284-2200; Kentish Town tube) also offers an impressive lineup of big-name acts from all over the world such as Oumou Sangare et Quatre Etoiles, The Australian Doors, Crash Test Dummies and John Mayall and the Bluesbreakers.

Other schedules well worth checking out are those of **Academy Brixton** (211 Stockwell Rd., SW9, 071/924-9999; Brixton tube) for popular rock; and **Apollo Hammersmith** (Queen Caroline St., W6, 081/416-6080; Hammersmith tube), a large venue for rock and pop talent. **Shepherds Bush Empire** (Shepherds Bush Green, W12, 081/740-7474; Shepherds Bush tube), another rock favorite.

Subterrania (12 Acklam Rd., Ladbroke Grove, W10, 071/282-2200; Westbourne Park tube). On Fridays and Saturdays after midnight this seems to be *everybody's* first choice. Subterrania attracts a mixed crowd who've definitely come to dance. Subterrania offers both live bands and the fabulous funky, jazzy, soulful DJed tunes of Jez Nelson on Saturday nights. Fridays are absolutely fabulous; the crowd is decked out in the most outrageous outfits, somewhere between the Miss Universe pageant and a football locker room. The music is a blend of soul, disco and rock. Dress is casual (except, of course, for Fridays) and the atmosphere relaxed. Admission ranges from £5–£10, depending on the performers. Occasional discount offers are available with advertisements. Reserve with credit cards by calling the box office or Ticketmaster (071/344-4444), or pick up tickets at Tower or HMV Records in Greater London.

The Limelight (136 Shaftesbury Ave., WC2, 071/434-0572; Leicester Sq. tube) has recently reopened with so many changes in decor, lighting, sound system, and management and ownership that it's a virtually new place. You can choose between The Dome and Club VIP, and on any given night you may hear house, garage, scream, dance, progressive house, jeep, urban, rap or swingbeat soul classics. Admission prices range from £5 before 11 p.m. to £10, depending on the DJ, MC and band, or a combination of these, with discounts frequently offered with flyers or advertisements, which are easily found around town.

POP QUIZ 1

Which of these bands did *not* have roots in John Mayall's Bluesbreakers? Mark-Almond Band, Cream, Ten Years After, Rolling Stones, Fleetwood Mac, Led Zeppelin, Humble Pie

ANSWER: Ten Years After

The **Marquee** (105 Charing Cross Rd., WC2, 071/437-6601; Tottenham Ct. Rd. tube) has been around *forever* it seems (actually, thirty-five years) and has always been a midsize, live-music venue for big-name rock bands—many, such as the Rolling Stones, before their names became household words. But even a successful club has to keep up with the times, so they've added several popular club nights (Thursday–Saturday), which change seasonally, making the Marquee one of the most popular venues for the over-eighteen leather-and-fishnet crowd. The music changes nightly with an emphasis on indie, rock, heavy, classic, and alternative. Not exactly a quiet night out, but energy abounds. The admission price varies, and there's a £1 discount for advance tickets. The Marquee is open until 6 a.m. on Saturdays.

Astoria (157 Charing Cross Rd., WC2, 071/434-9592; Tottenham Ct. Rd. tube) is a live-music venue during the week for harder-than-average rock and an audience teeming with purple-haired, pierce-lipped London youth. On most Saturdays, however, it undergoes a metamorphosis to become the scene of a hard-core rave. It's the perfect place for it, too, with two dance floors that hold about 1,600 and lots of room on the balcony above to chill out and watch the action. The club has a stated policy banning drugs and weapons, which may make you wonder what goes on at places where such is *not* the policy. Entry ranges from £7–£15, depending on the promoter. Bottled lager goes for about £2.30, mineral water for £1 and fast food is available to fuel your partying body and dancing feet until the 8 a.m. closing.

For an eclectic range of music with a great Tex-Mex menu, try **Break for the Border** (5 Goslett Yard, WC2, 071/287-1441; Tottenham Ct. Rd. tube). Live bands perform every night from 8 p.m., followed by a DJed party until 3 a.m. The tequila and beer flow like water, and the experience is a nearly guaranteed good time out. The admission is free except Friday and Saturday after 11 p.m. when there's a £4 entry fee. Dress and attitude are casual.

One of the most enduring and popular live-music clubs in London is **Borderline** (Orange Yard, W1, 071/734-2095; Tottenham Ct. Rd. tube) with a long list of impressive performers including Pearl Jam, REM, Suede and Lenny Kravitz (in his very first appearance in the U. K.). Its small size (the club accommodates fewer than three hundred) makes this a terrific place to experience big-name bands, which usually command much larger, less-intimate spaces. Even if the band playing is one you haven't heard of yet, chances are it's up-and-coming and you'll be able to tell everyone you saw them way back when. After the live gigs, the bands on stage are replaced by the wilder, more self-assured dancers, leaving the spacious dance floor to those who just want to dance in a relaxed and informal atmosphere. If you tire of jumping around, there's lots of space to chill or play a few games of pinball. By midnight the queue winds around the block, and the line inches along slowly as only one person is allowed to enter for every person who leaves. The admission ranges from £2–£6. Liquid and solid refreshments are available. Open Wednesday–Saturday until 3 a.m.

With theme nights, uplifting music and a "positive attitude only" policy at the door, **The Gardening Club** (4 The Piazza, WC2, 071/497-3153; Covent Garden tube) is one of the most popular clubs not just in London, but in the entire U. K. This interesting club, decorated with more drapery than Tara, not only changes themes each weeknight but offers one unique club night each month, Sunday being Queer Nation. The entry tab ranges from £5–£12 with beers going for about £2.50. The club also has a cappuccino bar. Open all week, weeknights until 3 a.m., Saturday and Sunday until 6 a.m., the line is long so be prepared to wait. Remember: don't bother going unless you're feeling upbeat. The folks at the door can spot bad vibes at one hundred paces.

If you're gay and it's the first Monday of the month, you simply *must* check out Kinky Gerlinky at **Equinox** (Leicester Sq., WC2, 071/437-1446; Leicester Sq. tube), a carnival-like, fabulous, freak-gown ball. It's truly a sight to behold. On any other night of the month, this club is still one of the best discos in the West End.

If you want to party until long after the rest of the town has awoken and opened shop never leaving the place you are in, visit the **Ministry of Sound** (103 Gaunt Street, SE1, 071/378-6528; Elephant and Castle tube). While enjoying a warehouse decor with sets that change frequently, you can move to hard house and garage music that you can feel in every cell of your body. Choose any one of three huge dance floors, take a break and lie back on some cushions to catch a flick at the cinema, or just stand back and enjoy the laser show. Top-name DJs keep this place pumping until 9 or 10 a.m., though the club is usually packed by 1 a.m. (Doors open around midnight.) Perhaps one reason the crowd is able to stay open so late—and this is just a guess—is that the Ministry's huge bars serve no alcohol, but they do serve plenty of energy-rich natural juices and psychoactive concoctions. Entry is £10–£12. Expect very long lines and serious security at the door enforcing a strictly over-twenty-one policy. But once you're past all that, you'll have a great time.

Was that a nine-foot whale's tail you saw in the middle of the dance floor? If it was, you've been to **Raw** (112a Great Russell St., WC1, 071/637-3375; Tottenham Ct. Rd. tube), a hot and sexy club with a distinctive aquatic motif. Open five nights a week, Wednesday–Sunday, each night has its own theme. Wednesday, it's Barbarella for "Queens of the Galaxy," where more come to be seen than to see. Thursday, you'll hear classic '70s soul, funk and disco while Friday is progressive house night. Saturday, it's Belly Button, featuring a wide range of danceable hits from garage to euro house and more. Keep your eyes peeled for the French Maid who hands out goodies and, yes, belly button wipes. Sunday, there's underground garage and hardcore. If you want to make it past the door, your dress and attitude must be sexy. The entrance fee is £8. Open until 5 a.m.

If it's rave you crave, try **Paradise** (105 Parkfield St., N1, 071/354-9993; Angel tube), which features an all-night rave revue on Saturdays until 10 a.m. There's a bar, of course, and snacks are available to keep your energy up. Entry is £10.

POP QUIZ 2

Elvis is The King, but who is God?

ANSWER: Eric Clapton

In a Victorian meeting hall complete with stage, balconies and high ceilings, adjacent to the University of North London, is **Rocket** (U. of N. London, Holloway Rd., 071/700-2421; Holloway Rd. tube), an incongruous, yet highly successful, location for raves and other club nights. Depending on when you go (and themes change radically from day to day and month to month), you might find yourself amid a wild, psychedelic, music-and-laser-induced trip or in the midst of salsa and lambada lessons at Club Brazil (every Wednesday). There are also plenty of one-nighters, so check the club listings. Admission charges vary widely, from £4 Wednesday, £7–£10 Friday and £10–£13 Saturday. Open until 6 a.m. Friday and Saturday.

Have a hankering to dance your pants off while the rest of London is reading their morning paper? Stricken with happy feet while everyone else is having tea? Not to worry. **Turnmills** (63b Clerkenwell Rd., EC1, 071/250-3409; Farringdon tube) is open twenty-four hours, and once inside you can lose all track of time. Turnmills attracts a varied crowd, including lots of neighbors from across the English Channel. This club-bar-cafe has a three-hundred-person dance floor (though the rest of the club accommodates far more people). The entry charge ranges from £6–£10.

If you're prepared to stand in line for hours to experience one of London's hottest clubs, check out **Club UK** (The Arndale Centre, Buckhold Rd., SW18, 081/877-0110; Wandsworth tube). The club attracts hordes that transcend age, sex and class barriers. The very impressive sound system in the Pop Art Room could blast you right out of your shoes, grinding out perpetual hard house. The Chill-out Room (aka the sex room) looks as if it were copped off the set of *Caligula*, though the traffic flow through here precludes any kind of relaxation or intimacy for any but the truly brain dead or wildly exhibitionistic. In the darker Disco Room, a partylike atmosphere prevails. Snacks (burgers and such) are available, and entry price runs about £10–£12. Open until 6 a.m. weekends.

Underworld (174 Camden High St., NW1, 071/482-1932; Camden Town tube) is young and retro and offers a good bargain at

£4 entry. Monday nights are Bubblicious with live bands and guests, while Thursdays are Hazard County—classic rock, disco, retro-garage, some industrial and rap. The club closes at 3 a.m.

For a break from pounding beats and up-to-the-minute trends, visit **Wildes** (13 Gerrard St., W1, 071/494-1060; Leicester Sq. tube) where an unpretentious crowd of mostly media and music-industry types comes to hang out. Eclectic nighttime promotions mean that you never know what you're going to find, so check the listings. On Friday nights Wildes is London's only all-women's club. Entry ranges from £3–£10; open until 3 a.m.

Whirl-Y-Gig (Shoreditch Town Hall, E1; Old St. tube) is a Saturday-night-only world-music happening for all ages. Have a global music dance experience and witness the club's famous parachute drop toward the end of the evening. Since no alcohol is sold on premises (it's strictly BYOB), children are allowed in; and it closes early enough (midnight) for you to still get some serious partying done at one of the other clubs, although Whirl-Y-Gig might be all the fun you need for one evening. Admission from £5–£7. Kids under twelve are admitted free. The lines are long, so come early.

WHERE IT'S AT   WHIRL-Y-GIG

The most accurate thing you could say about Whirl-Y-Gig is that it's almost impossible to describe. From toddlers with their parents to fresh-faced adolescents, from hip young teens to nostalgic hippies, Whirl-Y-Gig attracts close to two thousand people each Saturday.

Whirl-Y-Gig is not a place, really—it's a *happening*. Organized by its promoters and held every Saturday night from 8 p.m. to midnight in Shoreditch Town Hall in Finsbury, London, this free-for-all is enhanced by the psychedelic light show, Day-Glo face painting, and a most amazingly diverse musical play list. A very laid-back but energized and down-to-earth crowd dances to indie, world, reggae, '70s funk and '60s freak-out music. There's no liquor or beer served (though patrons often bring their own)—but that doesn't mean many folks are without "mood enhancement" or "mind expansion."

At the eleventh hour, the mood changes with the introduction of ambient, chill-out music, such as Brian Eno or Deep Forest. The disparate crowd joins together for the famous parachute games that have the entire club sitting in a circle on the floor. A huge circle of fabric is rolled out and everyone grabs a piece of the edge and lifts it in unison. It whooshes up and out like a billowing sail, much to the delight of any still-conscious children and those having a mind-altering good time.

Gay

Many clubs, such as **Equinox, The Gardening Club, Wildes** and **Raw** offer gay and lesbian nights. Check the local listings.

Britain's—and one of Europe's—largest and best-known gay club, **Heaven Under the Arches** (Villiers St., WC2, 071/930-9604; Charing Cross or Embankment tube) is built in the railway arches below Charing Cross station. The club has a huge dance floor that holds over one thousand, several bars including a lounge and a top-notch sound system. Its club nights are renowned, often talked about years later. Wednesday night's Fruit Machine is a very camp, very outrageous scene, particularly with the addition of the Powder Room, the West End's only drag bar in which the famous and infamous can sometimes be spotted. (Regulars were gabbing about RuPaul's visit for months!) Open from 10 p.m.–3:30 a.m. though it starts to get crowded by 11 or 11:30 p.m. **The Fridge** (Town Hall Parade, Brixton Hill, SW2, 071/326-5100; Brixton tube) in a former movie theater, has mixed gay nights on Tuesday and Saturday and a women-only shindig with fun themes the first Wednesday of the month. There are special effects galore as well as go-go dancers in cages. There's plenty of dance floor, including the stage, and music is both live and DJed. Admission ranges between £5–£8, and things keep hopping until the wee, wee hours of early dawn.

Jazz and Blues

It used to be that London, a city generally known for its musical hipness, had pitifully few jazz clubs. Fortunately, that has changed over the last few years. From large, elegant clubs that attract internationally renowned artists to smaller, more-obscure venues that cater to

less-traditional musical tastes, it can now be said that London has
music for jazz enthusiasts of all tastes.

Ask a Londoner to name a jazz club and nine out of ten will say
Ronnie Scott's (Frith St., W1, 071/439-0747; Leicester Sq. or
Piccadilly Circus tube). Featuring well-known artists and an international audience, this famous club has been bringing celebrated musicians to London since before many of today's performers were born.
People come here to listen; it's a serious *faux pas* to talk while the
music is playing. For variety, on Sundays you can hear rock, soul and
world music. Upstairs, a Latin disco pulls in its own crowd. Try to
arrive by 9:30 p.m. or book ahead. Open Monday–Saturday from
8:30 p.m.–3 a.m., the admission is £12 (students £6), AE, DC, MC, V.

SPOTLIGHT ON   RONNIE SCOTT

Although Ronnie Scott's name has become synonymous with his
famous jazz club in London, he is an outstanding tenor saxophonist
as well. Born in London in 1927 to a musician, Scott started playing
the saxophone in his early teens, influenced heavily by Coleman
Hawkins. When he was sixteen, he joined Johnny Claes's swing band
and continued to play with various big bands through the late '40s
including those of Ambrose, Jack Parnell and Ted Heath. Just after
the war, he joined the ranks of the British musicians who played on
the transatlantic ocean liners, including the *Queen Mary,* mostly as a
way to experience the modern jazz being performed by such lumi-
naries as Charlie Parker, Dizzy Gillespie and Bud Powell.

In 1948 he and Johnny Dankworth, along with other jazz musicians, founded Club Eleven, one of the few places in Great Britain
for the performance of modern jazz, but two years later, after a
police drug raid, the place was closed down.

Scott and Tubby Hayes formed the Jazz Couriers in 1957 and
together they put several recordings on vinyl including *The Message
from Britain* and *The Jazz Couriers in Concert* before opening the club
that bears Scott's name in 1959, mainly as a venue for idolized
American jazz artists.

Inside Ronnie Scott's

Scott continued to perform with big bands as well as with younger modern jazz players such as baritone sax player John Surman and drummer Tony Oxley. The Ronnie Scott group, including trumpet player Dick Pearce and Irish guitarist Louis Stewart, performed regularly in the club throughout the 1970s.

The **100 Club** (100 Oxford St., W1, 071/636-0933; Tottenham Ct. Rd. tube) also attracts big-name artists. The place has been around for quite a while and though it's beginning to show some wear and tear, the quality of the performers more than compensates for the condition of the club.

Don't allow the name **Pizza Express** to put you off. This is no greasy 'za joint with wanna-be musicians. At each of its various locations (10 Dean St., 94 Golders Green, 227 Finchley Rd., 7 Rockley Rd. in Shepherds Bush, and 11 Knightsbridge, Hyde Park Corner) you can enjoy some very impressive jazz with your inexpensive gourmet pizza, salad, fancy dessert or tea. Pizza Express has hosted such musical greats as George Shearing (composer of "Lullaby of Birdland") and the popular and entertaining jumpin-jive Honkin Hepcats. **Pizza in the Park** overlooks Hyde Park and offers cabaret presentations of international artists at 9:15 p.m. and 11:15 p.m. (9:15 and 10:30 on Sundays).

Cafe by day, **WKD** (18 Kentish Town Rd., NW1, 071/267-1869; Camden Town tube) becomes a jazzy-funk-blues-soul venue once nighttime rolls around. Wednesday–Sunday are club nights with live performances. One of the most popular nights is Cruella, an all-women's night the last Wednesday of every month. Entry is £3–£4 and beers are under £2. The club stays open until 2 a.m. on weekends.

For jazz seven nights a week, it's the **606 Club** (90 Lots Rd., SW10, 071/352-2953; Bus 11 or 12), a classic one-hundred-person basement jazz club (sans the miasma of nicotine, thank goodness). Every great jazz artist who has ever set foot in London has played this place, either on a sanctioned gig or after playing one of the other clubs in town. Unlike many other quality live-music venues, the 606 is also a first-rate restaurant with moderately priced (£9–£12) entrees. If you want to listen to music without eating, you can sit in the bar in back, but due to local laws if you don't eat, you can't drink. Sitting way back there, too, you miss the up-close-and-personal ambience diners enjoy with the stage in the middle of the restaurant. The 606 is open until 2:30 a.m. Door policy prohibits single men or women, probably to keep the pick-up scene to a minimum.

Tenor Clef (1 Hoxton Sq., N1, 071/729-2476; Old St. tube), situated logically above the Bass Clef, offers some of the best combos and soloists in jazz. It's the kind of informal and comfortable setting where the performers might chat with the audience during break. The admission charge is £3. Food and drink are available. Tenor Clef is open until 12:30 a.m. Set above a used bookstore, **Vortex** (139–141 Stoke Newington Church St., N16, 071/254-6516; Bus 73) is a down-to-earth jazz bistro serving simple, hearty food (£3–£5 per entree), catering to a mostly intellectual crowd. Though off the main circuit, Vortex is a cozy place to hear very listenable jazz.

Bull's Head (Barnes St., SW13, 071/876-5241; Hammersmith tube, then Bus 9/Barnes Bridge BR) offers live modern jazz that many feel is the best in town every day. A good place to take a break from walking or shopping, if you find yourself in the neighborhood. At the **Hand and Spear** (Heath Rd., Weybridge, Surrey, 0932/

845-035; Weybridge BR) you can hear a range of styles in addition to jazz, everything from stirring Celtic rock to soulful Scottish blues. **Dingwalls** (Camden Lock, top of Camden High St., NW1, 071/267-1999; Camden tube) offers jazz Sunday–Thursday, sets at 9 p.m. and 10:30 p.m. Open from 8 p.m.–1 a.m. **The Vortex Jazz Bar** (139–141 Stoke Newington Church St., N16, 071/254-6516; Stoke Newington BR) offers jazz every night plus Sunday lunch.

Folk, Roots and Country

In England "folk music" is generally synonymous with "Irish music," but if you scout around, you'll find pubs and cafes that offer folk-rock, traditional English ballads, and even a British version of country and western. (Remember the Stones's "The Girl with the Far-Away Eyes"?) Most of these performances come free with the purchase of drink or food, but additional donations are always welcome. Check weekly listings in *Time Out, What's On* or *Loot* for specific pubs and performances. What follows is a small sampling. **Mean Fiddler** (24–28 Harlesden High St., NW10, 081/961-5490; Willesden Jct. tube) is a vast club with wraparound balconies and several bars, stage, dance floor and pub-style seating that offers a menu of soulful, acoustic funk to roots music, Texas swing to rip-roaring blues. The club is open from 8 p.m.–2 a.m.; entry is about £4. **Weavers** (98 Newington Green Rd., N1, 071/226-6911; Highbury and Islington tube) features everything from Cajun bands to lone singer-songwriters playin' their guitars. Shows start at 8 or 8:30 p.m. and run until about midnight; admission is about £5. Back in the '60s, the **Troubadour Coffee House** (265 Old Brompton Rd., SW5, 071/370-1434; Earl's Ct. tube), a dark, wooden den, was *the* place to go for folk music; even Dylan sang here when he was but a wee pup. The bohemian aura lingers, though the beatniks are gone. The Troubadour still offers a nice selection of folk and jazz every Wednesday (admission £2.50) and Friday–Saturday (admission £5). On Monday for £2 the club sometimes sponsors rather large poetry readings at which local poets read from their works. **Hourican's Pub** (209 Liverpool Rd., N1, 071/607-5519; Angel/Highbury and Islington tube) often has traditional Irish music sessions as does the **Archway Tavern** (Archway Roundabout, N19, 071/272-2840; Archway tube), which also has lunchtime gigs. **St. Georges Tavern** (44 Lambeth Rd., SE1, 071/928-4688; Lambeth

North tube) has traditional sessions nightly starting at about 8:30
p.m. A bit farther out of the center of the city is **Whittington and Cat**
(89 Highgate Hill, N19, 071/272-3274), which has regular trad sessions from 9 p.m., free with drinks.

Black Lion Kilburn (274 Kilburn High Rd., NW6, 081/624-1520;
Kilburn tube) features Celtic rock and Irish ballads from 9 p.m. The
cover is £1. **Heathcote Arms** (334 Grove Green Rd./Richmond Rd.,
E11, 081/539-1369; Leytonstone tube) is another popular spot, featuring everything from Appalachian flatfooting to Cajun to swing to
jitterbug.

Cecil Sharp House (2 Regents Park Rd., NW1, 071/485-2206;
Camden Town tube). Built in 1930, Cecil Sharp House is now the
home of the English Folk Dance and Song Society. The Society hosts
weekly folk dance and music lessons and performances. Tuesday
evenings at 8:00 the Sharps Folk Club, a friendly and participatory
gathering of performers with folk lovers more (£2 cover, £1.50 for
performers). The building also houses a music shop that sells traditional sheet music, recorded music and instruments. The **London
Irish Centre** (Hartfield Rd., SW19; Wimbledon tube) often has
lunchtime concerts and sessions, from trad to Celtic rock and singer-
songwriters.

SPOTLIGHT ON CECIL SHARP

Cecil Sharp (1895–1924) believed that a true folk song was not one
with a single composer, but rather a tune whose words and music
evolved over the years, embellished by many, taking on new meaning
for generation after generation. As such, these songs had a deep cultural and historical meaning worth preserving, as one would preserve any monument to one's society. Sharp dedicated his life to
collecting and cataloging folk songs in England and America, and
his methods and publications formed the backbone and influenced
the direction of the folk-song revival in Great Britain.

A music teacher by trade and the principal of the Hampstead
Conservatory of Music, Sharp first became interested in the art form
when he heard a gardener singing a folk tune. Sharp wrote down the

words and music, launching his life's work of collecting and publishing over five thousand folk songs and ballads, taking copious notes about the traditions and related customs that went with each. So committed was he to this pursuit that he spent several months in the Appalachian Mountains of the U. S. adding hundreds of songs with roots in the English folk tradition to his collection. He founded The English Folk Dance Society (now The English Folk Dance and Song Society) in London. The music compiled by Sharp and his fellow members of the E.F.D.S.S. had a great influence on British composers of the day such as Ralph Vaughn Williams and Benjamin Britten, who recognized these folk tunes as the foundation of English music.

In 1930 Cecil Sharp House was built in London, "in memory of Cecil Sharp who restored to the English people the songs and dances of their country." Sharp's books, manuscripts, papers and photographs are stored here in the Vaughn Williams Library, which also houses a multimedia archive for folk song and dance, including material dating back to the seventeenth and eighteenth centuries.

World

Africa Center (38 King St., WC2, 071/836-1973; Covent Garden tube). In addition to being a cultural and political center in London, Africa Center is also one of the best places to hear African music—and eat African food. More a social club (with a small bar and the Calabash Restaurant) than a nightclub or disco, the dance hall, which holds only about 150, frequently hosts an impressive array of internationally recognized artists such as "Zimbabwe's James Brown" Thomas Mapfumo or the powerfully exciting jit-jive Bhundu Boys. Friday night is Limpopo Club with a DJ and live band and features strictly African sounds; Saturday the music is African-based which means it may be Latin, Cuban, Caribbean, soul, or jazz. Dress is casual but smart; entry costs from £5–£8. Beers go for the bargain price of about £1.70. Open until 3 a.m.

For Latin music, try **Bar Rumba** (36 Shaftesbury Ave., W1, 071/287-2715; Piccadilly Circus tube). On Friday and Saturday night until midnight there's a Latin party (followed by regular club nights with mostly dance music). Beer is £2.20, tapas bar included. Entry £3–£5 charged after 9:30 p.m. Open until 3:30 a.m. If you love Latin dancing, or would like to learn, try the **Bar Madrid** (4 Winsley St., W1, 071/436-4649; Oxford Circus tube), a young, hip, continental club where you can have lambada lessons on Monday, samba lessons on Tuesday, salsa on Wednesday and reggae on Friday. By 9 p.m., there's a healthy crowd of twenty- to forty-year-olds, having a blast learning the steps. Once the lessons are over, the bar begins to fill up. There's a Brazilian restaurant upstairs, but tapas are available at the club. Open until 3 a.m.

Depending on the night, **The Bass Clef** (5 Coronet St., 071/729-2476; Old St. tube) offers Latin (La Salsita on Fridays), African (Club Mabouya on Saturdays), funk and jazz rap (Wednesday's Fusebox) and east-west trance fusion (Joi on Thursdays). On Mondays, Norman Jay's Original Rare Groove Show packs in the regulars with good reason. This relatively small club (population 200) closes at 3 a.m. Food is available, and beers run about £2. Entry ranges from £3–£5.

The name **Jazz Café** (5 Parkway, N1, 071/916-6060; Camden Town tube) may be somewhat misleading, as more often than not the music has funk, groove or world rather than traditional jazz combos. The bands are, nevertheless, at the top of their form and include the Bhundu Boys, Jazz Warriors and Courtney Pine. Admission is £5–£12; items from the food menu run about £10. Open until 2 a.m. weekends. For some of the best jazz-funk and salsa nights, check out **HQ** (Camden Lock, NW1, 071/485-6044; Camden Town tube). HQ is half-restaurant with an eclectic menu and half-dance club with DJs often playing the latest music from Rio, accompanied by live salsa and Afro-Cuban jazz bands. Club nights vary, so check the local listings. Admission is £3–£6. The club closes at 2 a.m.

If you feel you can't fully appreciate Latin music without knowing the dance steps, why put off your pleasure any longer? Head to **London School of Salsa** (7–9 Islington Green, N1, 071/923-4574; Angel tube) in, to be honest, a not-exactly-attractive back alley, and take some lessons. Lessons begin at 5:30 p.m. and continue until 9 p.m. by which time you're ready to enjoy the club that follows and its 300–person dance floor. On Thursdays it's salsa; Fridays, Cuban; Saturdays, Colombian and mambo loco on Sundays. No alcohol but plenty of soft drinks (50p–£1). Open until 3 a.m.

Music with Dinner

Many ethnic restaurants feature live music, sometimes with accompanying singers or dancers. Enjoy flamenco music with your paella or the strains of a sitar with your vindaloo. Try **Cleopatra Taverna** (146–150 Notting Hill Gate, W22, 071/568-1616; Warren St. tube) for live Middle-Eastern music, belly dancers and good, old-fashioned plate-smashing along with your moussaka and retsina. **The Elysée** (13 Percy St., W1, 071/636-4804; Tottenham Court Rd. tube) offers friendly hosts, good Greek food, bouzouki music, dancing and, of course, enough plate-smashing to make you wish you were their wholesale supplier. The **Al Basha** (222 Kensington High St., W8, 071/938-1794,5,6 or 938-1030,8938; High St. Kensington tube) has great Lebanese food along with live entertainment including singers and belly dancers. Open late. For Turkish music, belly dancing and a full Turkish menu, try **Turqoise Restaurant** (228 Edgware Rd., W2, 071/724-0832).

At **Tiroler Hut** (27 Westbourne Grove, W2, 071/727-3981) your host, Joseph, will entertain (or perhaps annoy) you with his accordian-cowbell-singing show. Joseph has made several TV appearances, so if you're in the mood for Alpine soul music, he's your man. For traditional English music, it's **Tiddy Dol's** (55 Shepherd Market, Mayfair, W1, 071/499-2357,8) with popular early English songs played on the rebec, cettern lute, and dulcian. For Gilbert and Sullivan fans, visit **Gilbert's House** (Grim's Dyle Country Hotel, Old Redding, Harrow Weald, Middlesex, 081/954-4227), now a hotel and restaurant in which you can enjoy a Gilbert and Sullivan concert with your Sunday dinner.

If you're very lucky, you may get invited to members-only **Las Estrellas** (2–3 Inverness Mews, W2, 071/221-5038; Bayswater or Queensway tube) for top-notch flamenco artists every Friday, Saturday and Sunday. This is no seedy Spanish restaurant where some relative of the owner stomps around in costume and high heels while the waiters pretend to be impressed, but rather a venue for some of the world's most celebrated artists including Antonio Varga (from the film *Strictly Ballroom*) and Paco Perez (lead dancer in the West End production of *Matador*) plus distinguished tango duos. Between sets members take to the floor to dance to the Spanish music. Light tapas are available and the Spanish Rioja flows freely. Membership is £100 and nightly admission from £5–£10 at this slightly off-the-beaten-track club, but perhaps you can convince one of the members to take you in as a guest. Hours are 8:30 p.m.–1 a.m.

FESTIVALS

For lovers of seventeenth- and eighteenth-century music, the month of June is synonymous with the **Lufthansa Festival of Baroque Music.** Many of the world's best early-music ensembles gather in the historic St. James's Church in Piccadilly (Piccadilly Circus or Green Park tube) and Wigmore Hall (Bond St. or Oxford Circus tube) for four weeks of baroque classics such as Jacopo Peri's *Euridice,* the earliest surviving opera; French and Italian harpsichord music; Handel oratorios; Montéclair cantatas and early instrument recitals. Concerts at both St. James's and Wigmore begin at 7:30 p.m. Tickets run £5 for unreserved tickets (some with restricted views) and £15 for reserved tickets in St. James's and range from £7.50 to £15 for Wigmore. For more information call St. James's box office (071/437-5053 between 11 a.m.–5 p.m., Tuesday–Saturday and from 6:30 p.m.–8 p.m. on the day of the concerts) or Wigmore Hall box office (071/935-2141, Monday–Saturday 10 a.m.–5:00 p.m. (until 8:30 p.m. on concert days). Credit cards are welcome, although a booking fee is charged. For tickets by mail: The Box Office Administrator, Lufthansa Festival of Baroque Music, St. James's Church, 197 Piccadilly, London, W1V 9FL, England.

The Greenwich Festival during the first two weeks of June is a full arts festival presenting music, theater, dance and more against a backdrop of settings in the London borough of Greenwich. There are classical concerts, jazz bands, big band music and other performances along the waterfront in a variety of locales—from Wren's Royal Naval College Chapel to the River Thames. For further details, contact the Greenwich Festival, 147 Powis Street, Woolwich, London, SE18 6JL, England; phone 081/317-1085, fax 081/316-5009.

During the last three weeks of June **The Spitalfields Festival** presents a delightful variety of classical music, from concerts by symphony orchestras to Cathedral choir performances to fully staged operas to chamber music. There are free lunchtime concerts on Thursdays and Fridays. For more information, call 071/377-0287.

The City of London Festival imports musicians from the world over for three weeks in mid-July. There are free open-air events in Broadgate Arena, evening jazz concerts, chamber music, choral and orchestral recitals in St. Paul's Cathedral as well as poetry and prose readings. For more information, write to City of London Festival, Bishopsgate Hall, 230 Bishopsgate, London, EC2M 4QD, England; phone 071/377-0540, fax 071/377-1972.

Notting Hill Carnival (the last weekend of August) is the biggest street festival in all of Europe. Caribbean music, food, costumes and floats let you take a sidetrip to Jamaica while visiting London. For more information, call 081/964-0544 or 969-3603. Take the tube to Notting Hill Gate, Westbourne Park or Ladbroke Grove for this gigantic Afro-Caribbean party.

In October there's the **London Bach Festival,** a two-week celebration of Bach's music played by international artists. Admission ranges from £5–£15. For a schedule of bookings, call or write the Festival Director, London Bach Society, Bach House, 73 High St., Old Oxted, Surrey, RH8 9LN, England; (in Old Oxted) 0883/717372, fax 0883/715851.

CHURCHES AND SYNAGOGUES

St. James Piccadilly (Piccadilly, 071/437-5053; Piccadilly Circus tube), designed by Sir Christopher Wren, often hosts classical music programs including lunchtime concerts for a donation and is the home of an Early Music Festival held in June. **St. Giles Church** (Cripplegate, EC2; Barbican tube) also sponsors evening, usually classical, concerts with prices ranging from £3.50–£6. **St. Anne and St. Agnes** (Gresham St., EC2, 071/373-5566; St. Paul's tube) usually holds several concerts or music with worship throughout the week, both in the afternoon, at about 1, and in the evening, at 7. **Southwark Cathedral** (Montague Close, SE1, 071/407-2939; London Bridge tube) occasionally has recitals in the afternoon.

The fantastic acoustics of the lovely, baroque **St. John's Church** in Smith Square (071/222-1061; Westminster tube) has made it one of the most popular places in which to hear classical concerts. Admission ranges from £3–£10. Box office hours: 10 a.m.–5 p.m., Monday–Friday. And last, but hardly least, is **St. Martin-in-the-Fields** (St. Martin's Pl., Trafalgar Sq., 071/930-0089; Charing Cross or Leicester Sq. tube), which you probably already know from the work of Neville Mariner and the Academy of St. Martin-in-the-Fields. If you happen upon a lunchtime recital (Tuesdays at 1 p.m.), you're

Leicester Square Half-Price Ticket Booth

sure to enjoy it though the famous orchestra is not playing. Free unless you're late, when you must pay £2.

MISCELLANEOUS
West End Theaters

The West End is the Broadway of London, the center of legitimate theater. As in New York, at any given time it seems as if at least five Andrew Lloyd Webber musicals are playing. Says Ned Sherrin, successful West End director and producer (*Side by Side by Sondheim*), "Everything changed because of Andrew. He has made it essential for a whole new generation of actors to be able to sing and dance. Now the London drama schools have a serious musical program for actors. Andrew has provided work for many London performers— two hundred actors for *Cats* and *Phantom*, another fifty for *Sunset Boulevard.*"

In addition the West End imports American revivals (*Guys and Dolls* and *Grease*) and, though it may be hard to believe, London does produce the occasional musical such as *Les Miserables* and *Blood Brothers* written by someone *other* than Lloyd Webber.

Leicester Square Half-Price Ticket Booth offers tickets at half price plus a small service charge for any seats left on the day of the performance. You may be approached by scalpers trying to sell you tickets while you're in line either at Leicester Square or at the theaters themselves. We suggest that you ignore them.

Pick up a helpful little booklet called *Going to a Show: A Guide to Buying Tickets in London* at any British Tourist Authority office in town.

SPOTLIGHT ON   ANDREW LLOYD WEBBER

When it comes to contemporary musical theater on both sides of the Atlantic one name immediately springs to mind: Andrew Lloyd Webber. Lloyd Webber, often in collaboration with lyricist Tim Rice, has written dozens of musicals including *Jesus Christ Superstar, Joseph and the Amazing Technicolor Dreamcoat, Evita, Cats, Starlight Express, Phantom of the Opera* and *Sunset Boulevard* that included such hit singles as "Don't Cry for Me Argentina" and "Another Suitcase in Another Hall" from *Evita*, "Memory" from *Cats,* and "I Don't Know How to Love Him" and "Jesus Christ Superstar" from *Jesus Christ Superstar.*

Although Lloyd Webber and Rice wrote *Joseph and the Amazing Technicolor Dreamcoat* in 1968, their other biblical musical, *Jesus Christ Superstar,* which came to Broadway in 1970, propelled the duo to international fame. Although the subject matter shocked many and was publicly denounced by evangelists such as Billy Graham, the album nevertheless topped the charts in the U. S., an unusual phenomenon for a cast album. The play, one of their most enduring, has been performed in more than forty countries and is still a favorite among student and repertory theater companies.

Cats, based on T. S. Eliot's *Old Possum's Book of Practical Cats,* was first produced in 1981 and continues to be one of the longest-running and most-popular shows on Broadway. *Phantom of the Opera,* a collaborative effort with Harold Prince, with lyrics by Charles Hart and Richard Stilgoe, was a huge success in both London and New York and garnered seven Tony Awards in 1988. Webber's most recent work, *Sunset Boulevard,* which has starred both Patti Lupone and Glenn Close, opened to rave reviews in London, Los Angeles, and New York.

Lloyd Webber has also composed several classical pieces including *Variations*, based on a theme by Paganini, and *Requiem* that, though not very well received by critics, produced a British top-ten song, "Pie Jesu," for his then-wife Sarah Brightman and boy soprano Paul Miles-Kingston.

Ballroom Music and Piano Bars

Many of the great hotels offer big bands and a dance floor for their diners. You can swing or samba between courses or just relax and enjoy the music. For the best of the best try the Savoy, the Ritz, or the Park Lane Hilton. **Kettners** (29 Romilly St., W1, 071/734-6112; Leicester Sq. tube) is a stylish haute-cuisine restaurant in Soho that has live piano music most evenings and weekends. On Sundays the music turns classical.

SPOTLIGHT ON THE BLACK CAT RHYTHM BAND

They play music that makes you smile and tap your toes. The Black Cat Rhythm Band, formed in 1983 by a group of London's finest free-lance, classically trained musicians, can be heard at London's Ritz Hotel most Saturday nights playing old favorites from Dixieland to Charleston to Cole Porter. Most of their tunes come from the era in which Broadway and the Hollywood film musical were vying for the attention of the public—those musically prolific years when such brilliant lyricists as Lorenz Hart and Ira Gershwin were inspiring the composers. If the Black Cat's version of "Jealousy" (by Bloom and Gade) doesn't make you want to pluck a rose from your table arrangement, clasp it between your teeth, grab a partner and tango across the floor, you're made of stone. And we dare you to sit still when they break into Irving Berlin's "Let Yourself Go" or "Puttin' on the Ritz."

The poignant strains of Wilfred Gibson's violin could bring tears to your eyes and John Elliot's sousaphone punctuates various songs with just the right touch of light humor. Many of the musicians in this group are quite versatile instrumentally, with the saxophonists doubling on clarinet, the guitarist strumming the banjo and the sousaphonist playing bass.

This musical tradition runs in the blood of their band's leader and main vocalist, Martin Hall Nicholls, whose father was a well-known band leader of the 1930s. Most of their inventive arrangements are scored by members of the group, often by Alan Gout, the group's musical director. If you find yourself in London on a Saturday night and feel like "puttin' on the Ritz," slip into your dancing shoes, head over to Piccadilly and give the Black Cat Rhythm Band a listen.

The Black Cat Rhythm Band

Cabaret

For a taste of the old-time Victorian music hall, visit **Cockney Cabaret and Music Hall** (18 Charing Cross Rd., WC2, 071/408-1001; Charing Cross tube). Patrons join the staff in singing along to honky-tonk piano while consuming vast quantities of East End fare (four-course Cockney meals) along with unlimited wine and beer—all for about £25. Open daily during summer months, Wednesday–Saturday other times, from 8 p.m. Another music hall, **The Water Rats** (328 Grays Inn Rd., WC1, 071/837-7269; King's Cross tube), is the head-quarters of the Grand Order of Water Rats, a charitable organization of the U. K.'s variety performers. Admission is £5 for the show and about £8 for dinner. Reservations are recommended.

A Classical Note

The **British Music Information Centre** (10 Stratford Pl., W1, 071/499-8567; Bond St. tube) frequently holds small classical evening concerts starting at 7:30 p.m. at very low prices, from £1–£6, often including wine.

Large Stadiums

And lest we forget the truly gigantic venues, there's the **Wembley Arena** (indoor) and **Wembley Stadium** (outdoor) (081/900-1234; Wembley Park or Wembley Central tube) for those mega-concerts that half the world attends.

✪ ANSWERS TO TEST YOUR MUSICAL I.Q.

Page 4

1. Herman (from Herman's Hermits)   **2.** Sting   **3.** David Bowie
4. Lulu   **5.** Luka Bloom   **6.** Freddie Mercury   **7.** Sid Vicious
8. Cliff Richard   **9.** Sade   **10.** Johnny Rotten   **11.** Elvis Costello
12. Cleo Laine   **13.** Adam Ant   **14.** Boy George   **15.** Elton John

Heart of England

Including Bath, Birmingham, Bristol, Cheltenham, Glastonbury, Gloucester, Henley-on-Thames, Hereford, Leamington, Lichfield, Ludlow, Malvern, Newbury, Oxford, Reading, Stratford-Upon-Avon, Warwick, Windsor, Worcester

BATH

For a full, day-by-day listing of what's going on in Bath, pick up a copy of *This Month in Bath,* free from the Tourist Information Centre and other places around town.

CONCERT HALLS

Michael Tippitt Centre (Bath College, Newton Park, 0225/873701) offers classical and jazz concerts during morning coffee (Monday–Saturday, 10:30 a.m.–noon) and afternoon tea (3 p.m.–5 p.m.). **Pump Room Complex** (Stall St., 0225/444477), adjoining the Roman Baths, is more a restaurant and conference center than a concert hall, per se. Listen to the Pump Room Trio while you enjoy a meal in these elegant Georgian surroundings. The complex also has an intimate concert room that seats about 120. Open daily, 9:30 a.m.–4:30 p.m. **Theatre Royal** (Sawclose, 0225/448844), built in 1805, is often referred to as the most beautiful theater in Britain. The theater offers a program of concerts, opera, ballet and drama. **Guildhall Complex** (Bridge St., 0225/315329) offers a wide variety of performances from classical Indian music to chamber music.

CLUBS AND DISCOS
Rock

The Tier Garden (under the Pulteney Bridge, not far from Tilley's Bistro, 0225/425360) offers live jazz and rock played by mostly local musicians, as well as DJ nights (and even comedy). There is a £3 cover. The hours are 9 p.m.–2 a.m. At **Moles** (George St., 0225/333448) you can hear some great rock, indie, jazz, funk and reggae...*if* you can get in. The catch? It's an exclusive, private club. But if you phone ahead you may get yourself on the guest list, or take a chance; go and try to persuade a member on line to get you in.

Jazz

Park Brasserie (Green Park Station at the junction of Charles St. and James St. West, 0225/338565) offers live music usually jazz, on Tuesday, Friday and Saturday nights (from 9 p.m. on) and for Sunday brunch. Green Park is basically a restaurant, so the music is more an accompaniment to your meal than the focus of your visit. Still, if you love music, this sure beats eating at a place with canned music.

SPOTLIGHT ON   ANDY SHEPPARD

He's a naturally gifted artist who's found himself in the right place at the right time. When Andy Sheppard was nineteen, he heard a friend's jazz records and decided he was going to play saxophone. In just three weeks, he was playing in public! During the late '70s, still living in his hometown of Salisbury, he founded Sphere, a jazz quartet. The group quickly picked up gigs across Europe, won a few awards and made several albums. Instead of doing the obvious, and moving to London to further pursue his career, he moved to Paris, where, it might be said, there was a greater appreciation of jazz. In France he developed his skills, playing with a variety of bands—from African groups to jazz rock to Laurent Cugney's band, Lumiere.

Sheppard moved back to Bristol in the '80s, just as a wave of interest in jazz washed over the U. K. His new group became one of the most popular in town. They entered the BBC's Young Jazz Band of the Year Competition of 1986 and, though they only placed second, Sheppard's mind-blowing playing caught the attention of Island Records, which signed them to its Antilles label.

Since then, Sheppard's *Introductions in the Dark* spent some time on the British pop-album charts, an unusual accomplishment for a jazz musician. His recording and performing schedules are relentless. He's recorded live at Ronnie Scott's and written music for the theater, dance, films, (including *Iceworks,* about Olympian skaters Torvill and Dean), a BBC radio production, incidental music for the 1993 HTV arts series *The Andy Sheppard Wrap* and more, much of it in collaboration with Steve Lodder. His performance schedule has included Europe and Africa. It's a rare British jazz artist who has made such an impact on the jazz scene in the U. K. as Andy Sheppard.

FESTIVALS

In this beautiful Georgian city, for two weeks from late May through early June, is the **Bath International Festival,** an arts festival featuring jazz, blues, opera and concert performances, as well as talks and exhibitions. Classical concerts are held in Bath's most elegant venues such as Bath Abbey, plus plenty of fringe and street events take place. Contact Bath International Festival, Linley House, 1 Pierrepont Place, Bath, BA1 1JY, England; phone 0225/462231, or fax (0225) 445551.

CHURCHES AND SYNAGOGUES

Holy Trinity Church (Monmouth Place) occasionally invites in the public for informal and formal concerts.

MISCELLANEOUS

If you're visiting Bath during the summer, check out the **Abbey Churchyard** where buskers often perform. There are also occasional outdoor Saturday night concerts such as classical quartets and opera at Iford Manor nearby. These concerts run about £6–£8 and you are welcome to come an hour early with a picnic dinner. For more information, contact Whitemans Bookshop, Orange Grove (0225/862122).

BIRMINGHAM

Birmingham, England's second largest city, owes its importance largely to the industrial revolution. An area rich in natural resources, it became one of Europe's primary manufacturing centers. During the 170 years from 1760 to 1930—the peak of the industrial revolution—Birmingham's population grew nearly three hundred percent, from 350,000 to well over a million. Being a city devoted primarily to industry, Birmingham was not, historically, a place known for its music, with one exception—each year, from 1768 through the start of World War I, it held a world-renowned music festival, premiering such pieces as Mendelssohn's *Elijah* and Edward Elgar's *Dream of Gerontius*.

Over the years, however, Birmingham has devoted more money and placed more emphasis on the arts. Consequently, it now boasts one of the finest symphony orchestras in Great Britain under the leadership of the very young and very brilliant Simon Rattle, as well as one of the most acoustically perfect symphony halls, making a sidetrip to Birmingham well worth your time. And though the traditional festival is gone, Birmingham does sponsor a Towards the Millenium Festival, an event that features music and the arts.

Birmingham has also contributed to popular music. The city has been the birthplace of many rockers including Black Sabbath, Duran Duran, Electric Light Orchestra and Jeff Lynne.

CONCERT HALLS

Birmingham Town Hall (Victoria Square, box office 021/236-2392, info 235-3942) has an ever-changing program ranging from jazz to musical comedy, from folk to classical. This landmark building in the heart of the city is a copy of the Temple of Castor and Pollux in Rome's classical Forum and has been a famous concert hall since it opened in 1834. Over the years, such musical masters as Elgar,

Mendelssohn and Dvořák have conducted their own work here. In the '60s, all-night jazz raves spilled people out into the streets at seven in the morning, and pop greats such as the Beatles, the Rolling Stones and Cliff Richard have all taken the stage here. The hall's famous forty-five-ton, six-thousand-pipe organ is one of the country's biggest and, though it is one hundred sixty years old, is still played in weekly organ recitals by Thomas Trotter. Recently, the hall has hosted Fairport Convention, Buddy Guy, Mary Chapin Carpenter, Tony Bennett, the Dubliners and Jools Holland. Concerts start at 7:30 or 8 p.m. and drinks and snacks are available from the bar. The box office is open from 10 a.m.–6 p.m. Monday–Saturday.

The acoustically perfect **Symphony Hall** (International Convention Center, Broad St., 021/212-3333 or 0839/222888 for information twenty-four hours a day) is the home of the renowned City of Birmingham Symphony Orchestra and its conductor, Simon Rattle. Tickets can sell out, so book early. Prices range greatly and can go as high as £20.

Alexandra Theatre (Station St., 021/633-3325) is the home of the D'Oyly Carte Opera Company, known worldwide for its Gilbert and Sullivan operas. This is also a good place to catch performances imported from London's West End. **Birmingham Hippodrome** (Hurst St., 021/622-7486) was originally an old-time music hall featuring big-name vaudevillians. A few years ago, however, the theater was completely renovated and turned into one of Great Britain's major opera houses. Tickets range from £5–£20, but many different discounts are available.

The **National Exhibition Center Arena** (past the airport and international train station, 021/780-4133) is a 12,300-seat concert and sports venue on the order of Wembley Arena where you may find the likes of Aerosmith, Lenny Kravitz, Sting and other notable performers. Check the local listings for performance schedules. Ticket prices vary with event, but be prepared to pay upwards of £15–£20 plus a service charge.

POP QUIZ 3

Who wrote Peter and Gordon's "Woman," "A World Without Love," "Nobody I Know," and "I Don't Want to See You Again"?

ANSWER: Paul McCartney who, back in the '60s dated Jane Asher, Peter Asher's sister.

SPOTLIGHT ON   GILBERT AND SULLIVAN

When I was a lad I served a term
as office boy to an attorney's firm.
I cleaned the windows and I swept the floor
and I polished up the handle of the big front door.

chorus: *He polished up the handle of the big front door*

I polished up the handle so carefully
that now I am the ruler of the Queen's Navy.

H.M.S. PINAFORE

Since 1875, the satiric and comic operas of Gilbert and Sullivan have played to people all over the world. Between 1871 and 1896, the two collaborated to create the words and music for thirteen operas.

William Schwenck Gilbert (1836–1911) was first a government clerk, then a lawyer, and finally a librettist. He was born November 18, 1836, in London. While at Earling School he wrote several student dramas, and on graduation went to King's College. The verses he wrote while studying law, first published in papers and magazines, were collected in two books: *Bab Ballads,* and *More Bab Ballads.* Until his collaboration with Sullivan, he was a successful, but not outstanding, dramatist.

Arthur Seymour Sullivan (1842–1900) was Victorian England's most famous composer of popular and sacred songs and oratorios. "Onward Christian Soldiers" is his best-known hymn. Sullivan was born in London, May 13, 1842, the son of a poor Irish musician. As a boy, he was a soloist with the Chapel Royal choristers. His pleasant manner and superior talents won him scholarships at the Royal Academy of Music in London and at the Leipzig Conservatory in

Germany. *The Tempest,* based on the Shakespearean play, won him fame before he was twenty.

Gilbert and Sullivan met in 1870 and within a year wrote their first opera, *Thespis,* and saw it performed. It was not successful, and the two did not again join efforts until 1875. Then they created *Trial By Jury,* which poked fun at the judiciary, for Richard D'Oyly Carte who, three years later, formed the famous D'Oyly Carte Company to produce Gilbert and Sullivan operas.

Gilbert's amusing rhymes and tricks of phrasing added color, variety, and vigor to his topsy-turvy plots. Sullivan's lighthearted tunes have been hummed, whistled, and played on sundry musical instruments ever since he composed them.

Although they were partners for years, the two were physically and temperamentally unlike. Gilbert was tall, sour, brusque, and short-tempered. Even so, he married in 1867. Sullivan was small, dark, suave, and pleasant; he never married. Gilbert was impatient with officialdom; Sullivan was a friend of the Prince of Wales and other royalty. Their differences brought on frequent spats. For example, the partners quarreled furiously over who should pay for carpeting their theater, The Savoy.

The pair's most successful operas were *The Sorcerer,* 1877; *The Pirates of Penzance,* 1879; *Patience,* 1881; *Iolanthe,* 1882 (thought to be their finest); *The Mikado,* 1885; *The Yeoman of the Guard,* 1888 (their biggest success); and *The Gondoliers,* 1889.

Gilbert's caricatures of government and officials angered Queen Victoria. She knighted Sullivan in 1883, but Gilbert had to wait for Edward to ascend the throne. Gilbert was knighted in 1907.

CLUBS AND DISCOS
Rock

As you might imagine, **The Steering Wheel** (Wrottesly St., 021/622-3871) has an automotive theme including race cars hanging from the ceiling in the glass roof. The club sports two dance floors, where the crowd dances to the latest DJ mixes, and one chill-out room.

Suggested dress is "outrageous or nothing at all." Open from 10 p.m. until late. **Bobby Brown's The Club** (52 Gas St., off Broad St., 021/643-4525), across the street from the huge National Exhibition Center (NEC), is way larger than it looks at first glance. The club is a converted warehouse full of cozy little hiding places for that intimate tête-à-tête. This place really cooks on the weekends; industrial and rave music play downstairs and music of the '70s plays upstairs. Wednesday is student night with big discounts on the cover and pints.

The Club (Central Hall, Corporation St.) offers club nights during the weekend. For the best in soul, try Deep Soul Megajam the last Sunday of the month at **Branston's** (Jewellery Quarters, Hockley). Two floors of funk, soul, swing, jazz and electro. By midnight this place is really cooking. Admission £7. Open 8 p.m.–2 a.m. At **Coast to Coast** (off Broad St.) on Saturdays is Brothers Sisters, a funky weekly from 9:30 p.m.–2:30 a.m. Entry is £3 before 11 p.m., £4 after.

Jazz and Blues

Ronnie Scott's (Broad St., across from the NEC, 021/643-4525) is affiliated with the famous London jazz club of the same name. Like its namesake, you can hear internationally recognized jazz artists every night except Sunday. Friday and Saturday it's a place to "see and be seen," and the trendiness of the crowd can be offputting, but, if you plan on being in town during the week, you'll find the crowd a lot more down-to-earth. Prices for shows vary, and there is a £6 cover (£3 for students), which you can beat by having a drink outside (weather permitting), but then you miss out on all that smoky, jazzy atmosphere.

Another club with live bands is **Waterworks Jazz Club** (Edgbaston, 021/454-0212). Shows start at around 9 p.m. **The Bear** (Bearwood Rd., Bearwood, 021/454-7020) often has interesting performers, and this is the place in which you may stumble on an interesting blues band. Prices range around £5–£6. At **Palms** restaurant (City Plaza, Cannon St., 021/643-3728) there's live jazz—generally solo pianists and duos—most weekend evenings during the dinner hour. There's no cover, but of course you are expected to eat.

Folk, Roots and World

The Hummingbird (Dale End, 021/472-4236) usually features live reggae and soul. You won't be disappointed, if what you want is to dance and have a good time. Cover charges vary from £2.50–£10. Take care when coming out of the club late. The nabe can be a bit rough.

SPOTLIGHT ON   UB40

Ali and Robin Campbell's father, folksinger Ian Campbell, formed the Ian Campbell Group back in the late '50s. Ian Campbell wrote the antinuke anthem, "The Sun is Burning," which appeared on Paul Simon's first album in 1965.

The parents' tradition of political and protest songs has been passed down to their children, who, along with Earl Falconer, Brian Travers, James Brown, Mickey Virtue, Norman Hassan and Astro, form UB40, a Birmingham-based reggae group that has topped both British and American charts with such hits as Neil Diamond's "Red, Red Wine" and their version of Elvis's "Can't Help Falling in Love," which was featured in the Sharon Stone film *Sliver*.

Beautifully illustrated sketches, drawn in music, have long been UB40's hallmark since their first concerts back in 1978 and continue to be with such poignant songs as "C'est La Vie" from their album *Promises and Lies*. That song was inspired by a Haitian woman who approached them at a U. S. concert in tears, telling a moving story of having witnessed some people sell their baby for twenty dollars. She'd made a promise to herself that this story would someday be

UB40

told in song. Another tune, "Sorry," examines the politics of racism with their usual keen eye for societal observation. One of their best-known early songs, "One in Ten," talks about unemployment in the U. K. ("One in ten" refers to the percent of jobless in Britain. The very name of their group is taken from the notorious Unemployement Benefits Form 40.)

This multiethnic group of musicians stays close to its Birmingham roots, having built a recording studio in its hometown while continuing to attract fans all over the world, as is evident by its impressive record sales to date—thirty-three million worldwide.

FESTIVALS

Towards the Millonium Festival, founded by Simon Rattle, conductor of City of Birmingham Symphony Orchestra and the late Michael Vyner, artistic director of the London Sinfonietta, runs for three months, February–April, and is celebrated in three cities: Birmingham, London and Cardiff, Wales, with a variety of musical and theatrical performances, talks and exhibitions. For information contact the Birmingham City Council, The Council House, Birmingham, B1 1BB, England; phone 021/235-4175, fax 021/235-4943.

The **Birmingham International Jazz Festival** during July offers free and not-so-free jazz and blues concerts by musicians from the world over, such as Art Farmer, Budapest Ragtime Orchestra, Jamma Caribbean Jazz Band, Hugh Masakela and Miriam Makeba. Throughout the month music can be heard on street corners and in parks, shopping centers, hotels and nightclubs. For a full list of events, call 021/454-7020.

While not a live music festival, worth checking out if you happen to be in town is the **Record and CD Collectors' Fair** at the Birmingham NEC, usually held the second weekend in July. This two-day event is the largest such fair in the U. K. With more than five hundred stalls filling up the Pavillion Hall, this is the place to find rare, old, out-of-print, hard-to-find and, yes, even new recordings, as well as videos, books, posters and memorabilia. Open 10 a.m.–5 p.m. (£2 before 2 p.m., £1 after). For further info, call 0273/463017 or 0860/709751.

MISCELLANEOUS

In the summer there are often free concerts in Cannon Hill Park with some impressive performers. Check the local listings and pray for luck.

BRISTOL

(See *Glastonbury*.)

CHELTENHAM

CONCERT HALLS

Everyman Theatre (Regent Street, 0242/572573) is actually two venues in one—the larger Main Auditorium with a capacity of six hundred fifty and the smaller Richardson Studio, which seats an intimate sixty. Both offer a variety of arts events. **Cheltenham Town Hall** (Imperial Square, 0242/523690) can seat up to one thousand. It plays host to many different kinds of events throughout the year, some of them musical including jazz quartets and classical concerts.

FESTIVALS

The Cheltenham International Festival of Music, held in the first half of July, is Britain's longest-running postwar arts festival offering performances of both commissioned new works and music by the old favorites, plus plenty of fringe concerts including jazz and folk. Some of the artists featured in the past have included the English Touring Opera, Music Theatre Wales, and York Piano Trio as well as late-night cabaret with Tomfoolery and Richard Rodney Bennett and afternoon choral concerts by the Westminster Abbey Choir and the Apollo Saxophone Quartet. For information: Cheltenham International Festival of Music, Town Hall, Imperial Square, Cheltenham, Gloucestershire, GL50 1QA, England; phone 0242/21621. To request a brochure, call 0242/237377.

GLASTONBURY [BRISTOL]

FESTIVALS

Imagine Woodstock '69 without the rain. Now add jazz performances, world music, cabaret, theater, circus, cinema, crafts, foods, holistic healing plus loads of stuff for kids and you have the annual **Glastonbury Festival,** held over a weekend at the end of June. The list of performers is mind-boggling, and this exciting festival has come a long way from the days when Marc Bolan played to fewer than one thousand people out in a field next to a farmhouse with free milk being ladled out by the dairy. Radio recordings by the BBC of a recent festival reached an audience of over five hundred million people in more than forty-five countries including China. Over the years, musical guests have included Peter Gabriel, Elvis Costello, Van Morrison, Johnny Cash, Jackson Browne, Dwight Yokum, Lucky Dube, The French Funk Federation—in all over one thousand acts on seventeen stages!

Tickets *must* be purchased in advance—none are available at the gate—and are £59 for the full weekend (plus £2 per ticket for postage and handling) and can be obtained from the festival office (Glastonbury Festivals Ltd., P.O. Box 352, Bristol, BS99 7FQ, England). Allow twenty-one days for delivery. No postal applications are accepted after June 7. You can also get your tix from ticket outlets such as Ticketmaster, Ticket Zone and most large record stores throughout the U. K. Or, to purchase by credit card, call 0272/767868. Tickets include camping, parking, tax and all on-site events. Children under fourteen are free when accompanied by an adult. For information on the latest performers and travel to and from the site, call 0839/668899.

SPOTLIGHT ON   BOY GEORGE

Art should never kiss the arse of conventionality.

BOY GEORGE

George's fascination with show biz began at an early age, as he watched the Saturday afternoon musicals such as *South Pacific* and

Forty-Second Street on TV, and enjoyed Fred Astaire, Ginger Rogers, Judy Garland and Marilyn Monroe. His father, a self-employed builder, would bring home piles of old records from house clearances. George would take them to his room and play them till they were worn through—thus learning to appreciate Bessie Smith, Pearl Bailey, Ella Fitzgerald, Dinah Washington, Frank Sinatra and Rosemary Clooney.

In the early '70s, dressed in high-waisted loons, a rainbow tank top and cork platforms, he fell in love with T. Rex and Davie Bowie. After he was expelled from school during a rebellious period, he became a punk, tuning into the Sex Pistols, Patti Smith, The Ramones and X-Ray Specs. A friend introduced him to the club scene and he was hooked.

Inspired by his friend, George experimented with frills and eyeliner. He left home at seventeen and went to live in Birmingham with Martin Degville (later frontman for Sigue Sigue Sputnik). Beckoned to London by the growing dandy culture of the budding New Romantic scene, he eventually performed with Bow Wow Wow at the Rainbow Theatre. His flamboyance got him fired, which convinced him it was time to start his own band—Boy George and the Culture Club.

They rose to the top of the charts with such international hits as "Do You Really Want to Hurt Me," "Church of the Poisoned Mind," and "Karma Chameleon," which was a number one hit and helped them win a Grammy as Best New Artists. The group disbanded in the wake of George's heroin addiction but after cleaning up his act, he scored a major comeback coup with the soundtrack for the controversial movie *The Crying Game.*

Says George, "Hendrix was more than a guitar solo, Ziggy was more than his stardust, Prince is much more than a pair of Cuban heels and Boy George is more than his eyebrows...."

POP QUIZ 4

Who recorded one of her big hits in German (under the title "Warten under Hoffen")?

ANSWER: "Wishing and Hoping," Dusty Springfield

Gloucester Cathedral

GLOUCESTER

FESTIVALS

The Three Choirs Festival during the last week of August is Europe's oldest choral festival. Founded in the music meetings of the Three

Cathedral Choirs—Gloucester, Hereford and Worcester in the early 1700s, it is rotated among these three cities (The festival will be held in Worcester in 1996). During the nineteenth and early twentieth centuries, many soon-to-be-eminent musical figures such as Elgar, Holst, and Vaughn Williams debuted their works here. This festival now sees performances of classical music from all periods and from all countries—from Schoenberg to Gershwin, from choral performances to chamber music, from organ recitals to full orchestral works. Adding to the enjoyment of this world-class musical event is the pleasure of attending these concerts in some of the country's most magnificent buildings. For more information or to make a reservation, contact The Festival Secretary, Three Choirs Festival Office, Community House, College Green, Gloucester, GL1 2LZ, England; telephone 0452/529819.

HENLEY-ON-THAMES

FESTIVALS

Henley Festival of Music and the Arts, held the week after the Henley Regatta in early July, is a four-evening program of concerts, opera, theater, art and solo performances with an emphasis on performances by young artists from the Henley area. Over the years, visitors have enjoyed the jazz sound of swing bands, musical comedy sketches, new operettas and classical symphonies. Information: Henley Festival Ltd., Festival Yard, 42 Bell St., Henley-on-Thames, Oxfordshire, RG9 2BG, England; telephone 0491/411353.

POP QUIZ 5

How old is Tommy, the Pinball Wizard?

ANSWER: 01

HEREFORD

(See Three Choirs Festival listed under *Gloucester.* The Festival is to be held again in Hereford in 1997.)

LEAMINGTON

(See Warwick Leamington Festival listed under *Warwick*.)

LICHFIELD

FESTIVALS

Residencies are one of the main features of the **Lichfield International Arts Festival** held for a week in mid-July. Artists-in-residence include soloists and trios as well as teachers who offer classes in both performing and composition at the area's senior schools. In turn the students perform the works at the festival. This major arts festival includes a film series, street entertainment, waterside exhibits, and alternative and nonclassical musical shows at the Arts Center. A spectacular fireworks display over Stowe Pool tops off the gala on the last night. For further information, contact The Festival Office, 7 The Close, Lichfield, Staffordshire, WS13 7LD, England; phone 0543/257298 or fax 0543/415137.

LUDLOW

FESTIVALS

Situated in the center of this historic and picturesque market town, Ludlow's Norman Castle and the fifteenth-century Parish Church are the setting for the **Ludlow Festival,** held over three weeks from the end of June through the beginning of July. The festival offers a cornucopia of planned events including concerts, theater, ballet and comedy as well as many events for children. Highlights from the 1994 season included fourteen-year-old Vanessa Mae, whom the BBC described as "the most exciting young violinist in the world," comparable to Heifetz, Menuhin and Kreisler. For the young folks, pianist Anthony Goldstone played and described Mussorsky's *Pictures from an Exhibition*. Information: Ludlow Festival Box Office, Castle Square, Ludlow, Shropshire, SY8 1AY, England; telephone 0584/872150.

MALVERN

FESTIVALS

John Evelyn, seventeenth-century diarist, called the Malvern Hills "one of the goodliest vistas in England." This is the setting of the **Malvern Festival,** two weeks of chamber and instrumental music by some of the country's finest artists with a program ranging from gala concerts to intimate recitals, from opera and choral works to string quartets. Founded in 1929 by Barnard Shaw, many of the events are now held in magnificent Madresfield Court, the country seat that served as a model for Evelyn Waugh's Brideshead. The Malvern Festival runs from the end of May to the beginning of June. For additional information about scheduling and events write to: Festival Secretary, Broads Bank, Malvern, Worcestershire, WR14 2HP, England; phone 0684/892200.

POP QUIZ 6

What glitter rock legend has a son named Zowie?

ANSWER: David Bowie.

NEWBURY

FESTIVALS

During the second two weeks of May, the beautiful Parish Church of St. Nicholas hosts the major concerts during the **Newbury Spring Festival.** This lovely town with the Kennet and Avon canal flowing through its center is a delightful setting for international musical artists such as the Polish National Radio Symphony Orchestra, Metalworks Gamelan, and the Beethoven Trio of Vienna. In addition to the world-class music are exhibitions of painting and sculpture as well as lectures by artists and art historians. The Festival's "Events Programme and Booking Form" is available from Suite 3, Town Hall, Newbury, Berkshire, RG14 5AA, England; phone 06350/48774/32421.

OXFORD

CONCERT HALLS

The Apollo Theatre (George St., 0685/244544) presents a variety of different performances, musical and otherwise, including rock, jazz and classical. Tickets start at £6 with student discounts available. **Holywell Music Room** (St. Algate's, 0865/276125) is one of Oxford's more famous venues as is the historic **Sheldonian Theatre** (Broad St., 0865/277299), built by Sir Christopher Wren.

FESTIVALS

Oxford Pro Musica is the city of Oxford's orchestra, and performances in their series **Beautiful Music in Beautiful Places** are held in some of the city's most historic edifices including the Sheldonian Theatre and in various college chapels. There are usually two concerts a week throughout the summer season. (The rest of the year, the orchestra is frequently performing abroad.) Shows begin at 8 p.m. and ticket prices range from about £3.50 to £9 with discounts for students. Contact the Old Rectory, Paradise Square, OX1 1TW, England; phone 0865/252365.

Music at Oxford, a series of weekend chamber concerts from late June through mid-September, includes performances in such awe-inspiring settings as Christ Church Cathedral and the Sheldonian Theatre or sometimes on the grounds of estates in the area. The music is mainly early Baroque, performed by ensembles and choirs from all over the globe (as well as local). For a schedule write to Music at Oxford, 6a Cumnor Hill, Oxford, OX2 9HA, England; telephone 0865/864056.

SPOTLIGHT ON   OUTBACK

The essence of Outback's sound is the didgeridoo, a traditional instrument of Australian aborigines. Made from a tree branch or trunk hollowed out by termites, sound is produced by blowing into it while buzzing the lips, similar to the way one plays a trombone. It produces a distinctly beautiful, deep drone that can be altered with the tongue and mouth.

Although a difficult instrument to learn, Outback's Dr. Graham Wiggins, an American-born, Oxford-trained physicist, taught himself the basics. Then he traveled to Australia and studied with aboriginal musicians, acquiring several traditionally crafted instruments in the process. Although rooted in the rhythms and phrasings of aboriginal playing, Wiggins's didgeridoo style also incorporates more percussive rhythms influenced by Afro-Cuban, jazz and modern dance music producing a sound that is at once unique and totally listenable.

If Wiggins' didgeridoo is the heart of Outback, English-born Martin Craddick's acoustic guitar is the backbone. Like Wiggins,

Outback

Craddick has traveled extensively, often busking with local musicians, and has developed his own distinctive style, influenced by rock, classical, flamenco, reggae and Celtic styles.

The two men met by chance in Oxford in 1988, began playing together and immediately began attracting attention as a duo throughout the U. K. After the release of their first album, *Didgeridoo and Guitar* on Hannibal Records, the duo formed a band, including Sagar N'Gom on West African percussion, Ian Campbell on drums and Frenchman Paddy LeMercier on violin. Together, they recorded *Dance the Devil Away* for Hannibal, an album of upbeat, toe-tapping world music with such cuts as "Cuban Connections," inspired by Afro-Cuban rhythms, and "Aziz Aziz," which recalls the sounds of Middle Eastern bazaars.

If you're lucky enough to be in town when Outback is playing one of its many live concerts at a festival, arts center, pub or even at a club rave, make it a point to see this unique and memorable group.

READING

FESTIVALS

Reading comes alive in the summer with two great festivals. Called "wonderful...bizarre...euphoric" by *Rolling Stone,* the **Womad Festival,** held for three days in mid-July at Rivermead, gathers an unbelievable lineup of musicians from every corner of the globe. During the last festival, Womad had such wonderfully diverse performers as Boukman Eksperyans from Haiti, Les Quatre Etoiles from Zaire, Kocani Orchestra from Macedonia, trance musicians from Morocco, Malagassy acoustic music by the Justin Vali Trio, pop prince of Algerian rai music Cheb Mami, Lucky Dube, and Drumfire!—a unique festival event by the world's finest drummers and percussionists such as Airto Moreira of Brazil, Xalam of Senegal, Khakberdy of Turkmenistan and many more. Plus, there are plenty of U. K. acts. Whirl-Y-Gig, London's famous club experience, is present with a global dance adventure; plus there are activities for children, an all-night global bazaar, a carnival of workshops and more. Weekend tickets are £40; day tickets are £17.50. Write to Womad

Ticket Office, The Hexagon, Queen's Walk, Reading, RG1 7UA, England; call 0734/591591 for reservations.

During the bank holiday, the last weekend of August, the *big one*, the **Reading Festival**, three days of the best acts in rock, indie, rap, jazz et cetera take to the stage at Little John's Farm. The fee for the entire weekend including camping will set you back about £55–£60, but if you're lucky, you'll see the likes of Red Hot Chili Peppers, The Lemonheads, Ice Cube and Primal Scream. For reservations, call 071/284-2200, for info call 071/284-4111.

STRATFORD-UPON-AVON

FESTIVALS

The **Phoenix Festival,** at Long Marsden Airfield, held for four days in mid-July, is a relative newcomer to the festival scene and has grown a bit each year of its short life. Organized by London's Mean Fiddler organization, it offers over three hundred acts on seven stages and includes an acoustic stage, a theater stage, a cinema, a circus area and an open-air bazaar as well as the usual food and drink. The music has a mostly rock and jazz flavor, having seen the likes of Squeeze, The Pogues, John Cale, Crash Test Dummies, Galliano, Gil Scott Heron and Herbie Hancock. The cost is £52 (plus service charge) and includes camping. For reservations, call 071/284-2200, for info call 071/284-4111.

For two weeks from mid-July to early August is the **Stratford-Upon-Avon Festival,** an annual celebration featuring music, drama and street entertainment. For further information, contact Festival Office, 2 Chestnut Walk, Stratford-Upon-Avon, Warwickshire, CV37 6HG, England; 071/284-1382.

MUSICAL MOMENTS *Ian Carr and John Taylor Record in the Southwark Cathedral*

Southwark Cathedral was William Shakespeare's parish church. A commemorative flagstone marks the spot where his younger brother,

Edmond, sixteen years his junior, is buried among what are now the choir stalls. Stained glass windows throughout the church depict scenes from Shakespeare's plays, and a reclining statue of the elder brother rests in the nave.

So it was appropriate that Ian Carr and John Taylor would record Carr's compositions inspired by Shakespeare's works here. In May of 1992 Carr, playing trumpet and flügelhorn, and Taylor, playing the cathedral's organ, over the course of two nights, recorded the music for the album *Sounds and Sweet Airs* (*that give delight and hurt not*) (on Celestial Harmonies). The album is an evocative blend of impressionistic jazz, containing such pieces as "Alas Poor Yorick" and "Such Sweet Sorrow." The title cut, "Sounds and Sweet Airs" (from *The Tempest*), was recorded between 5:00 and 6:00 a.m. on the second night, and a dawn chorus of swallows and swifts can be heard in the background.

WARWICK

FESTIVALS

For the first two weeks of July, the towns of Warwick and Leamington play host to classical musicians from all over the world performing well-known favorites as well as new compositions at the **Warwick Leamington Festival.** Although international orchestras, opera companies and soloists abound, the Warwick Arts Society is well-known as one of the leading promoters of chamber music in Britain. Formerly known as the Warwick Festival, it was renamed in recognition of Leamington's Royal Pump Room now being used as the festival's main venue. Still, you'll be able to enjoy the magnificent setting of the Warwick Castle and the annual Fireworks Concerts at the beginning of the festival in the Pageant Fields, landscaped in the eighteenth century by Capability Brown. For details, contact Warwick Leamington Festival, Northgate, Warwick, CV34 4JL, England; call 0926/410747, fax 0926/407606.

WINDSOR

FESTIVALS

The Windsor Festival is held in early fall (September or October) in this historic town. Concerts are held in and around Eton College and Windsor Castle. What a way to see the interior of this famous residence! You can tell all your friends you went to hear some music at the Queen's house. For further details, contact Windsor Festival, Dial House, Englefield Green, Surrey, TW20 0DU, England; phone 0784/432618.

WORCESTER

FESTIVALS

For two days toward the end of October, every three years, Worcester celebrates one of its most illustrious townsmen and one of Britain's greatest composers, Sir Edward Elgar, with the **Elgar Choral Festival.** This relatively new festival (1994 was only its third year) is held in and around Worcester Cathedral and in such historical buildings as College Hall, the Chapter House, and the Guildhall. Primarily a competitive festival, there are also classes and opportunities for all to participate in music-making. Performers compete in any one of a variety of categories, from church choirs to children's choirs to instrumental solos, the only stipulation being that their performance piece be by a British composer. For further details, write to the Festival Administrator, Far Netherbury, Old Road, Lower Wick, Worcester, WR2 4BU, England; phone 0905/426304.

(See Three Choirs Festival listed under *Gloucester.* The Festival will be held again in Worcester in 1996.)

SPOTLIGHT ON EDWARD ELGAR

Edward Elgar is the foremost English composer of the beginning of the twentieth century. Born at Broadheath near Worcester in a house that now houses the Elgar Birthplace Museum, Elgar was raised in a musical atmosphere. Though trained as a violinist, he also learned to play several other instruments and taught himself orchestral composition. His earliest job was a strange one: Elgar served as bandmaster at the county lunatic asylum from 1879–1884, but then went on to something more ordinary—succeeding his father as organist of St. George's Roman Catholic Church, Worcester, where he remained from 1885–1889. From 1905–1908, he served as professor of music at Birmingham University.

Elgar began to devote himself seriously to composition at about the time of his marriage to his piano pupil, Alice Roberts, in 1889. By the turn of the century, he was widely acknowledged as the greatest English composer since Henry Purcell, who had lived 200 years before. In 1904 Elgar was knighted, and that same year he was honored at Covent Garden, London, in a three-day Elgar Festival, which history records as an all-out bash. In 1924 he was created (which, in "royal-speak," means appointed) Master of the King's Music.

Although his work includes songs, chamber music and instrumental compositions, Elgar was at his best in the larger forms of orchestral composition. His style was a romantic one, deriving to some extent from the German music of the earlier part of the twentieth century of which he was very fond. A master of musical technique, original and varied in his musical ideas, Elgar's most significant compositions are *The Black Knight*, 1893; *The Enigma Variations*, 1899, a portrait of his friends, each lovingly depicted in characterful and entertaining music—his first great success and possibly his most popular work; and *The Dream of Gerontious*, 1900, a magnificent choral setting of Cardinal Newman's poem. Other famous works by Elgar include the five *Pomp and Circumstance* marches, 1901–1930, which have been used in almost every American graduation ceremony since then, and the first of which contains the melody later known as "Land of Hope and Glory," a BBC Proms favorite; *Falstaff*, 1913, a symphonic poem; the cello concerto, 1919, perhaps Elgar's best-loved work, a nostalgic masterpiece that was his last major composition; and *Nursery Suite*, 1931, dedicated to the royal princesses Elizabeth and Margaret.

Central

Including   Burnley, Buxton, Derby, Knutson, Liverpool, Manchester, Sheffield, Wigan

BURNLEY

CLUBS AND DISCOS

Angels (0282/35222, 0836/544661) hosts a large crowd that dances to various DJs in this multilevel club, complete with a laser show, 24K sound system, and constantly changing visuals. Chances are pretty good that you'll be able to get in on any given night, but the earlier you arrive, the better your chances. The club opens at 9 p.m. and closes at 2 a.m.

BUXTON

CONCERT HALLS

In the heart of this Peak District spa town, **Buxton Opera House** (Water Street, 0298/72190), a lovely Edwardian theater, features more than just opera, though most concerts are classical. Most begin around 7:30 p.m. Tickets range in price from around £8 to £15.

POP QUIZ 7

Which son of a composer of classical music wrote his first piece, "The Toy Theatre Suite," at age eleven?

ANSWER: Andrew Lloyd Webber

FESTIVALS

Although the focus of the **Buxton Opera Festival,** held during the last two weeks of July, is on opera, don't let the name deceive you. The festival offers a diverse program not only of opera and classical recitals, but of jazz, cabaret and performances by upcoming artists. In 1994 the Earl of Harewood, one of the most influencial movers and shakers in British opera, became the festival's managing director, adding to the already considerable prestige of this celebration. For further information, contact Buxton Opera Festival, 1, Crescent View, Hall Bank, Buxton, Derbyshire, SK17 6EN, England; phone 0298/70395, fax 0298/72289.

DERBY

CLUBS AND DISCOS

Progress at the Wherehouse Club (110A Friargate, 0332/360-5370), set in a Victorian warehouse, retains its former character with lots of bare brick and industrial decor. Overly casual dress is frowned upon by the powers that be, and it's unlikely you'll be admitted if you are dressed too informally. Also, be prepared to show identification, as no one under twenty is permitted. Two dance floors hold close to seven hundred, but still we suggest that you arrive early if you have your heart set on getting in, as the lines grow as the night wears on. Members and their guests get priority, but if you're a friendly sort, perhaps you can make a friend. Open from 9 p.m.–2 a.m.

SPOTLIGHT ON   BLUR

Fax machines, shopping malls, virtual reality: for most, these are symbols of progress—devices that enhance our lives and precipitate cultural and technological advancement. But for Blur (Damon Albarn, vocals; Graham Coxon, guitars/vocals; Alex James, bass; Dave Rountree, drums), who've called their album *Modern Life Is Rubbish,* they're merely trivial signs of waste and stagnation.

"I really don't view the '90s as having a place in history at all," says Albarn, with a confidence that borders on cockiness. "We've progressed as a society to the point where we've hit a standstill, and the only thing to cling to is nostalgia. What we're standing on today is all the rubbish that's accumulated over the last thirty or forty years, and that nostalgia is the new modern age.

"I just love that '60s and '70s style because it wasn't rock and roll. It was more like really great folk songs that spoke about mundane, day to day experiences. I love listening to good songs. I don't understand the point of recording three or four minutes of noise without having a good melody."

Blur was formed in the summer of 1989 when Coxon met James at a London art college. Soon after, they hooked up with Albarn, whose arrogance, intelligence and rambunctious stage presence fueled the band's identity, and drummer Rowntree, whose sparse, skillful beats gave the other instruments room to groove. Leaping into the past with wit and attitude, Blur injects modern pop with the freshness and vivacity of a bygone musical era.

KNUTSFORD

FESTIVALS

The Cheshire County Council sponsors a variety of events in the expansive Tatton Park, many of them musical, including orchestral performances; organ recitals; concerts of English song; a **Medieval Fair** in mid-July with music, dance and authentic costumes; popular artists in concert; a **Dickensian Street Fair** the first week of December and a **Christmas Concert** in mid-December. Call 0565/654822, fax 0565/650179 or write to Tatton Park, Knutsford, Cheshire, WA16 6QN, England, for a complete schedule.

LIVERPOOL AND ENVIRONS

Before 1964 few Americans had ever heard of Liverpool. Enter John, Paul, George and Ringo, and instantly, Liverpool, a city of about 500,000, was on the map. For Liverpudlians the Beatles are both a blessing and a curse. Certainly, there's a great deal of pride for their most famous historical export, especially for those with firsthand memories of the Fab Four.

For some residents of this once-bustling port city, the "Beatles Era" exists as a reminder of a time when Liverpool's shipping economy was booming and a live music scene was, indeed, alive; when young English merchant sailors arrived at the Albert Docks on boats from America with their personal cargo of the newest releases by Elvis, Chuck Berry, Buddy Holly and other early rockers. Rock 'n' roll and R&B were, up to that point, distinctly American sounds. Liverpudlians translated the sound, creating their own Mersey Beat, igniting the musical spark that later became the British Invasion.

For the younger generation, the attitude about the Beatles ranges from historical pride to near revulsion, from hype overload to complete indifference. Said one twenty-something-year-old native, "By the time I was in my early teens, I was like 'Oh, no! Please! Not 'Penny Lane' *again!*' " Tourists may react with an equally wide range of attitudes. For those fans hoping to experience the unique musical excitement of Liverpool in the early '60s, a certain degree of disappointment should be expected.

Still, there's lots to see and hear. Your visit will be much more enjoyable if you open yourself up to what's going on in the music scene now. You'll find it a city full of humorous and genuinely unpretentious folk who are eager to share with you the rich history of this working-class city.

FLASHBACK **TICKET TO RIDE [The official Beatles bus tour]**

Sitting in a sweltering, white tour bus, packed outside the Tourist Information Center by Clayton Square, it occurred to me that any resemblance between the experience of the next two hours and the feeling I have about the brilliant group I have loved for most of my life would be purely coincidental.

Elizabeth, our perky tour guide in a purple suit, took us through what might be called a "Magical History Tour," cheesier than an economy pack of Kraft singles. Fab Four selections were piped in during our trip through stop-and-go afternoon traffic. Unfortunately, the speakers had all the high fidelity of a cheap, transistor radio, which didn't do much to enhance Ringo's vocals on "Act Naturally." Just as I'd sit back and begin to enjoy a favorite tune, it was interrupted by the nasal voice of our chipper guide.

As I heard familiar strains of "Penny Lane," I thought it strange that we were now in the middle of the Liverpudlian suburbs. I'd been expecting to have the playing of the song coincide with a visit to the bustling Penny Lane I'd imagined for years. Suddenly, the bus stopped and we all got out and walked a few steps to a brick wall with a small, white sign reading "Penny Lane." The lane, in fact, is not a busy thoroughfare at all, but a narrow suburban road facing a public park. The lot of us dutifully snapped photos of the corner as if there were an invisible celebrity posing by the wall and we were all excited papparazzi.

The lane leads to the bus "shelter in the middle of the round-about," once a late-night hangout for prefame Beatles and their mates, now reincarnated as Sgt. Pepper's Licensed Bistro featuring pizza, kebobs and beer. From this roundabout fan out the commercial streets with more of the bustle associated with the song. There is a barber shop, a bank and indeed, "blue suburban skies," when it's not cloudy or pouring rain.

As we gawked and snapped away at various streets of row houses, fraught with Beatles significance, the residential Liverpudlians seemed rather bemused by us. To them, it's just their home. Outside Paul McCartney's childhood residence, I asked the woman of the house if she minded the droves of tourists. She was busy manicuring her small garden plot and replied that she actually liked it; that it helped "show that there are pretty parts of Liverpool as well."

I did learn a few new morsels of tasty Beatles trivia. For example, Paul's "Let It Be" was written for his mum, Mary, who always used the title's mantralike words of wisdom, "Let it be, Paul. Let it be," to calm her excitable son.

To say that the actual sites on the tour are disappointing is a wee bit of an understatement. Then again, to a dyed-in-the-wool Beatlemaniac, their historic significance is notable. The details given by the guide can get fairly esoteric. We're shown the bus shelter that

John's mother, Julia Lennon, had been crossing the street to reach when she was struck by a car and killed.

Other highlights include Strawberry Fields (an orphanage—not a field), the childhood homes of John, Paul, George and Ringo, the maternity hospital where John was born and the location of George and Paul's primary school (reopened in September 1995 as the Liverpool Institute of the Performing Arts, funded by McCartney).

Among the international tourists with itchy camera fingers jockeying for a better view, I strained to enjoy myself. I ended the tour with a desperate need to hear a favorite Beatles tune, any Beatles tune, loud and uninterrupted.

MICHAEL GOLDFRIED

CONCERT HALLS

The **Blue Coat Arts Center** (School Lane, 051/708-9050) features regular programs of music and dance as well as other performances and exhibitions by local, national and international artists. **Liverpool Empire Theatre** (Lime St., Merseyside, 051/709-1555), the city's largest, features a variety of acts including concerts, opera, musicals, ballet and drama. Prices range from £5 and up, depending on the performer. Check local listings in the *Liverpool Echo*. **St. George's Hall** (Lime St., 051/225-3938) is one of the best examples of neoclassical architecture in all of Europe. Its former name was the Concert Hall and Crown Courts of Liverpool. After being renovated somewhat, it is now a popular venue for concerts and musical events, as well as exhibitions and conferences. The Royal Liverpool Philharmonic Orchestra plays at **Philharmonic Hall** (Hope St., 051/709-3789), which features performances by national and international artists. For rock and pop performances, check the schedule at the **Royal Court Theatre** (Roe St., 051/709-4321).

To the northeast, in St. Helen's there's the **Citadel Arts Center** (Waterloo St., 0744/35436) selected by the *Liverpool Echo* as 1990's "Venue of the Year," *the* place to see contemporary music, jazz ensembles and more. Also in St. Helen's, **Theatre Royal** (Corporation St., 0744/451175) offers a variety of events including musicals, shows, plays and music hall performances.

Across the Mersey in Wirral is the **Floral Pavilion,** the penninsula's largest theater, offering a varied program of appearances by national and international musical stars. Up the coast, in Southport the **Southport Arts Centre** (Lord St., 0704/540404) has two auditoriums offering a wide range of events running the full spectrum of the performing arts.

CLUBS AND DISCOS

Club 051 (1 Mount Pleasant, Merseyside, 051/709-9586) is huge, "The Hacienda of Liverpool," with flashing blue lights, a heavy-duty sound system pumping hard rave beats and enough smoke machines for a Hollywood set. Touted by regulars as having the best rave music in Liverpool with both live and DJ house and techno every Friday and Saturday and frequent visits from DJs from other rave hot spots in the U. K. and abroad. The crowd is primarily very young, white and straight, with dress ranging from hip to casual. Some weekends feature all-night raves with live techno bands. The usual hours are 9 p.m. –2:30 a.m., but there's usually a line outside by 10 p.m. for entry on a first come, first served basis. Admission is £5 with average club prices for drinks. If you're driving, there's a security-patrolled car park for more than five hundred cars.

Right next door and up a long flight of stairs is **The Beat Bar Club** (1 Mount Pleasant, second floor, 051/708-9128), which seems small by comparison. On the night we visited, the crowd was sparse enough to allow elbow room, a rare commodity at a rave. And while it's nice to have some breathing room on the '70s-style-disco dance floor, the smaller numbers of patrons might indicate something about its popularity among the locals. This might be due to the fact that it's a little more out of the way. Look for a painted sign of *Yellow Submarine*'s Glovie, pointing you in the right direction. This club plays more soft rave music, which tends to be charty with intermittant segments of vocals and melody but don't confuse this with "soft rock." This ain't no "easy listening." Guest DJs; no live music. Admission is £3; club prices on drinks. Hours: 10 p.m.–2 a.m.

Another massive rave hot spot is **The State** (Dale St., 051/236-4616), an immense dance club with the look of a converted music hall with ornate ceiling glass and molding. Frankie Goes to Hollywood, the '80s pop sensation, made a music video here. Presently, The State is equipped with great psychedelic lighting, top techno DJs and young, dressed-up kids. Bouncers here aren't known for their charm or progressive attitudes, but then again, where *are* they? Live techno on Mondays and Fridays. Admission varies nightly,

but hovers around £6. Hours: Monday 10 p.m.–2 a.m., Friday 10 p.m.
–3 a.m., Saturday 9:30 p.m.–2 a.m.

Up the block is one of the most popular gay clubs in town,
Reflections (25 Dale St., 051/236-3946). There are a good number
of both men and women of all ages. The club itself is divided into
four bar areas with separate dance floors for each. There's a men's
bar that is like a pub washed in black light, a women's bar with music
ranging from k. d. lang to serious dance music, a high-energy hard-
core rave and a low-key piano bar—the latter being completely
deserted when we were there. Sandwiches and hot snacks are available into the night. Although the music is very good and widely varied, this place tends to be as much a place to cruise as to dance.
Admission is a bargain at £1. Open from 10 p.m.–2 a.m.

FLASHDACH   THE CAVERN· Birthplace of the Beatles

I remember when the Beatles used to play at the Cavern. I was about
sixteen or seventeen. To be honest, I didn't think they were that spe-

Raucous confines—the Cavern

cial at the time. The club itself was a sweat shop. Remember—we all wore suits and ties at that time—and down in the celler, there'd be puddles of sweat on the floor. We'd all be soaked. It was one hell of a time. Live rock and roll music had just arrived from America. There was no drinking, no drugs, and it was nothing to go out three or four nights a week to hear live music. There were pubs, halls—about a hundred groups playing in the Merseyside area.

I went to the Cavern a lot and the Beatles didn't always get top billing. Thinking back, the difference between the Beatles and the other bands was that they didn't dress up in little suits. They were unkempt, they were larkin' about, eating and drinking, laughin' and jokin' with all the girls—all of this taboo, mind you—but they definitely held the interest of the audience more than any other band. All the other bands had this clean-cut image, emulating Bill Haley and the Comets. The Beatles, on the other hand, wore their street clothes, whatever they were wearing that day. These beatnik types were only a minority in Liverpool. The majority of us dressed smart—slim ties, three-button jackets, very short hair.

NEMS was the main record shop—Brian Epstein's place—everyone bought their 45s there. [It was Epstein who saw the Beatles' potential and cleaned up their act for America.] When the single "Please, Please Me" first came out, Epstein promoted it at his store, and it was his hype that helped it climb to the top of the charts.

During the last year they played at the Cavern [1963], their gigs were so packed with screaming teenage girls, you could hardly hear the music. Even outside of the club, they were so hounded by fans, day and night, they had to move out of their families' homes into secret flats.

JOHN, AGE 55, CONSTRUCTION MANAGER, LIVERPOOL

It can be argued that a visit to Liverpool is not complete without a trip to the **Cavern Club** (Mathew St., 051/236-1964), although for you purists we should mention that this is *not* the original location where the Fab Four had their famous lunch sessions. The original

Cavern Club, also on Mathew Street, opened in 1957 as a venue for skiffle groups but quickly became the main scene for the beat groups that emerged in the early '60s. From February 1961 to August 1963, the Beatles played 275 lunch gigs. In 1973 the Cavern closed due to lack of interest, but a replica was later rebuilt (with some bricks from the original Cavern) and opened. You descend a long, winding staircase with images of life-sized Liverpudlians and the Beatles, in their various styles of dress, painted on a brick wall. Once inside, the low, vaulted brick ceiling and close walls can help you imagine the Beatles playing here. The early '60s mods and rockers have been replaced by mid-'90s teeny boppers, young students and curious tourists. The owners, Cavern City Tours, claim to play every kind of music, but more often than not you'll hear retro '50s and '60s. Open 8 p.m.–2 a.m. with drinks at pub prices. Be prepared to stand in line starting at 10 p.m.

PUBS

Bold Street in central Liverpool is, in general, a good place to hustle up a midnight snack at one of the dozens of eateries or carouse at one of the late-night bars with juke-box music spilling out into the street. If you're in the mood to hear some live music in a pub atmosphere, try **Rosie O'Grady's** (Wood Street off Bold St., 051/709-6395). Depending on the night, you might hear traditional Irish folk music, American blues or basic electric rock and roll. This pub has a remarkably mixed crowd with many students, older locals and even some rowdy types in a very sociable atmosphere—it's a place to talk with friends, drink and listen to music—not a place to see and be seen. Admission is £2 after 10 p.m. on weekends, free other times. Hours are Monday, Tuesday and Sunday, 11:30 a.m.–10:30 p.m.; Wednesday–Saturday, 11 a.m.–2 a.m.

Rosie O'Grady's is part of a chain of Irish live-music bars sprinkled throughout Liverpool. Another in the chain (and probably the best of the lot) is **Flannigan's Apple** (18 Mathew St., near Williamson Sq., 051/236-1214), right in the heart of Beatle country, with live music seven nights a week. The ground floor of the pub is large and inviting, with wood ceilings, Irish and nautical paraphernalia and hanging, antique light fixtures. The crowd is a nice mix of students, business folk and walk-in tourists. Downstairs is the live venue area, where the crowd is thicker and a bit younger. For those looking for a taste of Ireland and its music without crossing the Irish Sea, Flannigan's Apple is the spot. Open from 11 a.m. to midnight, occasionally until 2 a.m.; from 11 a.m.–3 p.m. a pub lunch is served, often accompanied by music from 1 p.m.–3 p.m.

Next door to the Cavern on Mathew St. is the **Abbey Road** (051/236-4554), teeming with Beatles memorabilia. Although the DJed music never rises above your basic chart dance tunes, if you're a true Beatlemaniac and haven't yet had your fill, it may be worth the trip, if only to see the wide range of Fab Four photos, paintings, the huge mural of the *Abbey Road* album cover and even a birth certificate or two. It's open from 11 a.m.–1 a.m.

☯ Test Your Musical I.Q.

1. Which Beatle was sickly as a child?
2. What is Paul McCartney's real first name?
3. Which popular British pop star did the Fab Four play backup for before they, themselves, became popular?
4. What was the title of John Lennon's first book?
5. Who's the shortest Beatle?
6. What was John's original band named?
7. Who was the manager of the Beatles?
8. What was the name of the drummer whom Ringo replaced?
9. What was the song that you played backwards to hear that "Paul is dead"?
10. Which Beatle's child is the oldest?
11. In the film *Help*, what were the bad guys trying to get that turned the boys' lives topsy-turvy?
12. Who owns the rights to the Lennon-McCartney song catalog?
13. Who produced most of the Beatles' big hits?
14. Which Beatle was born last?
15. What was George Harrison's first hit?
16. What song was recorded by both the Beatles and Anita Bryant?
17. In what city did the Beatles play their final concert?
18. Who sits perfectly still, day after day?
19. Whose drawing made the film *Yellow Submarine* come to life?
20. What is the album *The Beatles* better known as?

(Answers on page 72.)

FESTIVALS

If you had to take a stab at what kind of festival Liverpool might host, what would be your first guess? If Beatles doesn't immediately pop into your mind, you haven't been paying attention. One might think, not entirely without justification, that if it weren't for the Beatles, Liverpool would rarely see a tourist. One thing's for sure—those guys at Cavern City Tours have certainly turned the Fab Four into a commodity and are milking them for all they're worth. **The Merseyside Beatle Festival,** however, may prove to be the most interesting and interactive of all. The last weekend of August, Beatles fans from around the world congregate in the lads' hometown for two days filled with live music, tours, films, video, a memorabilia fair, auction and more. For more information about the festival or on package weekends, contact (guess who?) Cavern City Tours, The Cavern, Mathew St., Liverpool, L2 6RE, England; 051/236-9091.

That same weekend, there's the **Mathew Street Fair,** with a carnival atmosphere, street entertainment and live music through the day. During mid-October in Wirral is the **International Jazz Festival** at various venues throughout the penninsula across the Mersey. Then, during mid-November, comes **The Wirral International Guitar Festival.** For more information on both of these events, contact Wirral Leisure Services, 051/647-2366.

CHURCHES AND SYNAGOGUES

The **Liverpool Cathedral,** the largest Anglican cathedral in Britain and the fifth largest cathedral in the world (designed to look hundreds of years older than it is) was created and completed within the twentieth century. It's worth a visit just for its architectural enormity, though it does occasionally sponsor concerts. Paul McCartney's *Liverpool Oratorio* debuted here in 1991. For information, call 051/709-6271.

MISCELLANEOUS

If you haven't already taken the Beatles bus tour, or in case you haven't had enough of the Beatles yet, there's always **The Beatles Story** down at the Albert Dock (Britannia Pavilion, 051/709-1963), brought to you by those folks at Cavern Tours. This walk-through shrine to Beatlemania allows you to "relive the sights, sounds, even smells of the Swingin' '60s." You can "take a trip to Hamburg, feel the Cavern beat, board the Yellow Submarine." Open "eight days a week" from 10 a.m.–6 p.m. (summer hours; shorter hours in winter). The admission is £3.95; group discounts are available.

MANCHESTER AND ENVIRONS

Considered England's second city, Manchester is surprisingly small with a walkable city center. Although not dangerous, a certain amount of street savvy is helpful when going out at night. Despite attempts to make the city more enticing for the failed Olympics 2000 bid, Manchester is a gray, postindustrial city where the friendly people and hopping nightlife offer a greater attraction than the physical surroundings.

Musical nightlife is dance oriented, and most clubs have DJs instead of live music, but some of the dance clubs here are considered to be the best in the country. There is a notable lack of small pubs with live music; there are some, but this is not the city to go to for acoustic, traditional folk-pub sessions.

Manchester has some excellent midsize venues for live jazz, rock and R&B. Most big-name artists make a stop in Manchester as part of their U. K. tour. Manchester also has a smattering of classical and opera halls. Touring West End musicals also make a temporary home in this "City of Drama."

There is a sizable gay population in Manchester, hosting quite a few late-night dance clubs. Most of these are in "The Village," a predominantly gay neighborhood located behind the Chorlton Bus Station, alongside the canal.

Throughout the U. K., Manchester is synonymous with the rave and techno-music culture. Throngs of sixteen- to twenty-five-year-olds can be found nightly, hypnotized to the pulsing rhythms of house, garage, trance and techno music. Though you may be a bit older than the gum-chewing, "ecstatic" crowd, it may be worth feeling a bit like a sociologist just to experience the compelling 4/4 bass line and buzzing psychedelic atmosphere.

In the warmer summer months, you might be lucky enough to catch an all-night, slightly underground, outdoor rave, usually held in a field outside the city center. Private promoters commandeer a field and provide DJs, a massive sound system and often a generous dose of good, old-fashioned trippy light show. Admission prices vary. Check flyers, placed discreetly in bars around town. Or ask around at the clubs and bars you visit early in the evening, as locals can be helpful in steering you in the right direction.

For specific information on who's playing where, check the weekly publication *City Life*, £1.20 at most newsstands.

Inside the Palace Theatre

CONCERT HALLS

Labatt's Apollo (Ardwick Green, 061/236-9922) features a variety of big-name musical acts from country to soul to rock. Within a few months, the Apollo hosted the likes of Jackson Browne, The Isley Brothers, Dwight Yokum and Santana. Prices range from around £7 to £20, depending on the performers. The theater holds about 2,600, so big acts can sell out quickly. Get your tickets at the box office or Palace Theatre, Opera House, HMV Records or Piccadilly Box Office. **Manchester Opera House** (Quay St., 061/236-9922) is more than an opera house. It's the place to see visiting performers from every genre of music from rock to country to classical.

The maroon, velvet-upholstered **Palace Theatre** (Oxford Street, 061/236-9922, Oxford St. tube) is a major venue for a variety of musical concerts, opera, ballet, cultural happenings and kiddie attractions, often featuring visiting performers from all over the world. During a recent visit, Bonnie Raitt was completely sold out. The much-smaller **Free Trade Hall** (Peter St., 061/834-0943) holds an audience of 320, so this isn't the place to see mega-stars, but it does occasionally host interesting performances, so check local listings. **Royal Northern College of Music Theatre** (124 Oxford Rd., 061/273-4504) is a relatively small venue with both an opera theater and concert hall featuring guest orchestras, finals for musical competitions, string quartets, student recitals and more. Ticket prices range from free (for some student recitals) to around £10 for more elaborate spectacles.

CLUBS AND DISCOS

Rock

Let's face it: regular clubgoers can be fickle, which means that what's this week's hot spot can be next week's video store. Before you go, check listings in the *Manchester Evening News* or pick up one of the free guides available in record stores, cafés and clubs.

If Manchester is the center of rave, **The Hacienda** (11–13 Whitworth St., West Manchester, at the corner of Albion St., 061/236-5051, 0891/550741) is at the very epicenter. Touted by those in the know as *the* premiere dance club in the U. K. and considered a national trendsetter, this warehouse industrial wet dream has three bars and a dance floor that holds one thousand two hundred house-raving maniacs. The birthplace of The Smiths, Stone Roses and New Order, this infamous club usually fills to capacity on Saturday nights, mostly due to the talents of such DJs as Graeme Park and Tom Wainwright. Buy tickets early from Dry Bar, Oldham Street, which has a free shuttle bus to the club. The Hacienda is close to The Greater Manchester Exhibition and Event Center (GMEX). Hours are Thursday 9 p.m.–2 a.m., Friday 10 p.m.–4 a.m., Saturday 9 p.m.–2 a.m.

WHERE IT'S AT   THE HACIENDA

Waiting in line to get into The Hacienda, you can feel the beat even before you hear it. Techno is known for being eminently danceable with a driving 4/4 baseline that grabs you from the first beat, and The Hacienda is the vortex of the vortex that is rave culture.

On the ground floor and the upstairs balcony, people dance by the hundreds. The dance floor is truly massive, and the sheer crush of sweaty, massed human bodies draws you into the communal trance. Downstairs the grooves are funkier, with elbow room and places to sit. Kaleidoscopic images project on the wall from a revolving disco ball. It's even possible to converse.

Swarms of teen members of Generation X, proudly displaying their newest postpsychedelic headwear and kitsch clothing and accessories, dance, stomp, and otherwise undulate, glassy-eyed and smiling, to the hypnotic rhythms. But these young ravers haven't totally cornered the market on the scene. There are still plenty of jean-wearing, T-shirted twenty- and thirty-somethings doing their thing.

At Flesh, the last Wednesday of every month, some people don't wear anything at all. Many Mancurians insist that Flesh is a *must* experience. The music is excellent and endless, including both live and DJed happenings. Considering the outrageous costumes and a debaucherous and campy atmosphere, it's possible to consider Flesh a night at the theater.

Band on the Wall (25 Swan St., 061/832-6625) is another major venue open six nights a week with both a wide mix of DJed club nights and top-notch live music by such artists as Lonny Liston Smith and percussionist Dade Krama. In addition, they have classes from sound engineering to jazz, a recording studio, two bars, with an interesting selection of beers and ales, and a vegetarian restaurant.

Home Nightclub's (Ducie House, Ducie Street, 061/237-3495; close to Piccadilly train and bus station) minimalist decor leaves plenty of room for a crowd of one thousand two hundred who come to hear live music and guest DJs every night. Admission prices range from £5–£8 (usually with a £1 discount for advance ticket purchase). Home stays open from 9 p.m.–3 a.m. At the same address is **Ducie Bar/Café,** open every Monday, Tuesday and Wednesday until 2 a.m. with free admission and £1 bottles of Stella, Pils and Heineken Export.

One of the most popular club nights in town is Fridays at **The Boardwalk** (Little Peter St.) with retro dance music. Admission £5, £3 before 11. It's open from 9 p.m.–2 a.m. **Jabez Clegg** (off Portsmouth St., 061/2772 8612) is a huge pub-style club with lots of rooms. The place is always completely packed and attracts a very young (read: U. of Manchester, "don't talk to anyone over thirty"), mixed and funky crowd. The music is mostly DJ, but it does occasionally have live bands on Saturday and Sunday nights. Open 11 p.m.–2:30 a.m., the place gets packed fairly early.

Outside Jabez Clegg

If it's live music you're after, try **Star & Garter** (18–20 Fairfield Street, 061/273-6726; near Piccadilly Station) features live bands almost every night and a late bar. **Flea & Ferkin** (Grosvner St. and Oxford, 061/274-3682; Oxford St. tube), a former cinema now a pub, with high ceilings and lots of big tables, also features live music, although, as one patron put it, "the quality of the bands is iffy," which it seems to compensate for through volume. The crowd consists of a lot of rugby boys at big tables and their adoring, giggling female groupies. Pub food is served for breakfast, lunch and dinner, and the pub makes its own beer. Flea & Ferkin is open 10:30 a.m.–11 p.m.

For rock concerts, check the schedule at **Manchester University Students' Union** and **Manchester Academy** (Oxford Rd., 061/275-2930), which sponsors several concerts weekly of local and international groups. Prices range from £4–£12. Recently featured were Indigo Girls, Pride and Sheep on Drugs. Tix are also available at HMV, Piccadilly Box Office and Royal Court.

FLASHBACK   **MORRISSEY**

"Big Morrissey fan?" I asked the young man seated across the street from Tower Records in New York's Greenwich Village one evening. Morrissey was still inside the store signing autographs, and there was a line of dedicated fans that went completely around the city block. Police were standing by, but the crowd, though enthusiastic, was tame.

"I'd say so," he smiled. "I just waited on line for 28 hours to get his autograph." Being the kind of person who wouldn't wait in line for twenty minutes for *anyone's* autograph, even if it were on a check, I was curious to know what inspired such devotion.

"His work is completely autobiographical. Other artists *say* their work is autobiographical, but it's really about how they want you to perceive them," he explained eloquently. "Morrissey's completely honest about his life—his actions offstage are completely consistent with his music.

"I started listening to The Smiths in 1986. [Morrissey was lead singer for the group until 1987.] What appealed to me was that they were very acoustic. It was a true sound, not embellished by a lot of studio pyrotechnics. Just raw talent. Them, their instruments, their music and their words.

"The Smiths were indisputably the best band out of England in the '80s." He took out the poster-photo of the singer and proudly showed me the autograph scrawled across the paper in silver marker.

TULLIO, AGE 22, STUDENT, JERSEY CITY, NJ

Gay and Lesbian

At one of the busiest pubs in Manchester, the **New Union Pub** (111 Princess St., corner of Whitworth, 061/228-6960; near Piccadilly bus stop), a very mixed gay crowd dances to pop and dance tunes. Sunday nights there are live drag reviews, Monday and Wednesday nights there's cabaret, Thursdays you can sing along with karaoke. Other nights and after the regular shows occasionally DJs play mostly golden oldies. The pub itself is over one hundred years old and has original stained glass art deco windows in many rooms, a full pub menu and outdoor seating by a canal waterfall. Though the dance floor is small, and the patrons range from leather-lovers, to drag queens, to nine-to-five suit types, to both straight and gay women, and ages range from eighteen to seventy, everyone gets along just fine. Says the proud manager, a woman in her seventies, "Over eight hundred people a night and never once an argument." Open 11 a.m.–11 p.m. except Sundays, noon–3 p.m. and 7 p.m.–10:30 p.m. The place is packed by 9:30.

Cruz 101 (101 Princess St., 061/237-1554) is a membership-only club, but don't let that dissuade you. Anyone can join, as 28,000 members can attest, and you can just come to the door for your membership. Except for the very crowded Monday nights when it has a live band, DJs play pop, dance, '80s stuff and cutting edge for a crowd of up to five hundred, dancing on two floors. This club attracts a very young, trendy crowd probably because it's free Tuesday–Friday with £1 drinks. (Mondays are £1, Saturdays, £4.) Hot pub food is available. Open 10 p.m.–2 a.m., though in July and August the club has a 4 a.m. license, which last we heard, it was trying to extend to twenty-four hours.

If you're looking for something a bit more upscale, try **The Mantos** (Canal St., 061/236-2667; near Princess St. buses), technically a "wine bar," though they serve every sort of drink. DJs play dance, house and garage music for a smallish, smartly dressed and often chi-chi crowd of gays and lesbians (and even straights) against very '90s, post-postmodern decor. Food is not available. Open from 11 a.m.–11 p.m., but by the end of the evening the place is packed. Owned by the same people is **Paradise Factory** (112–116 Princess St., 061/228-2966; a short walk from any station in City Center). The capacity crowd of about six hundred is young (eighteen to thirty), hip, trendy—even outrageous, nay, flamboyant. The club has better music than most places (not so much mainstream stuff) and it does sometimes have live bands. Light snacks are available. It's open from 10 p.m.–4 a.m. Admission ranges from £5–£7.

POP QUIZ 8

What member of glam-and-glitter group Queen was born in Zanzibar?

Answer: Freddy Mercury

Jazz and Blues

Jazz (25 Swan St., 061/832-6625, credit card bookings, 061/832-0183) has top-name international jazz performers and changes its bill weekly. Acts have included Lonnie Liston Smith—the godfather of jazz funk—and Deirdre Cartwright Group—led by a top London fusion guitarist. Advance tix may be purchased at the box office or from Decoy Records, Piccadilly Box Office and HMV. Check the schedule at **Day and Night Café** (26 Oldham St., 061/236-4597), an intimate venue, formerly a "chipper" (a fish and chips shop), that often features jazz performers, folk artists and world musicians as well as stand-up comedy and plays. Although the decor is not the most posh, the cosmopolitan crowd doesn't seem to mind. Businesspeople sit contentedly next to musicians with dreadlocks; tables are peopled by artists and young, hip folks. Pleasant, unpretentious atmosphere and an impressive, inexpensive organic restaurant menu make this place a favorite of regulars. Musicians use the basement as a practice room, and there's talk of that space being opened as another club. The music ranges from experimental and fusion jazz to obscure indie and rock. Open from 10 a.m.–2 a.m. with music from 10 p.m.–2 a.m. The cover is usually under £4.

Up the block is "the infinitely funky" **P. J. Bell's** (85 Oldham St., 061/834-4266), a more-established venue for music including jazz, soul, Latin, reggae and indie with a permanent dry ice haze and colored lights on black walls. This club is considered one of the hippest places in Manchester to hear live music in a relaxed and intimate atmosphere. If you're in luck, P. J. Bell himself, reputed by regulars to be a gregarious man, passionate about jazz and new musicians, will be there. Dress is hip to casual, and the crowd seems to appreciate the superior sound system. Admission ranges from £2–£5. Open from 9:30 p.m.–2 a.m. With room for only 250, it can get pretty packed on the weekends, and admission is first come, first served. Listed earlier but worth mentioning again is **Band on the Wall** (Swan St.) for some hopping fun on jazz nights with such groups as The Dirty Dozen Brass Band—an old-fashioned New Orleans marching band—or Lightnin' Willie and the Poor Boys—a rockabilly Texas import. **The French Brasserie** (The Downs, Altrincham) features the occasional jazz combo as well. Every Thursday night there are live blues and R&B acts at **The Castle Hotel** (66 Oldham St., 061/236-2945). Admission is free.

POP QUIZ 9

Which group, formed as a parody of the Beatles, had a big hit with "All You Need Is Cash"?

ANSWER: The Rutles (members of Monty Python's Flying Circus in their Beatles parody)

Folk, Roots and World

Poynton Folk Centre (Park Lane, Poynton) can be counted on for traditional folk, Celtic, Cajun and more. At **White Swan** (Green St., Ladybarn, Fallowfield) you can hear live bands nightly. During a recent visit to **The Roadhouse** (Newton St., Piccadilly) the band Gondwana was playing featuring Goldrick, Frankinsence and Myrrh, who were touted as "the three kings of Celtic groove." **O'Shay's** (80 Princess St., 061/236-3906) tries to be as Irish as is possible in Manchester. The live Irish folk and rock seven nights a week draw a broad mix of students and people of Irish descent, both young and old. The pub is very spacious and provides plenty of wooden tables to sit down and throw back a few pints of Guinness with your mates.

The crowd can get very spirited especially when it hears some of the traditional songs that everyone seems to know. O'Shay's is open from 11 a.m.–11 p.m. with occasional extended hours. No cover charge; pub prices for drinks. It serves basic Irish pub food for lunch (12 p.m.–12:30 p.m.) and dinner (7 p.m.–10 p.m.); the tab ranges from £2–£3.

Manchester Cajun Club (High Lane, Chorlton, 061/368-8769) is "a celebration of all things rootsy." It has two dance floors and music that won't let you sit still featuring old-style Cajun music, Cajun dancing and Cajun food. In September the club hosts the Cajun Fest (*mais, bien sûr!*) with various bands as well as dance workshops. Bands change nightly, sometimes weekly, often with a different band on each dance floor. Tickets are usually around £4 in advance and £5 at the door.

FESTIVALS

Manchester Cathedral (Victoria St.) is one of the sites for **Cathedral Classics**, the summer festival of music in cathedrals throughout the country. Prices range from £3–£9. For tickets and information contact the Halle Box Office, Albert Square, 061/834-1712, or for full festival details call the prerecorded info hot-line in London, 071/928-9257, on twenty-four hours. In a completely different direction, check out the **Edale Bluegrass Festival** in the Derbyshire Peak District. Plenty of British and American musicians are fiddling around the first weekend in June. Call 0457/861-1789 for details.

How sweet the moonlight sleeps upon this bank!

Here will we sit, and let the sounds of music

Creep in our ears; soft stillness, and the night

Become the touches of sweet harmony.

SHAKESPEARE

CHURCHES AND SYNAGOGUES

Manchester Cathedral, in addition to being one of the featured locations of the Cathedral Classics, also features its own recitals, usually

Thursdays at 6:30 p.m., at nominal prices. (For example, tickets for a recent organ recital were £3, £2 for students.)

SHEFFIELD

CLUBS AND DISCOS

The Leadmill (6–7 Leadmill Rd., 0742/754500) is located in a converted Victorian flour mill and has a spacious dance floor and ambient lighting. Wednesday is '80s night. Thursdays you step back into time another decade or two with classics from the '60s and '70s. On Fridays DJs deliver funk, jazz, hip-hop and Latin. On Saturday nights there are live bands as well, but arrive early unless you enjoy spending your evening standing in line. In addition to the bar, there's also a cafe. And if all that doesn't make you want to rush right over, their toilets were voted best in Britain. The Leadmill is open from 10 p.m.–3 a.m.

A recent sampling at **Beluga** (Carver St.) gave us acid jazz on Wednesday and the best of British funk and jazz grooves on Thursday. Admission is under £2 before 10 p.m. (sometimes it's free!), £2 thereafter. Hours are 9 p.m.–2 a.m. **The Music Factory** (London Rd.) is smack dab in the center of the student quarter. Wednesday's fairly new Skat is particularly popular here with a selection of jazz, Latin, funk, soul and rap. There's a chill-out room with live jazz and a great Asian and Caribbean menu at student-type prices. Entry £4; open from 9 p.m.–2 a.m.

CONCERT HALLS

Lyceum Theatre (Tudor St., 0742/760621) is a major venue for opera, ballet and musicals. **Sheffield City Hall** (Barkers Pool, 0742/735295/6) is really three halls in one. The largest, Oval Hall, is the place for concerts, with its almost-two-thousand-five-hundred capacity. Concerts are sometimes held in the smaller Memorial Hall, which seats about five hundred. The Central Suite is mainly standing room only.

WIGAN

In and around Wigan for one week in mid-July is the **Wigan International Jazz Festival** with street performances, late-night shows, workshops and, of course, the usual evening concerts at various locations about town. The most expensive tickets are £12 and the least expensive are free. For more information, a schedule and listing of venues, contact the Tourist Information Centre, Trencherfield Mill, Wigan, WN3 4EL, England; 0942/825677.

ANSWERS TO TEST YOUR MUSICAL I.Q.

Page 69

1. Ringo   **2.** James   **3.** Tony Sheridan   **4.** *In His Own Write*
5. Ringo   **6.** The Quarrymen   **7.** Brian Epstein   **8.** Pete Best
9. "Revolution #9"   **10.** John's (Julian)   **11.** A sacrificial ring owned by Ringo   **12.** Michael Jackson   **13.** George Martin
14. George   **15.** "Something"   **16.** Meredith Wilson's "Till There Was You" from *The Music Man*   **17.** San Francisco, August 29, 1966
18. "The Fool on the Hill"   **19.** Peter Max   **20.** The White Album

North

Including Alnwick, Appleby, Billingham, Blackpool, Bradford, Durham, Great Grimsby, Harrogate, Huddersfield, Hull, Lake District, Leeds, Wensleydale, York

ALNWICK

FESTIVALS

For one week in mid-August, at and around Alnwick Market Place and the Playhouse Arts Centre, is the **Alnwick International Music Festival,** celebrating song and dance from around the world. There are free open-air concerts during the day and evening performances at 7:30 for £3. For further info, contact the Chairman, Georgian Guest House, Hotspur St., Alnwick, Northumberland, NE66, England; 0665/602398.

✪ Test Your Musical I.Q.

Which of these artists are from the U. K.? (Part 1)

1. **a)** Dire Straits or
   b) Men at Work
2. **a)** Cream or
   b) Bread
3. **a)** Elvis Costello or
   b) Elvin Bishop
4. **a)** Belinda Carlisle or
   b) Kate Bush
5. **a)** The McGarrigle Sisters or
   b) The Thompson Twins

6. **a)** Wayne Fontana and the Mindbenders or
   b) ? and the Mysterians
7. **a)** The Tubes or
   b) Squeeze
8. **a)** Stawbs or
   b) Strawberry Alarm Clock
9. **a)** Steely Dan or
   b) Steelers Wheel
10. **a)** Aerosmith or
    b) the Smiths

(Answers on page 96.)

APPLEBY

FESTIVALS

The strains of jazz can be heard emanating from an ancient Cumbrian castle during the **Appleby Jazz Festival** held over a weekend in mid-June. A long list of very notable British modern-jazz performers will be making their unique brand of music in this idyllic setting nestled between the Pennines and the Lake District. For further details, write to Appleby Jazz Society, Bongate Mill, Appleby, Cumbria, CA16 6UR, England.

BILLINGHAM

FESTIVALS

For eight days in mid-August, the town of Billingham comes alive with its **International Folklore Festival** with over five hundred artists and ensembles of dancers and musicians from nearly a dozen countries. Over the thirty or so years that this festival has been in existence, it has played host to the Peking Opera; the Korean National Dance Troupe; the Hungarian State Folklore Ensemble; and a group from the Rang Bahar Academy of Indian Dance, Music and Drama in Ahmedabad, as well as local folk presentations such as Northern Clog Dancing and Cleveland musicians. Prices for events range from £1–£7. For further information or a program, write to the Festival

Office, Municipal Buildings, Town Centre, Billingham, Cleveland, TS23 2LW, England; call 0642/558212.

BLACKPOOL

CONCERT HALLS

The Winter Gardens Complex (Church St., 0253/27786) consists of the main Opera House, which seats close to three thousand music lovers, and the smaller Pavillion, which holds a still-generous five hundred. Other concert venues in Blackpool include **The Grand Theatre** (Church St., 0253/28372) and **The South Pier Theatre** (The Promenade, 0253/43096).

CLUBS AND DISCOS

Nellie Dean's (150 North Promenade, Blackpool), though only a couple of years old, is currently the hot club in town offering the best in mainstream jazz. The bill changes nightly.

BRADFORD

CLUBS AND DISCOS

With its eight bars, including a revolving cocktail lounge, and three-thousand-person capacity, **The Maestro** (110 Manningham La., 0831/480507) was voted best nightclub in England in 1991 and 1992. Dress is casual but smart. Open from 9 p.m.–2 a.m. While you're there, check out the luxurious marble bathrooms of which the club is very proud.

SPOTLIGHT ON TASMIN ARCHER

Like a shot, Tasmin Archer's first single, "Sleeping Satellite" from her *Great Expectations* album, sped to the top of Britain's pop charts, earning her the 1993 BRIT Award, England's equivalent of the Grammy, for "Best Newcomer."

Archer hails from the gritty northern city of Bradford. In the tradition of Judy Garland, Chaka Khan and Edith Piaf, the sheer size of her swelling voice contradicts her diminutive frame. Born to Jamaican immigrant parents, the young Archer found little direction for her yearning for music. Although the members of her family love music, they are not musicians. At church and at school, the belting strength of her voice was ill-suited to the genteel British choir aesthetic. Nevertheless, she persisted in writing songs that she taped into a Walkman in her bedroom and seizing every singing opportunity that came up.

Tasmin Archer

After leaving school, Archer began leading a double life, working at go-nowhere factory jobs by day and singing with bands at night. She remembers jumping on stage and belting out a tune with a local pub group "when I'd had a few too many." Though her vocal range and power were largely unappreciated by her first proper group, Dignity, one member, Philip Edwards, recognized her distinctive talent and nurtured the budding singer, shoring up the confidence that various setbacks had shaken. When Edwards opened a recording studio, he brought her in to sing back-up vocals for various groups, a situation that proved frustrating for Archer; she was forced to hold back or risk overpowering the other singers. Eventually, Edwards introduced her to John Hughes (guitar) and John Beck (keyboards). Their collaboration proved a winning combination, and as the Archers they've begun a steady climb to success.

FESTIVALS

One of the fastest-growing and most-lauded festivals in Britain is the **Bradford Festival,** held for three weeks from mid-June to early July. Say the organizers, "Right from the start, Bradford Festival set out to demolish class and race barriers and create an event that would become a byword for creativity, originality and sound community relations." Not content to let its audience come to them, the festival took touring companies to perform in hospitals, old-people's homes, youth clubs and council estates. The festival's formidable schools' program encourages participation by the next generation of artists and performers. Bradford, an ethnically mixed city, embraces the heritage of its various subpopulations and augments these artists with others booked from overseas, making this a very diverse program. Incorporated into the festival is the popular Mela (a traditional Indian fair), which attracts Asians from all over Britain.

The rest of the program includes folk music, jazz, world music, classical concerts, street entertainment, dance, theater, cinema and visual arts. For more information, write to Bradford Festival, Room 2, The Wool Exchange, Bank St., Bradford, W. Yorkshire, BD1 1LE, England; or call 0274/309199, fax 0274/724213.

DURHAM

FESTIVALS

During the first weekend in August is the **Durham Folk Festival,** a gathering of musicians and folk dancers from all over the U. K. It's all free, and the city will even let you camp along the river gratis (this weekend only), but it gets crowded fast, so set up early. Festival tickets run about £12 for the weekend. For more information, pick up a brochure at the tourist office or call 091/384-4445.

GREAT GRIMSBY

FESTIVALS

At the mouth of the River Humber is the town of Great Grimsby, which comes alive the first weekend of July with the **Grimsby International Jazz Festival.** Performances are held at the King George V Stadium and will set you back £25 in advance or £30 at the gate. You can purchase day and evening tickets separately, as well. There are special weekend hotel packages available for about £85 including festival entry. Contact Great Grimsby Borough Council, Municipal Offices, Town Hall Square, Great Grimsby, South Humberside, DN31 1HU, England; phone 0472/245036.

HARROGATE

FESTIVALS

Set amid some of Britain's loveliest countryside in the heart of North Yorkshire, for three weeks from late July to mid-August is the **Harrogate Arts Festival.** This elegant town is known for its ancient spa and prize-winning gardens. Concerts are held in both historic settings, such as the magnificent ninth-century Ripon Cathedral, to the new Harrogate International Centre. This diverse arts program offers an impressive program of events including chamber concerts, visits by international orchestras, celebrity recitals, opera, jazz and cabaret, as well as dance, drama and street theater. For information, contact Festival Office, Royal Baths, Harrogate, North Yorkshire, HG1 2RR, England; phone 0423/565757.

MISCELLANEOUS

(See Harewood under *Leeds*.)

HUDDERSFIELD

CONCERT HALLS

Huddersfield Town Hall (Ramsden St., 0484/422133) serves as a venue for a variety of events, many of which are musical. Check the local listings for a schedule.

FESTIVALS

Huddersfield Contemporary Music Festival is considered by many as one of the most successful and significant new-music events in all of Europe. During the last two weeks of July, leading composers and critics from across the globe, along with audiences numbering in the thousands, gather in the lovely countryside to enjoy exciting new music and performances by both established and cutting-edge musicians. Performances are held in magnificent Victorian halls and in a new Italianate-style theater. The program includes a range of events from major classical orchestral concerts to smaller, more-intimate solo recitals as well as talks, films, workshops, exhibitions and multimedia work. For further details, write to The Festival Office, Music Department, The University of Huddersfield, HD1 3DH, England; phone 0484/425082.

FLASHBACK   PINK FLOYD

I sank my weary body down on a crude wooden bench in a clap-trap, two-table restaurant high in the Nepalese Himalayas, exhausted from a full day of trekking. I scanned the sparse menu: eggs, dahl with rice, pizza.

A telephone, an electrical outlet and a toilet were a week's walk away. Everything in the village that had not been grown or made locally had been carried up the mountains on the backs of humans. I ordered the pizza made of ketchup and yak cheese melted on Tibetan bread, along with a cup of *chai*.

The waiter casually plunked a cassette into a tinny, battery-operated tape deck. Suddenly, in a part of the world where even the wheel is a rumor, the room was filled with the exotic, timeless, ethereal strains of Pink Floyd.

Kathmandu was filled with great music, but out here on the trail it was a delightful surprise. It was at the same time incongruous and totally logical and appropriate. After all, it's been the trekkers—young, hip and usually stoned—who've brought Western music to Nepal.

A fellow traveler, an Israeli guy, was the most gorgeous hunk of manflesh I'd ever met. He was a huge Pink Floyd fan and requested that their tapes be played wherever he went. If I heard Pink Floyd when I walked into a place, I knew there was a good chance he was inside. Everywhere it seemed, no matter how little else the local café and lodge owners had in the way of material possessions, there was always a cassette player and at least one Pink Floyd tape. Good thing, too, because for all his stunning good looks, my pal was a nasty s.o.b., sullen, moody and rude—the kind of guy who kicks chickens—and Pink Floyd was the only music that had charm enough to soothe his savage breast.

Pink Floyd always brings to mind my three-week trek in Nepal and my stunning but tragically flawed friend, whose love of Pink Floyd and good looks may have been his only redeeming qualities.

ADRIENNE GUSOFF

HULL

FESTIVALS

Shiver ye timbers at the **Sea Shanty Festival** for a weekend in mid-September in the historic town of Hull, on the north shore of the River Humber. To celebrate the town's long maritime history, traditional sea chanteys are performed against the setting of traditionally rigged sailing ships. For further information, contact the Tourist Information Centre, 75/76 Carr Lane, Hull, Humberside, HU1 3RQ; or call 0482/223559, fax 0482/593959.

LAKE DISTRICT

FESTIVALS

For the first two weeks of August, Ambleside on the shores of Lake Windermere is the place to be for both students and lovers of classical music. **Lake District Summer Music** offers not only concerts and chamber music recitals, but summer school courses and individual classes by international teachers and musicians to pianists, string players and ensembles. On Wednesday, Thursday and Friday afternoons, master classes, which are open to the public, are held at Charlotte Mason College. For a schedule of events and courses, contact Lake District Summer Music, 72 Greenhill, Wirksworth, Derbyshire, DE4 4EH, England; phone 0629/823733.

The Windermere Festival, held the first week of July, provides some of the only *real* entertainment of the summer in this neck o' the woods. In addition to folk music and dancing, there's also plenty of other mayhem such as traditional Westmoreland wrestling contests, regattas and even bungee jumping. For information, write to Tourist Office, Gateway Centre, Victoria St., Windermere, Cumbria, LA23 1AD, England.

LEEDS

Leeds prides itself on being a twenty-four-hour city with entertainment for all tastes. To find out what's happening when you're in town, pick up one of the many informational brochures available with listings for special events such as the *City Centre Bulletin*, the tiny pamphlet *What's On in Leeds,* and *Leeds Nights,* or check the local papers.

CONCERT HALLS

Leeds Grand Theatre and Opera House (46 New Briggate, 0532/459351, 440971) is the main venue in town for classical concerts, opera, musicals, and serious theater. **The Civic Theatre** (Cookridge St., 0532/4776962, 455505) features musical theater, concerts and drama. **Leeds Town Hall** (The Headrow; call Civic Theatre for information) is the home of the Leeds International Concert Season and also hosts other musical and theatrical events.

CLUBS AND DISCOS

The Gallery (9 Lower Merrion St., 0532/450923) is really three clubs in one: Ricky's, Arcadia and The Gallery. Saturday nights, enjoy jazz-funk in this hip decor. Monday is student night; Tuesday, hear rock and indie bands; Wednesday is all jazz; Thursday is '70s disco, soul and funk. The bar offers many kinds of beer as well as soft drinks. Open from 9 p.m.–2 a.m. If you're into partying a little later, try **The Music Factory** (174 Briggate, 0532/470480), which opens at 9:30 p.m. and hops until 3:30 a.m. The smartly dressed crowd parties on three dance floors, surrounded by original back-drops, drapery and corrugated metal. If you're driving, there's a one-thousand-car parking lot opposite the club.

| SPOTLIGHT ON | DAVID BOWIE |

One might never have suspected, examining David Bowie's rocky early career, that he would later have such a profound influence on so many aspects of rock music including glam, disco and punk. None of his first groups—The King Bees, The Mannish Boys and The Lower Third—recorded with any success. At this point he abandoned his birth name, Jones, taking Bowie (after the knife) as a stage name, to avoid confusion with the already-famous Monkees lead singer. Contracts with Pye and Decca labels as a soloist in the late '60s produced several pop love ballads, some of which made the British charts only in re-release, years later.

Bowie dropped out of the music scene for a while, spending a few months in a Buddhist monastery in Scotland without taking his vows. From there, he moved on to an apprenticeship in Lindsay Kemp's mime troupe—training that would serve him well later on. In 1969 he reemerged to record *Space Oddity* for Mercury which became a huge surprise hit. The sudden fame and attention prompted Bowie to create Ziggy Stardust, a fictional, decadent, rock superstar, a character who eventually became indistinguishable from Bowie himself.

Bowie's flair for theatrics, highly fashionable yet androgynous style and Nietzsche-influenced lyrics made his performances some of the most well-attended in rock history and left him with a string of gold records. As a producer, he revived the flagging careers of Lou Reed (*Transformer*) and Mott the Hoople (Bowie wrote "All the Young Dudes"). His acting career, though not a spectacular success overall, included the Broadway production of *The Elephant Man* for which he received critical praise.

Bowie is acknowledged by most as rock's most influential performer of the '70s, and well into the '90s he remains an important personality.

Consider also **The Warehouse at the Warehouse** (Somers St., 0532/461033), the bilevel, two-dance-floor club close to the Leeds train station where there's no dress code, just an "attitude code." To keep the regulars regular, the club also features a weekly soap opera. Open from 10 p.m.–2 a.m. If you want to get started a little earlier, try the very large **Orbit** (South Queen St., Morley, 0532/528202, a bilevel club featuring laser shows and two chill-out rooms.

If an upbeat pub atmosphere is more to your liking, try the glitzy, ultramodern **The Boulevard** (Headrow), with youth-oriented disco nights on Thursday and Friday. **The Duchess of York** (Vicar Lane) is another popular place, where you can hear top-notch up-and-coming bands every night.

The Observatory (40 Boar Lane), with its impressive domed interior, is a favorite singles hangout featuring a busy dance floor and a balcony where you can just stand back and watch the action. The club features resident DJs nightly. Mondays and Wednesdays are student nights; Tuesday is rock night. The club has a huge selection of beers and ales and serves hot meals and snacks to help you keep your energy up.

For the over-twenty-five crowd, there's **Digby's** (York Place, 0532/443590), which attracts a more sophisticated crowd by playing varied DJed music. Entry ranges from £3–£6, depending on the night. **Mr. Craig** (New Briggate, 0532/422224) is a narcissist's paradise, what with nearly every surface either mirrored or covered with silver fittings. Fridays and Saturdays attract an older, smartly dressed crowd and DJs play popular mainstream stuff. Monday is Student Night. Closed Thursdays for private parties. Admission ranges from £2–£6, depending on the night.

FESTIVALS

During the first weekend of July at Roundhay Park is the fantastic **Heineken Music Festival**. The first band goes on stage at 7:00 p.m., but get there early as attendance runs about fifty thousand for this free event featuring performers from all over the country. At Leeds Town Hall for four days during the first week of July, enjoy the **Leeds Conductor's Competition** featuring Britain's leading young conductors vying for this coveted award. Admission to the competition is free, and tickets for the gala final concert on Saturday night range from £5–£15. Tickets available from Civic Theatre Box Office. Call 0523/455505, 476962.

On a Saturday in mid-July from noon well into the night the town fills with the sound of buskers, all doing their own thing, during the **National Street Music Festival**. Local cafés serve at streetside tables giving the city a continental atmosphere. During the August Bank Holiday (the last weekend in August), Chapeltown comes alive with the sights and sounds of the **West Indian Carnival**. In addition to parades, street performances, music and costumes, there's a huge concert on Sunday in Potternewton Park, featuring stars from Britain and abroad playing irresistable reggae.

CHURCHES AND SYNAGOGUES

Leeds Parish Church of St. Peter-at-Leeds (Kirkgate, 0532/452036), built in 1841, has a daily offering of choral worship featuring both a boys' choir and men's choir.

All one's life is music, if one touches the notes rightly, and in time.

RUSKIN

MISCELLANEOUS

Enjoy **Opera in the Park** at Temple Newsam Park on a Saturday night in mid-July. Throngs gather in the park, wearing anything from ripped jeans and T-shirts to black tie, for this free event featuring excerpts from the world's favorite operas. Admission by free ticket only, available from The Bond Street Centre (0532/445701), the Civic Theatre Box Office (0532/476962, 455505), or the Grand Theatre Box Office (0532/459351, 440971) or send a self-addressed envelope to the Information Centre, Civic Hall, Leeds, LS1 1UR, England. For more information call 0532/478197.

Granary Wharf features festival markets every weekend with street entertainment ranging from Latin bands to folk singers. Walk the magnificent grounds of Harewood by day, then stick around and enjoy **Music at Harewood**, a series of outdoor evening classical concerts at Harewood House, a grand eighteenth-century home, estate and museum located just seven miles outside of Leeds. There's always something interesting going on at Harewood in addition to the music series, which in the past has featured Kiri Te Kanawa and the Prazak String Quartet. Ticket prices vary and are in addition to admission to the grounds. Call 0532/886331 for details and a schedule. There is bus service to Harewood Village from central Leeds (and Harrogate) every half hour.

WENSLEYDALE

FESTIVALS

Seventy-six trombones and scores of other brass instruments from all over the world play alongside British bands at the **International Brass Festival** in Wensleydale, North Yorkshire, during the last week of August. For further information, contact Wensleydale Music Arts Centre, Town Hall, Leyburn, N. Yorkshire, DL8 5AN, England; phone 0969/22725.

YORK

CONCERT HALLS

Grand Opera House (Cumberland St., 0904/654654) and the **York Theatre Royal** (St. Leonard's Pl., 0904/623568) both hold an audience of about 1,000 for opera, theater and musical concerts. **Sir Jack Lyons Concert Hall** at the University of York (Heslington, 0904/432447) is a newer but smaller venue that seats about 325.

FESTIVALS

For two weeks in mid-July the city of York takes a giant step into the past during the **York Early Music Festival,** Britain's largest festival of early music. Within the city's medieval churches and abbeys and amid the ancient architectural splendor of this city, which dates back to pre-Christian days, music lovers from around the world gather to hear gothic choirs, Renaissance music and more, including costumed characters and street performances. The goal of the artistic advisors is to make early music accessible and enjoyable for people of all ages and backgrounds. For further details, contact York Early Music Festival, 65 Rawcliffe Lane, York, YO3 6SJ, England; phone the box office at 0904/658338, fax 0904/612631.

✪ ANSWERS TO TEST YOUR MUSICAL I.Q.

Page 83

1-a,   2-a,   3-a,   4-b,   5-b,   6-a,   7-b,   8-a,   9-b,   10-b

South Coast

Including Arundel, Bournemouth, Brighton, Canterbury, Chichester, Lewes (Glyndebourne)

ARUNDEL

FESTIVALS

Arundel Castle, ancestral home of the Duke of Norfolk, is the focal point for the **Arundel Festival** held for ten days in late August through early September. The festival, featuring an international mixed-arts program, takes place in a variety of historic settings in the vicinity of this small Sussex town, not the least impressive of which is the Open Air Theatre beneath the battlements of the Castle. Open-air events include an opening night concert accompanied by the Theatre of Fire's amazing annual pyrotechnic display, Jazz Night, and Festival Dance as well as Shakespearean performances. Although billed as an arts festival, there is a heavy emphasis on music including concerts and performances by international artists. For a brochure, contact Arundel Festival Society, The Mary Gate, Arundel, West Sussex BN18 9AT, England; call 0903/883690.

BOURNEMOUTH

CONCERT HALLS

The Pavillion Theatre (Westover Rd., 0202/297297), recently renovated to its former splendor, is a 1500-seat theater and a wonderful place to see concerts, musicals, and "summer spectaculars." There are full catering and bar facilities within the complex. **Tregonwell Hall** (Exeter Rd., 0202/297297) and the larger **Windsor Hall** (seats up to four thousand) are both part of the **Bournemouth International Centre,** both major concert venues for the south, featuring international artists the likes of Tina Turner, Elton John, Simply Red, Tom Jones, A Ha and many more. Bar and restaurant facilities are located in the complex.

SPOTLIGHT ON   PHIL COLLINS

He was already a respected member of a very popular rock band, Genesis, when Phil Collins went out on his own. He'd just gotten divorced from his first wife and he put together *Face Value,* an album full of personal songs, so private that even his ex-wife asked, "How can you let everyone know all this stuff?" But to Collins, that's what writing music is all about—making strong statements about what's going on inside, despite his stiff-upper-lip British background.

Collins's music comes from his gut. So much so, in fact, that while in the recording studio he'll often sing the lyrics spontaneously and write them down later. That's how he wrote "In the Air Tonight," which topped the charts on both sides of the Atlantic, "There's a Place for Us" and "I've Forgotten Everything," a tune the songwriter sees as a Hoagy Carmichaelesque song about trying to get over a love affair.

Married again and the father of a young daughter, Lily, he and his wife Jill sometimes live in Los Angeles, in a house once occupied by Cole Porter. He also maintains a home with a studio in Sussex. Having his own studio is important to him because it permitted him to make a truly solo album, *Both Sides,* with a coherent mood throughout. Collins played all the instruments and produced the album alone. "I didn't want anyone to muck about with the demos," he said.

In addition to recording and touring, Collins also keeps his fingers in other pots, most notably the Hollywood film industry. No stranger to acting (he starred as the Artful Dodger in a West End production of *Oliver!* when he was fourteen), he's appeared in a few films and television programs. He'd like to expand his role as a composer of film scores. He says, "I would really like to compose a proper orchestral soundtrack with themes and variations. It's somewhere between performing music and acting; it's about the power of matching music to visuals."

Phil Collins

FESTIVALS

The relatively new **Bournemouth International Festival,** held for two weeks at the beginning of June, features a wealth of stars in an innovative and varied program designed to appeal to a broad audience of music lovers. This seaside town was voted "Resort of the Year 1992–1993" by the English Tourist Board, which means that when you're not listening to music, you can kick back and enjoy the beach. For a program, contact Bournemouth International Festival, Suite 2, Digby Chambers, Bournemouth, BH1 1BA, England; phone 0202/297327.

Music is the language spoken by angels.

LONGFELLOW

BRIGHTON

Brighton is to England what San Francisco is to the U. S.—the gay mecca—with plenty of shops, restaurants and nightclubs oriented toward gay lifestyles. Also called "The Las Vegas of England," this often outrageous seaside resort, though hardly elegant, is almost always fun, regardless of sexual preference—as long as you're willing to let your hair down.

CONCERT HALLS

Brighton Centre (King's Rd., 0273/202881) is the largest civic hall in the south and offers widely varied programs. **Gardner Arts Centre** (University of Sussex, Falmer, 0273/685861) presents a mixed program of music, theater and other performances.

CLUBS AND DISCOS
Rock

For years, Brighton's major club has been **Escape** (10 Marine Parade, 0273/606906). A bar by day, by night it attracts some of the area's biggest-name DJs and a good-looking, trendy crowd. Admission is £4–£5, and no sportswear is allowed. There are two dance floors teeming with a mixed crowd dancing to soul, hip hop, funk, swing, house and more. Open until 2 a.m. Vying with Escape for best club in town is **Zap** (Kings Road Arches, 0273/821588). Zap offers different clubs nightly, including Saturday's Coco Club, which pumps out music until 5 a.m., one of the latest closings in town. There are ministages along the dance floor where the less-inhibited dancers can shake their booties for the rest of the crowd. Plenty of good chill-out space gives patrons opportunities to just sit and talk. There's a very liberal door policy here; the entry fee runs about £6. If you're going to club hop, before heading over to Zap try **Shark Bar,** right on the waterfront. Many stop here for preclub drinking, and some even stay to dance though it's pretty small (holds 180). Shark Bar appeals mainly to a selective older crowd. The club closes at 3 a.m. Food is available.

Paradox (West St., 0273/321628) is a huge place (holds 1,200) that plays mostly commercial dance tunes. Its once-a-month (Monday night) gay night, Wild Fruit, was voted one of the top ten clubs in the U. K. by *DJ Magazine.* Thursday nights you'll find mostly students undoubtedly due to the free admission before 10 p.m. and cheap bar prices before 11 p.m. On Saturdays no one under twenty is admitted. No "trainers" (running shoes or sneakers) are allowed. Light food is available. Paradox is open until 2 a.m.

✪ Test Your Musical I.Q.

Which of these artists are from the U. K.? (Part 2)

1. **a)** Cat Stevens or
   b) Stray Cats
2. **a)** Dusty Springfield or
   b) Leslie Gore
3. **a)** Birds or
   b) Yardbirds
4. **a)** UB40 or
   b) B-52's
5. **a)** Lynard Skynard or
   b) Def Leppard
6. **a)** Mott the Hoople or
   b) Motley Crue
7. **a)** Iron Butterfly or
   b) Iron Maiden

8. a) Three Dog Night or
   b) Bonzo Dog Doo-Dah Band
9. a) Blood, Sweat & Tears or
   b) Average White Band
10. a) Bay City Rollers or
    b) New Lost City Ramblers

(Answers on page 105.)

Gay and Lesbian

Revenge (32–34 Old Steine, 0273/606064), an all-gay, members-only club, is Brighton's number-one gay club. Until a couple of years ago, it was strictly men, but women are slowly joining the party in this bilevel club with a fantastic view of the Channel.

Another great little venue is the **Warehouse** (54 Meeting House Lane, 0273/208050) set in The Lanes, a warren of mazelike streets. Although the dance floor is small, it's got plenty of nooks and crannies to chill out including a balcony that overlooks the crowd and a bar up a spiral staircase in a turret. The bad news is that you'll need a membership to get in. The good news is that memberships are free. The bad news is that you have to apply forty-eight hours in advance. The good news is that Brighton can keep you entertained for the two days you'll have to wait. Food is available. The Warehouse is open until 2 a.m.

Were it not for music, we might in these days say, the Beautiful is dead.

DISRAELI

FESTIVALS

The **Brighton Festival,** the last three weeks in May, claims to be "the largest and most comprehensive arts festival in England," and includes opera, symphony concerts, ensembles, string quartets, premieres of new pieces (often by new artists), international dance, international theater companies, world film, literature and visual arts exhibitions. Contact The Brighton Festival Society, 21–22 Old Steine, Brighton, BN1 1EL, England; telephone 0273/713875, 6, 7, fax 0273/622453.

Tomb of Edward, the "Black Prince"—Canterbury Cathedral

CANTERBURY

FESTIVALS

The two-week **Canterbury Festival** held in mid-October offers more than two hundred arts events, including cabaret and song in the Festival Club, opera, jazz, street performances, dance, walks and talks and fireworks. Many of these events are held in historic settings such as the Canterbury Cathedral, Dover Castle and Margate's Theatre Royal. Although most of the fun can be found in the cathedral city of Canterbury, many events stretch out into the surrounding coastal towns such as Margate and Dover and inland through East Kent. For more information, write to the Festival Office, 59 Ivy Lane, Canterbury, Kent, CT1 1TU, England; call 0227/452853.

POP QUIZ 10

How many members made up the original Thompson Twins?

ANSWER: Seven

CHICHESTER

FESTIVALS

The Sussex cathedral city of Chichester celebrates for seventeen days in early to mid-July during the **Chichester Festivities,** a flamboyant feast of the arts, from classical music to jazz and opera, and including comedy, theater, dance, films, exhibitions, children's events, poetry readings and raucous street entertainment. Enjoy a concert in Chichester's magnificent nine-hundred-year-old Cathedral or a "champagne" concert at Goodwood House. For a program or ticket information, write to Administrator, Chichester Festivities, Canon Gate House, South Street, Chichester, West Sussex, PO19 1PU, England; call 0243/11200.

WHERE IT'S AT   GLYNDEBOURNE FESTIVAL OPERA

Back in the 1930s, John Christie, whose family owns the large estate upon which the Glyndebourne Opera takes place, decided, almost on a whim, to build a theater in which to present opera. His ideas didn't come entirely from left field. After all, he was an opera aficionado and his wife the soprano Audrey Mildmay. He had the stage constructed in a quaint room built to seat an audience of three hundred.

Over the years, the Glyndebourne Festival Opera has attracted opera lovers in formal dress, who've paid up to £150 per ticket to listen to the music and enjoy the lovely grounds. Glyndebourne has built a reputation as one of the finest companies in the country, at once reserved yet always fresh. Back at the start, they presented operas in their original languages, at a time when other companies were translating the librettos into the language of the audience.

Sir George Christie, son of the opera's founder and current chairman, decided in 1987 that Glyndebourne needed a new theater. The old one had too many limitations, both technical and practical (lack of air conditioning, for example). With much fanfare, the old hall was demolished at the end of the 1992 season and a grand new theater built, seating four times as many opera lovers, at a cost of £49.5 million. The ambience of the new theater was kept as close as possible to the old. Builders used one-hundred-year-old pitch pine from old buildings and docks. There's been no added glitz. Like the old theater, the new one is comfortably unostentatious. Technically, however, there have been improvements that, one hopes, will permit more elaborate and inspired productions.

LEWES [GLYNDEBOURNE]

FESTIVALS

The Glyndebourne Festival Opera season is more "season" than "festival," though one can't deny the festive air, as opera lovers, many of whom having come down on the train from London in full dress, enjoy both the delights of this first-class opera company as well as the magnificent, rolling grounds of the private estate on which the event is held. The season lasts from the end of May through late August and sees over eighty thousand music lovers during that time. For a season's schedule and ticket information, contact Glyndebourne Festival Opera, Glyndebourne, Lewes, East Sussex, BN8 5UU, England; phone 0273/812321, fax 0273/812783.

✪ ANSWERS TO TEST YOUR MUSICAL I.Q.

Page 101

1-a,   2-a,   3-a,   4-a,   5-b,   6-a,   7-b,   8-b,   9-b,   10-a

East Coast: East Anglia, Norfolk and Norwich

Including Aldeburgh, Bury St. Edmunds, Cambridge, King's Lynn, Norwich

ALDEBURGH

FESTIVALS

Aldeburgh's half-century-old **Festival of Music and the Arts,** held from early to late June, offers a remarkable range of music in a short time. Considered by many classical music lovers as one of the best of its kind in the country, the festival was founded by Benjamin Britten in 1946. The 1995 season began with the world premiere of *The Wildman,* a new piece of musical theater by eminent composer Nocola LeFanu and librettist Kevin Crossley-Holland. The title character, completely naked and covered in hair, was, according to legend, trawled up by an Oxford fisherman and imprisoned in Oxford Castle during the reign of Henry II. For more information on the festival, contact the Aldeburgh Foundation, High Street, Aldeburgh, Suffolk, IP15 5AX, England; phone 0728/452935 for a brochure, for tickets 0728/453543, fax 0728/452715.

BURY ST. EDMUNDS

FESTIVALS

For two weeks in mid-May, this attractive market town in the heart of East Anglia hosts the **Bury St. Edmunds Festival.** Although fairly new among British arts festivals, it has quickly become one of the most highly regarded. The festival schedule is packed with classical concerts, jazz performances, late-night cabarets and choir recitals, as well as dance, theater, walks, lectures and other events held in a variety of venues around town including the Georgian Theatre Royal and Bury St. Edmund's Cathedral. For further information, contact the Festival Office, Borough Offices, Angel Hill, Bury St. Edmunds, Suffolk, England.

CAMBRIDGE

CONCERT HALLS

Cambridge Corn Exchange (Wheeler St., 0223/357851) offers everything from variety shows to Cambridge Philharmonic performances, from operas to international, star-studded extravaganzas. Concerts generally start at 7:30 p.m.–8:00 p.m. and admission ranges from £7–£12. Student standby discounts of fifty percent are available.

CLUBS AND DISCOS

Depending on the night, you might find jazz, blues, folk or rock at any of the clubs below. It's best to check their schedules to see who's playing. **The Junction** (Clifton Rd., 0223/412600) features both live music gigs ranging from the acoustic folk-rock strains of the Indigo Girls to hard house music and indie and disco. Doors open for performances at 7 p.m.; nightclub is open from 10 p.m.–2 a.m. Tickets range from £5–£9. **5th Avenue** (Heidelburg Gardens, Lion Yard, 0223/64222), open Wednesday through Saturday, changes its theme nightly and holds dance parties on the weekend. Stand in line early if your heart's set on getting in. Dress smartly but casually and be over eighteen. Open from 9 p.m.–2 a.m. Admission can be as low as £3.50 with a flyer.

Other places to hear various kinds of live music are **The Boat Race** (East Rd., 0223/60873) and **Flambards** (Rose Crescent, 0223/358108). **Caffe Piazza** (Regent St.) occasionally features live jazz and Latin music nights, so if it's jazz you crave, you might check out this club. Pick up a *Cambridge Nightlife Guide,* "the most sought after information leaflet," at many places around town for a day-by-day schedule of events.

FESTIVALS

You have no excuse to be bored while visiting Cambridge during the summer. There are at least half a dozen different festivals, many of which happen simultaneously. In addition to fairs, film festivals and sporting events, many of which are free, there are several festivals either dedicated to or with a heavy emphasis on music.

Cambridge Summer in the City is a program of arts and entertainment events sponsored by the Cambridge City Council. Most every day, from June through September, there's *something* going on, though not all of it is musical. Still, you might find yourself in town on a Sunday afternoon when there's a jazz band playing on Jesus Green or during an exhibition of international folk music and dancing, an outdoor performance of a traditional choir or a Sinfonia concert. For a thirty-two-page booklet, contact Cambridge City Council, Leisure Services, The Guildhall, Cambridge, CB2 3QJ, England; information hotline 0223/463363.

Music Around Cambridge Summer Festival, mid June through mid-September, is a cornucopia of classical music from medieval times to the present day, including opera, early-music ensembles, vocalists, quartets and chamber music, most held in churches and chapels around the university. Themes change yearly. For tickets and information, contact Arts Box Office, Market Passage, Cambridge, CB3 9AD, England; phone 0223/352001.

The Cambridge Folk Festival at the end of July features an impressive roster of international folk stars on two main stages as well as workshops, ensemble playing and special events for children. There are two campsites with offsite parking. These sites usually sell out well in advance, so book early. To sate your hunger and thirst, there are all-day bars and food stalls. Standard advance weekend prices are £34 per person, dailies at £18, with substantial discounts for city residents and those with Leisurecards. (Camping fees are not included.) Children are free. For festival tickets and camping reservations, contact Folk Festival Box Office, P.O. Box 385, Cambridge, CB2 3QT, England; call 0223/463346, to pay by credit card 0223/463347.

POP QUIZ 11

Which female composer, known for her outrageous fashions and romantic involvements, wrote *The Wreckers* and *March of the Women*?

ANSWER: Ethel Smyth

SPOTLIGHT ON   ALEXIS KORNER

Regarded by most as the granddaddy of British blues, Alexis Korner inspired an entire generation of musicians, who, in turn, continue to inspire others. Born in Paris in 1928, Korner spent his early years living in various countries including Switzerland, France and North Africa before his family finally settled in London at the outbreak of World War II. He taught himself boogie-woogie piano by listening to Jimmy Yancey recordings and after the war played guitar in Chris Barber's "trajazz" band. In the early '50s, he played in a skiffle band. In the late '50s, inspired by American blues legend Muddy Waters, Korner began playing his own version of the blues along with harp player Cyril Davies.

By 1961 the two had formed Blues Incorporated, a major influence in the blues revival in the U. K. and the U. S. in the early '60s. From this and subsequent Korner groups came the founding members of Cream, The Rolling Stones, Led Zeppelin, Fleetwood Mac, Pentangle and Humble Pie including Mick Jagger, Brian Jones and Charlie Watts, John Mayall, Eric Clapton, Ginger Baker, Jack Bruce, Graham Bond and Robert Plant.

In 1970 he was persuaded by producer Mickie Most to front a studio band, Collective Consciousness Society, which had several hits including the Led Zeppelin song "Whole Lotta Love" in 1970. His inimitable husky voice brought him work doing advertising jingles and voice-overs and later as a BBC radio DJ.

From the second to last week in July is the CN.FM (Radio) **Cambridge Fringe,** three weeks packed with musicals, opera, dance, concerts, comedy, theater, poetry readings, workshops, even bell-ringing demonstrations. Ticket prices are per event and range from free to £6. For information and reservations for all shows: Arts Box Office at the Arts Cinema (open Monday–Saturday from 10 a.m.– 8 p.m.), Market Passage, Cambridge, CB2 3PF, England; phone 0223/352001. **The International Arts Festival** is held the second and third weeks of July and is another packed program of music, theater, film, spoken word, dance, visual arts and workshops from around the world. The 1994 season offered such musical delights as roots music from Madagascar, the thirty-two-piece Pan-African Orchestra and the stunning musical drama of France's Pascal Theatre Company. For a brochure and schedule call the box office at 0223/412600 or, for credit card bookings, call the twenty-four-hour festival hotline at 0710/344–4444 (subject to a service charge). Or, you can write to The Kirin International Arts Festival Box Office, The Junction, Clifton Rd., Cambridge, CB1 4GX, England. Student and senior discounts are available.

SPOTLIGHT ON   IAN HOBSON

Ian Hobson began piano lessons when he was four years old, at an age when most young boys can hardly sit still or concentrate on anything for more than five minutes at a stretch. Years of study, combined with a great natural talent, have made Hobson one of the most respected pianists and teachers in the world

Born in Wolverhampton, England, Hobson later studied at the Royal Academy of Music at Cambridge University with pianist Sidney Harrison and organist Arnold Richardson and completed his degree with a dual major in both instruments at nineteen. He continued his education in the United States at Yale, adding harpsichord and conducting to his studies. In 1977 he began performing on the competition circuit, so critical to professional musical careers, ascending from fifth place at his first Van Cliburn competition in 1977 to first at Leeds in 1981. These prizes provided him with opportunities to appear with Sir Georg Solti and the London Philharmonic (playing Beethoven's Second Piano Concerto), with Henry Mazer and the Chicago Symphony (performing Rachmaninoff's Third Piano Concerto) and with Dennis Russell Davies and the Pittsburgh Symphony (playing Shostakovich's Second Piano Concerto). Though he always remained true to the piano, conducting also called to him, and he continued his musical training at the Aspen and Tanglewood music festivals with Leonard Bernstein, Seiji Ozawa and Gustav Mayer.

Hobson has an impressive discography on EMI and Arabesque (his current label) including Godowsky's technically demanding

Eighteen Studies on Chopin Etudes, Twenty-Four Preludes by Rachmaninoff and *Piano Works* by Robert Schumann. He is in the process of recording the complete Beethoven sonatas and Brahms's complete variations.

More than anything else, it is Hobson's diversity, sensitivity to subtle detail and virtuosity which are most remarked upon by critics and reviewers. Tim Riley of *CD Review* (February 1993) wrote "Hobson...makes you hear new things even in the most familiar Schumann." Dean Elder of *Clavier* (September 1990) wrote "[Hobson's] transversal of Rachmaninoff's seventeen études-tableaux, works of great diversity, depth and grandeur little known to the public, is miraculous." *Digital Audio* wrote "Hobson...offers the best [Johann Nepomuk] Hummel ever put on record." Hobson now teaches at the University of Illinois at Champaign-Urbana, but his performance, conducting and teaching schedules take him all over the world.

KING'S LYNN

FESTIVALS

Only an hour-and-a-half by train from London, this historic coastal town with its pristine coast and countryside is the perfect setting for a festival—small enough to be completely immersed in the goings-on of the **King's Lynn Festival,** held annually the last two weeks in July. Considered one of the preeminent music and arts festivals in all of Britain, King's Lynn attracts performers the world over. The variety of orchestra, opera and chamber music performances, open-air concerts, cabarets and classic film showings make this a feast of the arts. Contact the Festival Office, 27–29 King St., King's Lynn, Norfolk, PE30 6LD, England; call 0553/773578.

POP QUIZ 12

What famous British Invasion group was called the Ravens and the Bol-Weevils before taking the name by which we know it today?

ANSWER: The Kinks

NORWICH

CONCERT HALLS

Although Norwich isn't on the main circuit for big concert artists, it does have its share of concert venues, most of which are pressed into service during the festival. They include **Norwich Arts Centre** (St. Benedict's St., 0603/660-3520, **Theatre Royal** (Theatre St., 0603/628205) and **The Waterfront** (139–141 King St., 0603/766266). The University of East Anglia has its own concert hall and imports performers, such as the Pogues and the Saw Doctors, chosen mainly for their appeal to the students.

FESTIVALS

During the second week of October the **Norfolk and Norwich Festival** offers eleven days of music and dance as well as theater, comedy, film, puppetry and exhibitions. You may enjoy performances on some of the organs in Norwich's historic churches and the Cathedral or hear concerts in many of the venerable houses in the region. Contact Festival Ticket Shop, The Guildhall, Goal Hill, Norwich, NR2 1NF, England; phone 0603/764764.

SPOTLIGHT ON   NOEL COWARD

Extraordinary how potent cheap music is.

NOEL COWARD

Although thought of mainly as an actor and playwright, Noel Coward (1899–1973) was one of this century's cleverest and most important songwriters. His first notable song, "Parisian Peirrot," was featured in the 1923 show *London Calling* starring Gertrude Lawrence, who later starred in many other Coward plays. Coward was quickly lauded as the young genius of the stage. By the late '30s, he'd written nine hit musicals, in which he often starred.

Coward spent much of World War II entertaining the troops and contributed songs, such as "London Pride," to the war effort. The satire of his "Don't Let's Be Beastly to the Germans," however, went right over the heads of the powers that be at both EMI (his record label) and the BBC, who refused to record or broadcast it because it was "pro-German."

Coward was greatly influenced by Gilbert and Sullivan and wrote his own operettas. He also wrote films, satires and comedy thrillers. As a nightclub artist, working with such entertainers as Marlene Dietrich, he was one of the highest-paid on the circuit. He died at age seventy-four in Port Maria, Jamaica.

Southwest: Devon and Cornwall Coast

Including   Dartington, Exeter, Sidmouth

Much of the southwest is covered by Dartmoor National Forest, and though wildlife makes its own lovely sounds, this area of the country does not hold much attraction for those in search of music made by humans. There are, however, a couple of notable exceptions.

DARTINGTON

FESTIVALS

For five intense weeks from the end of July to the end of August the **Dartington International Summer School** offers master classes, open rehearsals, participatory choir, chamber music and workshops for musicians at all levels of experience. This residential musical banquet draws together brilliant professionals, gifted amateurs, dedicated dilettantes and fascinated listeners and music lovers from all over the world. The program includes lectures, composition workshops, advanced opera courses, jazz, conductor's master classes, orchestra and early-music classes and recitals. Tuition and full board range from £195–£575 a week, based on accommodations, but Dartington offers a scholarship program enabling serious students to attend at greatly reduced rates. For further information, contact Dartington International Summer School, Dartington Halls, Totnes, Devon, TQ9 6DE, England; call 0803/865988, fax 0803/868108.

MUSICAL MOMENTS "Tommy" Wins a Grammy and Five Tony Awards

It took twenty-five years, but finally Pete Townsend's rock opera, *Tommy*, has taken its proper place in musical history. Originally an album, *Tommy* is the story of Tommy Walker, a boy who, as a result of a traumatic childhood experience, becomes deaf, dumb and blind. His only means of expression is by "playing the silver ball," eventually becoming "The Pinball Wizard," an icon whose followers expect the world from him. Although it never won a Grammy it was one of the most popular albums of the early '70s. So beloved was it that Ken Russell made a star-studded movie version, packed with big-name stars such as Jack Nicholson, Ann-Margret, Roger Daltry, Elton John, Eric Clapton and Oliver Reed.

And now, finally, *Tommy* has been reincarnated as a theatrical musical. *Tommy* broke day-after-opening ticket sales records by selling half a million dollars worth of tickets in one day. The next day, it broke its own record. The show went on to win five Tony Awards on June 6, 1993, including Best Original Score for Townsend. *Tommy* has also won six Drama Desk Awards and three Outer Circle Awards. The cast, choreographer, scenic designer and technical personnel have also won a variety of awards. And, of course, Tommy, the Pinball Wizard, also has a pinball machine named after him.

EXETER

CONCERT HALLS

Exeter University Great Hall (Stocker Rd., 0392/263519) offers a varied schedule of British and international artists such as Christy Moore, The Saw Doctors and Manic Street Preachers appealing primarily to a student crowd. For more general, less rock-oriented musical events, there's **St. George's Hall** (Market St./Fore St., 0392/265866, 422137).

Also worth checking out is the **Exeter and Devon Arts Centre,** which offers a full program of arts including music, dance, classes, films, community programs, and so on. The **Cabaret Theatre** there offers a variety of concerts ranging from zydeco bands and jazz ensembles to electric blues and experimental works. Call 0392/421111 for a program.

CLUBS AND DISCOS

The Quay is dotted with dozens of venues, which offer club nights featuring such genres as rock, rave, house and indie. During the summer, the town is filled with lots of young, foreign students to whom the clubs cater. Try the **Box Disco** (Commercial Rd., 0392/59292), which has been around for a while, but don't be afraid to try the new clubs along The Quay.

✪ Test Your Musical I.Q.

Match each British Invasion band to its big hit:

1. The Troggs	**a)** "Glad All Over"
2. Wayne Fontana and	
The Mindbenders	**b)** "Summer Song"
3. Manfred Mann	**c)** "Ferry 'Cross the Mersey"
4. The Tremeloes	**d)** "Gloria"
5. Dave Clark Five	**e)** "Do Wah Ditty Ditty"
6. The Foundations	**f)** "Whiter Shade of Pale"
7. Freddie and the Dreamers	**g)** "We Gotta Get Out of This Place"
8. Gerry and the Pacemakers	**h)** "Game of Love"
9. Chad and Jeremy	**i)** "Silence Is Golden"
10. Herman's Hermits	**j)** "I'm Telling You Now"
11. The Kinks	**k)** "Needles and Pins"
12. Peter and Gordon	**l)** "She's Not There"
13. Procul Harum	**m)** "World Without Love"
14. The Searchers	**n)** "Friday on My Mind"
15. The Hollies	**o)** "Build Me Up, Buttercup"
16. Them	**p)** "Bus Stop"
17. The Zombies	**q)** "You Really Got Me"
18. The Easybeats	**r)** "I'm Henry the Eighth, I Am"
19. The Animals	**s)** "I'll Never Find Another You"
20. Seekers	**t)** "Love Is All Around"

(Answers on page 119.)

FESTIVALS

The Exeter Festival held from the end of June through mid-July, features over two hundred events, both indoors and out. There are local bands and international orchestras, street entertainers and classical soloists from around the world. There are rock and roll, world music, folk music, opera and chamber orchestras plus ballet, modern dance, theater, lectures and discussion groups, films and slide shows, a crafts fair, children's programs and a black-tie masked ball in Powderham Castle. Exeter's own "last night at the Proms" is held beneath the stars in the National Trust's lovely Killerton Gardens with programs to appeal to every musical taste. For further details, contact the Festival Organizer, Festival Office, Civic Centre, Exeter, EX1 1JN, England; phone 0392/265-2000, fax 0392/265-2654.

CHURCHES AND SYNAGOGUES

The Cathedral of St. Peter sponsors concerts, often choral recitals. Call 0392/55573 for a schedule.

MISCELLANEOUS

Throughout the summer, the Exeter City Council sponsors **Music in the Parks** at a variety of locations about town including the Belmont Pleasure Ground, St. Thomas Pleasure Ground, Heavitree Pleasure Ground and Northernhay Gardens. All events are free. Call 0392/265871 for details.

PUBS

Bowling Green (29–30 Blackboy Rd. on The Quay, 0392/422527) serves up live R&B, reggae and rock to university students. On Wednesday and Sunday nights there's live music in a laid-back atmosphere at **Vines** wine bar (Gandy St., 0392/213924). If folk

■ POP QUIZ 13 ■

Which piano man early in his career, as a member of Bluesology, backed up such artists as Patty LaBelle and the Bluebelles and Billy Stewart?

ANSWER: Elton John

music's more to your taste, and you find yourself in town on a Tuesday evening, stop by **The Mill on the Exe** (Bonhay St., 0392/431791). For jazz, it's **The Jolly Porter** (St. David's Hill, 0392/54848) on Wednesdays.

| SPOTLIGHT ON | SANDY DENNY |

Sandy Denny's career as a vocalist and songwriter, though tragically brief, was full of memorable musical highlights. Remembered mainly as the bluesy, bittersweet lead voice of Fairport Convention, she also enjoyed a brief solo career and was lead singer for the short-lived Strawbs and Fotheringay.

Denny is best known for moody English folk ballads, but she also recorded rock and country tunes as diverse as Chuck Berry's "Memphis," "When Will I Be Loved," and Ernest Tubbs's rockabilly "Walking the Floor Over You," which she sang in a southern accent. She seemed to regard *every* song as a folk song. Denny appeared on Led Zeppelin's song "Battle of Evermore" and on the Who's orchestrated *Tommy*. Her best-known composition is "Who Knows Where the Time Goes," which was only the second song she ever wrote.

Said Joe Boyd, Denny's producer and a good friend, in an interview with the *Boston Globe*, "Sandy always brought a tremendous amount of energy to her sessions. [The other members of Fairport Convention] were all well-behaved, soft-spoken, middle-class boys and she was like a tornado hitting the group. She drank and swore more than they did, and she'd kid them on sensitive subjects."

But Denny was insecure about her rather plain and pudgy appearance. Though she had a sweet face, she never perceived herself as glamorous like so many other performers. She was, however, always confident about her vast talent. She rarely toured as she had a fear of flying, which, in a way, proved ironic; she died in 1978 at age thirty, of injuries sustained after a fall down a flight of stairs in her own home.

SIDMOUTH

FESTIVALS

For the first week of August various venues in and around the Devon town of Sidmouth host the **Sidmouth International Festival of Folk Arts,** a major festival of music and dance, drawing participants and folk-music lovers from around the world. For further information, contact Festival Office, 6 East St., Sidmouth, Devon, EX10 8BL, England.

POP QUIZ 14

Which progressive rock band of the '70s took its name from the title of a W. H. Davies book?

ANSWER: Supertramp, from *Autobiography of a Supertramp*.

ANSWERS TO TEST YOUR MUSICAL I.Q.

Page 116

1-t,   2-h,   3-e,   4-i,   5-a,   6-o,   7-j,   8-c,   9-b,   10-r,
11-q,   12-m,   13-f,   14-k,   15-p,   16-d,   17-l,   18-n,
19-g,   20-s

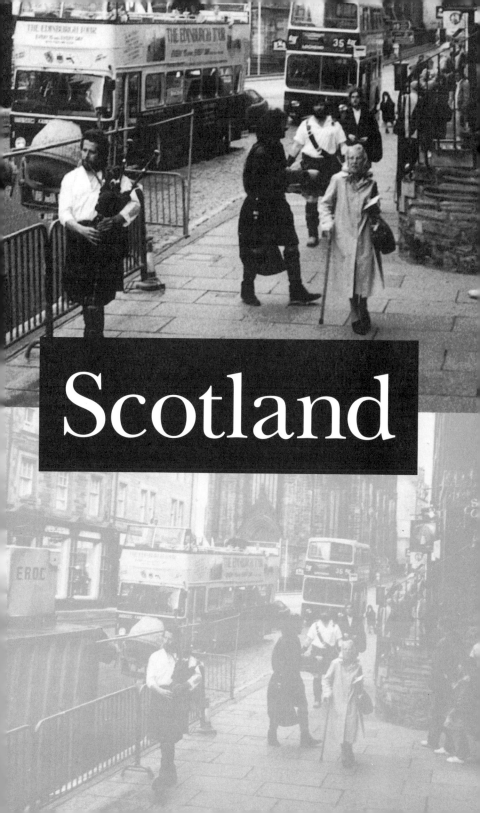

Scotland

Scotland

Including Edinburgh, Glasgow, Aberdeen, Inverness, the North including the Isle of Skye, the Central Highlands, Arran, and the Borders

A bouncing tennis ball is the best analogy to describe Scotland's musical history. In the Middle Ages music developed gradually and peacefully in the churches and at court. But then came the fourteenth century, which was largely disrupted by English aggression directed toward Scotland's fruitless quest for independence; musical development during this period was *not* a high priority.

But then came the fifteenth and sixteenth centuries, which marked another flowering of both church and court music. But, in the mid-sixteenth century, Scotland had to deal with an anti-music national church, and in the seventeenth century the country was abandoned by a fugitive royal court, and music was once again consigned to limbo. In the eighteenth century the musical traditions were revived by Scottish aristocracy, only to be disdained by the nineteenth-century masses who, like their counterparts in Ireland, turned to the more-fashionable music emanating from Mother England.

The twentieth century continues the struggle; one look at the modern musical scene, and you're instantly time zapped back into the world of knights, swords and haggis. On the one hand, you have the bagpiping establishment holding fast to its tradition of a piping discipline handed down through the ages like family jewels. On the other, you have the freewheeling folk-group renegades who've adopted the pipes as their own in the continuing war for a larger share of the musical marketplace.

Until now, the piping establishment has survived thanks to patronage rather than popularity. Anyone who was anyone in the

Scotland of old, in fact, probably had a piper on the books. And what was a war without the blood-curdling drone of the great highland pipe? The military connection actually continues to hold fast with a never-ending supply of piping contests and military tattoos. These interminable events inevitably draw big-name sponsors and pipers from all over the world who come to challenge each other at what in the Gaelic is called *piobaireachd* (*pibroch* or great music).

Bagpiping—Scotland's resilient tradition

However, lest you forget that we're talking music—not the Crusades—let's move beyond bagpiping to fiddlers and harpists who, unlike their blowhard counterparts, have managed to move into the present with a minimum of fuss—and certainly not for lack of a historical context! The fiddle has been part of Scottish culture for about as long as the bagpipe—King James IV, after all, had fiddlers on his payroll in the fifteenth century.

Is it just attitude then that makes bagpipers such prima donnas and other musicians just plain folks? Unfortunately the answer seems to be yes. Fiddle music, like piping, is also divided into what can be considered classical and folk traditions. In the eighteenth century, in fact, many Scots went to Italy to study fiddle music and brought back not only the classical tradition but a shipload of fine violins, which were soon adapted by local artisans and turned into a steady stream of exquisite reproductions.

But, unlike piping, the classical string tradition has consistently felt itself to be *augmented*—not divided—by the country fiddling that reaches its creative zenith in those incessantly robust jigs and reels. The classically trained giant of nineteenth-century fiddle virtuosity, Niel Gow, who was a prolific composer and an extraordinarily gifted player, lies comfortably in the historic archives of fiddle music alongside James Scott Skinner, the most famous rural fiddler of all time—the "King of the Strathspey."

Tis God gives skill,

But not without men's hands;

We could not make Antonio Stradivari's violins

without Antonio.

GEORGE ELIOT

Regardless of internal battles, both piping and fiddling benefit as art forms from the adoring attentions of large numbers of devoted fans (as does the *clarsach* or Scots harp, which had just about fallen into extinction until it was revived in the '70s by Alison Kinnaird and a few of her enthusiastic colleagues). Both are part of a concerted effort to reconcile the past with the present—to break new musical ground while holding fast to the traditions that have made Scotland a steadfast musical giant.

The best of these new traditionalists combine the various elements of Gaelic musical culture with an exuberant use of traditional instruments: accordian, violin, pipes, acoustic guitar and tin whistle—and often layer the mix over a rolling beat that ranges from folk to jazz to rock.

The revival of Scotland's musical heritage has also been boosted by the steadily growing number of folk festivals. Never a week goes by, in fact, when there isn't a folk festival *somewhere* in Scotland. From the Edinburgh Festival, which lasts ten days and is one of the largest of its kind in the world, to the smaller, calmer venues in rural areas such as Keith and Orkney, Scotland's folk festivals are veritable extravaganzas of entertainment.

The revival trend isn't relegated strictly to acoustic music. Equally swayed by the seductive lure of traditionalism has been the world of rock and roll, which has recently begun to pay special attention to Celtic heritage. The problem for rockers, however, is that—like their musical counterparts in other countries—they would love to be able to spread their traditional culture beyond their own borders. And

✪ Test Your Musical I.Q.

Match the groups and artists with their hometowns:

1. The Buzzcocks
2. Shirley Bassey
3. Jeff Beck
4. Duran Duran
5. Kate Bush
6. Petula Clark
7. Joe Cocker
8. Tim Curry
9. Sheena Easton
10. Gang of Four
11. Ian Dury
12. Van Morrison
13. Ten Years After
14. U2
15. Rory Gallagher
16. Annie Lennox

a) Aberdeen, Scotland
b) Sheffield, England
c) Manchester, England
d) Glasgow, Scotland
e) Nottingham, England
f) Cardiff, Wales
g) Billericay, England
h) Epsom, England
i) Dublin, Ireland
j) Ballyshannon, Ireland
k) Glenageary, Ireland
l) Surrey, England
m) Birmingham, England
n) Belfast, Northern Ireland
o) Plumstead, England
p) Cheshire, England

(Answers on page 185.)

that task is not easy, partly because the British rock industry is dominated by London and partly because of a worldwide perception of Scottish music as all tartans and kilts that leaves little room for hard-rocking, electric instrumentation.

Nonetheless, Scotland's rockers keep rocking. And in their determination to succeed they take encouragement from the most tangible sign of success thus far produced by the Scottish Record Industry Association—a Scottish record chart. Extracted from U. K. data collated by Gallup for the main listings, it is published weekly in a number of regional papers and used as the basis for a BBC television show on Friday nights, thereby giving Scottish acts some prominence. The Scottish Record Industry also plans to mount a Scottish-music awards ceremony, which would be on the same scale as Canada's Juno awards and would serve, among other functions, as a vehicle for bringing emerging Scottish acts to the attention of the world market.

EDINBURGH

Edinburgh is a city that believes in investing in the arts. For traditional theater buffs there's the city's incredible Victorian gem—the Royal Lyceum Repertory Theatre. For those tending toward the more avant-garde, there's the Traverse, known worldwide for its daring and innovative work. And for film buffs the city has over twenty movie houses.

Arts galleries are tucked away in quiet streets, in mews and closes with changing exhibitions of painting, photography, jewelry, tapestry and ceramics. Permanent collections are housed in the National Gallery of Scotland and its associated Gallery of Modern Art, and historic portraits can be found at the National Portrait Gallery, which illustrates a nation's history.

But nowhere is Edinburgh's artistic sensibility more evident than in its panoply of music venues—from the fine Edwardian King's Theatre, host to quality touring productions, opera and ballet to the vast, refurbished Playhouse, which offers London's West End musicals as well as rock concerts. There's the magnificently refurbished Festival Theatre with world-class facilities, which was opened in June 1994 for opera and touring productions, and the mammoth Usher Hall, which serves as the home of the Royal Scottish Orchestra. And if musical desires run towards the smaller-scale, there's the intimate

Queen's Hall, presenting the Scottish Chamber Orchestra, as well as recitals and jazz ensembles. In fact with its many clubs and discos and its tradition of Scottish evenings with traditional fare, bagpipes and other music, Edinburgh is justly deserving of its reputation as a world-class capital of arts and entertainment.

Song brings of itself a cheerfulness that wakes the heart to joy.

EURIPIDES

CONCERT HALLS

Classical music is the city's enduring passion, and its many concert venues bear testimony to the breadth of this passion. For starters there's **Usher Hall** (Lothian Road, 031/228-1155), which holds over 2,500 people and is the home of the Royal Scottish Orchestra. Tickets range from £5–£20 and sell out early, so book in advance. Students, senior citizens, registered unemployed and Young Scot Cardholders are entitled to standby tickets on the day of performance for £3.50, and there are free foyer talks introducing the evening's performance from 6:30 p.m.–7 p.m. at the entrance by the main doors. The highlight of Usher Hall's season comes at the end of May when it is home for a week to the Scottish Proms, a series of concerts modeled after the London Promenades. Tickets for the Proms range from £4–£20 for individuals, £7–£38 for a three-concert series and £13–£69 for a six-concert series. Book extremely early, as this is the premier event of Edinburgh's classical season.

Additional concert venues include the more intimate **Queen's Hall** (Clerk St., 031/668-2019), which houses the Scottish Chamber Orchestra (ticket prices range from £3.50–£15 with £5 off for seniors and schoolchildren) as well as classical, rock, folk and jazz concerts; King's Theatre (2 Leven St., 031/229-1201) with a capacity of over 1,300 houses the Scottish Opera as well as performances ranging from operetta to light musical theater. Ticket prices range from £3.50 in the upper circle to £35 in the stalls, and there is a £6 discount on the day of performance for seniors, the disabled, and children under sixteen. King's Theatre can be reached by buses 9, 10, 11, 15, 16, 17, 23, 27 and 45.

The **Edinburgh Playhouse** (18–22 Greenside Place, 031/557-2590) is Scotland's new international theater offering a wide range of performance genres including (in 1994) Barry Manilow's play "Copacabana." Ticket prices range from £7.50–£19.50.

St. Giles Cathedral (look for the spires that can be seen from everywhere in the city, The Royal Mile, 031/225-9442, 225-4363) includes a magnificent organ and the exquisite Thistle Chapel. Concerts are held regularly—mainly at noontime—and are free. Another church to check out for concerts is **St. Mary's Cathedral** (Palmerston Place, 031/225-6293), which has evening concerts and charges about £5.

CLUBS AND DISCOS

The club scene here is young, lively and very casually dressed. Admissions generally run in the £5 range, and most clubs are open until 3 a.m. although there's generally a 1 a.m. or 1:30 a.m. curfew, which means that you have to be inside by that time and done with your hopping from one club to another. Old Town, especially around High Street and the area around the University of Edinburgh, is probably the place you'll want to check out first for its vast array of live music venues and traditional pubs. New Town is best known for the multiplicity of its rock clubs and for its lack of cars. Minding this info and the fact that Edinburgh is a relatively safe city even in the wee hours in mind, check out a few of the following:

The Cathouse Rock Club (Victoria St., 031/225-3326) is open from 11:30 p.m.–3 a.m.; admission £4. **Stone's** (24–26 Frederick St., 031/220-1226) is both a rock and a blues bar with live bands most nights from 8 p.m. on. **The Rockin' Horse** (Victoria St., 031/225-3326) is open from 11 p.m.–3 a.m.; free admission before 11 p.m., £2 after 12:30 a.m. **Madogs Bar and Restaurant** has a slightly older crowd (you can even find some over-thirties here) and pretty good food. Open until 3 a.m. Friday and Saturday; special prices on drinks from 5 p.m.–10 p.m.

Vertigo (21 Lothian Rd., no calls) has good DJs and loud, infinitely danceable music. Ditto **AJ Ramsays** (39–41 Broughton St., 031/557-0627), which also adds to its roster of gentle promotional rhetoric this contention, "All other bars are dog shite." **EXS** (Chandwick Place, 031/225-2266) has house, funk and soul on Friday free, garage on Saturday for £5 and a changing roster on Sunday for £4. Attitude rules here, so dress accordingly.

| SPOTLIGHT ON | THE PROCLAIMERS: AS GOOD AS THEIR NAME |

We always wanted a strong name. We wanted something with a gospel feel to it that indicated strength in the vocal delivery, a sort of spiritual element.

CRAIG REID, OF THE PROCLAIMERS, MAY 1989

The Present

The Proclaimers have just released their first album in five years. *Hit the Highway* is strong, simple, honest and urgent. As the title track puts it bluntly, "Your way? No way. You do it my way. Or you can hit the highway."

Hit the Highway is the naked truth. It's the uplifting sound of unstinting individualism. It's individual...inspired...stirring. Stand up for what you are. Go your own way. Or hit the highway.

"If you're a bit shady or cowardly," says Craig, "you're gonna sell dummies, sidetrack, all the time."

The History

They've always done it their way. While children in Edinburgh, Cornwall, and Auchtermuchty in Fife, the twins, Craig and Charlie Reid, were rabid music fans. At home, it was Merle Haggard, Jerry Lee Lewis, Hank Williams and Ray Charles. At school, it was punk bands such as the Hippy Hasslers, Blag Flag and Reasons for Emotion. Out of this collision of styles and attitudes came The Proclaimers in 1983. Over the next three years, the duo built up a fervent following in the pubs of Edinburgh and Inverness.

People latched onto and identified with these two characters—straight (nice jeans'n'sweaters, thick glasses, sensible haircuts), but individualistic. After a series of favorably reviewed live performances

The Proclaimers made their television debut on January 30, 1987, playing its song, "Letter From America." Immediately afterward, the TV station was jammed with curious callers. Two weeks later, Craig and Charlie did a four-song set in the boardroom of Chrysalis Records in London. Two weeks after that, they began recording their debut album. Nine days later, it was finished. In eight months, the record had gone gold and a rerecording of "Letter from America" went to number three on the singles charts.

Sunshine on Leith, their next album, came out the next year. It sold well throughout Europe and America and went platinum in the U. K., Canada and New Zealand. "I'm Gonna Be (500 miles)" from the album was a worldwide hit single, occupying the top slot in Australia for five weeks.

Then out of the blue, via the efforts of actress and Proclaimers fan Mary Stuart Masterson, "I'm Gonna Be" became the theme song in her film *Benny and Joon,* and in the summer of 1993 the song sold nearly a million copies. The parent album sold another 450,000 copies. The Proclaimers toured the U. S., playing to sold-out crowds, and then repeated the tour in Venezuela, Brazil, Malaysia, Slovakia, Austria, Canada, Germany and Holland. But with characteristic conviction, the duo refused to rerelease the single in the U. K. It had been a substantial hit there already, they maintained.

By the time of their American debut, *Hit the Highway* was complete. It had, however, taken five years. "It's not that we were sitting with *nothing,*" says Craig. "We could have had an album out two or three years ago, but it would have been mediocre. Mediocre or bad. And there's no point in doing that."

Honesty is paramount with these boys. In The Proclaimers' view, there's no crime worse than faking it. As Charlie put it when asked why the album took so long to materialize, "It had to be the best thing we'd ever done, or there'd be no point in putting it out. I couldn't sleep at night if it wasn't a step up. It takes as long as it takes."

The Proclaimers

The Venue (15 Calton Rd., 031/557-3073), with two floors, big crowds and lots of special effects, has a changing lineup and a hip crowd, as does **Cas Rock** (104 West Port, 031/229-4341) where admission ranges from free to £3.50 and Sundays bring R&B jam sessions at which all musicians are welcome.

One of the hottest places in town currently is **The Subway** (69, the Cowgate, 031/225-6766) with a changing roster and lots of people dressed in black leather, as well as "Junefest" (Edinburgh's answer to Glasgow's Mayfest)—an extracharged month filled with hot bands (fourteen every week, two per night). The music ranges from indie to rock, from reggae to thrash to hardcore, and it's all loud. Admission runs about £3.

POP QUIZ 15

Who was the first British artist to have a hit reach number one in the U. S. without the song ever having entered the U. K. charts?

ANSWER: Lulu, "To Sir with Love."

Café St. James (25 St. James Centre, 031/557-2631) has over-twenty-five disco nights Thursdays, Fridays and Saturdays. Plopped on the roof of the St. James Centre, the café has small curtained windows, lots of atmosphere, good food and generally a very contented crowd. **Legends** (71, the Cowgate, 031/225-8382) has musicians' jam sessions on Sundays and about a million promotionals on other nights. (On Thursdays each time a loud siren goes off all drinks are 60p for the next ten minutes.) Got the picture? **Sneaky Pete's** (73 Lower Cowgate, 031/225-1757) attracts the black leather and Doc Martens crowd. The magic follows.

If you like Latin music and thought you might have to check your fancy for the rest of this trip, take heart. On the second Friday of every month, head for **La Belle Angele** (behind the Pelican on the Cowgate), which turns into "Club Latino" (trust us, this is no joke) and offers salsa and other variations on tropical music. Admission: £4. Don't even *think* about going unless you have a feathered boa.

The **Citrus Club** (Lothian Rd., Grindlay St., opposite the Lyceum Theatre, 031/229-6697) features reggae managed by two Jamaican MCs who flip-flop from live music to canned. The crowd is mixed (ages sixteen to forty) and hours are from 11 p.m.–4 a.m.; admission is from £3–£8 depending on the night. If reggae is your thing, you might also want to check out **Innovation Records** (11 Blackfriars St., off High St., 031/557-4688), which stocks all kinds of items related to reggae, thereby proving that there's more to Scotland than haggis, whiskey and mountains (although they're worth checking out too)! Chrissie and Roland, the owners, carry the complete reggae single and album chart as well as West Indian food (salt fish, dragon stout, super malt—all excellent), hair and skincare products and an attitude about serving as a meeting place for other-than-white-people that's altogether refreshing.

JAZZ

The Tron Tavern (9 Hunter Sq., 031/220-1550) has jazz on Wednesdays and Sundays at 8:30 p.m. Admission is generally £3, and the food is good.

Four places with no cover are **The Bank Hotel** (Royal Mile/South Bridge), which has jazz bands from 8:30 p.m. on (it also serves good pastas and salads) Thursdays through Saturdays, but just about every minute during the Edinburgh Festival (check the Festival listings); **Fat San's** (Fountainbridge), which features jazz performers from 7:30 p.m.–10:30 p.m.; the **Granary Bar** (in the Hilton Hotel on Belford Rd.); and **Old Orleans** (on Grisley St.) where performers go on at 8:30 p.m.

Conan Doyle's (71–73 York Place, 031/557-3700) has jazz on Thursdays at 8 p.m. for about £3, good food and a wide selection of beers. The **Traverse Theatre** (next to Usher Hall) has a fifteen-piece jazz band every Monday at 8 p.m.; admission is £3. And **Platform 1** (Rutland St. in the West End, 031/225-2433) has a jazz lunch every Saturday from 12:30 p.m.–3 p.m. featuring the Alex Shaw Trio.

PUBS AND TRADITIONAL MUSIC

As with other cities throughout Scotland and Ireland, traditional music is a must in Edinburgh. It's not just the music. The whole of the culture is contained in every informal session in which musicians jump up from the floor to jam with the band, or in which the band lives down the road. Trad music is not about performance; it's about getting together—a form of socialization that dates back to single-digit centuries. The attitude toward musicians in pubs says it all: pubs don't hire musicians per se. They merely leave a space for musicians to gather much in the same way that they leave space for any other activities deemed essential to social gatherings.

SPOTLIGHT ON ▮ BATTLEFIELD BAND

The Background

Inspired by a rich heritage of Celtic music and fired by the strength of today's Scottish cultural scene, Battlefield Band creates a music of rare passion, relevance and joy. Refusing to be limited by their musical heritage, they mix old songs with their own material, playing a unique fusion of ancient and modern instruments—bagpipes, fiddles, synthesizers, guitars, flutes, citterns and accordian.

The Reviews

The Scotsman
Battlefield Band have long since cracked the problem of mixing electric and acoustic instruments without simply resorting to cranking up the volume.
Christchurch Press, New Zealand
The Battlefield Band fully deserved their three encores and obviously

enjoyed being paid to do something they enjoy. Given the reaction the group got, it will not be "will ye no' come back again," but when.
Aachener Volkszeitung, Germany

This group writes new songs that are already classics. They prove that folk music doesn't have to be a dusty antique. The instrumentalists and singers are true to their homeland, and sing about history, legends, politics, and the Scottish sense of fun.
St. Louis Dispatch

You feel like you're in the middle of the greatest party in the world.
South China Morning Post

The group comes on strong as both musicians and entertainers. Let's hope they come back to Hong Kong next year.
Washington Post

This is a traditional band that knows how to be modern. And the ability to roll with the changes while keeping its roots intact is the reason the Battlefield Band has been garnering fans as diverse as rock-oriented German youth and grandparents with little children on their laps for the last twenty years.

The Musicians

ALAN REID—keyboards/guitar/vocals
Alan is a founding member of Battlefield Band. He does much of the band's singing, and although he started off playing guitar, he has now become famous (notorious?) for introducing keyboards into traditional music, first using a pedal organ, then electric piano. He currently uses a bank of synthesizers and adapts these modern instruments to the service of a living tradition. A composer first and foremost, Alan's songs have recently become part of the band's strongest material.

ALISTAIR RUSSELL—guitar/cittern/vocals
Alistair was brought up in northeast England but, with Scottish parents and the middle name McKenzie, has never been far from his roots. After several years of playing semiprofessionally, Alistair teamed up full time with Tom Napper (*Tripping Upstairs*) playing mainly in Scotland and Ireland and then spent some time playing

solo, issuing a well-received album, *Getting To the Border.* Since joining
Battlefield in 1984, Alistair has shared most of the singing with Alan.
His fluent French and German have proven very useful during the
band's many foreign tours.

IAIN MacDONALD—highland pipes/flute/whistle

Iain is the youngest of three brothers from Glenuig in Inverness-
shire, all renowned for their exceptional piping skills. His career in
piping was nurtured by pipe major John MacKenzie at the Queen
Victoria School in Dunblane. On completion of his studies and after
a spell as a fish farmer, Iain joined the Gaelic Repertory Company
"Fir Chlis" with whom he played pipes, flute, and whistle. In 1990 he
joined Battlefield after acting as a stand-in on a trip to Australia.

JOHN McCUSKER—fiddle/whistle/accordian/keyboards

John is the youngest member of Battlefield, but don't let his youth
fool you. Musically he is not only highly accomplished in all his
instruments, but is exceptionally mature in his compositional skill.
John played fiddle with the Lararkshire-based band, Parcel
O'Rogues, once described as "Scotland's secret weapon against New
Kids on the Block."

Battlefield Band

Here are a few of the better musical pubs to check out. In the old town, the **Black Bull** (12 Grassmarket, 031/225-6636) is a lively bar with a cosmopolitan clientele and live folk music most nights. **Deacon Brodies** (435 Lawnmarket, 031/225-6531) is dedicated to the memory of the infamous Edinburgh character who sat on the Town Council by day and robbed shops and houses by night (later to reemerge as the inspiration for that other terrible split personality, Dr. Jekyll and Mr. Hyde). **Ensign Ewart** (521 Lawnmarket, 031/225-7440) is the nearest place to Edinburgh Castle where you can eat, drink and listen to great traditional music. And for fans of cask ale, there's **The Royal Oak** (1 Infirmary St., 031/557-2976), a gathering place for fans of trad.

New Town also has its great music pubs. Among them are **Auld Hundred** (100–104 Rose St., 031/225-1809) which is popular with businesspeople and shoppers at lunchtime and a young, slightly boisterous crowd in the evening. **Beau Brummel** (99 Hanover St., 031/225-4680) is one of Edinburgh's hottest pubs in the evenings—a traditional, old-time city bar. **Finsbury Park** (3 South Saint Andrew's St., 031/556-1124) is on three levels, comprising pub, gallery bar and nightclub. It's a bit more urbane than the others—crowdwise and musicwise. If all this talk about music leaves you hankering to sing along, head for **Victoria and Albert** (15–17 Frederick St., 031/226-4562) where you'll enjoy traditional food (we'll leave you to judge what that means) and a good ol' sing-along in Olde-World surroundings.

If you're over on the West End, you're in luck musicwise, but you've probably already figured that out. Three of the best trad bars are **L'Attache** (3 Rutland St., 031/229-3402), which is a wonderful cellar bar and a main venue for live music in Edinburgh; the **Burnt Post** (133–135 Lothian Rd., 031/228-5407), a happening nightspot smack in the heart of everything else that's going on; and the **Granary** (42–45 Queensferry St., 031/220-0550), which many people feel is a unique traditional music pub—both because of its music and the large, lively crowd. **Bannerman's** (the Cowgate, 031/556-3254) has live music every night; Friday and Saturday being Gaelic folk. The crowd is mostly students and people from the youth hostel, but in summer it's just about all tourists. No admission charge, and drinks are the standard cost—about £1.60 pint.

For those of you in South Edinburgh, head for the **Gold Medal** (58 Dalkeith Rd., 031/667-1816), which is close by the Commonwealth Pool and provides good music as well as food; and the **Southern Bar** (22 South Clerk St., 031/667-2289), a southside bar popular with students. The music tends a bit toward rock.

FESTIVALS

If festivals are your main thing when it comes to music enjoyment, you've come to the right place. Edinburgh is *the* festival city of Scotland, boasting not only one of the largest festivals in the world—the Edinburgh International Festival—but also a constant festival calendar starting at the beginning of August.

Let's start with the biggie. The **Edinburgh International Festival** runs from mid-August through the first week of September. An amalgam of over nine hundred productions in the fields of theater, dance, and music, this forty-seven-year-old festival draws performers from all parts of the globe and each year has its own theme—generally something classical. It goes without saying that you'd better book early—way before you get here—if you want to see any of the main events. Tickets go on sale in early April and are generally sold out by the end of May.

Prices range from £4–£44, but you can buy different kinds of passes that reduce the cost (for example, "rover passes" that entitle you to certain reductions and "half price" passes). For information and tickets, write to The Edinburgh Festival Office, 21 Market St., Edinburgh, EH1 1BW, Scotland; call 031/225-5756. If you're up for paying a booking fee, you can also get tickets from either Edwards & Edwards in London, 071/379-5822 or Edwards & Edwards in New York, 212/944-0290.

If this festival sounds too serious, you might want to check out the more spontaneous **Festival Fringe** which has grown around the edges of the big festival to include over five hundred amateur and professional companies presenting theater, children's shows, folk music, poetry, mime, revue and various exhibits. The Fringe is generally younger, weirder, and—in the minds of many visitors—much more fun than its granmammy. Full-price tickets for any one event are rarely more than £6, but you can often pick up free tickets from actors or musicians dying to be heard, if you hang around any of the Fringe haunts: the **Fringe Club** at Teviot Row, the **Gilded Balloon** on the Cowgate or any of the assembly rooms at the festival itself. For info and tickets, write to the Fringe Office, 180 High St., Edinburgh, EH1 1QS, Scotland; call 031/226-5257, 5259.

When it rains it pours, so at approximately the same time as the other two, you have the **Military Tattoo** which usually starts about a week before the Edinburgh Festival and lasts until the end of August. A great celebration of martial music and military skills set on the Castle Esplanade, this is Scotland's tribute to its historical fighting force complete with military bands, bagpipes, drums, and more tartan plaid than you ever imagined existed. Be prepared to be a little chilly since it's outdoors, slightly wet if it rains since it's an all-weather happening, and sitting next to an older couple from Missouri who will think this is the greatest thing they ever saw. (Believe it or not, this event draws over two hundred thousand people annually.) For more info and tickets (which range from £6–£16), write to Military Tattoo Office, 22 Market St., Edinburgh, EH1 1QB, Scotland; call 031/225-1188.

And then there's the **Edinburgh International Jazz Festival,** which takes place for one week at the beginning of August and draws the cream of the jazz crop from all over the world. Free performances are scattered throughout the week and there is usually one all-holds-barred free performance to open the festival. Events are held lunchtimes, afternoons, and evenings in a variety of venues throughout the city. Again, book early. This is a *major* festival with *major, major*

OBSERVATIONS ON *Scottish Traditional Music Made by Peter McMillan, Proprietor of the High St. Hostel*

There's a big difference between Irish and Scottish traditional music. Irish music is sweeter, more melodic. Its history is tied into roving harpists and angelic bards who traveled from village to village bringing peace and pleasure. Scottish music on the other hand is powerful; it has staccato rhythms that can't help but remind you of war. It's definitely not "easy listening," but what can you expect—it was our war music—all those kilts and tartans and bagpipes marching into battle!

FLASHBACK | THE WILDEST NIGHT OF MY LIFE: NEW YEAR'S EVE, 1992–93

We started at my flat and proceeded to go from one pub to another. At the stroke of midnight we were at one pub on High Street, and the Pogues were on the stage. Scotland has this thing called "snogging" which means "kissing," and so we were "snogging" everybody—cops, strangers, everybody—for about three hours. Then at three, we went to yet another pub and just kept going until it got light out.

The next day, January 1, is a holiday where everybody continues to party with music. January 2 is also a holiday—it's the day everybody recovers and even though I really needed till about January 5 to feel fully back in form, I still remember that New Year's Eve as the night of my life.

CONNIE LYNDON, CANADIAN STUDENT

crowds. For more info and tickets (from £8–£20), write Jazz Festival Office, 116 Canongate, Edinburgh, EH8 8DD, Scotland; call 031/557-1642.

Edinburgh's **Lesbian and Gay Festival** is held the first week of June and draws an ever-increasing crowd of participants from around the U. K. and internationally. For more info, call 031/556-0079.

Edinburgh Hogmanay Celebrations are year-end celebrations held in various venues over a three-day period and culminating in a massive Hogmanay spectacular in the Royal Mile and Princes Street areas of the city. For more info, contact Pete Irvine, Unique Events, 25 Greenside Place, Edinburgh, EH3 1AA, Scotland; call Pete at 031/557-3990.

Feb Fest is a ten-day festival of new works in music and theater that takes place in the middle of February. Three shows a day are performed at the Bedlam Theatre, and ticket prices range from £5–£10. Contact Martin Danziger, Bedlam Theatre, 2A Forrest Rd., Edinburgh, EH1 2QN, Scotland; call the theater at 031/225-9873, 9893.

The **Edinburgh Peace Festival** is a two-week event in the beginning of March, which takes place in various venues and celebrates peace. Concerts, ceilidh and multicultural events round out the program. Contact Ray Newton, 1 East Silvermills Lane, Edinburgh, EH3 5BG, Scotland; call 031/556-1083.

The **Edinburgh Harp Festival** is a five-day event at the end of March that consists of classes, workshops, concerts, and exhibitions. Tickets are available from the festival administrator beforehand as well as from Queen's Hall (one of the many venues) during the festival. Contact John Campbell, Festival Administrator, "Clarsair," 14 Bells Mains, Gorebridge, EH23 4QD, Scotland; call 0875/820532.

The **Edinburgh Folk Festival** takes place at the same time as the Harp Festival (are there no other dates for these things?) and includes *ceilidh*, song and instrument workshops and a lively Festival Club. Contact the Festival Organizer, Folk Festival Office, POB 528, Edinburgh, EH10 4DU, Scotland; call 031/556-3181.

In the middle of June, there's another jazz festival, the **Leith Jazz Festival,** which happens in the Leith shore area and includes large and small bands, traditional and modern jazz and parade bands on the street. This is—obviously—a smaller, more local event, but it has a laid-back style and flavor that shouldn't be missed if you're any kind of jazz fan. Contact Alan Thompson/Willie Greenfield, Capital Enterprise Trust, 141 Leith Walk, Edinburgh, EH6 8QN, Scotland; call 031/553-5566.

MISCELLANEOUS

Scotland's Crowning Glory is a performance tribute to the ancient tradition of Scottish music. Housed in the Scandic Hotel (80 High St., The Royal Mile, 031/557-9797), the performance includes the The Clann pipers who formed in 1983 and have been featured in many films portraying realistic battle enactments (most notably *Highlander,* starring Sean Connery); the Angela Forsyth Dancers; the Robert Black Band whose lead member, Robert Black, is considered to be Scotland's finest accordianist; and the Pipes and Drums of the Glencorse Pipe Band with Pipe Sergeant Iain Dewar. Together, these people attempt to give you an idea of what it was like to live in the bonny Scotland of old when bagpipes thundered across the Highlands announcing untold battles and brutalities. All this over a three-course meal featuring traditional Scottish fayre. The price is £34.95. Reserve early.

FOCUS ON SCOTTISH FOLK MUSIC

Scotland is a bilingual country, and its folk music falls roughly into two categories defined by the two tongues: Gaelic and Scots. To define the music even more precisely, there's "highland" music, sung in Gaelic, and "lowland" music, sung in Scots.

Highland songs were originally divided into those used to coordinate movement in communal tasks such as rowing, reaping, and corn grinding (these were called "waulking" songs and tended to have series of meaningless syllables in the refrains such as *hao ri ri, o ho lebh o, ho ro eile,* etc.), and those used to lighten solitary tasks such as spinning, churning and nursing infants.

Another popular form of Highland folk music is *puirt-a-beuls,* or "mouth music." Puirt-a-beuls are instrumental dance tunes sung to words and exist for all the common dance forms—strathspeys, reels and jigs. *Port* (plural *puirt*) means "a tune for a musical instrument." So *puirt-a-beuls* implies the substitution of the voice for an instrument. Recently puirt-a-beuls have become very popular with young Scots involved in the folk-song renaissance.

Any listing of highland (Gaelic) folk songs would be incomplete without reference to the fascinating "fairy songs" which, according to tradition, are the works of "fairy composers." The songs are concerned both with "little people"—children—and with supernatural creatures such as the waterhorse (*each-uisge*), which takes human form to entice and woo a maiden. The theme of nearly all fairy songs is that of a love affair between a fairy and a mortal.

In contrast to highland folk songs, which can take a variety of different forms, the folk songs of lowland Scotland can be divided into only two categories: the ballads and the songs. The difference between the two lies mainly in the treatment of subject matter: the ballad is objective and the song subjective, often expressing the personal feelings of the composer.

The songs of Robert Burns are probably the most famous examples of historic lowland songs although there's currently a great renaissance of new songs. Ballads, on the other hand, have not enjoyed as strong a rebirth; the old ones are actively sung only in Aberdeen and the northeast, where versions of the finest have been collected by Gavin Greig and others.

Scotland's great bard, Robert Burns

Hail Caledonia (Carlton Highland Hotel, North Bridge, 031/556-7277) is another "realistic" enactment of Scottish musical culture, this one a bit more low key. There's highland dancing with bagpipes and accordians and audience participation and a three-course meal featuring Scotch broth, roast sirloin and apple frenchie with Drambuie cream. The crowd tends to be middle-aged and upscale. The price is £30. For a more genuine "Scottish evening," you might try to catch a performance mounted by the **Edinburgh Folk Club** (031/339-4083) which often stages Wednesday night ceilidhs at the **Café Royal Circle Bar** on West Register St. Shows start at 8 p.m., and admission is about £5.

Another possible *real* Scottish session can often be had at the **Caledonian Brewery** (Slateford Rd.), which often sponsors *ceilidhs* with the Auld Reekie Band. Tickets are £10, buffet included, and can be gotten through the ticket center at Waverley Bridge. Yet another good shot at a real Scottish ceilidh session is the Haymarket *ceilidh* dances run by **Walpole Hall** on Chester St. There's a live band and traditional dancing. Bring your own refreshments. Smoking is prohibited. (Don't take this lightly; there's hardly any other place where this rule holds.) The admission price is £2–£3. For days and times (usually 7:30 p.m.) contact Ken Gourlay, 031/553-9147).

And finally, when you're in Edinburgh you definitely won't want to miss a slightly different aspect of the piping culture. If you're not going to one of the aforementioned shows (or even if you are, you daredevil), you *must* visit one of the many pipe-makers' shops and maybe even pick up a chanter or two. Among those you may visit are the following two—both will blow your mind. **The Bagpipe Centre** (49 Blackfriars St., 031/557-3090), has an incredibly impressive array of bagpipes, tin whistles, harps, accordians, fiddles and other Scots instruments, in addition to sheet music, tapes, records, CDs and any other form of musical geegaws you can imagine. The Centre is a very small store off High Street with lots of the atmosphere you came to Scotland to soak up. Bagpipes run from £350 to over £2,000 depending on whether they're mounted in ebony with nickel-silver ferrules or mounted in African blackwood with imitation-ivory ring caps.

At **Clan Bagpipes** (13a James Court, Lawnmarket, The Royal Mile, 031/225-2415) visit proprietor Joe Hagan if you want to have your bagpipes remounted with silver. This will cost you £700, probably a bargain considering that you get a silver eighteen-piece Edinburgh Hall Mark along with nine ferrules, three ring caps and bushes, five slides and one sole. You can also have your bagpipes hand-engraved, with a thistle runic, a zoomorvic or your own design for £340. Don't miss this place!

Speaking of bagpipes, you might be lucky enough to catch the Royal Scottish Pipers' Society in a recital of bagpipe music. These events happen from time to time at **St. Cecilia's Hall** (the Cowgate, 031/667-1011); tickets run about £3.

Joe Hagan—Pipemaker

GLASGOW

Nobody was more chagrined at Glasgow being chosen "European City of Culture for 1990" (a title bestowed by the ministers of culture of the twelve member-states of the European Economic Community) than Edinburgh. Sure, other U. K. cities were also dismayed, especially since no British city had ever been chosen for such an honor. Edinburgh's consternation, however, had to do with a long history of competition with its sister Scottish city during which it had never wavered in its deep-rooted feeling that it—and it alone—was the seat of Scottish culture.

But things were changing under Edinburgh's very nose, and, apparently, nobody in the capital city noticed. For starters, there was the long-enduring dearth of resident opera houses in Scotland. Opera in Scotland being a very serious business, there were calls from every quarter in both cities for a remedy to the situation. And for forty years Edinburgh had *talked* about the need for a resident center. But Glasgow—upstart that it is—just went ahead and *did* it, sneakily converting one of its all-purpose theaters, the Theatre Royal, and in 1975 inviting the internationally acclaimed Scottish Opera to make the Theatre its home.

And then there's the case of resident symphonies. Somehow, it seems, Glasgow was able to lure to its bosom not only the BBC Scottish Symphony Orchestra but the Scottish National Orchestra, which makes its home in a new eighteen-million-pound concert hall on Buchanan Street, a replacement for the St. Andrew's Hall, which burned down in 1962.

In the art of sculpture, even a torso is enough to reveal the master; while in music, coherence and completeness are indispensible in every individual composition, however small.

SCHUMANN

As if that weren't enough, an opera department was recently added to the Royal Scottish Academy of Music and Drama; among its recent productions was Robin Orr's *On The Razzle* based on the play by Tom Stoppard. And to cement its reputation as Scotland's foremost opera city, the biennial Glasgow International Early Music

Festival was established in 1990 and presented the first modern production of Marazzoli's *La Vita Humana* that year to rave reviews. In addition the National Youth Orchestra of Scotland, the highly regarded Scottish Ballet and the Royal Scottish Academy of Music and Drama all make their home in this humble city, as do Scottish Television, the Citizen's Theatre, and over two hundred cultural organizations.

While it may take something of a backseat to Edinburgh when it comes to festivals, Glasgow's calendar is no slouch. The biggest and best festival is Mayfest, a general celebration of the arts, which runs for three weeks. Following that are a series of jazz, folk music and choral festivals that definitely establish Glasgow as one of Europe's foremost festival cities. And that's not even considering its hot, contemporary-music scene or the prestige of serving as the home base for the College of Piping's blend of self-importance and historical legitimacy.

More than anything, though, the stature of the previous European Cities of Culture—Athens, Florence, Berlin, Paris, and Amsterdam—gives the best indication of Glasgow's international reputation for cultural events. With a place alongside these colleagues, Glasgow continues to advance the cultural renaissance it has enjoyed over the last ten years. And what becomes clearer with the realization of every new cultural endeavor is that its selection by the EEC was neither an accident nor a question of savvy marketing. The honor was the result of a very concerted effort by a very committed population to raise its city above the ashes of industrial decay and turn it into a world-class cultural destination.

CONCERT HALLS

The Glasgow Royal Concert Hall (2 Sauchiehall St., 041/332-6633; Central and Queen St. British Rail stations [BR]) is a multipurpose venue with excellent acoustics. The facility holds over 2,500 people and draws performers from Pavarotti to the Royal Scottish National Orchestra. This is also the home of the Scottish Proms, a two-week-long series of special concerts that take place in mid-June (tickets for these are very difficult to get—book way in advance). A restaurant within the hall is open from 10 a.m.–late Monday through Saturday and 5 p.m.–8 p.m. on Sundays. Ticket prices vary from £5–£20,) reservations are essential. **King's Theatre** (294 Bath St.,

041/248-5332; Charing Cross BR) is one of Britain's premier venues for plays and large-scale musicals. There is an entertainment room, which accommodates forty, available for preperformance and intermission drinks. There's also a Crush bar, which holds eighty, for postperformance entertainment. Ticket prices range from £5–£20.

The Mitchell Theatre (Granville St., 041/227-5033; Charing Cross BR) is a multiuse theater and conference complex that opened in 1980 on the site of the famous St. Andrews Hall, which had been almost completely destroyed by fire. The original facade with its ornate columns has been lovingly preserved. Inside, the complex can accommodate a total of more than eight hundred people. Two bars are available: one which opens one hour before performances, and a coffee bar which is open from 10 a.m.–4:30 p.m. and during intermissions. Tickets range from £5–£20. **The Royal Scottish Academy of Music and Drama** (100 Renfrew St., 041/332-5057; Central and Queen St. BR) includes two theaters and two concert halls which are generally used for performances, generally classical. Ticket prices range from £3–£17.

The Scottish Exhibitions and Conference Center (041/248-3000; the complex has its own railway station, which is four minutes from Glasgow Central BR) consists of five halls with a total capacity of more than twenty thousand. Musical offerings focus mainly on rock. Ticket prices range from £5–£15. **The Theatre Royal** (282 Hope St., 041/332-3321; Central and Queen St. BR) is the home of the Scottish Opera and is the most prestigious venue in Glasgow. Tickets sell out very early, although you might be lucky and get same-day seats if you arrive at the box office when it opens at 10 a.m. on the day of performance. Prices range from £4–£25.

Tramway (25 Albert Drive, 041/422-2023; Pollokshields East from Glasgow Central BR) is Glasgow's premier venue for contemporary performing arts. Its bar is open during performances only. Ticket prices range from £4–£20.

SPOTLIGHT ON GLASGOW OPERA

For a brief period during the end of the nineteenth century, Glasgow seemed to rival Edinburgh as the "artistic capital" of Scotland. By 1880 artistic stars were streaming into Glasgow, Scotland's largest city, to perform on its stages. One of the first major operatic stars to perform in the city was the Italian diva Angelica Catalani, who appeared in 1808 at the Theatre Royal on Queen Street. Over the course of the next ten years, Glasgow became an important stop for professional opera touring companies. Italian groups appeared often; in 1877 the noted Carlo Rosa Opera Company made the first of its many visits; a few years later, the Beecham and British National companies brought works ranging from *Carmen* to *The Golden Cockerel.*

A huge step forward for local operatic activity was the founding in 1905 of the Glasgow Grand Opera Society, which was set up to help touring companies work through that century's version of red tape. In 1934 the Society gave the British premiere of *Idomeneo* and the following year *Les Troyens.*

In more modern times Glasgow has continued its artistic prominence with respect to opera. In 1974 Scottish Opera got a permanent home when it purchased Glasgow's Theatre Royal and, as part of its 1975 gala opening in the converted theater, the company performed *Die Fledermaus.* Since then operas by Scottish composers have featured prominently in the repertory, notably Iain Hamilton's *The Catline Conspiracy* and Thomas Wilson's *Mary, Queen of Scots.*

The Tron Theatre (63 Trongate, 041/552-3748; Central and Queen St. BR), situated in the unique eighteenth-century Tron Kirk, is in Glasgow's historic Merchant City. Contemporary music, folk music, and dance events are the main attractions here. There are also two bars: the Victorian Bar, which holds eighty people and the more-intimate Chisholm St. Bar, which can accommodate up to twenty-five. Ticket prices range from £5–£15.

The Winter Gardens Glasgow Green (Candleriggs, 041/227-5511) offers summer celebration concerts—mainly chamber events featuring Scottish performers. Tickets are £7.

CCA (350 Sauchiehall St., 041/332-0522) offers a wide variety of musical venues. Ticket prices range from £5–£14. **The Old Atheneum** (179 Buchanan St., 041/332-2333) also offers many different kinds of performances with varying ticket prices.

If you're having trouble getting tickets for any of these halls, or if you need to buy tickets at the last minute, try **The Ticket Centre,** which might be able to help for a small fee. Phone lines are open from Monday–Saturday from 9 a.m.–9 p.m. and Sunday from noon–5 p.m. Call 041/227-5511 for ticket availability and prices. Two final concert venues: **Henry Wood Hall** (Claremont St., 041/332-3868), a former church now used for classical concerts, ticket prices about £8; and the **Glasgow University Chapel** where you can get tickets only at the door on the night of performance at 7:45. Prices are generally £5.

CLUBS AND DISCOS

What you'll soon discover about Glasgow clubs is that they're mainly venues for very young people. That doesn't mean you're not welcome if you don't fit that age bracket—quite the contrary. In fact, Glasgow is named by many travelers as one of the best cities for ignoring the "age thing." You judge. All clubs shut their doors at 12:30 a.m. in an attempt to control street violence, which doesn't seem to be much of a problem. After that, it depends on the club; some stay open until 3 a.m., some until 4 a.m.

King Tut's Wah Wah Hut (272 A St. Vincent's St., 041/221-5279) is not nearly as cheesy as its name suggests. It's actually quite funky and tasteful—and very popular. All kinds of music are featured here: rock, indie, pop and new music, all of it live. The food is pretty good, too, with pastas and meat dishes priced from £2.50–£5. Afternoons, there's a financial crowd in for drinks. Call ahead to check on the size of the crowd. Sometimes you just can't get in, and it's best to know that in advance, right?

Bennet's (90 Glassford St., 041/552-5761) offers dance and techno music—both live and canned. It's a mostly gay place, but also caters to a mixed crowd who, says Perri, a frequent patron, "likes to get down." Lots of black lighting and very crowded on weekends. Admission is about £4.

The Garage (490 Sauchiehall St., 041/332-1120) has two halls: an upstairs attic and the "big hall." The whole place holds about three hundred people, and it's a mixed crowd—mostly students and working-class people. The music varies. Monday is club night, Thursday has reggae, Saturday features disco with a great DJ and Sunday has soul, rock and retro. Admission: £3–£4.

SPOTLIGHT ON   **MOUTH MUSIC: LOCAL COLOR GOES GLOBAL**

In 1991 Scottish TV producer Martin Swan embarked on a project to bring together the ancient *puirt-a-beul* (a cappella music for dancing) of Scotland and the high technology of the modern global neighborhood. The result was **Mouth Music,** which quickly became a sensation in Europe and America, topping the World Music charts and garnering critical raves on both sides of the Atlantic.

Now, after touring, changing, and growing, Mouth Music has become a six-piece band, a crew of Scots with roots in rhythm and blues, rock, traditional folk and high-tech TV. It's the passionate voices of Michaela Rowan and Jackie Joyce, dynamic vocalists who sing in an array of languages: Scots, Gaelic, French, English and Xhosa. It's the thumping bottom of ex-New York Pig funker Quee MacArthur's bass. It's the reedy wheeze and electro-blip of Andy Thornburn, professional potato inspector and accordian and keyboard master. It's the rhythms of the world of James Macintosh, inveterate busker and former drummer for Swamptrash. And it's the electronics and fiddle of Martin Swan, a Scot who has the shakes and rattles of Reunion Island stuck in his brain.

Mouth Music's music is a study in contrasts—a densely layered musical map of the world, where African grooves meet rhythm and blues, where Eno meets Enya. It is not unusual for the group to go from easygoing hip-hop rhythms to swirling washes of mysterious voices and synthesizers, from Celtic funk to Brazilian grooves to Arabic rhythm and violins.

The band's latest album and recent live concerts have reveled in these contradictions, and the press has responded. *Musician* called Mouth Music "a rave blend of the ethereal and the funky, the ancient and the orbital," while *SPIN* called it "a serene mutant hybrid of Gaelic a cappella and dubbed-up Afro-pop." The *San Francisco Bay Guardian* said, "Mouth Music makes time and space implode in a weird, psychedelic roots experiment, and you can dance to it!"

"I want people to be baffled and excited and confused," says Martin Swan. "A lot of dance music is low on harmonic content. A lot of songwriter music is low on rhythm and energy." Not so Mouth Music. Through a mixture of high-tech production and brilliant performances, this group takes popular music one step closer to a truly international sound with strong rhythmic grooves and powerful harmonies. Swan sums it up, "These are songs that people will remember after they've walked away."

Nice-n-Sleazy (421 Sauchiehall St., 041/333-9637) sometimes—but not always—lives up to its name. Usually this happens on weekends when the club gets raucous and loud and draws a crowd of twenty-somethings with the occasional missing tooth. If you want to hear local bands, from indie to thrash to cowboy, this is where you come. It's also a favorite watering spot of The Cranberries. Admission is from £2–£3, and there are frequent drink promotions. The pub is upstairs; the dance floor, which holds about three hundred people, downstairs.

One very popular club for the over-twenty-two crowd is the **13th Note** (80 Glassford St., 041/553-1638). Craig Tannock, the proprietor, says it's a "mellow alternative." The atmosphere is relaxed and informal; the music is mixed. Tuesday has "Kazoo Club"—a forum

Mouth Music

for new bands (alternative, acid jazz, indie, etc.). Saturday has a basement jazz club (modern, rock, fusion); Saturday afternoons a sixteen-piece jazz band plays; Sunday is indie and alternative, as well as a comedy club. The admission is usually free; Saturdays it's £3–£4. The food is good and ranges from veggie to homemade rashers.

Here are a few other clubs for you to check out. **The Railway Inn** (Busby, 041/644-2534) specializes mainly in blues and draws a very mixed crowd. **BJ's** (Croft St., Kilmarnock, 0563/44722), offers roots reggae bands as well as more-traditional rock. At the **Cotton Club** (5 Scott St., 041/332-0712) the Wednesday night DJ, Raymond Davren, tries his best to recreate a John Travolta feeling. The admission is £3. The **Lady Hamilton Lounge** (129 Nelson St., 041/429-1783) has live bands and bar lunches daily and attracts a very mixed, somewhat-upscale crowd. The **Cathouse** (9 Brown St., 041/248-6606) is a twenty, rock-oriented club on two floors with an early opening and especially cheap drinks until 11 p.m. Trad rock happens upstairs, contemporary rock downstairs.

Eruption (474 Sauchiehall St., 041/353-1927) tends toward techno music—loud—with plenty of smoke and big crowds having lots of fun. The admission is £5. **Club Xchange** (25 Royal Exchange Square, 041/204-4559) is a gay club with upfront dance tunes from DJ "Suave" Gav. Happy hour: 11 p.m.–12:30 a.m.

At **Frampton's** (1235 Maryhill Rd., 041/945-5999) you're assured of everyone being at least twenty-one. No one younger is allowed in. The club has a "smart dress only" policy, which means no jeans, and live music seven nights a week including Saturday and Sunday afternoons. The admission ranges from £5–£7. **Hepburn's** (26–30 London Rd., 041/552-3204) also caters to the over-twenty-three crowd. Wednesday nights, it's karaoke; Friday and Saturday, live bands; Sunday nights, disco.

And finally, for Latin music fans, there're two options. The first is **Club Havana** (High St.), which features DJs playing the likes of the Gipsy Kings, Tito Puente, Gloria Estefan and so on. Go early or forget about getting in. Admission: £4 between 8 p.m.–9 p.m., £6 after. Quote from DJ Jazz: "Outside the nights are hardly tropical, but inside, things are hot. The music changes the atmosphere. As soon as you step through the door, it just doesn't feel like Scotland anymore." At the second, **Club Cubana** (Speaker's Corner), there's Latin dancing with DJ Tchico. Hot tapas and cool Cuban cocktails. All proceeds go to the Scottish Cuba Defense Campaign.

JAZZ

Nico's (375 Sauchiehall St., 041/332-5736) has jazz on Sundays along with poetry readings. Happy hour on Sundays is from 5 p.m.–11 p.m. The admission is £3. **Curlers** (256 Byres Road, 041/334-1284) has live jazz bands three nights a week (the nights vary), karaoke on Sundays and "pop quiz" on Tuesdays. Admission is free. **The Halt Bar** (160 Woodlands Rd., 041/332-1210) has jazz Sundays, Tuesdays, Wednesdays, Thursdays and Saturdays. Free admission; bar food is available all day. **Jules' Bar and American Grill** (Forte Crest, Bothwell St., 041/248-2656) has live jazz from 10 p.m.–1:30 a.m. *and* great food. **The Kelvin Park Lorne Hotel** (923 Sauchiehall St., 041/334-4891) also has late-night jazz as well as jazz festival specials in the hotel.

COUNTRY

Though Glasgow doesn't have many country-music venues, it does have two really good ones: **The Tolbooth** (11 Saltmarket, 041/552-4955), which has American country-and-western on Friday and Scottish country (not very different from Scottish traditional except for the addition of a few instruments such as the banjo) on Saturday and Sunday. **The Grand Ole Opry** (Paisley Rd., 041/429-5396) has what you came for every Friday, Saturday and Sunday.

POP QUIZ 16

Which Scottish hippie-mystic singer and composer went on to write music for films including *If It's Tuesday, This Must be Belgium* and *Brother Sun, Sister Moon?*

ANSWER: DONOVAN

PUBS AND TRADITIONAL MUSIC

As we've said again and again, you *must* hear some traditional music while in Glasgow. The only other option is to head for the same sort of clubs and concert halls you'd check out in any other city. If that's the case, you're just going to have to let go of this sense of yourself as musically savvy.

The Scotia Bar (112 Stockwell St., 041/552-8681), which bills itself as the oldest bar in Glasgow, is a good start. Scotia has lots of regulars. It's a "people's" pub, says one inebriated regular with pride. Women feel safe here, say most of the others. There's music on Wednesday, Thursday and Saturday afternoons, all free. Mostly an over-thirty crowd. **Clutha Vaults** (167 Stockwell St., 041/552-7520) has traditional music on Saturday and Sunday, no admission charge. This club participates in the Glasgow Folk Festival and encourages musicians to play seriously (as opposed to drinkin' and havin' fun). Sometimes customers play. It's a younger crowd here than at Scotia's although both clubs are owned by the same person.

The Victoria (Stockwell St., 041/552-6040) is a different spot from Victoria Bar (159 Briggait St.), which is also a traditional place. This one serves the twenty-to-forty crowd, is very casual and laid-back and has lots of old posters on mahogany. On Wednesday, there are impromptu music sessions. Filled with "sincere and lovin' people" says one woman with spiked hair and a Guinness in hand. There is no admission charge.

Brewery Tap (1055 Sauchiehall St., 041/339-8866) occupies the ground floor of two Victorian houses. The pub has dark walls papered with sheet music and looks across Kelvingrove Park to Kelvingrove Museum and the university. The clientele consists of young professionals, musicians and students. Trad groups play most nights; jazz enthusiasts take over on Sunday afternoons. Admission is free.

FESTIVALS

Glasgow, like Edinburgh, has lots of "impromptu" festivals as well as the scheduled ones. The biggest of the scheduled is, of course, the **Mayfest,** which is a three-week-long event often beginning in late April. Founded eleven years ago, this festival combines the best in theater, dance, popular music, classical music, visual arts and film. Less formal and pretentious than the huge Edinburgh festival, Mayfest thinks nothing of inviting country music star Vince Gill to perform alongside the Rachmaninoff Trio. This doesn't mean that tickets are any easier to get than in Edinburgh, so book early. Bookings open March 1. Prices range from £5–£20. For information, write to Ian McKay, Mayfest Office, 18 Albion St., Glasgow, G1 1LH, Scotland; call 041/552-8000.

She was born in Bellshill, Scotland, the youngest of six children. Her early musical influences speak to the diversity she would later exhibit in her own recordings: Motown, Barbra Streisand, rock and '70s soul. She learned the ropes singing on the local club circuit in Scotland—an internship that soon led to a recording contract with EMI records.

But it's what happened next that established her as one of the all-time record breakers for quick and dramatic debuts. Her first album, *Sheena Easton,* clicked immediately and turned gold in America for sales in excess of 500,000 copies.

And as if that wasn't enough, Easton next appeared on-screen in the opening title sequence of the James Bond film *For Your Eyes Only* singing the title tune, which promptly became a number four pop hit.

In 1983 television fans got a special treat when Easton starred in her own NBC-TV special, "Sheena Easton...Act One" with guests such as Kenny Rogers with whom she zoomed to the top of the country charts via their duet, "We've Got Tonight." This was followed by her HBO special concert, "Live At The Palace."

Easton's 1991 album, *What Comes Naturally,* reinforced her position as one of pop music's most distinguished vocalists. In a further demonstration of the diversity of her talent, Easton herself wrote three of the songs on the album: "The Next Time," "The First Touch of Love," and "Half a Heart."

Beyond her recording success, Easton is a top concert attraction around the world, having performed at sold-out concerts in major arenas in the U. S., U. K., Canada, Japan, Hong Kong, Bangkok, Singapore and Taipei.

Her latest album, *No Strings,* is Easton's tenth. Included are eleven timeless classic songs performed with a contemporary edge and a jazz flavor. Why would this icon of pop music do a lushly arranged album of standards that were written before she was born?

"I've always had this vision of doing an album of very classy songs with contemporary arrangements, and here I was working with a producer/arranger who had the same vision, surrounded by musicians who had become as excited as we were," she says. "But the most amazing part of the whole thing was that we cut the songs with drums, bass and Patrice [artist/arranger Patrice Rushen] on piano, live, in a two-hour session with just three takes. More than that, we had fun doing it. It must have been like that in the early days when everything was live with no layers or overdubs of technology. We were all there living it and experiencing it together for one moment only. It can't get any better than that!"

The **Glasgow International Jazz Festival** takes place in the first ten days of July. It's Britain's biggest festival of jazz, blues and Latin music, featuring special performances and master classes. Advance booking is necessary. Tickets may be ordered from April 1 on. For more information or to order tickets, contact Marek Kolodziej, 18 Albion St., Glasgow, G1 1LH, Scotland; call 041/552-3552. Every Glasgow jazz club and hotel has special events during this time, so check the local listings.

The **Glasgow International Early Music Festival** gets underway early in August and lasts for one week. Various venues are involved in the presentation of concerts, opera, fringe and community events. Advance booking is necessary. For tickets and information, write Scottish Early Music Consort, 22 Falkland St., Glasgow, G3 4TH, Scotland; call 041/334-9229.

The **World Pipe Band Championships** are generally held for one day in mid-August. This is the main competitive gathering of pipe bands from all over the world, and there are six grades of competition, highland dancing and heavy events (ones that involve muscles). There is also a grand finale and a march past massed bands. For further information, contact Mr. J. M. Hutcheson, R.S.P.B.A., 45 Washington St., Glasgow, G3 8AZ, Scotland; call 041/221-5414.

The **Glasgow International Folk Festival** takes place for one week in late June at the Tron Theatre. Whether your specific interest lies in the waulking songs of the Harris tweedmakers or the latest in political street songs, this is where you'll want to be. For tickets and information, call the Tron Theatre at 041/552-3748.

One of the impromptu festivals that has become a little more formal in recent years goes simply by the name of **Streetfest.** Taking place at the same time as Mayfest, it seems to be Glasgow's answer to Edinburgh's Fringe Festival. Venues include Argyle St., Buchanan St. and Sauchiehall St. among others. Check the local listings for events, locations and times. Also check out **Shoppersfest** which takes place in the Drumchapel Shopping Centre (next to the Mercat Theatre) at the same time as Mayfest and Streetfest. Like Streetfest, this is another impromptu program of free afternoon entertainment featuring musicians, mimes and puppeteers.

Just north of Glasgow on the A82, in Dumbarton, you'll find the **Dumbarton District Festival** during the third week of July. Music, dance, *ceilidhs* and a spectacular town parade round out this festival. Contact Dumbarton Tourist Information; 041/0389-42306.

West of Glasgow in the small town of Paisley is the site of the **Paisley International Organ Festival,** which takes place during the first week of August. This is one of Britain's major music events, combining an international organ competition with a wide-ranging program of concerts, master classes and talks. Tickets are sold out months in advance, so book early. Contact Jeanette Fenyo, Paisley Abbey, Scotland; 041/889-8311.

Also in Paisley is **The Paisley Festival,** a weeklong festival of music, dance, visual, and performing arts that takes place throughout the Renfrew District in late May. Tickets are available from the Paisley Town Hall, the Paisley Arts Centre or by contacting Diane Hutchison, Abbey Close, Paisley, PA1 1JF, Scotland; 041/887-1007.

Just ten miles southeast of Glasgow between Hamilton and Motherwell you'll hit upon an outrageous rock festival, **The Tennents Live Festival,** featuring umpteen rock groups—some you've heard of (Primal Scream is usually a regular); some you'll wish you'd *never* heard of. The event takes place during three days in late July; ticket prices are £23.50 for one day and £39 for the weekend. Buy tickets by credit card or get information by calling 031/557-6969.

| SPOTLIGHT ON | THE TANNAHILL WEAVERS: LIVELY CELTIC SPIRITS |

Born of a session in Paisley, Scotland, and named for the town's historic weaving industry and local poet laureate, Robert Tannahill, the

Tannahill Weavers have a unique combination of traditional melodies, driving rhythmic accompaniment, and rich vocals that make the group's performances superb and unforgettable. As one review recently noted: "The Tannahill Weavers—properly harnessed—could power an entire city for a year on the strength of one live concert alone. The music may be old-time Celtic, but the drive and enthusiasm are akin to straight ahead rock and roll."

The band members include Roy Gullane who plays guitar, banjo and mandolin and sings lead vocals. His ready wit and seemingly endless collection of jokes and tall tales make the Tannahills' performances a comic delight.

Kenny Forsyth plays the highland bagpipes, Scottish small pipes and whistles. Kenny is solo piping champion in such far-flung places as Japan and Indonesia. He has won military piping championships as well as a world championship on the Scottish small pipes.

John Martin, one of Scotland's finest fiddle players, started winning fiddle competitions and made his first radio broadcast for the BBC at the age of fourteen. He has since played with Contraband, Ossian, and Easy Club, and is much in demand as a *saisán* (session) player as well as being involved as a traditional musician in various theater, film and television productions.

Les Wilson plays bouzouki, keyboards, guitar, bass pedals and harmonica and is a seasoned musical campaigner, a veteran of both folk and pop groups. He also does studio saisán work, teaches vocal arranging and does studio work for German radio and television. In addition, Les's fine singing voice ensures that the Tannahills will long maintain their tradition of strong vocal harmonies.

Phil Smillie plays flute, whistles and bodhran. His lovely high-tenor vocals give the group's harmonies their beautiful distinctive quality.

With the release of their tenth and most recent LP, *The Mermaid's Song* on Green Linnet, the group is firmly established as one of the premier groups on the folk concert stage. From reflective ballads to footstomping reels and jigs, the variety and range of the material they perform is matched only by their enthusiasm and lively Celtic spirits.

MISCELLANEOUS

An absolute must for anyone visiting Glasgow is a visit to the **College of Piping** (McPhater St. Church, Cowcaddens, 041/334-3587) where you can just poke around or—are you ready for this—take one (or more) classes in bagpipe playing. Classes run £10 for adults and £8 for those under eighteen. If you're going to be around for a week or more, you might want to sign up for a term (£20), which allows you to take series of evening classes. The classes are highly recommended. You can also get a subscription to their publication, *The Piping Times*, which describes everything the dear old lads have been up to

SPOTLIGHT ON	THE CLANN: HOW THE GROUP GOT STARTED

As a group, we were always interested in clan warfare and how the pipers led the battles. We were also inspired by the music; we felt from the beginning that this was a deeply significant part of our culture.

We started off doing a weekend here and there. Then after a while, we all realized we'd like to do this more—that this was the most interesting thing we'd ever done. We started doing dances, hotel gigs; and then our big break came when Sean Connery asked us to be in his film, *Highlander.* Since then, we've started these regular shows at the Scandic and are quite thrilled to be part of this process of sharing our history with visitors. The pipers start off the show; then we explain how piping was used in clan warfare, the methods of weaponry and battle. Then the singers and dancers take over, showing the tradition of highland dancing. All in all, I think it's a great way for newcomers to Scotland to learn a bit about our history.

ALISDIAR MACPHERSON, THE CLANN

between issues. It costs $35 in the U. S., $42 A in Australia, $50 NZ in New Zealand, £15.25 in the U. K. and £18 in the rest of Europe. If you're game, send your check to The College of Piping, 16–24 Ostago St., Glasgow, G12 8JH, Scotland.

If you're not up for classes, at least take in one of the dozens of piping shops around town. One of the best is **R.G. Hardie & Co.** (24 Renfrew St., 041/332-3021), which has as one of its seals, this: "By appointment to Her Majesty the Queen Bagpipe Makers," and advertises itself as being the "sole manufacturers of the famous Airtight Seasoning." You'll long remember the array of items in this store, even if you don't buy anything.

ABERDEEN

Aberdeen is the cultural capital of the north, and—partly due to the oil industry—has a fairly lively nightlife, although most of it revolves around pubs and hotels. What clubs exist tend to cater to a very young clientele, which makes the ubiquitous no-jeans-and-sneakers rule rather odd.

CONCERT HALLS

His Majesty's Theatre (Rosemount Viaduct, 0224/641122) presents opera and other musical theater. Tickets range from £5–£15. Ditto **The Hall at Haddo House** (off B9005, twenty miles north of Aberdeen, near Methlick, 0224/641122).

The Music Hall (Union St., 0224/632080) has seasonal programs centered around the Scottish National Orchestra, the Scottish Chamber Orchestra and other touring groups. Tickets range from £4–£20.

CLUBS AND DISCOS

Most clubs in Aberdeen are loud, and include the kinds of lighting effects that were popular in the bigger cities twenty years ago (mirrored glitter balls that spin—the John Travolta feel). Music ranges from the banal to the forgettable, and if you decide to order a drink, expect to pay a lot. With this in mind (don't be discouraged—it's all in the attitude) you might want to check out the following three establishments on Union St.: **The Cotton Club** (491, 0224/647544) where the blue-collar crowd manages to look as though they're having great fun; **The Soda Fountain** (492–494, 0224/647544), which does in fact serve soda; and **Eagles** (120, 0224/640641).

PUBS AND TRADITIONAL MUSIC

A better bet than discos and rock clubs is a trip to one of Aberdeen's pubs. For starters, the drinks are cheaper. And, although the music

FLASHBACK	THE BIG SURPRISE

I had bummed around Europe for about five months when I started to run out of money. I'd already decided I wasn't going home; for one thing I had told everybody I wasn't coming back for a year, and I certainly wasn't going to show up in Lincoln admitting that I'd blown all my money in half the time I'd said. I was a college graduate and all now; my reputation was on the line. So I started asking around, and next thing you know, I've got this job on an oil rig in Aberdeen. Now Aberdeen might have seemed great if I wasn't in dire financial straits, but I was hard up for cash, and on first glance the city looked like a dump. One week later, it still looked like a dump, plus I knew nobody. So one night, I went out by myself to The Cotton Club because I'd read about it in the local paper. The band was just okay and the atmosphere seemed a little cool friend-makingwise. I got a drink and stood over on the side. Long story short, I was there about a second when this group of guys and gals comes up, takes me by the hand, pulls me out to the dance floor, and introduces themselves. We danced for about an hour straight, and then I went out with them to a few pubs and then on a walking tour of the city and then to one of their places where I wound up living for the next four months. They became my best friends, and from that night on, Aberdeen seemed like one of the friendliest, nicest places I'd ever seen. Funny how that happens.

JAMIE BRENT, LINCOLN, NEBRASKA

schedule can tend towards the sporadic, you have a much better chance of hearing something memorable. Try the following:

Chuchill's (13–17 Crown St., 0224/586916) has, in addition to occasional local music, an extensive menu with generous portions and very reasonable prices. **The City Bar** (25 Netherkirkgate, no phone) is just off the shopping center and has lots of brass rails and ornamental geegaws for your viewing pleasure, in case the music doesn't materialize.

Don View (Ellon Rd., Bridge of Don, 0224/703239) is on the outskirts of the city overlooking the River Don. Much of the clientele consists of businesspeople or people involved in the oil industry, and they all seem to know each other. **Leathan Arms** (Cookston Rd., Porthlethan, south of Aberdeen, no phone) has an 'olde worlde' theme—mock ceiling beams with many ornaments, lots of pictures on the walls and soft lighting. **Star & Gartor** (Crown St., no phone) is a busy place just off Union St. Recently refurbished to look old, it has a split-level customer area, which is generally filled with shoppers and businesspeople.

FESTIVALS

The **Aberdeen Arts Carnival** runs for six weeks starting in mid-July and encompasses music, theater, literature and comedy events plus exhibits and free entertainment. Most events take place at the Aberdeen Arts Centre. This event is lots of fun. Ticket prices are £3 and up and are available starting June 1. Contact A. Deans, Administrator, 33 King St., Aberdeen, AB1 1JE, Scotland; 0224/635208.

Aberdeen Live runs for one week in the middle of July and is basically one big street party with indoor and outdoor performers, a street parade and a circus and beer festival in Union Terrace Gardens. Music performances take place each evening of the event, and many of these are free. Contact Alan Forrest, Arts and Recreation Division, City of Aberdeen, St. Nicholas House, Broad St., Aberdeen, AB2 6AJ, Scotland; 0224/276276.

The **Aberdeen International Youth Festival** runs for ten days at the beginning of August and is held in various venues throughout the city. Included are youth orchestras, choirs, dance and theater groups from around the world. Also part of the Festival are a visual arts program, the Shell Expo Music School, and AIYF Dance School. You'll see lots of talented Scottish youth looking very serious.

Bookings open June 13. Contact Nicola Wallis, 3 Nutborn House, Clifton Rd., London, SW19 4TQ, England; 081/946-2995. Tickets are also available from the Aberdeen Box Office: 0224/641122.

The **Aberdeen Alternative Festival** is the third largest festival in Scotland. Popular music, arts and street entertainment—all of them of the "pushing-the-envelope" style of art. The Festival takes place in various venues for ten days in mid-October. Contact Duncan Hendry, 10 Belmont St., Aberdeen, AB1 1JE, Scotland; 0224/635822.

✪ Test Your Musical I.Q.

Which of the following bands and musicians is not Scottish?

1. Tannahill Weavers
2. Hamish Moore
3. Bothy Band
4. Sweeney's Men
5. Annie Lennox

(Answers on page 185.)

Near Aberdeen, in the town of Kincardshire, you'll find the **Stonehaven Folk Festival** going on for three or four days in mid-July. Most musicians are Scottish and local, but some come from as far away as bonny ol' England. Contact Pat Tavendale, 56 Brickfield Rd., Stonehaven, Kincardshire, KI2 3JE, Scotland; 0569/63519. Also in Kincardshire is the **Banchory Festival of Scottish Music** which takes place in mid-May in the town hall and the Burnet Arms Hotel. There are competitions for fiddle, accordian and piano, along with evening concerts. Contact Mr. D. Menzies, 19 Dalvenie Rd., Banchory, Kincardshire, KI4 2AL, Scotland; 03302/2705.

The **Buchan Heritage Festival** is an annual festival of traditional music, song and verse, which takes place in mid-May in Ritchie Hall just outside Aberdeen. Advance booking is necessary, and bookings open May 1. Tickets are available from Mrs. M. Lowe, South Tarwathie, Strichen, ST4 7EJ, Scotland; 07715/344.

In mid-June, you can head for the **Turriff and District Pipe Band Contest,** which takes place in Turriff, just outside Aberdeen. This event includes a pipe-band contest, massed bands, and a highland dancing festival. This is one of the best pipe-band events in Scotland. Prices: £2 adults, £1 children. Contact Mr. W. Hepburn, Ardachaidh, Market St., Turriff, TU3 6BN, Scotland; 0888/62401.

Just west of Aberdeen, near Aboyne and Deeside, you'll find the **Aboyne and Deeside Festival,** which takes place during the first week of August. Held in Aboyne, Kincardine, O'Neil, Tarland, Dinnet, Torhpins, Lumphanan, Finzean and other centers in Deeside, the events include music, drama, puppetry, visual arts, crafts, sports and entertainment. Bookings open June 1, and advance tickets (£2–£4) are necessary. Contact Mrs. Ann Moffat, 2 Eastwood Terrace, Aboyne, Aberdeenshire, AB34 5AW, Scotland; 03398/86572.

INVERNESS

Inverness is usually used as a base for touring outlying areas in the Highlands, an area rich in castles, distilleries and majestic scenery. This being the case, you won't find great entertainment options in Inverness every night. What you *will* find are an amazing number of festivals—many among the best to be experienced anywhere in Great Britain.

For classical music, opera and dance in Inverness proper, look into the offerings of **The Eden Court Theatre** (Bishops Rd., 0463/221718), which presents music, film and pop concerts for prices ranging from £3–£8.

Local hotels provide the main source of nightly music options, but only sporadically. Check the **Cummings Hotel** (Church St., 0463/233246) or **McTavish's Kitchens** (High St., 0463/702406).

WHERE IT'S AT　BAILNAN HOUSE: A HOME FOR HIGHLAND MUSIC

In spring of 1993 Bailnan House opened its doors to the public as a center for the study and playing of Highland music. The house was bought by the Bailnan Trust twenty years ago for one pound. It then set about a long-term renovation and development project, raising over eight hundred thousand pounds to restore the building to its former Georgian splendor and to create a center for the performance, study and development of traditional Highland music.

The building now houses three exhibition rooms, which chart the development of Highland music using videos and listening points at which visitors can choose pieces of music from over six hours of specially researched and commissioned CDs.

The exhibition includes sections detailing the very first music, which was inspired by the sounds of nature, as well as sections on musicians of today. There are also sections that cover different facets of the Highland music tradition such as work and communal songs, piobaireachd songs and Highland fiddle music. Three videos explore the history of Highland music in the social context of the area and look at the music and the instruments themselves in detail. There are also three rooms dedicated to performance, study and practice for individual musicians and musical groups.

Regular musical performances are held on Thursday, Friday and Saturday evenings. A store sells some of the best of Highland music as well as a wide selection of books on music; a cafe in the basement serves fine cooking with a Scottish flair at good prices.

Over the next few years, Bailnan House plans to develop a library to house books, manuscripts, recordings and artifacts dealing with Highland music. The House is also investigating the use of sophisticated telecommunications technology to network with organizations of similar interests in the U. K. and Europe.

Bailnan House is located at 40 Huntley Street, Inverness. Hours of operation and performances vary, as do fees. For further information, call Lucy Conway, Manager, at 0463/715757.

PUBS AND TRADITIONAL MUSIC

Your best bet for more consistent musical sources lies, as usual, with the town's pubs—and even here, check before going to see if you've hit on the right night. If you do, you'll get an amazing array of local musicians, some of whom will sit in a corner havin' a few pints, and then—seemingly out of the blue—get up without consulting anybody and do a few numbers.

One good pub is **Brahan Seer** (Balnafettack Rd., 0463/243111). This pub has superb views across the town and Firth. The style is modern. **The Copper Kettle/Eagle Bar** (50 Baron Taylor St., 0463/233307) is one of Inverness's oldest pubs and is built on two levels—a pub lounge on the ground floor and a coffee house/tea room upstairs.

Finlays's (Tonmahurich St., 0463/231335) is tucked away from the busy town center. The pub has brass fittings on the bar and split-level seating and is more for people who want to relax than for those with a definite agenda. Translation: music may or may not happen regardless of what anyone may say in advance.

The **Glen Mhor Hotel and Restaurant** (9–12 Ness Bank, 0463/234308) has three bars and a restaurant: Nico's Bistro Bar, Nicky Tams Pub and The Cocktail Lounge. Music may be scheduled in any of the three although rarely in Nico's. **The Phoenix** (Academy St., 0463/233685) has sawdust floors and "real ales." Music is sporadic. Call first.

FESTIVALS

The **Inverness Music Festival** goes on for three weeks in March and takes place in various venues. There are competitive classes for solo, duo and ensemble in vocal music (including Gaelic), keyboard, string, woodwind, brass, chamber music, jazz, composition and Scottish country dancing. Despite being held in winter, this is a widely attended event, so it's best to book early. Tickets are from £1–£5. Contact Elizabeth Davis, Festival Secretary, 4 Bruce Gardens, Inverness, IV3 5EN, Scotland; 0463/233902.

The **Inverness Folk Festival** is a three-day event in early April that mixes traditional and contemporary and song and instrumental, with special emphasis on Celtic music. This is a very funky festival. Bookings open March 1. Contact Ms. J. Sinclair, 13 Union Rd., Inverness, IV2 6DL, Scotland; 0463/238586. The **Inverness Mod** is a competitive festival encompassing vocal and instrumental, plus crafts, which takes place in mid-June in the Cummings Hotel, Rose Street Hall and Black Hall. Adults pay 50p; children are free. Contact Betty MacRae, 17 A Lovat Rd., Inverness, 1V3 5EN, Scotland; 0463/ 236946.

The **Inverness Festival of Music and Dance** takes place in various venues throughout the region, including the Eden Court Theatre. It's a three-day event in mid-July—a colorful festival of music and dance performed by over two hundred young people from around the world. Performers wear traditional costumes. This event sells out early; bookings open July 1; prices are £5–£6. Contact Jim Morrison, Community Education Service, Highland Regional Council, 3 High St., Dingwall, IV15 9HL, Scotland; 0349/64962.

The **Inverness Country Music Festival** goes on for three days in late July and includes concerts, dances and cruises on Loch Ness.

(Remember when you're out there and think you see something big and black—the whole thing's been scientifically disproved.) As you would expect, this shindig sells out very early. Tickets go on sale March 1. Contact Mrs. A. Carmondy, 56 Kilmuir Rd., Inverness, IV3 6EP, Scotland; 0463/221268.

FLASHBACK   MICK JAGGER AND ME

It was 1991 and, like every other tourist in Inverness, I found myself out on this tour boat on Loch Ness with binoculars smashed against my face looking for—guess what? After about ten minutes of searching the horizon, I got bored and started panning my binoculars this way and that across the lake. At one point, I caught a glimpse of this beautiful, yachtlike essence gliding across the water and a lot of what looked like rich people on the deck. I fixed my binoculars on them, and sure enough, there he was, Mick Jagger, with his arm around some gorgeous red-haired woman. He was pointing to the water, and she was laughing. I was tempted to fix my binoculars on the spot he had chosen for his joke, but I couldn't take my glasses off him. I grabbed a few people next to me and said, "Look, there's Mick Jagger." But they weren't interested, and so I spent the rest of the trip watching him and wishing passionately that I was on that ship.

KATRINA HOPSON, CHICAGO

The **Inverness Tattoo** is a very big event, running for six days in late July at Northern Meeting Park. It includes pipes and drums, regimental bands, highland and country dancing, ceilidh and sessions. If you can get into this one, you'll experience a real part of what Scotland is about. Tickets are about £4 for adults, £2 for children, and are available from the Inverness, Loch Ness and Nairn Tourist Boards or by contacting Mr. R. Wood, 18 Annfield Rd., Inverness, IV2 3HX, Scotland; 0463/234511 (days).

The **Marymas Fair** is held in mid-August in various venues throughout Inverness. It's a reenactment of traditional sixteenth-century craft stalls and demonstrations, entertainment and refreshments. The Fair features lots of pageantry and includes a procession and the crowning of a Marymas queen. This event is for people who like the atmosphere usually found at renaissance fairs. Contact Mrs. O. M. Moore, 2 Queensgate Arcade, Inverness, IV1 1PQ, Scotland; 0463/715760.

POP QUIZ 17

Which Scottish-born rock diva's real first name is Griselda?

ANSWER: ANNIE LENNOX

The **Carrbridge Festival of Music** takes place during one week in mid-September at the Struan House Hotel on the outskirts of Inverness. Contact Patrick Blease, Pine Ridge, Carrbridge, PH23 3AA, Scotland; 04798/31646. Just east of Inverness, in Nairn, you'll find the **International Festival of Music and Dance,** which takes place for two weeks in mid-July. Tickets range from £1–£3. Contact Dan Farrell at 0667/52055.

A little farther east is the **Elgin Fiddlers' Rally** consisting of approximately 120 musicians (fiddlers, accordianists, double bass players, pianists, and drummers) playing Scottish music with guest singers. It takes place in late September in Town Hall at Elgin. Advance booking is necessary. Contact Mrs. D. Allan, 21 Birnie Place, New Elgin, Morayshire, IV30 3EB, Scotland; 0345/542100.

Just north of Elgin, there's the **Lossiemouth Folk Festival,** a three-day event in mid-July featuring *ceilidh*, sessions, concerts and children's entertainment. Phone Neil and Irena Paterson at 0343/546968.

Southeast of Inverness, you'll find the **Grantown Festive Fortnight,** two weeks (beginning of August) of events, music and song. There is entertainment nightly in the Highland capital of Strathspey featuring local bands and guest artists at various venues. Contact Aviemore and Spey Valley Tourist Board, Grampian Rd., Aviemore, PH22 1PP, Scotland; 0479/810363.

Also in Strathspey is the **Badenoch and Strathspey Music Festival** which takes place for five days in mid-March. There're competitions in music, speech (including Gaelic), country dancing and piping. Tickets are a whopping £1 for the day and £4 for the festival. Contact Mrs. Morage Campbell, Kinvaid, West Terrace, Kingussie, PH21 1HA, Scotland; 0540/661797.

THE NORTH, INCLUDING THE ISLE OF SKYE

FESTIVALS

The **Harris Arts Festival** takes place in various venues on the Isle of Harris during the last week of March. Included are classical and folk music, dance, poetry, storytelling and visual arts. This is a very hip event in an even hipper locale. The same event is repeated in late August. Tickets for both are available from the Harris Tourist Information Center, Pier Rd., Tarbert, Isle of Harris, Western Isles, IV3 7LN, Scotland; 0859/2011. Another Isle of Harris festival is the **Harris Gala,** a fortnight (two weeks for the less literary) of events, dances, ceilidhs, dancing, piping, raft and boat races, barbeques, football and everything else that these folks can pack into fourteen days. Tickets are available by contacting K. M. MacDonald at 0859/2237.

The Clan Donald Junior Clarsach Competition takes place on the Isle of Skye. (Talk about hip places—this is it!) This is a Celtic harp competition for kids throughout the Highlands. Visitors are welcome, and, if you go, you won't believe the number who absolutely excel on this harp thing. This free event takes place in mid-May. For more info, call Donella Beaton at: 04714/227. Another Isle of Skye event is **Skyefest,** a weekend in mid-June including half marathon, street fayres and live music—a real happenin'. This event is also repeated in mid-August for another weekend go-around. Contact Nick Lawton at: 047032/399.

The **Feis an Eilein** is a program of concerts, theater, exhibitions and workshops dealing with Gaelic themes. This festival takes place during one week in mid-July at Sabhal Mor Ostaig and various other venues on the Isle of Skye. Advance booking is necessary; tickets range from £5–£10. Contact Duncan MacInnes, Deall (Community Arts), Ostaig House, Teangue, Sleat, Isle of Skye, IV44 8RQ, Scotland; 04714/207.

The Isle of Skye is a great one for festivals and **The Gaelic Concerts,** which take place for one week in mid-August in Portree, Tigh na Sgire, Park Road, is one of the best. It's a summer program of Gaelic concerts featuring fiddlers, dancers, accordianists and singers presenting a series of lively evenings and ceilidhs. Tickets are £4 and available at the venue cited above. Telephone 0478/612341. Since we only categorized the previous listing as *one* of the best, we can also include in that honorific the **Dunvegan Castle Music**

Festival, a week of evening concerts that take place in mid-July in the eighteenth-century drawing room of Skye's magnificent Dunvegan Castle. The repertoire is mainly devoted to European chamber music, clarsach and piping recitals. Advance booking is necessary; tickets are £6. Contact John Lambert, Dunvegan Castle, Dunvegan, Isle of Skye, IV6 4DR, Scotland; 047/022206.

The **Skye Folk Festival** takes place for one week in late July and includes evening concerts and *ceilidhs* by local bands, bands from

FOCUS ON   LEANAIDH AN OIBRE IAD

The cairn commemorating the MacCrimmons at Borealg on the Isle of Skye is set by the western shore of Loch Dunvegan, little more than a league from the ancestral home of the Chiefs of Clan MacLeod at Dunvegan Castle. Here was founded and grew to fame the first college of piping that brought the art of playing the Great Highland Pipes to full flowering and immortalized the name of MacCrimmon.

Set in the cairn is the following inscription: "The memorial cairn of the MacCrimmons of whom ten generations were hereditary pipers of MacLeod and were renowned as composers, performers, and instructors of the classical music of the bagpipe. Near to this spot stood the MacCrimmon School of Music, 1500–1800. The work carries on."

The cairn at Leanaidh an Oibre Iad

the rest of Scotland and international poo-bahs. Optional pub saisáns happen at lunch and after events. Telephone Mrs. Henriksen: 0478/612506. The **Gaelic Music Festival** takes place in mid-August for two weeks at the An Tuireann Arts Centre in Portree, Isle of Skye. This is another of Skye's wonderful series of concerts celebrating local Gaelic musicians (and you can't *believe* the talent here—just hang out on a street corner and it's almost certain you'll be serenaded by some fiddler or accordianist) as well as national musicians. For tickets, contact Rosie Somerville at 0478/613306.

And while you're in the Hebrides anyway, head for the southernmost isle in the chain for the **Isle of Barra Festival/Feis Bharraidh** which takes place during two weeks early in July at various venues. This is a festival of Gaelic song, dance, and drama. Advance booking is necessary. Contact Margaret Ann Beggs, Secretary, CSS Office, Castlebary, Isle of Barra, PA80 5XD, Scotland; 0871/4667.

Off the north coast, there's the **Orkney Traditional Folk Festival** which takes place in late May in various venues in Stromness up in the Orkney Islands. Included here are folk music, competitions, talks and children's events. A kind of low-key affair, but then again if you've come all the way up here, you're probably feeling pretty low-key yourself. Advance booking is necessary for this one. Booking starts May 1. The ticket prices are £2–£5. Contact Mr. J. Mowat, Dept. STB, POB 4, Stromness, Orkney, ST8 4VX, Scotland; 0856/850773.

And while you're in Orkney, hang out until June and catch the **St. Magnus Festival,** a compact six-day festival encompassing music, drama, poetry and the visual arts. Advance booking is necessary; tickets £2–£4. Booking opens May 1. Contact Mrs. D. Rushbrook, Strandal, Nicolson St., Kirkwall, Orkney, KW15 1BD, Scotland; 0856/872669.

If you head down to Keith, you'll find the **Keith Festival of Traditional Music and Song,** one weekend in mid-June devoted to traditional music and dance. This is the biggest and best-known traditional festival in North Scotland. Concerts and competitions, workshops and impromptu sessions take place. Call Mr. J. Smart at 0343/820074. Up the road from Keith and a bit west, you'll find the **Festival of Scottish Music** taking place in mid-June in Elgin's Town Hall. This is a one-day event. Contact Mr. I. H. Cruickshank at 0343/842234.

Traveling back through Inverness, there's the **Highland Traditional Music Festival,** which takes place in Dingwall, Ross-shire for three days in late June. This is a gathering of the best of traditional music of the Highlands with guests from other countries. Tickets are £16 for adults, children under fourteen are free, and advance booking is necessary. Tickets go on sale June 1. Contact Rob Gibson, Rudha Alainn, Knockbain Rd., Dingwall, IV15 9NR, Scotland; 0349/63270.

The Gordon District takes up a lot of very green space in the wonderful area north and northwest of Aberdeen. Here's where you'll find **The Doric Festival,** which takes place for one week in mid-October in various venues throughout the district. This is a celebration of Doric culture featuring traditional entertainment and activities ranging from music and drama to storytelling, poetry reading and exhibitions of farming traditions. Top entertainers participate. Tickets are available from the Leisure and Recreation Department at 0467/620981.

FOCUS ON   THE BAGPIPE

How, when and where the bagpipe originated is a mystery, but by two thousand years ago or so bagpipes were already sounding the war music of the Roman infantry, and their keening was heard wherever the legions marched. In successive centuries the instrument became established in infinite varieties throughout Europe and in parts of Asia, notably India.

After the end of the Middle Ages, however, the tradition of bagpiping faded or died in country after country with the single exception of the Highlands of Scotland. There it has flourished to culmination in the great highland bagpipe, the *piob-mhor.* Elsewhere the bagpipe has survived in its older form, but usually as a musical relic of esoteric communities. And now, in the second half of the twentieth century, the music of the Scottish pipes swells across a world far beyond the ken of the Romans.

It has been more than four hundred years since the MacCrimmons—hereditary pipers to the Chiefs of Clan MacLeod—brought the nurturing of centuries to full fruition in their mastery of the piob-mhor. At their College of Piping in Boreraig, Isle of Skye, generations of MacCrimmons became legends in their own lifetime. Many distinguished families of pipers trace their expertise back to Boreraig, and among modern masters and pupils the influence of the MacCrimmons still dominates.

While the repressive measures taken after the crushing of the 1745 Rising ended one epoch in the history of piping, they heralded another. The piob-mhor was played in secret at home, but with the formation of the Highland regiments and expatriation of countless Scots, the pipes were carried across the sea, heard and loved over a wider area than ever before. Today there are more pipers in more countries than ever, and the College of Piping (which contributed information for this mini-history lesson) in Scotland was founded to serve them and their heirs and successors.

THE CENTRAL HIGHLANDS AND ENVIRONS

The Highlands are Scotland's "souvenir area." Strewn with castles, green countryside and coastal plains, the area boasts of being able to make you feel as if "you've nothing better to do than to spend hours gazing at a blade of grass," which may speak well for tranquility and getting rid of stress, but less well for organized entertainment. The Highlands are not the place to go if you're looking for hot rock clubs and cool jazz venues. When it comes to festivals, however, there's hardly a better destination.

FESTIVALS

Perth is one of the larger cities in the area of the Highlands. As such, it has a number of wonderful festivals. Among them is the **Perthshire Musical Festival,** which takes place during twelve days in mid-March in the town's City Hall. This is a competitive event encompassing music, Scottish country dancing and verse speaking. Tickets are 50p. Contact Mr. William Neish at 0783/31979. Also in Perth is the **Perth Festival of the Arts** which takes place during most of May in various venues throughout the city. Music, dance, opera, drama and visual arts are all part of this festival. Advance booking is necessary. You can buy tickets from March 1 on. Tickets are available at the Festival Box Office, Perth Theatre or by contacting H. J. Calder, 35 Kincarrathie Crescent, Perth, PH2 7HH, Scotland; 0738/21672.

The **Strathearn Summer Music Festival** is a three-day event that features many musical styles (folk, rock, jazz, classical, brass) and takes place the first week of August in various venues throughout Strathearn, Perthshire. Advance reservations are necessary. Tickets go on sale in mid-July and are available from the Crieff Tourist Information Centre, 0764/679465.

Near Perth, you'll find the **Dunkeld and Birnam Arts Festival** going on for three days late in June. All kinds of music and arts and crafts are involved here. Tickets are available from the Tourist Information Centre, Dunkeld, Scotland; 0350/727688. Another great musical event near Perth is the **Summer Music in Balquhidder** series of concerts each Sunday night from late June until the end of August. The concerts include mostly classical, chamber and traditional music, but you never know. Held in a wonderfully quaint church (the kind you travel thousands of miles to see), tickets are £5 for adults and £3 for children. Contact Rev. J. Benson, 08774/235.

SPOTLIGHT ON   DOUGIE MACLEAN

Singer/songwriter, record producer and magical performer, Dougie Maclean has been at the forefront of the Celtic music revival since the early '70s. A former member of such respected bands as the Tannahill Weavers and Silly Wizard, Maclean is now performing both as a solo artist and with his own band. He also has a record company, Dunkeld Records, which boasts among its artists some of the finest folk musicians in Scotland. And in his uniquely down home way, Dunkeld's record covers are all done by his wife, Jenny ("...my lovely Jenny," in the words of one of his songs), who is a painter with an unmistakable style.

Dougie's songs, according to the U. K. trade paper *Folk Roots*, "lodge in your braincells and nudge at your heart." He plays "flowing guitar, scorching fiddle, unique didgeridoo, and sings—as they say in ole Scotland, 'like a lintie.' "

Of the eclecticism in his musical style, Maclean has this to say, "There are creative musicians and interpretive musicians. I love singing traditional songs, and I wouldn't stop doing that because there's such a strength and honesty in them. But I see myself mainly as a creator. Even when I'm playing fiddle, I like to do mostly my own tunes, because there are so many good players around doing the traditional ones. It all comes down to wanting to do the complete thing, from writing the song through to arranging it and recording it.

"My albums aren't concept albums or anything like that, but there's usually a thread running through them. [One of my albums] is called *Whitewash,* and that's a sort of play on words. There a whitewashed cottage on the cover, but I get angry about things being covered up—whitewashed—and that comes out in some of the songs."

Three events have recently brought Maclean's name and music to a wider audience. "Caledonia," a song he had written fifteen years earlier while on tour in France and suffering from homesickness, was used as the soundtrack of a 1991 Scottish television commercial, and quickly zoomed to the head of the Scottish singles chart. Another Maclean piece, a track from *The Search* instrumental album, was used on the soundtrack of the 1992 hit film *The Last of the Mohicans* starring Daniel Day Lewis. And late in 1993, the BBC screened a forty-minute film, *The Land—Songs of Dougie Maclean,* to critical acclaim.

Maclean, who lives in an old schoolhouse in Dunkeld, regularly visits the U. S. and recorded his 1991 album *Indigenous* in Nashville, where it quickly caught the attention of American country stars including Kathy Mattea.

Despite his newfound international success, however, Maclean's feet remain firmly in Scottish soil. "I have my nice wee cottage and I want to live there forever. That's a contented feeling and it gives you a clear picture of why you're doing things. I could have tried to push myself over the last two or three years with major labels. There are lots of ways I could have compromised what I believe in, but I wouldn't be happy. I don't want that much out of music."

The **Crail Festival** takes place during ten days late in July at various venues in this very pretty small town out on the coast from Perth. Included are drama, arts exhibitions, concerts and recitals, competitions and children's workshops. Call Jill Sanderson at 0333/50909. If you have three days to listen to great blues, head to Blairgowrie (near Perth) for the **Blairgowrie Folk and Blues Festival** in early August. Catch the music at various venues throughout the town. Included are traditional Scottish music, modern folk-blues, concerts, ceilidh dances and informal pub sessions. Don't miss this one. Reservations are accepted beginning on May 1. Tickets are available through Catherine Jones, Brooklin Mill, Riverside, Blairgowrie, BL2 7HH, Scotland; 0250/873090.

The **European Brass Band Championships** are held in Falkirk, which lies between Edinburgh and Glasgow. It's a four-day event in the first week of April and is held in Falkirk Town Hall on Bridge St. Nowhere else will you see such an amazing assemblage of shining brass instruments being bandied about by young people with rosy, peachy cheeks and hopeful expressions. Ah, youth! For tickets and info, contact Craig Murray or Janet Clark, Leisure Services Dept., 0324/24911. At approximately the same time in Falkirk, you can also catch the **National Youth Music Festival,** which includes Scottish schools, solo and quartet championships, and European youth brass championships. This one is held in the Town Hall in Stirlingshire. Ticket information can be had by contacting Craig and Janet at the above phone number.

Pitlochry has other things besides souvenir shops selling shortbread and whiskey. One of them is the wonderful **Pitlochry Festival** held during seven days in the beginning of April in the town's Festival Theatre (just over the Aldour Bridge). Up to seven plays a day are included in the goings-on; also featured are Sunday concerts and fringe events including foyer shows and musical exhibitions. Advance booking is necessary; prices range from £9–£13.50. Contact the box office at 0796/472680.

But Pitlochry's *pièce-de-résistance* is its ongoing series of **Pitlochry Highland Nights,** which take place every Monday night from late May to mid-September. These are outdoor evenings of traditional Scottish entertainment—pipe bands, highland and Scottish country dancing (with audience participation), traditional songs and accordian music. If it rains, it's held in the Town Hall. Price: £2.50–£4 for adults. Children are 50p–£1. Go to the Recreation Centre on Ferry

| FLASHBACK | MY MOMENT IN THE SPOTLIGHT |

For some reason, I'd decided to tour the British Isles with my saxophone. Two or three days into the trip, I kind of regretted it since the damn thing weighed a ton when added to my regular bag. But I have to admit that those few-and-far-between minutes when I'd plop myself down on some empty grassy field and blow became memories that I hold dear to this day.

The dearest memory of that trip, though, happened during the Dundee Jazz and Blues Festival [see p. 178] in June of 1992. I had heard of it from some travelers and headed over to Dundee to see what it was all about. The first night I bought a ticket to a performance that was billed as being "The Highland Swing Troupe," and of course, I brought my saxophone. I sat in the back and halfway through the performance, started to play along on my sax softly enough so that I hoped I wouldn't be heard from the stage. Well, maybe that's a lie. Maybe I always intended to be heard. At any rate, I *was* heard and, at one point, the lead horn player invited me up to play. At first I said no, but he persisted, so I slogged up to the stage, my knees shaking. We played together for the next ninety minutes. It was my first time ever in front of an audience, and I was petrified. But man, was it ever great!

CHRIS ANGELI, BOULDER, COLORADO

Road at 8 p.m. or contact Mrs. G. McNab, Laigh of Cluny, Aberfeldy, PH15 2JU, Scotland; 0887/840302.

In Stirling's Old Town, you'll find a wonderfully historic festival, **The Royal Stirling Summer Events,** consisting of historical reenactments, medieval markets, *ceilidhs*, fiddle evenings, guided tours and outdoor music of all sorts. This celebration starts in early May and runs through the whole summer. For more info on what's going on and where it happens, check with K. Russell in the town's Department of Community Services at 0786/432353, 5, 7. Another Stirling historical moment can be experienced by attending the **Stirling Tartan Festival,** a variety of events held throughout the Royal

Burgh of Stirling ranging from pipe-band performances and highland dancing displays to a traditional family *ceilidh*. Despite its obvious appeal to tourists, this is a good look at traditional Scottish
culture. For tickets, contact the Stirling Tourist Information Centre
at 0786/475019.

Slightly southeast of Pitlochry, you'll find the **Dundee Jazz and
Blues Festival,** which swings into being the first week of June in both
the Dundee Repertory Theatre and the town's Tay Park. This is a
music-packed week of the very best in jazz and blues. Tickets, which
are necessary in advance, are from £3–£10 and are available from
the Dundee Rep Theatre or by contacting Chris Campbell, Dundee
Tourist Board, 4 City Square, Dundee, DD1 3BA, Scotland;
0382/23141, ext. 4284.

Near Dundee during the first week in September is the **Kirriemuir
Traditional Music Festival** which features Scottish traditional music
including ceilidhs, competitions, dances and pub sessions. The tickets cost £2–£3 and are available from the Tourist Information
Centre; telephone 0575/74097.

In Fife, which is near Edinburgh, there's a great traditional festival considered one of the best in Scotland. It's the **Auchtermuchty
Festival Traditional Music Weekend** and it takes place during three
days in mid-August in various venues throughout the tiny town of
Auchtermuchty. Included are dances, *ceilidhs*, concerts, a barn
dance, open-air music and a street dance on Sunday afternoon. This
one is a *real* event—don't miss it. The ticket prices are £3.50 for
adults and £3 for children. Contact Traditional Music Weekend
Secretary, c/o Auchtermuchty Community Centre at 0337/828907.

Dunoon (all the way over in west Scotland, northeast of Arran
Isle) sponsors a wonderful event, **The Dunoon Jazz Festival,** which
takes place in sixteen venues throughout the town during three days
in mid-October. The scenery is fantastic and the music no less so.
Contact Russell Cowieson at 0369/3118.

ARRAN

PUBS AND TRADITIONAL MUSIC

The gorgeous island of Arran bills itself as a "Scotland in Miniature"
and so it is—both geographically and musically. This is one place you
won't want to miss if what you came to Scotland to hear are the tradi-

tional sounds of pipes and drums and accordians and fiddles. Since the place is so small—less than twenty miles long—almost anyplace you turn will have a small pub with musicians about to break into a jam. But in case you need more direction, here are some you should check out.

The **Aldersyde Hotel** (Lamlash, 0770/600219, 600732) is an all-year-round live-music venue in which, no matter when you get there, you'll definitely hear music.

The **Lochranza Village Hall** presents occasional concerts. Tickets are £4 and are available by calling 0770/830304. Other concert-type halls include **Lamlash Hall** and **Whiting Bay Hall,** both of which feature various music programs. Call 0770/302680, 600280 for more information.

The **Festival Bar Club** (in the Ormidale Hotel, Brodick, opposite the golf club) offers good food, a beer garden and regular music sessions. **Duncan's Bar** (two minutes from the pier, 0770/302531) has a large selection of real malts and ales (Marston's Pedigree, Boddington's and Theakston XB) as well as regular jazz and folk nights. Call for more specific information.

The **Douglas Hotel** (Brodick, 0770/302155) has live folk music every Wednesday and Sunday during which you're inevitably going to wind up singing along—everybody else does! The **Breadalbane Hotel** (Kildonan, no phone) has live music most nights and good snacks available all day. And finally, there's the **Kiscadale Hotel** (Whiting Bay, 0770/700236), which has regular live music and pretty good bar meals.

SPOTLIGHT ON ▌JEAN REDPATH

Her voice has been described as sounding like a human cello. Her vast repertoire ranges from near-operatic interpretations of semiclassical works to folk songs of lovelorn damsels and homeless gypsies. Recognized on both sides of the Atlantic as the foremost interpreter and champion of traditional Scottish music, Jean Redpath is a household name among folk music fans for her scores of record albums and hundreds of concert appearances.

She started her career in 1961 when she arrived in the United States with eleven dollars to her name, wowed a crowd at a hootenanny in

San Francisco and accepted a job in Philadelphia. But after begging and borrowing her fare across the country, she arrived to find that the club owner had skipped town. The next day, she lucked into a ride to New York City with some new friends and went with them to a Greenwich Village apartment where yet another hootenanny was taking place, this one with the likes of Bob Dylan and Jack Elliott and the Greenbriar Boys. Six weeks later, Redpath did her first show at Gerde's Folk City; the rest is history.

Since then, she has won a recording career and worldwide acclaim that includes among its honors the MBE (Member of the British Empire), which was awarded by Queen Elizabeth II in 1991.

Redpath, who characterizes herself as having been a "mezzo since the age of eight," has a clarity of voice and a depth of emotional character that have made it possible for her to capture a wide audience despite her specialized genre. Although she prefers to sing a cappella, she'll also use a guitar—if only in the most minimal fashion. When she sings with other instrumental backing, she prefers the sound of the violin, the cello and the oboe.

Redpath's fame as a musician isn't very surprising. "In my family, it was assumed that one could turn one's hand to something musical," she says. "My mother was one of twelve musicians, and my father one of three…I had the piping and the drumming on one side of the family and my mother's siblings all played or sang something—all self-taught—usually keyboards because that was what was around."

Over the last thirty years, Redpath has represented Scottish music to the world. "I don't think the Scots are any different from anybody else," she says. "They'd just prefer if you thought so. We're an emotional race who for reasons best known to ourselves, decided that in everyday life we should not be demonstrative, emotional or romantic. But those feelings had to go somewhere, so they went into music."

Nowhere have these feelings found a better home than in the music of Jean Redpath. A sense of drama suffuses her many albums (most on Philo Records, a subsidiary of Rounder). On *Jean Redpath*, the myth-based "Silkie" tells the tale of a creature that is half-woman and half-seal. (See p. 181, the original "silkie" myth.) *A Fine Song for*

Singing offers musical arrangements of such poems as William Butler Yeats's "The Song of Wandering Aengus" and the "Captive Song of Mary Stuart," which recounts the tale of the sixteenth-century queen who recklessly married her second husband's murderer, was chased out of Scotland to the unwelcoming shelter of neighboring England and after nineteen years as a prisoner was beheaded for treason by her cousin Elizabeth Tudor.

Redpath's largest project is recording the 323 poems and ballads of Scottish poet laureate Robert Burns set to native folk melodies. After fifteen years, seven albums, and eighty-six songs, she only has 237 numbers to go. Is she sick of Burns and his odes? "You wouldn't have to look further than Burns if you want to spend a lifetime on Scottish music," she demurs. "Musically he was very consciously preserving a whole vocal and pipe-and-fiddle tradition. His work ranged from very formal songs full of classical allusions, written in standard English, to the simple Scottish dance melodies that everyone knows. He was a universal kind of bard, the voice of the common man. And it's remarkable how much his lyrics still have relevance today."

Despite her beautiful voice and the depth of her knowledge of Burns and Scottish songs, however, Redpath facetiously refers to herself as a musical illiterate. She never learned to read music and isn't especially concerned about it. "I work with my ears and with the audience's ears," she says. "You don't have to be able to read the musical notation or understand how to play the instrument if you just hang loose and let the stuff react."

"THE SILKIE"

A traditional scottish tale (This tale has been adapted by Jean Redpath and recorded on her album *Jean Redpath*.)

A long time ago a fisherman who cast his nets by the sea one night chanced to see a Silkie lay her skin down upon the rocks. Now a Silkie is a seal by day, but by night appears as beautiful a human creature as ever has walked the Earth. The fisherman gazed upon the Silkie woman and thought he had never seen anything more fair.

When she was out of sight, he took the sealskin from between the rocks and hid it in his own house. Returning to the shore he found the Silkie weeping her salt tears into the sea.

"Lass, why are you crying like your heart is going to break?"

"Och, Sir, my heart is breaking indeed, for without my skin I cannot return to the sea and I do not know how to live upon the land."

"Then," said he, "you must come with me and be my wife." So she went with him and married him and raised him fine children.

Then one day she found her skin hidden behind a wall in her house. Taking the skin to the sea, she became a seal once again, returning to the home which had never ceased its calling.

Jean Redpath

But the big event in Arran is the **Arran Folk Festival,** which takes place during six days in mid-June on the Isle of Arran and draws musicians and tourists from all over the world. This is a well-established festival with concerts and dances, workshops and saisáns all around the Isle, concentrated on Lamlash and Brodick over the final weekend. The spiritual center is the glasshouse bar and lawns of Brodick's Ormidale Hotel. Book tickets and accommodation early for this one; by early we mean possibly the year before. Call the Isle of Arran Tourist Board for more information: 0770/700406, 302416.

Just west of the Isle of Arran is the Isle of Bute with its own series of festivals. The first and biggest (well, maybe by only a few hundred people) is **The Isle of Bute Jazz Festival** which happens during three days in late May. This is a very successful and popular event (book early) featuring different styles of jazz, and presenting both younger and more experienced soloists and bands to an audience of all ages. Again, advance booking is necessary. Contact Phil Mason, "Shalunt," Isle of Bute, PA20 0QL, Scotland; 070084/283.

The other big Bute event is the three-day **International Folk Festival,** which takes place in late July and features everything you'd want a folk festival to feature—*ceilidhs*, dances, busking competitions, beach parties, informal music saisáns and street music. For more information, contact Danny Kyle, Director, 126 Renfrew Rd., Paisley, PA3 4BL, Scotland; 041/887-9991.

THE BORDERS

Music, when soft voices die, vibrates on the memory.

SHELLEY

A part of what's called the Borders area actually approaches the environs of Edinburgh and Glasgow and their artistic lives. But farther afield, the flavor gets distinctly more traditional, especially in the area surrounding the wonderfully verdant Galloway Forest Park. The area boasts much festival activity, most of which takes place, as you would expect, in the warmer months of the year.

Girvan is on the west coast smack in the middle of the Galloway Forest area. It has two festivals—one a jazz event, the other an authentically traditional festival well worth the trip. The **Girvan Folk Festival** takes place during the last weekend of April in various venues throughout the town. Included are concerts, ceilidhs and endless saisáns of informal dance and song. The weekend ticket price is £17, and tickets are available from 16 Annandale Gardens, Crosshouse, Kilmarnock, Scotland; 0563/44855. The **Girvan Jazz Festival** takes place during the third weekend in September. Tickets are available by contacting Mr. R. Jardine at 0465/2128.

The **River Tweed Festival** takes place in various venues throughout the Scottish borders and Berwick-upon-Tweed. It's a month-long festival in May celebrating the River Tweed; there are river sports, cycling, music, theater, hot air balloons and lots of other wonderful events and activities. For tickets, contact the Scottish Borders Tourist Board at 0750/20055.

Right on the border is Kelso with its **Pipe Band Festival** held on one day in early May in Floors Castle where pipe bands play on the forecourt lawn. Contact the Kelso Tourist Information Centre at 0573/23464. In that same area, you'll find the **Selkirk Scottish Music Festival,** a full weekend in late May of Scottish music, dance, games, pipers, drummers, massed bands, pipe and brass concerts and street entertainment—what more could you want? Contact Mike Firth, Ettrick and Lauderdale District Council at 0750/23139.

Dumfries is west of the border and entertains itself with a wonderful little event, **The Dumfries and Galloway Arts Festival,** in late May to early June, which takes place in various venues. Advance booking is necessary. Contact the Gracefield Arts Centre, 28 Edinburgh Rd., Dumfries, DG1 1JQ, Scotland; 0387/60447. Dumfries also hosts the **Dumfries Guid Nychburris Festival,** which—you guessed it—is mainly a Gaelic event taking place for one week in mid-June, and consisting of various indoor and outdoor activities culminating with a traditional ceremony and the crowning of the "Queen of the South." Contact Mr. A. Marshal at 0387/54805.

West of the border you'll find the **Largs Viking Festival** with everything from opera to battle reenactments, musicals to fireworks, and dances to lectures. It takes place the last weekend of August in the Barfields Pavillion/Kelburn Country Centre. Prices £1.50–£6. Contact R. E. Fergusson-Taylor at 0475/675030. And finally there's the **Gatehouse of Fleet Spring Festival of Music, Arts, and Crafts** in Kircudbrightshire (south of Galloway State Forest, on the coast) which has a program encompassing concerts, ceilidhs, arts and crafts exhibitions, historical exhibitions, outdoor events and pub sing-alongs. This is a wonderful festival that takes place during three days in late March and is substantially less commercial than others in the area. Advance booking is necessary; bookings open March 1. Contact George McCulloch, 4 Carneys Corner, Gatehouse of Fleet DG8 2HW, Scotland; 0557/814030.

✷ ANSWERS TO TEST YOUR MUSICAL I.Q.

Page 125

1-c,   2-f,   3-l,   4-m,   5-o,   6-h,   7-b,   8-p,   9-d,   10-k,
11-g,   12-n,   13-e,   14-i,   15-j,   16-a

Page 163

4a. Sweeney's Men

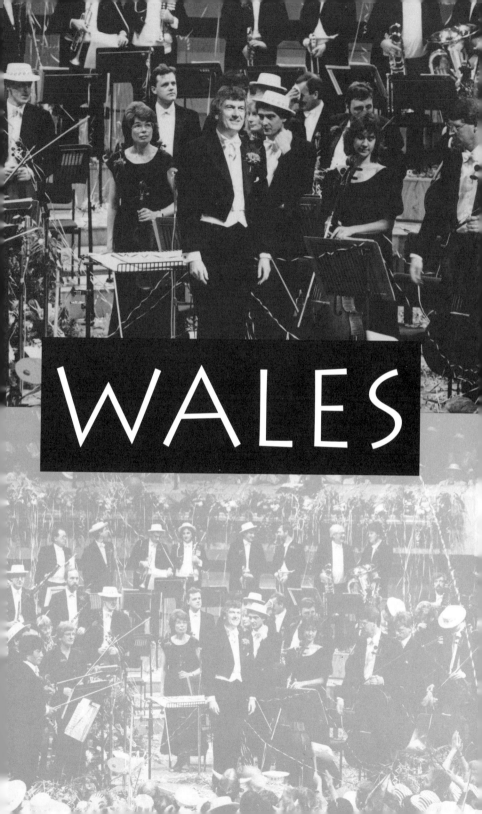

WALES

Wales

Including Cardiff, Swansea, Newport, Greater South Wales, Mid-Wales, and North Wales

Wales is the most westerly of the three countries on the island of Great Britain. An extremely small country (8,016 square miles), Wales has been united politically, administratively and economically with England ever since the passage of the 1536 Act of Union whose unstated purpose was to rid the affected countries of their "non-English ways." Wales was luckier than the rest of Britain, however. For whatever reason, the Act had less impact on the Welsh than on the unfortunate Irish and Scots, whose native culture was practically obliterated. For the most part, Wales has been able to preserve a cultural identity that, while sharing characteristics with its larger neighbor, is, nevertheless, quite different from it.

The most obvious manifestation of Wales's native culture is its language. The Welsh language, a variation of the Gaelic that was spoken by the Celts, evolved in the sixth century. It does not include the letters *j, k, q, v, x* and *z*. In many words, you'll find double consonants; *dd, ff* and *ll*, for example. *Dd* is pronounced as *f* and *ll* sounds much like *thl*. Knowing this, you should have no trouble pronouncing *Lanfairpwllgwyngyllgogerychwyrndrobwlllandysiliogogogoch*, a village in Wales with the world's longest place name. It means "Church of Saint Mary in a hollow of white hazel, near to a rapid whirlpool, and Saint Tysilio's Church of the red cave."

Difficult though it may be to outsiders, the Welsh language continues to serve as a key element in the country's myriad cultural traditions—especially its music. The ancient bardic songs, in fact, can still be heard exactly as they were originally performed over five hundred years ago. And while the early twentieth century may have seen a drop in interest in the country's native musical forms, there is currently underway a strong revivalist movement whose goal is to preserve and expand traditional music performed in Welsh.

The Welsh are an extremely musical people. They love to sing, and nearly every town has some sort of resident choral group. Government assistance is generous and supplied through the Welsh Arts Council which, in addition to arranging tours of Wales by British and foreign orchestras, also gives support to amateur music-making societies as well as to a great number of national festivals. The Welsh National Opera Company, for example, operates under the direction of the Council, and, because of this relative freedom from the need to raise funds of its own, has become one of the leading companies in Britain.

Another Council-supported activity is the tradition of *eisteddfod* (pronounced *eye-steth-vod*), or competitive festival, which is, perhaps, the most individual of Welsh cultural institutions and the culmination of hundreds of smaller local and school eisteddfod. Held annually in North and South Wales on alternating years, the venue for the national event results from the invitation of a particular town or area, and the festival is generally housed in a transportable hall or pavillion. It is always sited on open ground that, for the duration of the festival, becomes a campus on which most of the cultural organizations of Wales also hold exhibitions illustrating their activities.

Held for one week in August, the National Eisteddfod consists of competitions in all genres of music performed exclusively in Welsh (participants compete for the title of Chief Bard), and sometime during the middle of the week the bardic circle, or *Gorsedd*, holds its ceremonies. Tens of thosuands attend the festival, and for its duration this wonderful event becomes literally the gathering ground for the nation. For information on either local eisteddfod or the Big Kahuna Eisteddfod, contact Eleri Twynog Davies at 0222/ 763777.

As you take in the music of Wales, you'll find that the country offers numerous discounts to those fitting the proper categories. One such discount is the YouthCard, which is a phenomenal way to save up to fifty percent off the price of tickets for shows at premiere arts venues. The card costs £4 a year if you're eighteen or under and £5 a year if you're nineteen to twenty-one. Call Cardiff Arts Marketing to get one at 0222/343964. Another substantial savings is given to parties of eight or more attending major arts events. These groups save up to one-third off the price of tickets. Families are also given priority with ticket reductions averaging forty percent.

CARDIFF

Established with the fabulous wealth of a vast coal empire, Wales' capital is fast moving beyond its mining roots and becoming one of Europe's finest maritime cities. The only urban center in a land of small villages, Cardiff is also the youngest capital in Europe. Despite its relative lack of elegance and sophistication, its over-three-hundred-thousand population expresses itself in a lively arts scene.

The Welsh National Opera, one of the world's finest companies, presents all its premier productions at Cardiff's New Theatre. Touring groups are welcomed at the New Theatre as well as at the Chapter Arts Center.

For live music, the choices are few but of excellent quality. The BBC National Orchestra of Wales and a multitude of famous names in popular, classical and rock music perform regularly at the two thousand-person-capacity St. David's Hall. And, for both visitors and residents alike, there's the new Cardiff International Arena opened by HM Queen Elizabeth II in October of 1993 where one can hear international rock and pop megastars.

For more detailed information on music in Cardiff, contact the Arts Council of Wales (Museum Place, 0222/394711) or pick up a copy of *Buzz*, a free monthly magazine listing arts venues. *Buzz* is available through the Arts Council or at various arts venues around town. To find where to get one near your hotel, call their office at 0222/667554.

CONCERT HALLS

St. David's Hall (Working St., 0222/236244 for information or 0222/371236 for the box office) is said to have the finest acoustics in Britain. This two-thousand-seat national concert hall presents a wide variety of musical entertainment including classical, jazz, rock and folk (as well as films, sporting events and lectures; make sure you find out the schedule or you're likely to end up in a crowd of beer-swilling rubgy fanatics). The Welsh Proms are also held here—a week-long event of classical music offerings resembling the London Proms with one difference: you're likely to be able to buy a ticket. That having been said, however, book early for popular events. Cardiff has only a few big-time venues, so the rush is on whenever somebody wonderful is performing. St. David's is located in the

St. David's

heart of Cardiff, alongside the busy St. David's Shopping Centre. The box office is usually open Monday through Saturday from 10:00 a.m. Charge cards can be used for telephone bookings right up to the last minute, and telephone reservations will be held for three days. Ticket prices vary according to performance and range from £1–£22. Dress nicely; jeans will get you a discreet little tut-tut. St. David's also has a program of lunchtime recitals with tickets for as little as £2. For info call 0222/371236, 235900.

The New Theatre (Park Place, 0222/394844) has a capacity of over 1,100 seats. Recently restored to reflect its Edwardian heritage, the Theatre now serves as the home of the Welsh National Opera, which is in residence each spring and autumn. One of Britain's four major opera companies, the W. N. O. is said by many to be the most dramatic and exciting of all. With this reputation, tickets—naturally—sell out early.

Those who *do* manage to get seats are entitled to attend a free preperformance lecture in the Upper Circle Bar of the theater at 6:15 p.m. And for *real* opera afficionados, there's OPERACALL (0891/600-1946), a twenty-four-hour interactive information line, which provides plots, ticket availability and backstage news. Calls cost 36p–48p per minute.

The **Star Centre** (Splott Rd., 0222/484637, 484647) offers musical revues and a variety of performances, which can sometimes include members of the Welsh National Opera. Ticket prices are in the £5–£7 range and are generally easier to get than at the more famous concert venues. The **Sherman Theatre** (Senghennydd Rd., Cathays, 230451) caters mainly to theatrical productions. On occasion, however, you'll find a wonderful musical revue or operetta. Tickets range from £4–£8.

Music was taught to Achilles in order to moderate his passions.

HOMER

The **Welsh College of Music and Drama** (North Rd., 0222/372175) presents a variety of musical venues with ticket prices in the £3 range. Evening performances take place in the Bute Theatre and lunchtime recitals in the Evans Room. Generally, there is no advance booking, but you should have no problem getting tickets if you call a few days in advance. **The Norwegian Seamen's**

Church (Cardiff Bay, 0222/372175) conducts occasional classical concerts, the most notable of which are the five programs that make up the early music series; £6.50 covers the price of the concert plus refreshments. The wooden church, a model of small-scale elegance, was built for Norwegian seamen in 1867 but gradually fell into disuse. In 1987 a trust was set up which led to the resiting of the building, now used as a cafe that sponsors arts exhibitions and concerts.

CLUBS AND DISCOS

Cardiff has a wide variety of venues for nighttime entertainment. From rock to folk to jazz to karaoke, the after-hours scene is lively, crowded, smoke-filled, and—for the most part—casual, although some places tend toward a bit of the old sartorial attitude. Students usually congregate in the dozens of places along St. Mary Street, but don't avoid that area completely if you're beyond the pen-and-book-bag stage; many of the clubs reach out to wider audiences with such popular fixtures as swing nights. Tuesday nights are almost universally student nights during which students (or reasonable facsimiles thereof) are entitled to hefty discounts on both admission and drinks. If you're into partying of the raucous, carefree variety, Tuesday nights will be your thing.

The **Llandaff Rowing Club** (The Boat House, Bridge Rd., 0222/566361) serves up a healthy mix of Brains Special Ale (Cardiff's signature brew) and great soul. Unfortunately, it's for members and their guests only, although rumor has it that admission policies will soon undergo revision. In the meantime, hanging around outside can sometimes gets you qualified as a bona fide "guest."

The **Club Metro** (Bakers Row, 0222/371549) specializes in *indie* Tuesday–Saturday. If you get there before 11 p.m., you can get in for £2. A slight bit of dressing savvy would be appreciated here, although you can get by with your same old duds. Such is not the case at the **Hippo Club** (Penarth Rd., 0222/226168), where the rock is serious and the outfits definitely on the creative side. The Club is open Thursday, Friday, and Saturday. The admission hovers in the £4 range.

If swing and soul is what you crave, **Liberty's** (St. Mary St., 0222/372765) is the place to be Saturday nights. Admission is £4. Other nights, the music varies; Fridays are devoted to top 40. **Sam's** (63 St. Mary St., 0222/345189) is one of Cardiff's premiere night spots. Thursday, Friday and Saturday are devoted to local and national bands, and you can find some pretty wild fiddlin'—depending on who's in town. Wednesday is cabaret night. Another thing that makes Sam's unique is the good food. Admission varies, but expect to pay somewhere in the £3 vicinity.

For those seeking mellow, head to **Tapas Cafe/Bar** (St. Andrew's Arcade, Queen St., 0222/227700), where on Friday and Saturday you can relax to the soothing sounds of flamenco guitar. Happy hour is Monday–Friday from 5 p.m.–7 p.m., admission ranges from free to £2. And for the karaoke fans in the crowd, the place to be is the **Queen's Vault** (Westgate St., 0222/383401) where on Wednesday, Saturday and Sunday you can sing to your heart's content. Thursday and Friday are devoted to dance music; admission hovers in the £2 range.

Two more for the hip crowd are **Lloyds/The Philharmonic** (High St., 0222/230678), where you should plan on dressing to impress; admission is £3 after 9 p.m. but free if you go early and hang out in the pub upstairs; and **Faces** (7 High St., 0222/226468), which has great acoustics and musical offerings ranging from groove to funk to soul to garage; free before 10 p.m., £2 after.

GAY AND LESBIAN

Four places rate a mention—all of them located in the Charles St.-Dispenser St. area where most of the gay and lesbian places are concentrated. The **Bel-Air Cafe Bar** (Dispenser St., 0222/378866) has a cabaret night on Fridays. **Exit Bar** (48 Charles St., 0222/378866) is open Mondays and Tuesdays from 6 p.m.–2 a.m., Wednesdays–Saturdays from 6 p.m.–12 a.m. and on Sundays from 7 p.m.–12 a.m. for high-energy mixed dancing. **Club X** (Charles St., 0222/645721) is open Wednesday–Saturday from 10 p.m.–2 a.m. **The Scene** (in the Riverside Hotel, Dispenser St., 0222/378866) has techno and high-energy music Friday, Saturday and Sunday from 10:30 p.m. until late. All clubs charge varying admissions. Expect to pay somewhere in the £3 range. Don't wear a tie!

FOLK, ROOTS AND COUNTRY

As you would expect, folk and traditional music is abundant in Cardiff. Again, as you would expect, crowds are mellow and dress is casual. Don't be surprised if you're dragged into a sing-along; the Welsh are all singers, and you'll often see people from the audience jump onstage with their fiddles, which they just *happen* to have brought along.

The following is a list of places that run traditional-music *saisáns*. Saisán nights vary, however, so be sure to call ahead. When you call, also ask about other saisáns. Traditional music is a spur-of-the-moment kind of thing, so you're likely to hear of saisáns going on that night at St. Donat's Castle, or in the home of Andy Morgan down on Penarthy Lane or who knows where.

Mulligan's (St. Mary St., 0222/644952)

Yellow Kangaroo (Elm St., Roath, 0222/472064)

Llantwit Major Rugby Club (St. Mary St., 0222/794461, Graham Morgan) is the home of the Heritage Folk Club, which generally meets on Thursday nights at 8:30.

JAZZ

Jazz in Cardiff is almost a religious calling, with clubs dedicating themselves to this kind of music as their life's work. Yes, they also try to make money, but you'll find an attitude about the jazz places that you won't find elsewhere—a camaraderie, insider attitude and commitment to luring the best of both the local and international scenes. As proof of the esprit-de-corps in the jazz community, members have invented the National Jazz Card, which can be had for £7.50—or the U.S. equivalent—by sending a check to the Welsh Jazz Society, 26 Castle Arcade, Cardiff, CF1 2YB, Wales. This card will gain you free entry to most of the jazz venues in Wales and many in the rest of Great Britain.

The new place in town is **Jake's Jazz Restaurant** (Mill Lane, 0222/226373). Here you'll find not only great jazz but sublime pizzas (if you think that's no great feat, try ordering pizza elsewhere in Cardiff). A three-course lunch plus any sweet on the menu, all accompanied by live jazz, will cost you just £6.99. Most performers take the stage on Sundays, which it so happens is *the* big jazz day in Cardiff. Expect to pay around £3 for evening admission; reservations are necessary for weekend gigs. Tuesday nights are "Happy Nights" when you can hear great jazz and eat cheap food. On every other Saturday the club imports its musicians from London.

The old-timer on the block is **The Four Bars Inn** (Castle St., 0222/340591), which features local and international performers in the upstairs room. At **The Philharmonic** (St. Mary St., 0222/222595), jazz bands play during Sunday lunch. Admission is free with lunch reservations. The **Guildhall Tavern** (St. Mary St., 0222/668008) also has live jazz during Sunday lunch. Jazz here tends toward the swing variety. **Sam's Bar** (Mill Lane, 0222/345189) has jazz during Sunday lunch as well as Sunday nights.

And, if your jazz tastes tend toward fusion, there's **The Juice Joint** (in the Clwb ifor Bach, Womanby St., 0222/232199), where on Thursday nights you can catch the likes of classic, acid jazz, or funky neapolitan rockers, or soul-jazz-funk or who knows? Admission here is in the £4–£5 range.

FESTIVALS

Cardiff is home to many kinds of music festivals—from those concentrating on the harp, to those featuring medieval music, to jazz festivals spread out on the Bay, to the national Eisteddfod, which has as one of its main events the crowning of a "Chief Bard."

For starters, there are the **Welsh Proms,** which take place during nine days in July at St. David's Hall (The Hayes, 0222/342611). The Proms is an annual series of concerts performed by some of Britain's leading orchestras. The last night of the Proms is traditionally the most exciting and the hardest to get tickets for.

In addition to the main event, there's music and entertainment in the foyers of St. David's Hall. There you'll find clowns, brass bands and strolling minstrels. Proms Showsuppers take place in the Celebrity Restaurant in St. David's—two courses for £11.95, with a cold buffet available in the bar starting at 6 p.m. on performance nights. Tickets range from £3.50–£18.50, and if you're planning on going, book a month or two in advance. For advance booking information, write the Box Office, St. David's Hall, The Hayes, Cardiff, CF1 2SH, Wales; fax: 0222/383726.

And the night shall be filled with music,

And the cares that infest the day,

Shall fold their tents, like the Arabs,

And as silently, steal away.

LONGFELLOW

The **Cardiff Festival of Music** also takes place in St. David's Hall (The Hayes, 0222/342611) and is a two-week event encompassing opera, theater, exhibitions and jazz performances. Although film and literature are also presented, music is at this festival's center with international stars joining some of Wales's most-talented musicians. The BBC National Orchestra of Wales, the Welsh National Opera and the Welsh Association of Male Choirs can all be heard. For advance booking, contact Louise Cogman, Publicity Office, St. David's Hall, The Hayes, Cardiff, CF1 2SH, Wales.

The *Eisteddfod Genedlaethol Frenhinol Cymru,* or the **Royal National Eisteddfod of Wales** (0222/763777), takes place during the first week of August. The venue changes annually—one year in the North, the next in the South. This is perhaps Wales's most culturally authentic event—a unique blend of music, drama, poetry, art and crafts. All events are conducted in Welsh with free simultaneous translation facilities. On Wednesday or Thursday of the festival week, a "Chief Bard" is crowned—someone who best represents the bardic tradition of ancient Wales. For advance booking information, contact Eleri Twynog, The Royal National Eisteddfod of Wales, Eisteddfod Office, 40 Parc Ty Glas, Llanishen, Cardiff, CF4 5WU, Wales; 0222/763737.

The **Dyffryn Gardens Festival of Music** (Dyffryn Gardens, St. Nicholas, 0222/593259, 593328) is a colorful event featuring a wide selection of musical moods from medieval madrigals to the dynamic sounds of the '60s—all held in the grand splendor of a fifty-five-acre garden whose grounds provide a stunning backdrop to the estate's Victorian mansion. The festival spans almost four weeks in late July through early August with six events taking place once or twice a week. Each event is accompanied by a deliciously appropriate menu, so the events appeal to food lovers as well as music lovers. The organizers are keen to encourage audience participation in the spirit of the festival, so visitors are asked to dress up in a costume suitable to the style, mood and era of the music of each event. Prizes are offered. Tickets range from £12 including buffet, to £20 including dinner to £30 for a family ticket (two adults and two children under twelve). For advance booking information, contact the box office at the previously listed number or write Dyffryn Gardens, St. Nicholas, Cardiff, CF5 6SU, Wales.

Europa Caerdydd, or **Europe Week,** is an annual festival that takes place during the second or third week of May in the streets surrounding the Old Library. The event consists of open-air music, crafts, carnivals, fireworks, food and drink, and encompasses contemporary and traditional bands from all over Europe. Musical offerings can range from Dutch Rockedelia, to indie types such as the Newcranes entertaining with their own brand of Ukrainian melodies, to hurdy-gurdy player Nigel Eaton. The celebration ends on a Sunday with a procession involving samba street bands and fireworks, and the crowd is generally decked out in masks. This fun event draws thousands of people and—best of all—it's free!

The **Cardiff Bay Jazz Festival** (tickets available from the Welsh Jazz Society, 0222/340591) includes a string of concerts, which usually take place during the last week of May and feature world-class performers. Principal concert venues surround the bay and are the Coal Exchange, the County Hall and the Norwegian Church. On the last day of the festival the streets of Cardiff Bay ring out with the sounds of New Orleans jazz, street music and samba. Admission to over twenty events can be had for as little as £10 with a "Bay Pass" (call the Welsh Jazz Society at 0222/340591 to get one). Individual events range from £5–£7.

WHERE IT'S AT   THE COAL EXCHANGE

One of the most remarkable transformations in Cardiff Bay has been that of the Coal Exchange in Mount Stuart Square from commercial hub to arts-and-entertainment center. Its imposing facade speaks of the days when Cardiff was growing fast to become the greatest coal-exporting port in the world, its wealth built on the "black gold" dug from the earth by the miners of the Rhondda and neighboring valleys.

The Exchange was built between 1883 and 1886, and it was here that Cardiff's leading businessmen—owners of shipping firms, coal mines and a variety of allied businesses—met to fix their deals, some with far-distant countries. Cardiff, which half a century before had been a market town of ten thousand people with a small coastal trade, had by then become a commercial center of importance on the world's stage. It was said at the time that wherever you stretched an arm on the trading floor of the Exchange you could touch a millionaire. In their silk hats and frock coats, they seemed to symbolize a prosperity that would last forever.

But the Great War of 1914 brought their world crashing down around their ears. Lost markets were never regained, oil came to challenge coal and Cardiff's decline as a port was every bit as dramatic as its growth.

The millionaires have all turned to dust, but the Coal Exchange building remains in all its architectural glory. Paired Corinthian columns, an oak balcony and rich wood paneling adorn the trading hall. Instead of dancing to the tune of commerce, however, the Exchange is now a pantheon of pleasure. Feet tap to traditional jazz and music of many kinds pulls in the crowds.

The Exchange is only one aspect of a major waterfront development project whose goal is to rejuvenate the 2,700 acres of the inner harbor and turn the whole thing into a huge business and entertainment complex that would eventually include the site of a national opera house. Currently, it has one neighboring musical venue, The Norwegian Seamen's Church, which hosts a wide variety of musical performances from classical to jazz to pop.

Cardiff's **Singer of the World Competition** (St. David's Hall, The Hayes, 0222/371236), which takes place in odd-numbered years, is the culmination of hundreds of Young Welsh Singers competitions (many of which also take place at St. David's). Famous celebrities such as Tom Jones (who hails from Pontypridd in Mid Glamorgan), Shirley Bassey and U2 take part in the surrounding events, and singers from all over the world flock to Cardiff to compete.

The *Gwyl Telynau'r Byd,* or **World Harp Festival,** takes place during the second week of June in a number of different venues ranging from St. David's Hall (which is where you can get general information and tickets, 0222/371236, 235900), St. John's Church, Howell's School, Cardiff Castle, the Four Bars Inn and others. The festival centers around harps—all kinds of harps playing all genres of music. There are jazz and folk concerts, symphony concerts and recitals, master classes and a trade exhibition of harps. National and international musicians perform, and the event culminates with a bonanza concert involving as many harps as can be crowded onto the stage. Individual tickets range from £6–£21, but there are special discounts for a series. For advance booking information, write to the Box Office, St. David's Hall, The Hayes, Cardiff, CF1 2SH, Wales.

The *Amgueddfa Genedlaethol Cymru,* or **May Fair,** takes place at the end of April and lasts approximately three days. The venue is a Victorian fairground near the Welsh Folk Museum (St. Fagan's, 0222/569441). The event includes a variety of traditional music and dance groups. Also included are craft demonstrations, Maypole activities, clowns and puppets. This is an enjoyable family event. Tickets are approximately £2, and family rates are available.

MISCELLANEOUS

Lunchtime recitals are a fixture at the **City United Reformed Church** (Windsor Place, 0222/372173, the Welsh College of Music and Drama). The music is of the very mellow variety—lute, flutes, guitar and so on. Concerts are free, but a collection is taken. A snack bar provides refreshments.

Masterclass is a new initiative in classical music broadcast every Sunday afternoon from 3 p.m.–4 p.m. on classic FM radio (100–102 FM). Each week, leading figures from the music world join amateur musicians to explore themes related to performance.

Cardiff Castle is a 900-year-old fortress standing in the heart of the city. After centuries of raids by marauders, it was lovingly restored in the nineteenth century by the third Marquess of Bute, who created an extravaganza of color and crafts that remains today. Occasionally, the Castle offers evenings of music and laughter at medieval banquets, which take place in the Great Hall. For ticket information, call Cardiff Marketing, 0222/667773.

Cardiff's top rock-music store is **Noble's Music** (Crwys Rd., Bridge, Cathays, 0222/499138), where you'll find a massive number of local and national artists represented. It's worth a stop just to bone up on who's who in Wales.

The last Sunday in June is National Music Day in Wales and the day on which the **Cardiff Bay Concert** takes place. Hundreds of musicians—violinists, cellists, trumpeters and trombonists—gather to produce a dramatic audio display accompanied by fireworks and a visual presentation beamed on a giant screen over Cardiff Bay. The event is free, but you must have tickets, which are available from a number of outlets bearing signs reading "Cardiff Bay Concert Tickets Available Here." Tickets are also available by mail from Cathi Thomas, Coordinator, Cardiff Bay Concert, BBC National Orchestra of Wales, Broadcasting House, Cardiff, CF5 2YQ, Wales.

If you want to swoon over luscious flutes, clarinets, saxophones, oboes and bassoons while conversing with the man who repairs, services, insures and, for all intents and purposes, serves as one of Great Britain's foremost woodwind-instrument specialists, go see Richard Wood at the shop that carries his name, 56 Brunswick St., Canton; 0222/236763.

The **Glamorgan Summer School** is your chance to learn from jazz masters in Britain's number one jazz summer school. The school's session is ten days, and tuition varies according to when you register and the accommodations you require. For more information, contact The Welsh Jazz Society, 26 The Balcony, Castle Arcade, Cardiff, CF1 2BY, Wales; 0222/340591.

SWANSEA

Apart from Cardiff, the main town in South Wales is Swansea with its beautiful seascape, dozens of parks and vibrant nightlife. The city also has a year-round schedule of festivals, many held in outdoor settings that take full advantage of its maritime feel.

You can make the easiest cultural transition when traveling from England to Wales by entering Wales from the south. The culture is more English in the South than in the North, which retains much of its traditional heritage. (Surveys show that while only ten percent of southerners speak the Welsh language, ninety percent of northerners do.) As a result, you'll find more mainstream musical venues but fewer all-out traditional hoe-downs. It's your call.

CONCERT HALLS

By far the most important concert hall in Swansea is the **Brangwyn Hall/George Hall** Complex (Guildhall, 0792/302489), named after the vibrant British-Empire panels that adorn the walls. Together, the halls have a total capacity of over two thousand. Buses 1, 2, 3, 14, 16 and 23 drop you at the Guildhall, which is just a short walk from the complex.

Brangwyn Hall offers a year-round schedule of large-scale classical productions ranging from the BBC National Orchestra of Wales to the Welsh Chamber Orchestra. Lunchtime concerts are occasionally presented, and if you time it right, you can get a tour inside the Hall's impressive organ, which sits like a vast, golden curtain behind the stage. Tickets for events in Brangwyn Hall range from £3–£10 with discounts for children, seniors, groups and students. Lunchtime concerts and organ tours are about £2. Dress is fairly formal, so it's probably best to save your jeans for another day. George Hall is accessed through the Brangwyn Hall entrance. The Hall is a show-case for small-scale musical performances, and ticket prices range from £3–£8.

The Brangwyn Bar and Buffet is open starting at 6 p.m. for the evening events and from noon for lunchtime concerts. Sunday lunch is available once a month in conjunction with a specific musical per-formance; call 0792/302253 to make reservations.

Tickets for most shows are generally available until showtime. For advance reservations, however, write to Sophie Black, Music Officer, The Guildhall, Swansea, SA1 4PE, Wales.

The **Patti Pavillion** (Guildhall, Victoria Park, 0792/302432) is in Victoria Park between Gors Lane and Francis Street, just a few min-utes away from Brangwyn Hall. The Patti Pavillion is used for infor-mal events such as participatory workshops or occasional barn dances, *twmpath* in Welsh. Tickets range from free to £2 and are gen-erally available. Dress is casual. The new **Dylan Thomas Theatre** (0792/473238), along the marina, offers large-scale musical produc-tions. Ticket prices are generally about £3.

St. Mary's Church (0792/302432) is the only church on Princess Way, which is in the center of Swansea. Classical music is presented here, and the acoustics are wonderful. Ticket prices range from £4–£10. You should book early as seating is limited. To get there, catch any bus to the Quadrant Bus Station. For bus schedules call South Wales Transport at 0792/580580.

The **Swansea Grand Theatre** (Singleton St., 0792/475715) holds over a thousand people and offers everything from the Welsh National Opera to punk-rock groups. Ticket prices range from £4–£16 (for the really big acts). The **Taliesin Arts Centre** (Swansea University Campus, Mumbles Rd., 0792/296883) hosts a wide range of musical events from semiclassical to traditional. Ticket prices are £4–£9. As you would expect, dress is casual.

CLUBS AND DISCOS

Outside of an ever-changing array of clubs along the waterfront that are almost exclusively patronized by very young disco afficionados, the club scene in Swansea is not one to make your head spin with choices. If you're into live jazz and blues, head for **Ellington's** (Duke of York, Princess Way, 0792/653830), which has a constantly changing roster of performers (including open-mike nights) and is very informal. The cost of admission varies, but expect to pay about £2. Another good jazz possibility is **The Singleton** (Singleton St., 0792/665987), which tends toward the New Orleans style of speakeasy music.

The college crowd tends to congregate in the funky Uplands area of town where you'll find the **Uplands Tavern** (43 Uplands Crescent, 0792/458242), where the music varies as do the hours. The admission charge is usually about £2. Next to St. Helen's cricket ground is **The Cricketers** (83 King Edward Rd., 0792/466524), which has mainly rock and stays open until 11 p.m.

FESTIVALS

The largest is the **Swansea Festival** starting in late September and running all the way until early November. This festival consists of a wide variety of classical concerts, jazz, opera, dance and art exhibitions. Taking up whatever slack is left with alternative offerings is the **Fringe Festival.** Venues vary as do ticket prices (generally in the £5 range). Contact Sophie Black, Swansea Festival Office, The Guildhall, Swansea, West Glamorgan, SA1 4PA, Wales; 0792/302432, fax: 0792/302408.

In late August there's the **Vale of Glamorgan Festival,** which runs for one week in various venues (some in Cardiff, some in Llantwit Major and some in Swansea). The festival is a celebration of some of the world's greatest living composers. Get tickets early; expect to pay from £5–£15 for single events. Contact St. Donat's Art Centre, St. Donat's Castle, Llantwit Major, South Glamorgan, CF6 9WF, Wales; 0446/794848.

The land of my father is dear unto me,
Old land where the minstrels are honored and free.

JAMES JAMES

In mid-August the **Pontardawe International Music Festival** takes place in the village of Pontardawe, seven miles north of Swansea (take bus 120 or 125). Musicians flood in from all over the world for this folk festival. Ticket prices are £20 for adults and £10 for kids eleven to sixteen, £1 for children three to ten. Contact Festival Office, The Cross Resource Centre, High St., Pontardawe, West Glamorgan, SA8 4GU, Wales; 0792/830200, 865324.

Another folk festival in the area is the **Gower Folk Day,** which happens on one day in either June or July. Tickets run about £5. Contact Joy Toole, Blue Anchor Cottage, Blue Anchor, Penclawdd, Swansea, SA3 1PJ, Wales; 0792/850803. Also in Gower is the **Gower Music Festival,** which takes place in mid-July for two weeks. This is a small-scale, classical-music festival in intimate Gower churches. Contact Mr. Maurice Broady, Publicity Officer, 58 Hendrefoilan Rd., Tycoch, Swansea, SA3 1PJ, Wales; 0792/207021.

And finally there's the **Swansea Sea Shanty Festival** in May. The festival consists of—what else—chanteys and folk songs. For details, contact Sara Selby, City of Swansea Leisure and Promotions Section, Rm. 165, The Guildhall, Swansea, SA1 4PE, Wales; 0792/302427.

MISCELLANEOUS

Though Wales is a very musical country, some types of music demand more of a visitor's attention than others. With this in mind, you should make every effort to catch some local or regional choir or band performances while you're here, since both choirs and bands (especially brass bands) are considered Wales's main claims to musical fame. Every town has them, and even the smallest choir or band in the tiniest backwoods town is of very high caliber. The following are lists of resident musical groups in Swansea. Performance dates and venues vary, but you can generally catch them at rehearsal sessions and if your schedules click, we can guarantee you won't be disappointed. For phone numbers, contact the Welsh Amateur Music Federation at 0222/394711.

Hemiola is a mixed choir that rehearses on Sundays at 2:30 p.m.; 11 Dryslwn Close, Penllergaer.

Cor Meibion Y Faerdref is a male choir that rehearses on Sundays and Wednesdays at 7:30 p.m.; 23 Twyn-y-Bedw, Clydach.

Gower Campanulae are seven bell ringers who rehearse Mondays at 8 p.m.; The Moorings, Llanrhidian.

The **Swansea Bach Choir** is made up of forty members and rehearses on Mondays at 7 p.m.; 51 Eaton Crescent.

The **Swansea Philharmonic Choir** has one hundred twenty-seven members and rehearses on Thursdays at 7 p.m.; 56 Mayals Ave.

The **Penyrheol Light Operatic Society** has forty-three members and rehearses Mondays and Wednesdays at 7:15 p.m.; 18 Pleasant Close, Gorseinon.

The **Cockett Amateur Operatic Society,** with fifty members, rehearses Thursdays at 7:30 p.m.; 27 Hendrefoilan Ave., Sketty.

The **Pennclawdd Brass Band** has sixty members who rehearse on Tuesdays and Thursdays at 7:00 p.m.; 55 Station Rd., Llanmorlais.

NEWPORT

CONCERT HALLS

The **Newport Centre** (Kingsway, 0633/259676) presents a regular schedule of musical performances in a huge theater holding over two thousand people. Tickets are about £5 and are generally available except for the more famous acts.

The **Dolman Theatre** (Kingsway, 0633/251338, 0495/272376) offers everything from opera to *Show Boat*. Expect to pay about £9 for better-known acts and book early.

CLUBS AND DISCOS

The **Inn On The River** (Taff Embankment, 0663/700070) is a rock club with good acoustics, heavy crowds and admission prices hovering around £3. The **Newport Centre**, in addition to being a concert hall, also has a rock club as part of its complex. The crowds are a little older than at the other clubs, and admission is about £3. **TJ's** (14–16 Clarence Place, 0663/220984) also has a somewhat older crowd, although once the music starts, the music is so good that nobody cares how old anybody is. Newport's **Bunker/Stage Door** (Stow Hill, 0272/442588) plays host to Conscious Club on Fridays, featuring garage and house music as well as DJs from some of the most famous clubs in South Wales for just £5 entry. And for jazz, there's the **Royal Mail** (0633/263339) and **Ye Olde Oak Stave** on Rogerstone (0633/892883). Call for admission prices.

FESTIVALS

The **Tredegar House Folk Festival** is a weekend of folk music and dancing in mid-May. For details, contact Marcus Music, Tredegar House, Newport, Gwent, NP9 76F, Wales; 0663/815612.

MISCELLANEOUS

As in Swansea, the Newport area's finest music often comes from its extensive network of amateur societies. The following are some good bets. For phone numbers, contact the Welsh Amateur Music Federation at 0222/394711.

The **New Venture Players** is a fifty-five-member amateur opera troupe that practices on Tuesdays at 7:30 p.m.; 54 Glaswick Crescent.

The **Severn Tunnel Band** is a group of forty-nine brass band players who rehearse on Mondays and Fridays at 6:00 p.m. and Tuesdays at 6:30 p.m.; 47 Mill Common, Undy, Magor.

The **Newport Philharmonic Choir** is made up of thirty-six vocalists who rehearse on Sundays at 3 p.m.; 41 The Moorings.

GREATER SOUTH WALES

MUSICAL HAPPENINGS IN OTHER PARTS OF GREATER SOUTH WALES

The **Fishguard Music Festival** takes place during the last week of July in the southwest Wales town of Fishguard, which is in the Pembrokeshire Coast National Park. The festival encompasses a wide range of arts activities with musical events taking precedence. The music ranges from Bach to Gershwin to traditional (although the major emphasis is on classical works), and there are music workshops as well as special presentations such as the winner of the Young Welsh Singers Competition, a prestigious national event. Also included in the festival are fringe events such as The Festival Club, where festivalgoers can mix with the concert musicians over a light meal and arts exhibitions by local and national artists. Tickets for individual events range from £3–£9, and discounts are available for blocks of tickets or a series. Contact Mrs. Marion Butler, The Festival Office, Fishguard, Pembrokeshire, SA65 9BJ, Wales; 0348/873612.

St. Donat's Art Centre presents a variety of musical offerings in an outrageously gorgeous ancient castle in Llantwit Major. For details of what, when and how much, call the box office at 0446/794848.

South Wales is a pretty good area for jazz. One particularly good club is a new one, **John Henry's** (at the Great Gorge Hotel, Cross St., Abergavenny, 854230). Local bands from South Wales are featured as well as national and international guest stars (especially in the summer). Other clubs include **The Blackwood Miners Institute,** (Blackwood, 0495/227206), **The Congress Theatre** (Cwmbran, 0633/868239), which has Sunday evening jazz sessions in the bar, the **Wentloog Resort Motel** (Castleton, 0633/680591) with alternate Thursday jazz sessions and **Plas-Y-Coed Inn** (Pontypool, 0495/762505) with jazz on Friday evenings and Sunday lunch.

If you *do* go to Abergavenny for the jazz, why not stay for some amateur musical offerings of which the town has many? Following are a few amateur rehearsal sessions you might want to check out. Call the Welsh Amateur Music Federation at 0222/394711 for complete information.

The **Abergavenny Borough Band** is a brass band made up of fifty-eight people who rehearse on Tuesdays and Fridays at 7:30 p.m. at 2 Llanover Close, Blaenavon.

The **Abergavenny Light Opera Company** gathers on Tuesdays at 7:30 p.m. at Plevna, Dragon Lane, Govilon.

The **Abergavenny Orchestral Society** practices on Sundays at 6 p.m. at Wern-y-Cwm, Llandewi Skirrid.

Also in Abergavenny is the **Abergavenny Arts Festival** held during the first week of August. Mainly a classical music event, this festival takes place at various venues including the gorgeous Llandaff Cathedral, the Canolfan Hamdden Leisure Centre and the Church of Our Lady and St. Michael. Among the performers, you're likely to find such native sons (and daughters) as the National Youth Brass Band of Wales and the National Youth Choir of Wales. Tickets are approximately £5. For info, contact the Welsh Amateur Music Federation at 0222/394711.

Music in the Mountains is an event in late August at Abergrave in the Upper Swansea Valley. Two days of cultural music from male choirs to Welsh fold performances take place outside and inside a natural cave setting that is Europe's largest show cave complex. Call the Welsh Amateur Music Federation (0222/394711) for further information and ticket prices.

MID-WALES

CONCERT HALLS

The Arts Centre (on the campus of the University College of Wales in Aberystwyth, 0970/622888, 623232) has galleries, a concert hall and a theater (the Sherman Theatre). Musical offerings are most often classical. Tickets run from £6–£12 and should be booked in advance even though the great hall holds over 1,400. **The Castle Theatre** (Aberystwyth, 0970/624606) presents mostly theater but occasionally has music. All performances are held in both Welsh and English.

SPOTLIGHT ON | **ROBIN HUW BOWEN: MASTER OF THE WELSH TRIPLE HARP**

Robin Huw Bowen has become a virtual one-man crusade in the promotion of the Welsh triple harp, the national instrument of Wales. Of the few harpists worldwide who are competent enough to play the triple harp, he is the only professional now specializing solely in this instrument and its music.

Bowen was born in Liverpool and, as a child, was fascinated by the music of the reknowned Celtic harpist Alan Stivell. In 1979 Bowen received a degree in Welsh Language and Literature from the University College of Aberystwyth, Mid-Wales. Soon afterwards, he began his pursuit of the triple harp, seizing every opportunity to learn the music and techniques of the old Welsh harpers by studying many of their old manuscripts and publications. By 1986, he had mastered the instrument well enough to pursue his musical career full-time.

Since then he has performed extensively around the globe as a member of the Welsh folk group Mabsant, and—since 1989—as a solo performer. Since 1990, he has also performed and recorded with the group Cusan Tan, consisting of Ann Morgan Jones (lead vocal and flute), Sue Jones Davies (back-up vocals and harmony), Bowen on triple harp and John Rodge on guitar.

When not touring, Bowen spends much of his time continuing his research into the Welsh harp tradition. In 1990 he set up his own press, Gwasg Teires, to publish books on traditional Welsh music. His first solo album was *Cyfarch Y Delyn* (*Honor the Harp*), and his latest—the first to be released in the U. S. (on Flying Fish Records)—is called *Telyn Berseiniol fy Ngwlad* (*The Sweet Harp of My Land*).

Although Bowen's repertoire closely reflects that of the Welsh harp in its heyday (mid-seventeenth to the end of the nineteenth century), his playing is far from being a museum relic from a past culture. His infectious, always sensitive, yet sometimes irreverant arrangements delight in taking the triple harp out of the parlor and into the public house for a wee bit of fun.

Robin Huw Bowen—Harpist

In Llandrinod Wells, there's the **Grand Pavillion** (Spa Rd., 0597/3532) for large-scale musical performances of all types. The hall holds six hundred on two levels, and ticket prices average £5.

Newtown has the **Theatr Hafren** (Llanidloes Rd., 0686/625007), which holds over five hundred people for musical performances of all types. Ticket prices are approximately £6, and the classical performances usually sell out way in advance.

Hereford is where you'll find **The Cathedral** (0432/275063), which serves as a showcase for classical performances. Ticket prices range from £4–£10.

CLUBS AND DISCOS

Aberystwyth has over fifty pubs, many of which have live music and even livelier crowds. The aptly named **Porky's Fun Bar** (Pier St.) stays open until 1 a.m. on weekends, two hours later than most others and draws a trendy disco crowd.

Both **The Bear Necessities of Life** (Marine Terrace, downstairs at the hotel) and its rival **Rummers** (Bridge St.) have live music Tuesday, Thursday, Friday and Saturday. Admission is about £3. Both clubs occasionally feature traditional music.

In Shrewsbury there's **Butler's** (49 Mardol, 0834/271568), an indoor-outdoor cafe with occasional jazz. **DJ's Night Club** (Penally, near Tenby, Dyfed, 0834/845279) rocks hard and heavy with a trendy crowd dressed to impress. You won't see any ties here. Admission is £4 before 10 p.m., £5 after.

FESTIVALS

Powys has **The Gregynog Festival** in June and July. The music includes classical, jazz and traditional. This is music-making of the highest standard in the unique setting of the mock Tudor mansion house at Gregynog. Also included in the festival are spectacular gardens, master classes and composers' competitions. Contact Anthony Rolfe Johnson, artistic director, at 0686/626965 or the festival director at 0686/650224.

The **Brecon Jazz Festival** is entering its second decade, swinging for three days in mid-August. One of Europe's most atmospheric and successful jazz festivals, this event takes place in twelve venues both indoors and in the open air—all within a few minutes walk of each other—in Brecon, a small market town at the heart of the Brecon Beacons National Park. Ranked alongside Newport and Nice, this festival draws big names from Wynton Marsalis to Pat Metheny to Sonny Rollins to... Locals and Welsh favorites also play, and the atmosphere of this big event has a small-town flavor. Ticket prices vary (£3–£10), and advance bookings are necessary for the really big acts. Write to Deborah Parry, Festival Office, Brecon, LD3 7EF, Wales; 0874/625557.

The **Gwyl Machynlleth Festival** takes place in late August for one week and includes chamber and choral music. Contact Ruth Lambert, Machynlleth Festival Y Tabernacl, Heol Penrallt, Machynlleth, Powys, SY21 ON2, Wales; 0654/703355.

Also in Powys is the **Festival of Celtic Dance** (Builth Wells and Llandrindod Wells, 0982/552907), a three-day event in mid-May that draws musicians and performers from all over the U. K. For more info, contact Mrs. Vicky Sennett, Wyeburn House, Castle St., Builth Wells, Powys, SY16 1JB, Wales.

If it's traditional music you're after, head for the **Llanfair Folk Fayre/*Ffair Werin Llanfair*** (Llanfair Clydogau, Dyfed, 0570/45379) on the last weekend in May. Here you'll find *ceilidh*, country music and Irish and Welsh traditional music. Also look for workshops, crafts, a children's area and camping. Individual tickets run about £3, weekender pass £20 (£15 prebooked).

Dyfed's claim to festival fame is the *Gwyl Werin Y Cnapan*, which takes place in July and presents most events in untranslated Welsh. If you're into sampling *real* traditional stuff, here's where you'll want to be. This is Wales's largest Celtic music festival attracting performers from various Celtic countries. Acts are a deft blend of local and first-class international talent. Tickets are about £10. For further information, contact Peter Evans, Trewerin, Stryd Lincoln, Llandysul, Dyfed, SA44 4BU, Wales; 0239/858955.

Another traditional event is the **Harvest Ffair Gynhaeaf,** which takes place at the end of August and includes musical performances—both scheduled and spontaneous—as well as arts, crafts, and workshops. Contact Chris Pace, Pengemallt, Glandwr, Whitland, Dyfed, SA34 OYD, Wales; 0994/419641, 0239/841431.

SPOTLIGHT ON   THE DYFED CHOIR

The Dyfed Choir, founded in 1967 by John S. Davies, soon gained a fine national reputation. From its early days, the choir has enjoyed a close relationship with the Fishguard Festival in Fishguard, Dyfed, and has worked with orchestras as diverse as the Royal Liverpool Philharmonic and the BBC Welsh Symphony.

The choir's sixty voices allow a wide range of music. When Christopher Barton succeeded John Davies as Music Director in 1985, he extended the choir's reputation for the late baroque and classical repertoires, so it is now as experienced and accomplished at singing Monteverdi as Mozart, Durufl as Dvorak or Bruckner as Bach.

In recent years the choir has become particularly interested in performing baroque music with period instrument ensembles such as the King's Consort, the Welsh Baroque Orchestra and the Gabrieli Players. For information on where and when you can hear the Dyfed Choir in performance, call 0437/720885, 720314.

MISCELLANEOUS

There are a great many talented amateur groups in mid-Wales whose rehearsals you might want to check on if you want to douse yourself in local color. For phone numbers, contact the Welsh Amateur Music Federation at 0222/394711.

Aberystwyth has the **Aberystwyth Silver Band,** a group of seventy brass instrumentalists who rehearse on Tuesdays at 7:30 p.m. at Delfryn, Pontrhydfendigaid, Ystradmeurig, Dyfed and the **Ammanford Town Silver Band,** which rehearses on Mondays and Fridays at 7 p.m. at 39 Penybanc Rd., Ammanford, Dyfed.

The **Cor Dyfed Choir** rehearses Tuesdays at 7:30 p.m. at Ty Olaf, Mount Gardens, St. David's, Dyfed. In Dyfed, you'll also find the **Kidwelly Festival Choir/ *Cor Gwyl Cydweli*,** a mixed choir that rehearses on Mondays and Wednesdays at 7 p.m. at 85 Water St., Kidwelly, Dyfed.

NORTH WALES

This part of the country will probably give you your best peek into traditional Welsh history. From the walled city of Caernarfon, where Prince Charles was appointed Prince of Wales in 1969, to the largely Welsh-speaking population of each town and village, North Wales is the place to go if you want a sense of what the music once was.

CONCERT HALLS

In Bangor you'll find the **Theatr Gwynedd** (Deiniol Rd. at the base of the hill, 0248/351708), which offers musical performances in both Welsh and English. Tickets sell out quickly and are generally around £4.

Bangor also has the **Prichard Jones Hall** (University College of North Wales, 0248/382181), which seats almost seven hundred people and presents classical concerts as well as a variety of other musical genres. Ticket prices range from £5–£7.50.

In Llandudno, there's the **Arcadia Theatre/Canolfan Aberconwy Centre** offering a varied program of musical events on the Promenade (0492/79771).

CLUBS AND DISCOS

North Wales has a few places you might want to pop your head into. Among them are **The Jenny Jones** (Abbey Rd., Llangollen, 0978/860653), where you generally have to make reservations; the **Theatr Clwyd,** which presents various musical offerings (The County Civic Centre, Mold, 0352/755114); and the **Alyn Hotel** (Station Road, Rossett near Wrexham, 0244/570638). All are informal, all are crowded and all are cheap (expect to pay from £2–£4).

In Bangor you'll find the **Student Union** (Deiniol Rd. near the tourist office) whose basement is *the* place for hot rock and sizzling reggae. The Student Union also has jazz in **Jock's Bar** every Sunday. Bangor also has the **Fat Cat Restaurant** (High St., 0248/370445), which offers a variety of musical genres including jazz duos on Sunday nights. Admission is generally about £3.

In Caernarfon there's folk music everywhere. If you fancy getting into the swing, you might first want to check out **Merlin Music** (old Market Hall, 0286/75755), which sells musical instruments from countries you've never even heard of. Then when you're properly suited up, head to **Parc Glynllifon** (outside the town; take bus 91 to Dinas Dinlle), an amusement and nature park where folk musicians flock on Saturday nights during the summer.

SPOTLIGHT ON **TIM PHILLIPS: VIOLIN MAKER EXTRAORDINAIRE**

Tim Phillips decided to become a violin maker in 1988. The easiest part of his decision was probably where to house the enterprise. He already had an old stone flour mill in Mochdre, near Newtown, that he'd been using as a workshop. Onto this he built, from local timber, a couple of workshops—one for violin making and one for varnishing. These buildings were soon to become known locally as "Tim's Folly," since the general feeling was that he had no business taking up something he knew nothing about. But as soon as the buildings were done, Tim set his mind to proving them wrong.

Late in 1992, he made his first pair of violins from local and untraditional wood—his "infidels" as he called them because, like infidels, they didn't conform to traditional shapes. They were guitar-shaped instruments without the four corners on the inside, and, surprisingly, they looked and sounded pretty good. That gave him confidence to continue making more unconventionally shaped violins. From there, he eventually moved into the more classical types, which he now makes almost exclusively using only selected woods.

The strangeness of Tim's having chosen this particular career path comes across very clearly in his answer to my very first question: does he play the violin?

No.

Had he had any previous experience making instruments?

No again. His only previous woodworking experience, in fact, had been confined to making gates, window frames and staircases, although he did once make a tea-chest bass. But these constructions, to him, were just what one did to make a living. They weren't part of what, today, he considers his art.

"If I was making a piece of furniture, I didn't care about the detail as long as it fit right together and the customer was happy. But violins I really care about. They have to be as right as I can make them."

Why violins, rather than other instruments?

"Because violins have an extremely strong sculptural side to them. My natural inclination is to do something with creative scope. The mystique of violins is also something that appeals to me greatly. If you have two violins exactly the same—the same thickness, varnishing, strings, soundpost setting—exactly the same technically, they'd still sound different. I like that, so much so that it's become an addictive passion."

What is the most difficult aspect of making a violin?

"Every aspect has its own problems. I think the main difficulty is trying to maintain every process the best you can do it, and not disregard any one as being less important than the others. They've all got to be of equal importance. You can't cut corners on any of it.

"A lot of beginners to violin making find that the scroll is the most difficult thing, which is frustrating because it has the least effect on the sound. Finishing and varnishing can be easy to make a mess of, and, if you do, a good instrument looks awful."

What advice does Tim have for prospective instrument makers?

"Get in there and go for it! There are books available. That's how I learned, in fact. At first, the whole thing might all look very daunting, but just take one process and understand it and do the best you can. Don't be despondent about things not going right, because it isn't easy and you can't expect to produce something wonderful and beautiful straight away. It doesn't matter. Just go for it!"

Today, Tim's instruments cost from a few hundred pounds for the "double axe" model to just under one thousand for top-of-the-line classical models in the more-traditional shape.

FESTIVALS

Festivals are where this part of the country *really* shines. For starters, there's the **Llangollen International Musical Eisteddfod** held in early July for one week. This festival attracts singers, choirs, instrumentalists and dancers from all over the world (over 12,000!) who come to compete in daily performances. If you don't get a ticket to a specific event, relax; you can have loads of fun just wandering around the field, looking at the representatives from over forty countries dressed in colorful national costumes. For further info, contact Mr. T. V. Jones, Llangollen International Eisteddfod Office, Llangollen, Clwyd, LL20 8NG, Wales; 0978/860236.

Then there's the **North Wales Music Festival** the last week of September in the Cathedral of St. Asaph in Clwyd, which offers a varied program of symphony concerts, recitals, jazz, choral and chamber music. Admission ranges from £3–£12; tickets sell out pretty early. For info, write to the North Wales Music Festival, High St., St. Asaph, Clwyd, LL17 ORD, Wales; 0745/584508.

Tim Phillips—Violinmaker

For jazz fans, there's the **Llangollen International Festival of Jazz,** which takes place on three days in late May in Llangollen. Here various styles of jazz are performed in a variety of venues throughout the town. You can buy either individual tickets for prices in the £5 range, or a festival ticket that covers all the events for about £15. Call Mr. Roy Potts, Festival Organizer, at 0978/860236.

Gwynedd presents the **Gwyl Conwy Festival** at the end of July for one week. This is a folk event unfolding in a beautiful farm setting. For info, call Steve Markham at 0492/572502. Another July festival in Gwynedd is the **North Wales Bluegrass Festival** (Trefriw, 0492/580454), which twangs up for three fiddlin' days on the first weekend of the month.

There's also the **Gwyl Beaumaris Festival** held in late May–early June in various venues. Involving just about the whole town of Beaumaris, from the fourteenth-century parish church to the town concert hall, this event mixes classical recitals, jazz performances, street music, folk dancing, a regatta on the strait and medieval battles in the castle. Ticket prices vary widely, and they sell out quicker than it takes to give away a free turkey on Thanksgiving. Contact Janet Green, Festival Director, 44A Castle St., Beaumaris, Gwynedd, LL58 8BB, Wales; 0685/876675. On May Bank Holiday weekend, Gwynedd also sponsors the **Great Llandudno Extravaganza,** which is mainly a street event taking place on the Promenade. Exhibitions, street musicians, parades and Victorian dress make this event fun.

If you're looking for traditional music, head for the *Seiswn Fawr* in mid-July. Most events are exclusively in Welsh, and acts combine local talent with input from the rest of Wales. This is a Welsh cultural event. Telephone 0341/423355. One final Gwynedd festival: the **Criccieth Festival of Music and the Arts,** which takes place in the summer and concentrates mainly on classical performers. For tickets, contact the Festival Office at P. O. Box 3, 52 High St., Criccieth, Gwynedd, LL52 OBW, Wales; 076/522778.

The **Towersey Village Festival** is held over the last weekend of August and is organized by Mrs. Casey Music, 7 Dove House, Watermead, Aylesbury, Bucks, Wales; 0296/394411. This wonderful event awash in local flavor costs about £27 for the entire weekend to attend, and the music spans a mixed and international range of folk-roots to cajun. There's also dancing, children's entertainment, workshops, circus performances, food and lots of casual jamming.

MISCELLANEOUS

North Wales is home to the very best of traditional music. Some amateur groups you might want to check out include the following. (Call the Welsh Amateur Music Federation for local phone numbers. You can reach the federation at 0222/394711.)

The **Operatic Players,** a group of thirty-three performers, gathers on Monday nights at 7:30 to rehearse at 66 Oak Drive, Colwyn Bay, Clwyd.

The **Deiniolen Band/***Seindorf Arian Deiniolen,* a brass band comprised of seventy members, rehearses on Sundays at 7 p.m. and Thursdays at 7:30 p.m. at Minafon, Clwt-y-Bont, Caernarfon.

The **Colwyn Choral Society** has eighty members who practice on Tuesdays at 7:30 p.m. at 51 Glanymor Rd., Penrhyn Bay, Llandudno.

The *Cor Godre R Eifl* is a thirty-three-member mixed choir that rehearses on Sundays at 8 p.m. at Einir Wyn, Fferm Cae Du, Abersock, Pwllheli, Gwynedd.

The *Cor Meibion Dolgellau A R Cylch* is a male choir made up of thirty-three members who rehearse on Wednesdays at 8 p.m. at Hafod y Grug, Pencefn, Dolgellau, Gwynedd.

The *Cor Merched Edeyrnion* is a female choir that rehearses on Mondays and Thursdays at 7:30 p.m. at 26 Llwch y Dre, Corwen, Clwyd.

Ireland

Ireland

Including Dublin, Wexford, Waterford, Cork, County Kerry, Counties
Galway and Clare, and Sligo

Music was an essential part of life in the everyday Ireland of monks,
farmers and warriors. The country's well-preserved collection of
medieval manuscripts bears witness to a wealth of musicianship—
whether in connection with banquets and ceremonies, warfare or
the casting of spells. But the most frequently mentioned musical reference has to do with—what else—the harp, which just happens to
be the country's national symbol.

While many instruments were used in twelfth-century Ireland—
among them the *tympan* and the *fidil* (string instruments played with
a bow) and the *piopai* (bagpipe)—the harp was in a class of its own.
Harpers, in fact, were the virtual VIPs of the time period; they even
had professional status at the courts of the princes and chieftains
who were their main patrons. Officially, they were classified as *bo-
aires*—nonnoble rent-paying freemen with property. This exalted status entitled them to "honor prices," which were additional
compensations accorded them in case of injury.

FOCUS ON   THE CELTIC HARP

Clairseach (pronounced *clar-shuk*) is the Irish word for the ancient
wire-strung harp that was prominent in Ireland from premedieval
times to the eighteenth century. In its present form, the harp first
appears in the sculptured stone crosses of ninth-century Ireland and
Scotland. In the nineteenth century it was routinely produced in

Dublin by John Egan as a small, portable, drawing-room successor to the old professional Irish harp.

From the earliest times, harpers in Ireland enjoyed the great prestige awarded all highly trained and skilled professions. Every family had its own harper. The harps were strung with thirty to thirty-six mostly brass strings and played resting on the left shoulder with the left hand plucking the treble strings and the right hand sounding the bass. The strings were plucked with the fingernails—not the fingertips as became increasingly popular in the seventeenth and eighteenth centuries.

When the old Gaelic society was destroyed by the English under the Tudor and Stuart kings, harpers survived by entertaining the new Protestant nobility. But eventually their prestigious position in society evaporated and today only a few of the ancient harps survive—most in the National Museum in Dublin.

That court harpers had such elevated status, however, only serves to point out the enormous differences between Ireland's musical development and that of the rest of medieval Europe. By the end of the eleventh century, Italy, Germany and France had all evolved from the traditional monotonal style of music to polyphony. An infinitely more sophisticated sound, polyphony developed in the monasteries and churches that were, for the most part, the sole repositories of that era's musical experimentation. As a result, the musical repertoire of continental Europe came to include the use of complex instruments such as violins, violas and cellos; on these were played such multilayered musical forms as fugues, madrigals and sonatas.

But in Ireland—between the various invasions (the Norman conquest being one of the more heinous) and the wars and persecutions of the middle centuries—church music (and thereby music-at-large) was denied its normal course of evolution. During the Cromwellian period (mid-1600s), monasteries were confiscated, organs removed and destroyed and church music totally suppressed.

As if that weren't bad enough, after the Battle of Kinsale in 1601 and the final passing of the old Gaelic order, even harp playing

| FOCUS ON | THE IRISH BAGPIPES |

The British Isles have a few distinctive types of indigenous bagpipes, the most important being the well-known Scottish highland pipes, the sweet-toned small Northumbrian pipes, and the Irish pipes, also called *Uillean* (pronounced *ill-yin*) pipes. Few rival the Uillean pipes, however, when it comes to sophistication and delicacy.

Although they're among the most difficult of instruments to master, in the hands of a great player the Uillean pipes sound completely effortless. The mother of the great Irish piper Seamus Ennis put it like this, "Seven years learning, seven years practicing, seven years playing, to make an Irish piper."

The Gaelic word *Uillean* signifies "elbow pipe," after the right elbow, which works the bellows. On the Uillean pipes, the tune is played on a pipe called a chanter, which has keys like a clarinet and is gently conical. The Uillean pipes are unique among bagpipes in two respects: the chanter can be made to sound a complete upper octave and accompanying chords can be made on three additional pipes called "regulators" provided with brass keys. These are opened with the lower edge of the right hand without interrupting the music of the chanter, in which a vibrato is often made by shaking a finger over one of the open fingerholes.

The piper, seated, ties a leather "popping pad" above the right knee, and places the bellows under the right elbow and the bag under the left upper arm. Against the pad, the piper can momentarily close the end of the chanter so that when all holes are also closed there's no sound. A rapid closure at the end, accompanied by a smart increase in arm pressure on the bag, causes the chanter to jump to the higher octave, in which it will continue to sound, while fingerholes are uncovered and the pressure is relaxed.

An open-ended chanter sounds continuously, like the Scottish pipes. A permanently closed chanter, like that of the Northumbrian pipes, contributes to a bubbling quality of sound. The Uillean pipes, with characteristic versatility, offer both styles of speaking. The apron also makes it a lot easier to overblow the chanter to reach the upper register.

The earliest bagpipes in Ireland—testified to in the fifth-century Brehon laws—were mouth-blown. In Tudor times they were a peasant instrument. During the seventeenth century, the musette-type of bellows-blown pipes became increasingly fashionable among upper and lower classes alike, notably in France and Ireland. By the early eighteenth century, the somewhat improved Uillean pipes were replacing the harp as the preferred instrument for most kinds of Irish music. During the latter half of the eighteenth century, the introduction of the keyed chanter, the regulators and other refinements by such makers as Egan of Dublin led to the emergence of what is perhaps the most sophisticated form of bagpipes in the world.

---

began to decline. The families that had patronized harpers were, for the most part, outlawed and their estates confiscated. And because none of the planters who took over the confiscated land were really keen on supporting native art forms, harp playing went from being a privileged calling to a humble one.

Things got even worse, musically speaking, toward the end of the seventeenth century. After the Treaty of Limerick in 1691, Ireland fell into a relative period of peace and the rural gentry—including the few native families who had not already been dispossessed—began to turn away from Irish music to music that was more European in style. The last and greatest of Ireland's vagabond harpers lived during this period: Turlough O'Carolan (1670–1738), who, although blind, composed many hundreds of songs, chiefly in honor of the patrons whose houses he visited.

But before the last vestiges of the harp tradition had died away, one last attempt was made to preserve them. Harp festivals were organized—at Granard from 1781 to 1785 and at Belfast in 1792. At the latter festival, Edward Bunting, a Belfast organist, took it upon himself to write down the tunes played by the harpers. His notes were later drawn on for his three-volume *Ancient Music of Ireland*, the first important collection of traditional music.

Toward the end of the seventeenth century, after the turmoil of the Jacobite wars had subsided, conditions in Ireland became somewhat more stable. One effect of the newfound calm was that Irish music entered into a period of relative prosperity, and this in turn led Dublin to become one of the most musically active cities in Europe. A large number of musical societies came into being around this time in Dublin, among them the Hibernian Catch Club, the oldest body of its kind still in existence. Concerts for charitable purposes were organized, and performances of ballad opera became the vogue.

Crow Street Music Hall was built by the Dublin Academy of Music in 1730 for "the practice of Italian musick" and the New Musick Hall on Fishamble Street was opened in October 1741. Here George Frederick Handel gave the first of his series of Dublin concerts on December 23, 1741, and on April 8, 1742, he gave the first public performance of the *Messiah* to rave reviews and general public ecstasy.

With the passing of the Act of Union in 1800 and the subsequent abolition of the Irish Parliament, Ireland's political power was once again returned to London. As a result, Dublin lost most of its significance as the center of social life, and the patronage of music by the nobility began to wane. In the eighteenth century Dublin had not only been a hub of musical activity, it had attracted eminent musicians from England and the Continent. In the nineteenth century the only important names to be recorded were those of Irishmen who lived and worked abroad, chief among them John Field (1782–1837), the Dublin-born pianist and composer of nocturnes and piano concertos.

SPOTLIGHT ON **JOHN FIELD**

Born in Dublin in 1782 and mostly educated there, John Field made his solo piano debut at the age of nine in what critics described as "an astonishing performance by such a child." A year after this momentous event, the family moved to London where the boy was apprenticed to Muzio Clementi, the famous Italian pianist who is often called the father of the piano sonata, and who shepherded his young charge through the early stages of a virtuoso's career.

The first landmark in Field's career as a composer came when he played his First Piano Concerto to rave reviews at a concert at the King's Theatre on February 7, 1799; he was just sixteen-and-a-half. Despite his youth, however, the young Field showed that his playing had a strain of dreamy romantic expression that added a new element to the sometimes-brittle virtuosity of his older contemporaries. And it was this element in his playing and in his composition that was to make him one of the most popular pianists and composers for piano of the first half of the nineteenth century.

After his apprenticeship with Clementi was completed in 1799, Field embarked on a public career and, although he toured with reasonable frequency thereafter, settled in Russia for the remainder of his life. His St. Petersburg debut playing one of his concertos in March 1804 created a sensation, and he instantly became the darling of fashionable society in the imperial capital. "Not to have heard Field is a sin against art and good taste," wrote one reviewer.

During the second half of his life, his prodigious work as a composer fell off considerably, however, both because of an addiction to alcohol and a painful cancer of the rectum for which he sought treatment in London in 1831. At that time, he played concerts in London and Manchester and met a new generation of pianist-composers including Mendelssohn, Moscheles, and the Englishman Sterndale Bennett. He spent a season in Paris in 1832–33 playing to much acclaim but also some criticism from the young turks of the piano whose style was more aggressive. (After hearing one of Liszt's assaults on the keyboard for the first time, Field asked his companion, "Does he bite?")

During the season Field spent in Paris, Frédéric Chopin eagerly attended one of his concerts. He could hardly do otherwise. People had often asked him if he had been one of the Irishman's pupils, so strongly were they struck by the similarity in their styles of playing. Like Chopin, every item in Field's compositional output included a piano; in addition to the seven piano concertos written between 1800 and 1832, there were several piano duets and many solo piano works: sonatas, romances, waltzes, études and rondos.

Today, it is Field's short, lyrical piano pieces—the nocturnes—that are his principal claim to fame. The remainder of his output, however, has gradually begun to enjoy renewed performance. This is particularly true of his piano concertos, which are increasingly recognized as providing not only a lasting testament to his soulful, gentle, elegant, expressive musical ideas, but also as reflecting an entirely new sensibility in European music.

But the Act of Union affected music other than classical. At the end of the eighteenth century, Ireland had also enjoyed a strong tradition of folk songs. And because Irish was still the language spoken by the vast majority of people, this tradition was able to hold its own even when English ballads became all the rage. But with the subsequent suppression of the Irish language in the schools and its gradual abandonment as the vernacular in the second half of the nineteenth century, folk songs eventually went the way of the harp.

So, despite its brief and infrequent periods of musical renaissance, by the first half of the twentieth century the general organization of music in Ireland was still far behind that of other countries. After World War I, the main advances were due to the development of broadcasting. Radio Eireann supported a symphony orchestra of sixty-five players that gave concerts twice a week in Dublin's Phoenix Hall. The broadcasts, relayed by stations at Athlone, Dublin and Cork, provided the main source of music for the Irish public. In Northern Ireland the BBC Belfast served roughly the same purpose.

Apart from broadcasting, recitals by artists of international reputation were given weekly during the season by the Royal Dublin Society. The Dublin Grand Opera Society held (and still holds) two seasons annually during which they offered programs of international stature. But, all in all, it is safe to say that music was not one of the great priorities of early twentieth-century Ireland.

In the last twenty years, however, Ireland has enjoyed a classical-music renaissance. Concert halls have been built or refurbished, and the country's many wonderful composers and performers have begun drawing from traditional Irish themes for their inspiration. Chief among these is Shaun Davey whose ever growing body of successful compositions includes *The Brendan Voyage*, inspired by the legend of St. Brendan's voyage to the New World eons before anyone had heard of Columbus, and *Granuaile*, the story of Grace O'Malley, Ireland's pirate queen.

MUSICAL MOMENTS *Granuaile: The Sixteenth-Century Pirate Queen*

Grace O'Malley, the sixteenth-century pirate queen (*Granuaile* is an Irish version of her name) was a remarkable figure. Not only do the facts of her life show her to have been every inch the swashbuckling warrior-queen of legend, but her lifetime also coincided with one of the most crucial turning points in Irish history.

When the English decided to legislate an end to indigenous Irish culture, many Irish chiefs were elected to accustom their countryfolk to English custom and law. Those who did not entered into conflict with both their neighbors and the Crown. Grace O'Malley steered a course between both sides as she pursued her career of, as she herself put it, "maintenance by land and by sea."

Her war and trading ships dominated the waters off the west coast of Ireland in defiance of the English authorities and the merchants of Galway who sought to monopolize trade themselves. Between voyages she stormed and defended castles, had two husbands, gave birth to three children, rescued her lover from shipwreck, watched the death-throes of the Spanish Armada on the storm-bound shores of the Atlantic and plotted rebellions in Connaught. Toward the end of her long life, O'Malley sailed her own ship to London where she gained both the sympathy and the respect of another great woman in history, Queen Elizabeth I.

This is the subject matter of the songs that Rita Connolly sings in the person of Granuaile, whether roaring defiance at the besiegers of her castle or tenderly mourning the loss of her husband, whether swearing vengeance on those who slew her lover or standing as a child on the lonely seashore of Clare Island watching her father sail out to sea. Here is brought to life not so much Granuaile, the legend, but Grace O'Malley, the person and with her the feel of the times.

Granuaile, composed by Shawn Davey, was first publicly performed at the Lorient Interceltic Festival in 1985. Since that time, it has toured the U. K. and Ireland on numerous occasions which included performances at the National Concert Hall, Dublin. Other festival performances have included the Queen's Festival in Belfast, the Edinburgh International Folk Festival and the New York Festival of the Arts. The work was performed for television at Greenwich, London, and featured as part of Ireland's cultural contribution to Expo '92 at Seville, Spain.

Classical music notwithstanding, the Ireland of today has also become a year-round destination for some of the world's many festival enthusiasts. Whether it be the biggest of the traditional lot, the All Ireland Festival (the *Fleadh Cheoil na hEireann*), which generally takes place in late August, or one of the smaller events like the Fife, a three-day rock-pop-trad event in County Tipperary, Ireland's festivals have developed into virtual "explosions" of music. The chief festivals with historical roots are the *Feis Ceoil* and the *Oireachtas*, both founded in Dublin in 1897 as the prototype for the wide network of music festivals enjoyed throughout the country today, and the *feiseanna* held annually throughout the country, particularly in Northern Ireland.

But the biggest news with respect to music in Ireland is probably the continued growth of the contemporary scene, especially traditional music and "rock trad" which combines the raunchiness of rock with the plaintiveness of Ireland's tumultuous history. In fact, if one takes an up-close look at this thriving phenomenon, one thing becomes instantly clear: while the total population of the island—including Northern Ireland—is less than five million, Ireland can arguably boast of having a talent pool larger than that of a nation ten times its size.

Consider U2, long held to be one of the world's most popular bands. Consider also Sinead O'Connor, Van Morrison, Enya, the Pogues, Clannad, Planxty, the Chieftains and Sweeney's Men. The list is long.

Now consider that Ireland also boasts a pop music knight of the realm, "Sir" Bob Geldof, who was honored by Britain's Queen Elizabeth for his founding of the Band Aid and Live Aid musical events (see page 229) which, in the late '80s, collected millions of dollars in relief money for the starving people of Ethiopia.

But Ireland's contemporary scene is about more than its superstars. Across the country you can hear traditional music in any one

---

LIVE AID WEMBLEY STADIUM LONDON BILL

12:15 p.m.–10 p.m. July 13, 1985

1. Status Quo
2. The Style Council
3. The Boomtown Rats
4. Adam Ant
5. Ultravox
6. Spandau Ballet
7. Elvis Costello
8. Nik Kershaw
9. Sade
10. Sting, Branford Marsalis and Phil Collins
11. Howard Jones
12. Bryan Ferry and David Gilmour
13. Paul Young and Alison Moyet
14. U2
15. Dire Straits and Sting
16. Queen
17. David Bowie
18. The Who
19. Elton John, Kiki Dee and George Michael
20. Freddie Mercury and Brian May
21. Paul McCartney
22. Bob Geldof and Bono Vox

---

of thousands of pubs where locals mingle with tourists to swill a brew and catch a bit of the old musical brogue. Although some of the music has now been written down, much of it is still passed directly from musician to musician.

FOCUS ON   THE BODHRAN: IRELAND'S VERSION OF THE DRUM

Bodhran (pronounced *boran*) is the Gaelic word for the big frame drum that has once again become a crucial part of the music scene as a result of the 1950s rebirth of Irish folk music. Before its present popularity, it was a little-known folk instrument of the west of Ireland (the first one was made, perhaps, from a winnowing tray) and was used in the Christmastime "hunting of the wren"—an old custom formerly known also in France and the Isle of Man, in which hunters used drums to scare the scrumptious little wrens from their hiding places in the brush.

The bodhran is like a large, deep tambourine without the jingles. It's held with one hand by a rope or crossed wires attached across the inside of the drum's casing. The other hand strikes the skin with a wooden beater knobbed at the ends, twisting the wrist to achieve a constant sound. By varying the stroke and applying more or less pressure to the inside of the drum's casing with the holding hand, a variety of sounds can be produced.

The instruments are mind-boggling in their ability to invoke both the mournful, haunting quality of Ireland's past and the hearty gustiness of a foot-stomping present. Besides the harp in its many incarnations, there's the bodhran (a goatskin drum), the penny whistle, the fiddle, the flute, the accordian, the concertina and, of course, the bagpipes.

One final note: the best of the country's musical entertainment continues to be the impromptu songfests that are the heart of the country's musical tradition. Whether you find yourself in one of the aforementioned pubs or in a country hotel such as the Rock Glen in County Galway, what will become obvious instantly is that every person in Ireland has a set piece. From "The Rose of Alandale" to the old standard "Wearin' o' the Green," informal singing is a national sport, and everyone within earshot is expected to participate. Don't worry about talent—gusto counts more than a perfect soprano. Don't worry about getting to bed early either; the best impromptu sessions go late into the night.

| FOCUS ON | THOSE OLD IRISH TUNES |

The Wearin' o' the Green

Oh! Paddy dear, and did you hear the news that's goin' round.
The Shamrock is forbid by law, to grow on Irish ground;
Saint Patrick's day no more we'll keep, His color can't be seen,
For there's a bloody law agin' the Wearin' o' the Green

The old Irish popular melodies trailed an aura of melancholy, nostalgia, grief and lovelorn yearning. Their lyrics embodied the purest romantic emotions and became the quintessential symbol of romantic expression. One of the best known, and the one most closely associated with the Irish political experience, is "The Wearin' o' the

Green" with its blatant anti-English lyrics and strong scent of nationalistic pride. The song is an ode to the shamrock, an Irish national symbol since before 1775, and foreshadowed the great migration to America that resulted from Britain's policy of repression. Although the British never forbade the actual wearing of the "green," they did discourage its symbolic use.

The melody dates back to the 1830s, and may be Scottish in origin. The lyrics are by the Irish-born playwright Dion Boucicault (1820?–1890) and were an adaptation of an earlier lyric from the turn of the century.

DUBLIN

You just can't avoid hearing music in Dublin. On the streets wherever you look you see buskers with well-tried tunes. In the pubs you'll find fiddlers and singers. And Dubliners walking down the street are very likely to be humming a tune to themselves. The heartbeat of the city pounds like a drumbeat.

Every night, in pubs and clubs, in concert halls and stadiums, music fills the city like a gigantic helium balloon. Traditional music thrives in sessions where folks get together and play, and ballad singers fill your soul with memories of days gone by. In fact, if you come across a Dub who's not writing a novel, you can bet that he or she is probably in a rock band.

In Dublin the definition of an introvert could be someone who has never busked on Grafton Street. This city may be noted for its grand concert productions, but much of Dublin's real productions are found on its streets. In fact, the citizens themselves provide all the entertainment a visitor could ever want. On Bloomsday many dress up in Joycean costume and march around the city reciting verse and singing. All the city is a stage, and the best performances you'll see during your stay are often spontaneous: a mime artist sending everyone into convulsions, a street artist painstakingly chalking great works onto the pavements or a would-be tenor breaking into heartrending song in a centuries-old pub.

But the Dublin sound extends beyond its thousands of amateur musicians. It's also the home of, among others, the world-acclaimed rock band U2 which, honing its art to perfection in one of the city's

Dublin street buskers

many high-tech studios, Windmill Lane, first captured not just a slice of Dublin, but the imagination of people from all over the world.

The walls of the Lane now stand in testament to this. The scribbles painted on the brickwork speak volumes. "U2, you have changed my life. Thank You," writes Joe. Theresa has this to say, "Always walk in gentleness and peace" and another philosopher writes, "War is like a pizza, it leaves red stains everywhere." There are messages from all over the world written on the walls, some, inexplicably, as high as fifteen feet from the ground.

Over time, the wall has come to symbolize more than just a feeling for one band. Someone has written *"La Gente Irlandese e quella Italiene hanno lo spirito vicino."* (The people of Ireland and Italy share the same spirit.) And others scrawl the praises of Hothouse Flowers, Something Happens and Depeche Mode, other internationally acclaimed bands.

Those bands and singers who preceeded U2, Bono, My Little Funhouse and all who have come to the fore since, owe something to Dublin, while the city itself is indebted to the writers and artists

SPOTLIGHT ON   U2

When the rock history of the '80s and '90s is finally written, U2 will take up more than its fair share of space. From their first album, *Boy,* which was released in 1980 to rave reviews (the band collected nine firsts in the Reader's Poll printed in *The Hot Press*—Ireland's leading rock magazine), to their most recent release, *Zooropa,* U2 has consistently managed to take the rock spirit of its native Dublin and serve it on a gilded platter to eager fans in every corner of the world.

Along the way, they've racked up a continuing series of "firsts"— chief among them the acclaim given to their 1987 release, *The Joshua Tree,* which established once and for all U2's worldwide stature. Within days of its release, the album went straight to number one in the U. K. chart (arriving fittingly on St. Patrick's Day), and one month later reached the same position in the U. S. Never in history had an album by an Irish rock band topped the U. S. charts.

In the next eight months, *The Joshua Tree* sold in excess of fourteen million copies around the world and topped the charts in twenty-two countries. And when *The Joshua Tree* tour started in Arizona in April, *Time* placed U2 on its cover, as "Rock's Hottest Ticket."

To most Irish people, all the notoriety was overwhelming. But for the Irish music industry, it meant a new feeling of confidence in the worth of the home product abroad. Since then, the band has continued to inspire confidence not only in its ability to deliver sales, but in its commitment to making the world a better place in which to live. Following the release of *Achtung Baby* in 1991, the band embarked on a world tour that culminated in a Greenpeace concert held in Manchester, England, to protest a proposed nuclear processing plant at Sellafield in Cumbria. The following day, U2 was involved in a Greenpeace action, delivering contaminated waste from the beaches of Ireland, Scotland, Wales and England to the plant where the waste originated.

U2's lineup consists of Bono (vocals), the Edge (guitar, piano), Larry Mullen, Jr. (drums) and Adam Clayton (bass). The band's most recent release, *Zooropa,* is a studio album of ten new songs, one of which is a collaborative effort with guest artist Johnny Cash.

who have given something of themselves in return. "Tread softly, you are treading on my dreams," writes Zoe on the Windmill Lane wall, slightly misquoting the great Irish poet, W. B. Yeats, and at the same time capturing perfectly the dreams and hopes of youth, an optimism and a zest for living that thrives in Dublin.

Dublin is an ancient city, but it has the character of a teenager and a style of youthful living all its own. Most people who live in Dublin are young; by some estimates, fifty-four percent of Dubliners are under twenty-one, and it is this generation that gives the city its vibrancy and its excitement.

Music, of all the liberal arts, has the greatest influence over the passions, and is that to which the legislator ought to give the greatest encouragement.

NAPOLEAN BONAPARTE

Dublin is a small city, one in which no one is anonymous. People will pass the time of day with you and talk as if they've known you all their lives. Whole areas of the city, Temple Bar for one, buzz with energy and creativity. Dublin has many things to offer, but most of all it offers the visitor a sense of hope, freedom and excitement. It is the city that spreads its dreams under your feet.

CONCERT HALLS

The National Concert Hall/*an Ceolaras Naisiunta* (Earlsfort Terrace, Dublin 2, 01/6711533, fax: 01/6712615) is the home of the National Symphony Orchestra. Its musical offerings also include jazz, opera and some pop. Tickets range from £5–£15, and reservations are strongly recommended. The National Concert Hall also includes the John Field Room Concerts, which are smaller events (mainly chamber), and for which tickets hover in the £5 range. The Carolan room presents lectures for £5 each for a series of four. Food is served in the Terrace Restaurant (lunch from £3.30 and three-course preconcert suppers for £9).

SPOTLIGHT ON DUBLIN OPERA

The prosperity and elegance of Dublin in the eighteenth century rivaled that of many cities on the Continent. From about 1740 on, the city enjoyed a vibrant concert life, attracting many eminent composers and singers (Handel's *Messiah* was presented in 1742).

With the arrival of *The Beggar's Opera,* which was heard in Dublin within weeks of its London premiere in 1728, the initial standard for opera in the city was set. The performance also created an intense theatrical rivalry among Dublin's many operatic venues. (At the time, "opera" meant a one-act play with songs [ballads] performed after the main drama.)

Despite the existence of a few noteworthy Irish composers, for most of the eighteenth century, Dublin's elite continued to favor music from the Continent—especially from Italy. In December of 1761 a traveling group of Italians including the famed De Amicis family introduced a new operatic form—the *burletta,* which had a more comedic style than Dubliners were used to viewing. Similar pieces were later presented by Galuppi, Pergolesi and Jommelli.

But in 1800 it all came to an end. With the passing of the Act of Union, London abolished the Irish Parliament and effectively transferred all power and patronage to London. The decision turned Dublin into an impoverished provincial town almost overnight. Thomas Cooke (1782–1848) and William Rooke (1794–1847) led the exodus of famous Irish composers who had to struggle in London for the rest of their lives.

By the turn of the century, however, an intense patriotic fervor had emerged, leading O'Brien Butler (1862–1916) to write *Muirghis,* the first opera set to a Gaelic text. Staged in 1903, its text was continuous, the airs reflecting the modal character of Irish folk melodies.

Over the next few decades, war and civil strife suspended any attempt at musical creativity. But when a new Irish state emerged in the 1920s, people turned once again to the arts.

Dublin has offered a continuous season of opera since 1941; Wexford has had an opera festival since 1951, yet Ireland still awaits a resident opera company.

Other concert halls with programs and ticket prices similar to the National Concert Hall are **The Gaiety Theatre** (South King St., Dublin 2, 01/771717); the **Olympia Theatre** (74 Dame St., Dublin 2, 01/777744), which has both early evening and midnight performances; the **Royal Hospital Kilmainham** (Kilmainham, Dublin 8, 01/718666); **St. Ann's Church** (Dawson St., Dublin 2, 01/767727); the **Hugh Lane Municipal Gallery of Modern Art** (Charlemont House, Parnell Square, Dublin 1, 01/741903); and the **Tivoli Theatre** (135–138 St. Francis St., Dublin 8, 01/453-5988).

And then there are concert venues that focus on mainly popular and rock music. (Ticket prices are in the £5–£10 range; most require early booking; don't wear jeans.) These include **The Baggot Inn** (143 Lower Baggot St., Dublin 2, 01/761430); the **National Stadium** (South Circular Rd., Dublin 8, 01/533371), which draws performers the likes of Jackson Browne; the **Point Depot** (East Link Bridge, Dublin 1, North Wall Quay, 01/366777), formerly a depot building, now a theater and concert hall with a capacity of over seven thousand and state-of-the-art acoustics; **McGonagles** (South Anne St., Dublin 2, 01/774402); **Bob's Backstage Bar** (35–37 East Essex St., Dublin 2, 01/775482); **RDS** (Ballsbridge, Dublin 4, 01/680645) with an over-six-thousand capacity; **The Wildebeest** (7 Johnson's Court, Dublin 2, 01/712276), which is a late-night venue for rock and jazz; and finally, the **SFX Centre** (23 Upper Sherrard St., Dublin 1, 01/745962).

SPOTLIGHT ON **JOHN O'CONNOR: PIANO VIRTUOSO**

Acclaimed for his eloquent style, dynamic technique and command of keyboard color—particularly in the classic and early romantic repertoires—Irish pianist John O'Connor gained widespread attention in the U. S. in 1986 with the first of the complete cycle of Beethoven sonatas, which he recorded on the Telarc label. Additional recorded cycles-in-progress include the piano concertos of Mozart with Sir Charles MacKerras and the Scottish Chamber Orchestra and the complete works of Irish composer John Field.

O'Connor performs extensively in Europe, having appeared with leading orchestras including the Royal Philharmonic, the Vienna Symphony, the Czech Philharmonic, l'Orchestre National de France and the Stuttgart Chamber Orchestra. In addition, he has made several tours of North America, including appearances with the Cleveland Orchestra, the National Symphony, and the orchestras of

John O'Connor

Montreal, Detroit and Dallas. In Japan O'Connor performed both in recital and in concert with the NKH Symphony and toured the former Soviet Union twice. In recent sessions he performed three complete chronological Beethoven sonata cycles at New York's Metropolitan Museum of Art, Boston's Gardner Museum and London's Wigmore Hall.

O'Connor's early studies began with J. J. O'Reilly at the College of Music in Dublin. He was subsequently awarded an Austrian government scholarship enabling him to study in Vienna with the respected pianist and instructor Dieter Weber and with noted Beethoven interpreter Wilhelm Kempff. In 1973 O'Connor was unanimously awarded first prize in the International Beethoven Competition in Vienna, an achievement followed by another prestigious award that year—first prize at the Bösendorfer Piano Competition.

A familiar figure on television and radio in Ireland, O'Connor is actively involved in improving educational and performing opportunities for young musicians there. He has been instrumental in the establishment of the GPA Dublin International Piano Competition. O'Connor lives in Dublin with his wife and two sons.

For cabaret, head to **Jury's Cabaret** (in the Jury's Hotel), which has performances nightly except Mondays from April through October. Others include **Braemor Rooms** (Churchtown, 01/298-1016), and **Doyle's Irish Cabaret** (Burlington Hotel, Leeson St., 01/660-5222).

In addition to going to the box office or calling the theater and charging tickets, tickets can also be secured at **Mega Records** at 65 Grafton St., which is open Monday through Saturday 9:30 a.m.–6 p.m. and Thursdays until 8 p.m. Tickets are also generally available through **HMV** record stores. **Brown-Thomas** on Grafton St. also has a ticket bureau.

CLUBS AND DISCOS

Don't get too excited if Dubliners talk about "the strip after the pub." What they're talking about is a strip of Georgian buildings in whose basements are housed several ever-changing nightclubs. Some serve food, but eating is very low on the list of priorities when people turn up at Leeson St. DJs are more usual than live bands, crowds are large and lively and just about all the clubs have a no-jeans code. Admission varies; expect to pay between £8–£12.

Given that the club scene is ever-changing, here are some of the more long-lasting regulars.

Annabels (in the Burlington Hotel, Upper Leeson St., Dublin 4, 01/605222) fashionable and stylish for all ages; **Clare's** (Mont Clare Hotel, 13 Clare St., Dublin 2, 01/619555); **Rumpole's Blues Bar** (18 Parliament St., 01/679-9202) a small place with a mixture of blues styles—Chicago, jazzy, New Orleans. Sometimes the music is swing; the crowd is mainly musicians, actors and theatergoers from the nearby Project Arts Centre, no food; **Lily Langtry's** (Judge Roy Bean's Restaurant, 45 Nassau St., Dublin 2, 01/679-7539).

The world-famous **Kitchen** (in the Clarence Hotel in Temple Bar, 01/677-6178) is owned by U2 (and, yes, you *might* just catch them there if you're lucky). Theme nights predominate here. The club is open from 8 p.m.–12 p.m.; **McGonagles** (21a South Anne St., Dublin 2, 01/774402), no cover; **Lillie's Bordello** (01/679-9204) was once a favorite of Julia Roberts, Kiefer Sutherland and just about every tycoon and high flier in the city. It's still hip; **The Night Train** (Basement O' Dwyers Pub, 7 Lower Mount St., Dublin 2, 01/761717); **P.O.D's** (Place of Dance, 01/478-0166) is where much of

SPOTLIGHT ON   SINÉAD O'CONNOR

With a voice as pure as Ivory Snow, twenty-five-year-old Sinéad (pronounced *Shin-NAYD*) O'Connor was launched on the world in 1986 when The Edge released its soundtrack album for the Irish film, *Captive*. Sinéad sang "Heroine," the only song on the record, and drew rave reviews for her emotionally charged voice.

Born and raised in Dublin, the young O'Connor was a lackluster student who preferred songwriting, poetry and adolescent escapades to schoolwork. When asked about the origin of her tremendous energy and drive, she often credits these early years and the influence of having been born Irish, "It seems everybody from Ireland is just naturally musical," she says.

Possibly the youngest person ever to emanate from the Irish rock scene, O'Connor hit the stage already a professional at the tender age of fourteen when her original composition "Take My Hand" was recorded by the Irish band In Tua Nua and became an instant hit. When her parents found out, they forced her to enlist in a Waterford boarding school, from which she soon escaped, fleeing to Dublin to join an acoustic/funk band, Ton Ton Macoute.

In 1985 Nigel Grainge of Ensign Records saw Sinéad performing in a Dublin rehearsal room and encouraged her to move to London, which she did. "I love Ireland, but I had to leave it because I didn't want to be an Irish folk singer. Most Irish musicians, at least the non-traditional ones, have had to leave the country to get record deals and proper management. U2 are the exception, not the rule."

Her "official" debut came soon after the move. While collecting material for her first album, *The Lion and the Cobra*, O'Connor did a prestigious support slot to U2 in Belfast. With her shaved head and fascinating vocals, she blasted onto the world stage and made a lasting impression as a consumately skilled performer.

Since then, she has alternately been praised and plagued by conflicting perceptions of her image. With the release of her 1992 album, *Am I Not Your Girl?* she has once again confounded fans who insist on viewing her as "rock's bad girl."

Sinéad

The recording consists of eleven penetrating renditions of classic stage and screen tunes from the midcentury heyday of popular songwriting and—in Sinead's words—pays tribute to a time in her life when "I'd go into my room and close the door and sing something like 'Secret Love' from Doris Day's movie *Calamity Jane.*"

Just another marketing vehicle for this chameleon of pop music? Not so, says O'Connor, who insists on moving beyond the image of rebellious hellion. "I've found it difficult over the last years because of not being perceived as a person," she says. "Basically I'm still just a young girl. I love people, and I want people to love me...people are always trying to make me out to be a bad girl, and I'm trying to say I'm not. I'm a nice girl, and I have a heart."

The original catalyst for *Am I Not Your Girl?* is an album in Sinead's extensive collection of show music. "What really started me wanting to do this was the Julie London album called *The Liberty Years,*" she says. "When I heard her brilliant, strippy 'Why Don't You Do Right?' I just wanted to be beautiful like her, and that song made me get off my ass to do it."

the in-crowd has migrated, and is particularly a haunt of the young set in music, advertising and modeling. There's a strict door policy here, although nobody knows from night to night exactly what the rules are; **Leeson Street Clubs** where admission is free, closing time is very late and you can get a glass of St. Emilion (well, maybe) because they have a wine license. Don't call; be like everybody else and pop in from one to the other: **Suesey Street, Strings, Leggs, Buck Whaley's** and **Bang Bangs** are the livelier ones.

For a *really* concentrated dose of Dublin's club scene, though, you'll want to hightail it on over to the **Temple Bar** area, a happenin' section of town beautifully situated along the River Liffey, which is flooded with clubs, pubs, shops and restaurants. Some of the clubs especially worth checking out include **Da Phat Kat Club** (Bedford Lane, Blue Note Club) which features "phreaky jazzadelic, funk and fusion" in a happenin' place open on Saturdays from 10 p.m. on. Admission is £4; £3 before 11:45 p.m.; **Well Fed Cafe** (Crow St.) where you're likely to encounter everything from jazz to poetry to a buddhist musical benefit for the Dublin Meditation Center. Admission is in the £6 range.

The Garage Bar (Essex St.) is open seven nights a week with varied musical offerings including Blues Mondays, Chill Out Tuesdays, Wednesdays Caffeine sessions (mad, bad, loud, noisy, grungy, rappin' and rockin'), Fridays Release the Pressure (enough said) and Saturdays Rhythm Zone where you'll find wall-to-wall people. None of these are live, but the crowds—mainly 18–25, loud, young and neon—make up for it.

SPOTLIGHT ON | THE POGUES: A FRENZIED BLEND OF PUNK ROCK AND IRISH TRAD

Spider Stacy: lead vocals and whistle

Jem Finer: banjo

Darryl Hunt: bass

Andrew Ranken: drums

Terry Woods: citern and mandolin

Philip Chevron: guitar

James Fearnley: accordian

They've hung out with Tom Waits; they've been endorsed by Dylan and U2; they've left an indelible mark on records by Steve

Earle and David Byrne. They're members of the Pogues, together eleven years, eight disks to their credit and a hellacious reputation that has catapulted them to the very top of the punk-rock field.

The Pogues' turbulent history starts in a place that's halfway between punk and a furious, frenetic sound from the squats of North London. Seemingly mad and unorthodox, the sound came together sometime in 1982 when ex-Nipple Erector Shane McGowan met up with ex-Millwall Chainsaw Spider Stacy to play a set of rebel songs at Cabaret Futura Club; they were pelted off with chips.

Not to be deterred, another ex-Nip, James Fearnley, was enticed into the fray, and after a few months spent training some of their own King's Cross drinking partners, Jem Finer, Andrew Ranken (then known as The Clobberer) and bass player Cait "Mrs Elvis Costello" O'Riordan (since replaced by Darryl Hunt), the group completed their roster and took the name *Pogue Mahone*, which is Gaelic for "Kiss My Ass."

The U. K. had never seen anything like them. Frenzied gigs around town saw Pogue Mahone's special musical blend appealing to a group of fans as wild as the band. The first single, "Dark Streets of London," came out in August 1984, and the band was snapped up by Stiff Records. Changing their name to The Pogues, they released their debut album, *Red Roses for Me*, in October 1984 and immediately attracted international acclaim. Their second album, the darker *Sodomy and the Lash*, released in September 1985, saw the group firmly established as internationally celebrated artists.

The group has continued to sell millions of records; it's their live show, however, that most endears the Pogues to their fans. On every St. Patrick's Day, they play a special show, tickets for which become the most sought-after of all shows that year.

The early '90s saw the Pogues tour the world almost nonstop, from Sydney to Tokyo, Los Angeles to Lisbon—a practice they still maintain; 1993 was spent making *Waiting For Herb*, their eighth record and one more to be proud of. No question about it, the future for this legendary band lies in expanding even further its adventurous musical edge.

The **Gardening Club** (3A Crown Alley) offers garage, house, discobeats, and funk. The admission is £6. **St. Andrew's Lane Theatre** offers "Reggae on the Island" every Wednesday night, with DJ Richie *alias* Limbo Man. The club is open 11:30 p.m. until late; admission is £5.

At **Rock Garden** (Crown Alley) you'll find live music seven nights a week with late bar and dancing. The club features mainly Irish acts and some really interesting English indie bands. Monday and Tuesday nights are breakthrough nights featuring five newcomers to the rock scene. Rock Garden attracts a very young crowd. **Bad Bob's** (34–35 Essex) is open until 2 a.m. and draws a young, hip crowd. It features various genres including indie.

COUNTRY

In some cases, *country* just means traditional Irish music with a few nontraditional (for Ireland) instruments (banjo for instance) thrown in. In most, it means what's called *ethnic country* which could include anything from American bluegrass to Polish klezmer. For the former, check out **Bad Bob's Backstage Bar** (35–37 East Essex St., Dublin 2, 01/775482), which tends toward a rock-country lineup—loud, loud, loud; for the latter, try **The Lower Deck** (1 Portobello Harbour, Dublin 8, 01/751423) and **Break for the Border** (Johnson's Place, 01/478-0300). On Wednesday nights, you can also catch "The boss of country music," Ray Lynan, and his band at **The Harcourt Hotel** (60 Harcourt St., Dublin 2, 01/478-3677). The hotel also has country disco music until "late."

SPOTLIGHT ON MARY BLACK

How do you stay true to your traditional roots and yet reach out to a new audience influenced by the more aggressive rhythms of rock, pop and country? Ireland's Mary Black seems to have found the answer.

Black's crystal clear voice is an instrument of uncommon beauty and expressiveness. Her gifts as an interpreter of both folk and contemporary material have made her a major recording artist in her native Ireland. Named "Best Irish Female Artist" in the Irish Recorded Music Awards Poll (IRMA) two years running, Mary Black is one of those rare talents who crosses musical boundaries and makes every song she performs her own.

Black's musical roots run deep. Her father, a fiddle player from a small island off the north coast of Ireland, and mother, who sang in the dance halls of Dublin, gave their five children a real love of music. While still in her teens, she was performing with her siblings in small Dublin clubs. Not yet twenty, she joined General Humbert, a folk band that toured Europe and released a pair of albums in the late 1970s.

In 1982 she joined forces with musician and producer Declan Sinnott to record her first solo album, *Mary Black*. The LP earned her a gold album in Ireland. Shortly afterward, Black became a member of the folk group DeDannan and toured extensively in Europe and the U. S. Black also continued her solo career, releasing *Collected* in 1984 and *Without the Fanfare* in 1985, an album that took her in a more contemporary musical direction.

"I started in folk music," she says, "but never felt there should be any boundaries in music. Fortunately, here in Ireland there's an openness about music that allows you to step outside of categories." Black's expanding solo career led to her departure from DeDannan in 1986, which set the stage for *By the Time It Gets Dark*, her first multiplatinum Irish album after three golds.

Black's album *No Frontiers* was released in 1989 and went straight to the top of the Irish charts, achieving triple platinum status. Meanwhile, she had come to the attention of Americans. In August 1993 she was featured on the cover of *Billboard* in a story hailing her as a "firm favorite to join the heavy hitting ranks of such Irish artists as Enya, Sinead O'Connor, and Clannad's Maire Brennan in the international marketplace."

Black's most recent album, *The Holy Ground*, entered the Irish charts at number one in June 1993 and was released in the U. S. in September of the same year. Over the next twelve months, her live

American performances were consistently sold out. From San Francisco to New York, the reaction from critics was neatly summed up in this headline from the November 15, 1993, *Boston Globe:* "Simply Spellbinding!"

Mary Black

JAZZ

Jazz venues are very popular in Dublin. The crowd is a slightly older one, dressed a bit more traditionally (which means no oddly colored hair or piercings in strange places) and food is generally part of the deal. A few of the better places include the **Gaiety Theatre** (South King St., Dublin 2, 01/771717); the **Olympia Theatre** (74 Dame St., Dublin 2, 01/777744); the **Wildebeest** (7 Johnson's Court, Dublin 2, 01/712276); the **Night Train** (downstairs in O'Dwyer's pub, 01/761717); and the **Blue Note Cafe** (5 Aston Quay, Dublin 2, Temple Bar area), which bills itself as Dublin's *only* jazz cafe (lunch specials are £4; three-course dinner with wine is £20).

PUBS AND TRADITIONAL MUSIC

Traditional Irish music is a must in Dublin. Music sessions, referred to either as *saisáns* or *ceilidhs,* are held in pubs as well as many other kinds of places around the city. Many of the pubs charge nothing for music if you consent to having a pint or two. Many others charge £2–£4 for the better-known acts. In most you'll see musicians sitting among the patrons one minute, up on the stage jammin' the next.

OBSERVATIONS ON *The Dublin Music Scene from One Who Knows*

Bryan is a street musician in the Temple Bar area of Dublin. To his way of thinking, Dublin's music scene has both its ups and its downs. "You walk around Dublin, you see people with guitars everywhere," he says. "But a lot of these musicians don't get the opportunity to really shine here or even play like they would if they were abroad. There's so much competition here, but it's all part of a never-to-be-realized dream. The reality is, if you want to make it, you go elsewhere. Sinead had to go to London. By tradition, we Dubliners emigrate if we're really serious about our music. There's not even a pop chart here. And *emigrate* is a relative term. If you come from the country, you come to Dublin; Dubliners go to London; Londoners go to New York—although that's been changing.

"There are no instant pop stars in Dublin. If you make it here, you've been around a long time. Even U2 bounced around the city for years before they hit the top of the charts—and where did they do it? Not here. Now they're popular here, but they had to go elsewhere first in order to make their name."

The pubs of Dublin are not simply places to have a drink. They are theaters for storytelling, backdrops for romance, homes away from home, keepers of the spirit of the city and—of course—repositories of Dublin's own blend of music and performance. In the best of places, you'll find throngs of people joyfully involved in pursuit of "the crack," which means—not what you think—but literally "having a good time." In specific terms they're drinking, shooting the breeze and listening to the music of the ancients.

Besides the pubs, you'll find music sessions in cultural organizations, restaurants, and small halls. Some of the best in all categories follow.

"Guiness" spoken here

In **Baggot's Inn** (143 Baggot St.), sessions are held both upstairs and downstairs, and the young and trendy crowd, all in black leather jackets, is giving it all it's got. **The Brazen Head** (20 Lower Bridge St.) has one special feature that no other pub can ever claim for its own: it's the oldest bar in town—established in 1198 as the first stop after the bridge on the way into the city.

The **Waterfront Rock Bar** (14 Sir John Rogerson Quay) is a bar and café on the river close to the offices of U2. There's late-night music and bar until 2 a.m. **Kenny's** (Lincoln Place) is the place where you're most likely to find "sessions"—occasions where musicians and pubgoers burst into spontaneous renditions of Dublin ballads. **O'Donaghue's** (15 Merrion Row) was originally famous for being the haunt of the famous musical group, The Dubliners. The tradition started by The Dubliners still lives on in this pub, and you're mostly likely to catch an informal singing session within these walls.

Slattery's (29 Capel St.) is the best-known pub for traditional Irish music, set dancing, rock and blues entertainment. Open seven nights a week. **Whelen's** (Wexford St.) is the place for music, comedy sessions, food, drinks and entertainment of all sorts. Then there's **Bad Bob's Backstage Bar** (35–37 East Essex St., Dublin 2, 01/775482).

Harcourt Hotel (Harcourt St., Dublin 2, 01/478-3677) has traditional music Tuesdays and Fridays. **Central Hotel** (Molly Malone's Tavern, Exchequer St., Dublin 2, 01/679-7302) has music nightly from 9:30 p.m.–11:00 p.m.; admission is free. **Barry Fitzgerald** (Marlborough St., Dublin 1, 01/874-0685) has music Thursday–Sunday nightly at 9 p.m. **Mother Red Caps Tavern** (Back Lane, 01/538306) has music every Tuesday, Thursday, Friday and Saturday at 9 p.m., also on Sunday afternoon from 12:30 p.m.–2:30 p.m.; the admission charge is £5.

Other pubs include **An Beal Bocht** (Charlemont St., Dublin 2, 01/755614); **Keating's Pub** (Mary St., Dublin 1, 01/873-1567), nightly sessions; **Searson's** (Upper Baggot St., Dublin 4, 01/660-0330), Thursdays and Saturdays at 9 p.m.

Clifton Court Hotel (Lanigans Bar, O'Connell St. Bridge, Dublin 1, 01/874-3535) free sessions nightly; **Wexford Inn** (26 Wexford St., Dublin 2, 01/780391).

FOCUS ON   THE COMMITMENTS: THE ULTIMATE MOVIE MUSICAL

DEREK: So what kind of music are we gonna be playing, Jimmy?

JIMMY: You're working class, right?

OUTSPAN: We would be if there was any work.

JIMMY: So your music should be about where you're from and the sort of people you come from. It should speak the language of the streets. It should be about struggle and sex. An' I don't mean muschy shite love songs about "I'll hold your hand and love you till the end of time." I mean riding, fuckin', tongues, gooters, boxes—the works.

OUTSPAN: What kind of music says all that?

JIMMY: Soul.

OUTSPAN/DEREK: Soul?

JIMMY: We're gonna play Dublin soul.

OUTSPAN: Dublin soul...

DEREK: Fuckin' deadly.

In 1992 an unpretentious little film by Alan Parker hit the screen. The story, adapted from Roddy Doyle's book of the same name, centered around Jimmy Rabbite, a young Irish "tosser" with a dream: to bring soul music to Dublin. During the course of the next few weeks, he put together a band consisting of Deco, a drunken lead singer described by author Doyle as having "a deep growl that scraped against the tongue and throat on the way out"; Dean, who inherited his sax when his uncle's lung collapsed; Billy Mooney, who auditions in a pawnbroker's window *before* paying to get his drums out; Joey "The Lips" Fagan, who becomes the group's lead trumpet and guru and "The Commitment-ettes"—Imelda, Natalie and Bernie.

The story line is simple: as the film progresses, growing harmony on stage is mirrored by growing dissent off it, and by film's end, when their performances reach heights that none had believed possible, the inevitable breakup occurs. Backstage after their last performance, the band self-destructs in a frenzy of fists and foulness at the very moment when contracts are being waved in front of their incredulous eyes.

Jimmy, interviewing himself on a mythical TV program in the mirror, tells us in the final scene how the band members have gone off to their own separate destinies. But he consoles himself with the knowledge that, for one brief moment, he altered their expectations of life and lifted their horizons.

While the well-chosen cast of characters (with its wonderful Dublin street language described by director Parker as "purple Joycian prose") long remained in the memory of every filmgoer, the heart of this movie was unquestionably its music. With twelve hard-hitting blues numbers blasting across the screen, the film raised to new levels the idea of a "music film." Here was the perfect blending of story and sound, of action and concert, of narrative and exposition. Nowhere before or since has a director put so much stake in a film's music without for one second compromising the story that he wanted to tell.

Parker's mission, as he enunciated it while the film was still being edited, was simple, "I wanted to capture a little of the spirit and spunk of the working class kids of Dublin's Northside. I also wanted to capture the wit and wisdom of Roddy Doyle's original novel. Our film is set in Dublin, Ireland, but it's about the hopes and dreams music brings to young kids everywhere, from Finglass to Philadelphia and Memphis to Minsk."

A Tosser's Glossary

For centuries the Irish were forced to speak English. They got their own back by using it better. From Wilde to Shaw and Beckett to Behan. But the truth is, the Irish haven't been using English for years. They have their own language. And it isn't Gaelic.

ALAN PARKER, DIRECTOR OF *THE COMMITMENTS*

ALL MOUTH AND BOLLIX Someone who has too high an opinion of themselves.

BLEEDIN' All-purpose adjective used for emphasis. As in "You bleedin' gobshite."

BOLLIX All-purpose word with multiple usage. As a noun, refers to the male genitals. As in "I'll bite your bollix you spotty fuck." Or refers to a person. As in "Wait 'till you see the little bollix waiting for you outside." As an exclamation, "Bollix!" means "Nonsense!" "Rubbish!" "Bullshit!" "In your bollix" means you're talking through your hat. Talking nonsense.

THE BUSINESS The sexual act. (Not always with someone else) As in "I bet he does the business every night."

GOBSHITE Derogatory noun referring to a person.

GOOTER Meaning unsure. Probably refers to the male sex organ.

POXY Lousy. Of no merit.

RIDE Sexual intercourse. As in "The odd ride would be nice."

SCOOP A glass of beer.

TOSSER A waster. An idiot. A jerk-off artist.

WILLIES Plural of willie: a little boy's gooter.

Songs Performed by the Commitments

"Mustang Sally"
Written by Bonny Rice
Originally performed by Wilson Pickett
"Too Many Fish in the Sea"
Written by Norman Whitfield and Edward Holland
Originally performed by The Marvellettes
"Mr. Pitiful"
Written by Otis Redding and Steve Cooper
Originally performed by Otis Redding
"Bye Bye Baby"
Written by Mary Wells
Originally performed by Mary Wells

"Show Me"
Written by Joe Tex
Originally performed by Joe Tex
"Take Me to the River"
Written by Al Green and Mabon Hodges
Originally performed by Al Green
"The Dark End of the Street"
Written by Dan Penn and Chips Moman
Originally performed by Percy Sledge
"Hard to Handle"
Written by Alvertis Isbell, Allen Jones and Otis Redding
Originally performed by Otis Redding
"Chain of Fools"
Written by Don Covay
Originally performed by Aretha Franklin
"I Never Loved a Man"
Written by Ronnie Shannon
Originally performed by Aretha Franklin
"Try a Little Tenderness"
Written by Harry Woods, Jimmy Campbell and Reg Connelly
Originally performed by Otis Redding
"In the Midnight Hour"
Written by Wilson Pickett and Steve Cropper
Originally performed by Wilson Pickett

The Oliver St. John Gogarty Bar and Restaurant (57–58 Fleet St., Temple Bar, Dublin 2, 01/671-1822, 671-1165) is a hip pub with live traditional music nightly and Saturdays from 4 p.m.–7:30 p.m. There is no cover charge. The bar is part of Dublin's **Traditional Irish Musical Pub Crawl,** which you will definitely want to check out if you're into traditional music. It takes place nightly at 7:30 except Fridays, is two-and-a-half-hours long and finishes up with a traditional session in **O'Donoghues** on Merrion Rd. For more info, call 01/478-0191.

The Commitments

Abbey Tavern (Howth Co. ten miles north of Dublin on the coast, 01/322006) has trad music with the Abbey Tavern Singers nightly at 9; reservations are essential; dinner is available in the restaurant; admission to ballads is £3. **O'Shea's** (Lower Bridge St., 01/679-3797) has music seven nights a week, 9:30 p.m.–11:30 p.m. Monday–Saturday, and Sunday from 5 p.m.–7:30 p.m. Pub food is served from 10:30 a.m.–8 p.m. in the square wood bar. The decor is mainly soccer memorabilia, there's no cover and no children are allowed.

Cultural Na Eireann (Belgrave Sq., Monkstown, Co., Dublin, 01/ 280-0295; take DART to the Seapoint Station), June through September has music seven nights a week. This pub is a *must* for atmosphere and quality.

Next to theology, I give to music the highest place and honor.

                                                        MARTIN LUTHER

For a taste of the literary side of Dublin's pub life, attach yourself to the **Dublin Literary Pub Crawl** (for info, call 01/540228), which walks you through the best and the boldest and mixes history with music and, of course, grog every Sunday–Thursday at 5 p.m. Meet at the Bailey, 2 Duke St., at 7:30.

FESTIVALS

While not as much of a festival town as its other U. K. counterparts, Dublin's scene still leaves you breathless with options. For starters there's the **Festival of Music in Great Irish Houses,** which provides classical-music lovers with not only great music but great venues in which to enjoy it. Every June, this unique festival is held in ten of the most beautiful period houses throughout Ireland. Included might be such Dublin landmarks as Dublin Castle and the Hibernian Hotel, as well as sites from other Irish counties—the magnificent Castleton House in County Kildare or Strokestown House in County Roscommon. Ticket prices for the various concerts vary from £12–£25 and sell out way in advance. Call 01/670-9266 for further information.

And then there's the other great one, the **Dún Laoghaire Summer Festival** (contact Rita Hughes, Festival Director, Dún Laoghaire, County Dublin, Ireland; 01/284-1888). This festival takes place in the last week in June in Dún Laoghaire, a Victorian village six miles from Dublin with its own yacht-filled harbor. Its varied program encompasses everything from musical happenings in the Maritime Institute (High St.) to sea-chantey concerts in nearby Dalkey Island. Tickets range from £6 for single events to £45 for multievent packages. Book early!

MISCELLANEOUS

During much of the summer, you can enjoy **"Music in the Park,"** an organized series of performances spread out through the city's many public spaces, among them St. Anne's Park, Bushy Park, Griffith Park, Herbert Park, Ellenfield Park, Palmerton Park, Fairview Park, Sandymount Green and St. Patrick's Park. Performances are generally held on Sundays from 3 p.m.–5 p.m., except for Merrion Square Park where they're from 12:45 p.m.–1:45 p.m. Complete information on these concerts can be had by checking any of Dublin's four morning papers, the *Irish Independent,* the *Irish Times,* the *Irish Press* and *The Stars* or by calling the Dublin tourist board at 01/747733.

The city of Dublin also sponsors a **"Jazz in the Park"** series in June that parks itself in various venues, among them Merrion Square Park, Mountjoy Square Park, Herbert Park and Jervis Street Park. Again, call the tourist board for up-to-the-minute details, or check the local paper.

Visitors to Dublin are generally curious about the city's many world-class musicians and how they got their start. To accommodate this interest, Dublin Tourism has set up what they call the **"Rock 'n' Stroll Trail,"** consisting of sixteen plaques erected at sites that were significant in the development of the musical careers of such Dublin natives as U2, Sinead O'Connor, Bob Geldof, the Chieftains and Thin Lizzy. For a map and more details, contact Dublin Tourism, 14 Upper O'Connell St.; 01/747733.

MUSICAL MOMENTS   *Band-Aid and Live Aid*

Sometimes rock musicians involve themselves in social and political issues and gain a worldwide audience for their causes. When Sting devotes his time and energy on behalf of rainforest preservation, the response is always overwhelming. So, too, when George Harrison organized a concert for the starving people of Bangladesh. The concert and subsequent album raised over a quarter of a million dollars—all of which went straight to the relief effort.

In the 1980s it was the Dublin-born grandfather of punk rock, Bob Geldof, who took on a social cause and turned it into a worldwide movement. Geldof, a frenetic, high-intensity type, had just gone solo after a spectacular seven-year career with the Boomtown Rats, generally considered to be the original innovators of Irish punk style.

His cause was Ethiopia which, late in the winter of 1984, had been ravaged by the worst drought in centuries. Millions of people were dying as a result; even where there were relief efforts, only a few hundred out of every thousand could be fed. Geldof's idea was to gather together as many pop stars as could be persuaded to record a single record. The proceeds generated would all be spent for food and medical supplies.

And so, on a wintry Sunday in November of 1984 reporters and TV crews swarmed around the performers, who would be known collectively as Band-Aid, as they filtered into Trevor Horn's Sarm West Studio in London. Boy George was there, having flown in from America on the Concorde. So were Bono and the rest of U2, Sting, George Michael and Wham, Simon Le Bon and Phil Collins. The twelve inch version of the record "Do They Know It's Christmas? (Feed the World)," had extra contributions from David Bowie and Paul McCartney, who could not make the recording session. American artists, including Stevie Wonder, Michael Jackson, Bob Dylan, Bruce Springsteen, Paul Simon, Tina Turner, Diana Ross and Ray Charles, followed Band-Aid's example. They recorded "We Are the World," which was written by Lionel Richie and Michael Jackson, and produced by Quincy Jones. Millions of dollars were generated, and Geldof himself went to Ethiopia to make sure the money was properly spent.

But Geldof didn't stop there. His next idea was even more outrageous. Why not a special live charity concert, with all proceeds going to the starving people? The logistics were monumental. Two stadiums were eventually used—Wembley in London and John F. Kennedy in Philadelphia. There was an around-the-world satellite link, as well as an on-the-spot video link-up; Sky-Lab flew over both concerts to pick up the transmission. The event took an entire day, starting simultaneously at 7:15 a.m. in Philadelphia, and 12:15 p.m. in London on July 13.

Of the six hundred million TV sets in the world, five hundred million were locked into Live Aid. Viewers were asked to donate money in return for viewing the concert event of a lifetime. Everybody who was anybody took part (as the London bill illustrates), and, in the end, millions of dollars were generated. Suffice to say that when Bob Geldof took the stage with the Boomtown Rats to sing "I Don't Like Mondays," the whole of Wembley erupted and sang the song for him.

For a great night of Irish music, song and dance, don't miss *Culturlann na h'Eireann*—the home of Irish traditional entertainment at Belgrave Square, Monkstown, County Dublin (01/280-0295). Sponsored by Comhaltas Ceoltoiri Eireann, Ireland's premier cultural movement, the Culturlann na h'Eireann consists of musicians, singers, dancers and storytellers who entertain at a big open fire while attendants serve a choice of refreshments. In addition to sitting in a beautiful setting and steeping in the drone of the bagpipes and the beat of the bodhran, you (if you like) will be guided through the country set dances. Sessions take place at various times throughout the week, and prices vary according to programs. Expect to pay about £15.

For a truly different experience, think about signing up for the *Scoil Eigse*, Dublin's summer school of traditional music. The school runs for one week in late August, and includes workshops and lectures on the fiddle, concert flute, whistle, two-row accordian, concertina, piob Uillean, harp, banjo, piano-accordian, traditional songs in English and Irish, traditional dancing and the Irish language. Participants include people of all ages, and the fee for entrollment is £40. For applications and further information, contact: CCE, Belgrave Square, Monkstown, County Dublin, Ireland; 01/280-0295.

The Castle Inn (5–7 Lord Edward St., Dublin 2, opposite Christchurch, 01/475-1122) hosts a *ceilidh* (Irish music session including both musicians and set dancers) and banquet nightly from May 1–September 30. Dinner is served at 7:30 p.m.—you can choose a wonderful four-course meal for £21 including the show, or you can have Irish stew and home-baked brown bread for £12 including the show. The show only is £7. This is an honest-to-goodness, genuine traditional-music venue—not at all like the shlock performances you often find masquerading as "real." Reservations are essential. Be aware that most people book well in advance.

Catch a *ceilidh* at The Castle Inn

WEXFORD

Traveling south from Dublin, you come to Wexford, a lively town with plenty of musical happenings—traditional *saisáns* held in the city's many pubs, late-night disco experiences and ballroom dancing at the city's larger hotels. Wexford is not one of the best places to visit if what you're seeking is rock; most places—even if they advertise themselves as rock clubs—tend to favor oldies rock music. Crowds, overall, are nicely dressed and over twenty-one.

CONCERT HALLS

The premier arts center is **Theatre Royal** (High St., 053/22244, 22240), which offers a variety of musical events including classical concerts, jazz and popular entertainment. Tickets range from £4–£15, and advance booking for important performers is usually necessary.

CLUBS AND DISCOS

The **Strand Hotel** (Curracloe, 053/37333) presents disco every Friday night with the sounds of the '60s, '70s, and '80s, and "Saturday Night Fever" on—when else—Saturdays. An outdoor barbecue is provided for those who care to eat while they're shaking their boodies. Thursday nights have disco music and a mineral bar and are reserved for teens. The crowd here tends to be of the over-twenty-five variety, and you rarely see a pair of jeans. **Bogart's Nightclub** (Rosslare) also has Saturday Night Fever with disco dancing from 10 p.m.–2 a.m., and, to get you ready, Happy Hour from 10 p.m.–11 p.m.

Rackards (Killanne, 054/55107) has a variety of different musical offerings: Irish and adult dancing on Thursdays (admission is £1), country on Fridays from 9 p.m.–2 a.m., disco on Saturdays (admission is £6) with various promotions (for example, free future admission to the "coolest guy or gal in shorts and shades") and traditional groups on Sunday afternoons and evenings for about £6. The atmosphere here may be closer to what you would expect of Ireland than at some other spots. **The Junction** (Redmond Square, 053/22316) has disco music (oldies generally) Fridays, Saturdays and Sundays from 10:30 p.m.–2 a.m. Over-twenty-threes only. Also offers teen disco on Tuesdays from 8 p.m.–12 a.m.

■ POP QUIZ 18

Which two of these performers are related to each other? Lulu, Sheena Easton, Albert Lee, Christy Moore, Luka Bloom, Alvin Lee, Tom Jones, Ray Davies, Kate Bush, Richard Davies

ANSWER: CHRISTY MOORE AND LUKA BLOOM ARE BROTHERS.

White's Hotel (George St., 053/22311) houses both the **Speakers Music Bar** and the **Ace of Clubs Disco,** which swings into action on Fridays and Saturdays from 10 p.m.–2 a.m. Admission to the bar is either free or minimal, to the disco about £6. White's is a rather proper place with nice decor and a laid-back atmosphere. **The Goat Bar Lounge** on Main St. has a different band and various styles of music every night. The crowd is mostly over twenty-five and the cover about £2.

Mooney's Lounge (The Quay) has '60s and '70s music on Thursdays and more updated fare on Fridays and Saturdays. The admission is about £5. Tuesdays and Wednesdays are devoted to traditional Irish music and there is generally no charge. The **Hotel Saltees** (Kilmore Quay, 053/29602) has disco dancing on Saturdays from 10 p.m.–1 a.m.; admission is £5; and you'll find easy-listening dance music on Sunday nights from 10 p.m.–2 a.m.

PUBS AND TRADITIONAL MUSIC

In summer Irish music can be heard several nights a week at the **Talbot Hotel** (053/22566). The pub has jazz on Sundays, too. The **Shelmalier Bart** in White's Hotel (George St., 053/22311) devotes many of its nights to traditional Irish fare. **Lamberts of Wellinstonbridge** is a great place to spend time sipping ale and partaking of sessions Thursdays through Sundays.

Tommy Roche's Pub (38 N. Main St.) drips with atmosphere as performers and patrons regale you with traditional Irish music and dance every Thursday and Saturday night at 9:30 p.m. The admission is about £1. The **Crown Bar** (Monck St., no phone) claims to be one of the oldest pubs in Ireland, and from the looks of the collectibles packed between its walls, they're not kidding. Military gear, swords, landscape paintings, helmets: take in all this stuff and you might not even notice the music! If that happened, you'd be really missing out on a great opportunity, so stop the gawking and prick up your ears. At the **Oak Tavern** (Enniscorthy Rd., about two miles north of town, 053/24922) you can gaze out at the pacific River Slaney while you sip your brew and mingle with the musicians, many of whom have been playing here for decades.

SPOTLIGHT ON NIGHTNOISE

For the past decade, Nightnoise has created a unique melding of musical influences by borrowing freely from such varied and time-honored musical genres as Celtic, jazz, classical and pop. With four albums to its credit, the group's most recent effort, *Shadow of Time,* marks the introduction of a new member.

Famed Celtic fiddler Johnny Cunningham has joined other long-time residents, Dublin-born guitarist and keyboardist Mícheál

O'Domhnaill (pronounced *Meehall O'Donell*), keyboardist and vocalist Tríona Ni O'Domhnaill (pronounced *Trina Nee*), his sister and flutist Brian Dunning.

Born in Scotland, newcomer Cunningham is known as a founder of the legendary Celtic folk band Silly Wizard. He has played in myriad folk and rock settings with Bob Dylan, Warren Zevon, Don Henley, the Waterboys, Bill Morrissey and others. His participation brings a new sense of common heritage and musical unity to Nightnoise.

The path leading to this point in Nightnoise's history dates back to 1979 when O'Domhnaill, a veteran of the traditional Irish groups Skara Brae and the Bothy Band (both featuring Tríona), was touring the U. S. with fiddler Kevin Burke. The traditional Celtic music scene was tapering off in Europe and just beginning to take hold in America. Smitten with Portland, Oregon, O'Domhnaill settled there in 1982. "I was tired of playing only traditional Irish music, which is fairly well set," he says. "Especially the accompanist's role, playing guitar, and I was ready to write my own music."

It was then O'Domhnaill struck up a friendship with American violinist Billy Oskay, and the pair recorded *Nightnoise*. "When it came time to do the second album," O'Domhnaill remembers, "we knew we needed additional players. So I invited Tríona and Brian and they liked Portland so much, they decided to stay as well."

Tríona, born in Dublin, ventured out on her own after the demise of the Bothy Band, and joined a North Carolina band, Touchstone, before answering the call from Nightnoise. Her virtuosity on piano, synthesizer, accordian and whistle adds to the group's instrumental variety and flexibility, but her singing—cited in the *New York Times* as "one of the glories of current Irish folk music"—may well be the jewel in the crown.

Brian Dunning had been a professional flutist in Ireland, playing regular classical and jazz gigs before coming to the U. S. in 1977 to study at the Berklee College of Music in Boston. "I remember hearing a flute solo on a tune by Them (with Van Morrison) when I was about sixteen," Dunning recalls, "and it really used to send me. But jazz became my love." So it's not surprising that Dunning's influences include both classical master James Galway and jazz great Hubert Laws. But it was after hearing Mícheál O'Domhnaill and Kevin Burke playing duets at a music festival in Birmingham, Alabama, that Dunning realized what direction his own music might take. "I jammed with Mícheál there and that really made me want to write music that had an Irish flavor but with the freedom of jazz."

From such diverse backgrounds and influences, Nightnoise's present-day configuration flows with a rare grace that suffuses each of their albums and creates music that is as lithe and magical as it is undefinable. Quips Brian Dunning: "I could be facetious and say, hey, it's not music; it's Nightnoise!"

Nightnoise

FESTIVALS

The main event of the year in Wexford is the **Wexford Opera Festival,** which takes place in late October when most tourists are gone and any who remain have traveled long distances for this extremely popular event. Held in various venues including a four-hundred-seat opera house set on a narrow, winding street, this festival draws opera lovers from all over the world who come not only for the music—which is first rate—but for the setting. Even if you're not a fan of opera, you'll understand why others are; this is opera at its most natural and unaffected. Advance booking is necessary, and ticket prices range from £4–£10. Contact the Theatre Royal, 053/22244, 22240.

Music is indisputably the most adequate medium of perception; and the very essence of all perception might with truth be termed music.

RICHARD WAGNER

WATERFORD

Legend has it that it was here, in Waterford County, that St. Patrick picked a shamrock to explain the Trinity. Whether that legend is true or apocryphal, Waterford, conquered by the Danes and fortified by Reginald one thousand years ago, today combines ancient history with modern industry. The Waterford Glassworks—with age-old designs produced in a modern setting hailed as the largest crystal works in Europe—testifies to the deftness of this blend.

So too with music. While not plentiful by the standards of other Irish cities, Waterford's scene is a charming combination of biker rock and early-music festivals. And the unique aspect of this blend is that you'll find both—and more—all on the same picturesque streets.

CONCERT HALLS

Large-scale concerts featuring big-name artists can be had at **The Forum** (The Glen, 051/71111) where tickets go on sale about a month before performances and sell out quickly. Ticket prices range from £5–£20. Half-price tickets are offered on the day of performance.

The **Garter Lane Arts Centre** (5 O'Connell St., 051/55038) offers plays and concerts—generally contemporary. Tickets range from £4–£13. The **Theatre Royal** (City Hall, 051/74402) is Waterford's public theater and presents an arts-extravaganza schedule—everything from plays to opera to musicals to rock concerts. The season runs from May to September; tickets go quickly; and prices range from £5–£20.

SPOTLIGHT ON   **THE CHIEFTAINS: IRISH LEGENDS**

The Chieftains are the most famous exponents of traditional Irish music in the world. For over two-and-a-half decades, they have uncovered a wealth of traditional Irish music accumulated over the centuries. The nature of their playing and their extensive use of improvisation ensure that no two performances are the same. Although their early following was a purely folk audience, the astonishing range and variation of their music has now captured much broader attention.

To date, the Chieftains have released about thirty albums. They've recorded with Art Garfunkel, Gary Moore, Jackson Browne, Elvis Costello, Ricki Lee Jones, Van Morrison, Ry Cooder, Tom Jones, Mick Jagger and Roger Daltrey. When they performed for Pope John Paul II at Phoenix Park in Dublin in October 1979, they broke all attendance records. As Paddy Maloney, the band's leader, put it, "It was [the Pope's] gig—we were just the opening act."

In 1976 the score of the feature film *Barry Lyndon* (for which the Chieftains were largely responsible) won an Academy Award. The group also composed and performed all the traditional music for *The Grey Fox,* a widely acclaimed film directed by Philip Borsos and starring Richard Farnsworth. For this effort, the Chieftains won the

1983 Genie, and the album from the soundtrack was nominated for a Grammy.

In 1983 the Chieftains first appeared in China on a two-and-a-half-week tour with performances in Beijing, Shanghai and the Heavenly City of Suchow. During this historic tour, the Chieftains became the first Western group to perform on the Great Wall of China. The trip was the subject of a film, *The Chieftains in China,* which had world-wide distribution.

In 1991 and 1992, the prolific Chieftains released *The Chieftains' St. Patrick's Day Album, Reel Music,* a few film scores and *the Bells of Dublin* with, among others, Marianne Faithfull and Elvis Costello. In 1993 they won not one, but two Grammys—for *Another Country,* voted best contemporary folk album and for *An Irish Evening,* which won best traditional folk album. Their 1995 album, *The Long Black Veil,* has also won critical acclaim.

CLUBS AND DISCOS

The **Bridge Hotel** (1 The Quay, 051/77222) has within it both the **Olympus Nightclub,** which offers various types of live music—some mostly generic rock (admission is £4) and **The Stores,** a great bar oozing old-style atmosphere. If you're into karaoke, the bar is definitely where you want to be; big rollicking crowds jam in to sing along with DJ Dermot Power's mixture of '60s, '70s and '80s hits.

SPOTLIGHT ON **ELEANOR MCEVOY**

Ms McEvoy…has the skills of a first-rate songwriter; she gives her songs full-fledged melodies and her lyrics are concise and plain-spoken—emotional snapshots without extraneous detail. She sings with a voice that is forthright and welcoming, from a breathy low register up to a clear mezzo-soprano.

JOHN PARELES, *THE NEW YORK TIMES* (FEBRUARY 12, 1994)

Praise for Eleanor McEvoy has been coming in nonstop—especially since the release of her most recent eponymously titled album, *Eleanor McEvoy*. While her fans have never had any trouble singing her praises, they've often had a hard time pinning down her musical genre. "People who've simply heard 'Only a Woman's Heart' may have expected my next album to be a soft folky thing," says the Dublin-based singer-songwriter-multi-instrumentalist. "But I've made a rock record."

And what a rock record she's made! For starters, it's netted her the Irish National Entertainment Awards' Best New Artist of 1993. *Hot Press,* the noted Irish rock-and-roll magazine, named her Best Solo Performer (over stiff competition that included the venerable Van Morrison), while its Reader's Poll voted her Best Songwriter and placed *Eleanor McEvoy,* which went gold within five months of its release, among the top debut albums of the year.

But let's go back to the song that started it all in the first place—"Only a Woman's Heart," the final word on shattered romance resting on a simple acoustic arrangement. The song initially gained attention as the inspiration for *A Woman's Heart,* a compilation album of Irish female artists which has sold over 250,000 copies in McEvoy's homeland to date (more than any other Irish album in history). But that's not all. *A Woman's Heart* then soared straight into the Top Ten where it stayed for over a year, and the album's namesake and hit single led to McEvoy's winning the Irish Record Industry award for Best New Artist in 1992.

The success of the album cemented McEvoy's place—not only as a local favorite but something of a heroine to the women of Ireland...and their men. So when Geffen A & R executive Tom Zutaut heard her performing it while he was vacationing in Ireland, he signed her on the spot. The result was *Eleanor McEvoy,* her debut solo album.

McEvoy's songs have been noted for their insightful lyrics and haunting sounds. But where does she get the ability to convey such a sense of compassion? "Your ability to sympathize increases in accordance with the amount you've suffered," she answers. McEvoy's songs go beyond the broken-hearted, however. "Life is all about relationships—not just male and female, but parents and children and friends," she says, "and these are the things that move me." Still, listening to her lyrics about ruined romance may lead you to believe that she's got rotten taste in men. "Oh no!" McEvoy laughs. "Most of them have been great guys, really, and some have stayed my best friends."

Eleanor McEvoy Talks About Her Songs

"Only a Woman's Heart": Oh, that one! More than anything, it's about mourning for your dreams. But it describes the kind of depression that a woman will get when a pen rolls off a table and suddenly it makes you cry. For me, if I feel that way, it's worth writing a song about—it exorcises a demon and helps me get over it.

"Apologize": There was this couple I knew; I didn't know them very well, but they had their troubles. The woman never confided in me, but whenever there were flowers in their flat, you knew. She left him after a while, and I felt more sorry for him, because I knew she'd be all right, but I felt he might never get over it.

"Go Now": When you break up with someone, even if it's amicable and you both know it's for the best, there comes a point where you just want him to leave. You're going to cry but you don't want him to see it—your pride is all you have left.

"It's Mine": Again, this is about not intending to get involved but it being inevitable. In the first verse it's the feeling of "here I go again," in the second the neighbors are all talking, wondering about the new romance, in the third you confess that you're so close to falling—you tell him not to be flirting, you can't bear it. But all the choruses say you want to be with him—you want his hands in your hair, a piece of his time—and inside you know you already are.

Metroland (in the Metropole Hotel, 051/78185) has a grab bag of musical offerings: Fridays bring pretty good rock bands followed by disco on a huge dance floor for £5; Saturdays it's reggae, rock and blues until 2 a.m.; Mondays and Tuesdays traditional sessions include dancing for £1. At the same address, you'll find the **Metropole Lounge,** which rocks a little harder than its sister-occupant. Admission here is generally around £5 and usually worth it. The crowd is hip; the atmosphere very smoky.

The Hibernian Hotel in Tramore has disco, rock, traditional and easy listening—seemingly dependent on who walks in the door and offers to perform. Don't bother calling, but go; the atmosphere is a good cross between contemporary and old-style Ireland. You must be over twenty-one. The **Grand Hotel** (Tramore, 051/81414) has musical and cabaret acts—comedy, magic, vocals and impressions—some of them hilarious—on Mondays, Tuesdays, Wednesdays and weekends. A four-course meal and show go for £10.95. For more traditional rock and somewhat younger crowds, head for **Bobby McGee's** (Michael St., 051/73057), or **Rorke's** (O'Connell St., 051/75049). Both feature hard-core rock, rave and heavy metal The admission at both places is £5 or £6.

PUBS AND TRADITIONAL MUSIC

Crokers Bar (The Quay, next door to the Bridge Hotel, 051/77222) has traditional sessions with MC Denny Corcoran on Wednesdays and Thursdays. Admission is either free or £1; this is a great place to sit back and watch professionals work—the acts at Crokers have been playing here for centuries judging from their blend of expertise and familiar banter. **The Old Pike Inn** (Dungarvan, 051/91173) has traditional music and dance sessions on weekends and some weeknights. A good example of an ol' Irish bar, this place has more than its share of resident characters.

The **Long Hall Tavern** (Kilmeaden, 051/84234) is a great place to go when you want to meet people. Trust us; you won't be feelin' like a tourist for more than ten minutes. Be prepared to be taken in hand. There's music on some nights; call before you go. **Harney's Bar** (Dunhill, 051/96154) has great dartplayers as well as traditional-music sessions in the back room on Tuesdays and Sundays.

SPOTLIGHT ON	THE CLANCY BROTHERS AND ROBBIE O'CONNELL

At an age when they could easily ride off into the Irish sunset, The Clancy Brothers and Robbie O'Connell continue to be what they've been for three decades—the most popular force in the Irish entertainment field. Since they first captivated American audiences in their numerous appearances on the Ed Sullivan show in the early '60s, the fabled quartet has continued to weave their magic spell with a blend of music, history, poetry, and wit.

The lineup consists of brothers Pat, Bobby and Liam Clancy and Robbie O'Connell, a nephew who joined the group in 1977. Pat is the eldest and one of a family of four boys and five girls born in Carrick-on-Suir in County Tipperary, Ireland. He emigrated to America in the early '50s where he soon became a major figure in the folk revival blossoming at the time in New York's Greenwich Village. It was Pat who developed the blend of emotion and theme that ultimately made the brothers' "obscure" Irish songs appeal to a mass audience. In the mid-'60s, he bought a farm in Ireland and continues to return there between tours to breed prize cattle and keep a herd of dairy cows.

Bobby has had a varied career as a solo performer, half of a duo with his sister Peg and a member of the Clancy Brothers. In the '60s he had a series on Irish television called "When Bobby Clancy Sings," and it wasn't until 1977 that he permanently joined the Clancy Brothers trio as a singer and instrumentalist playing guitar, banjo, harmonica and bodhran. He still resides in the original family home in Carrick-on-Suir where, between tours, he carries on the family insurance business started by his father.

Liam is the youngest of the original group and, from an early age, displayed an artistic disposition that manifested itself mainly in theater. Before he was twenty, he was producing, directing and designing sets for plays on both sides of the Atlantic. In 1972 after singing with his brothers for over a decade, Liam went solo, basing himself in Calgary and becoming an established TV performer with his own Canadian Emmy-Award-winning series. He rejoined his brothers in 1990, but still manages to perform with other groups and keep his finger in the theatrical pie.

Robbie O'Connell was born in Waterford, Ireland. He began playing guitar and singing at thirteen, and soon became a regular performer in both England and the States. In 1977 he joined the

Clancys and today, in addition to his work with the brothers, he maintains a solo career and has recorded several highly acclaimed records for the Green Linnet Label. The second of these, *The Love of the Land,* was voted the best acoustic album of 1989 and in 1991 he won a prestigious Boston music award as Outstanding Celtic Act and was featured in the highly acclaimed TV series, *Bringing It All Back Home.*

Together, The Clancy Brothers and Robbie O'Connell have carved out a name synonomous with the best in Irish folk songs. As author Pete Hammill once wrote, the group "takes the music, reaches into the past and brings back the true poetry of the Irish heart, its genuine tragedy, its lyric passion, its bawdy pre-Norman humor. They turn their music into art."

The Clancy Brothers and Robbie O'Connell

Admission is usually free. **Bridgie Terrie's** (The Pike, Dungarven, 051/91312) is a steak-and-seafood restaurant as well as a great place to enjoy music (on summer Sundays, it takes place in the beer garden). Wood paneling, attic alcoves, smoke-darkened prints—you get the picture. There's rarely a charge for admission. **T. H. Doolan's** (32 George St., 051/72764) has traditional music and folk sessions on an irregular schedule. Call ahead. **Reginald's** (The Mall, 051/55087) lies within the walls of Reginald's Tower. You'll probably find yourself sitting in some rocky niche with a brew in your hand toasting by a fire, staring in fascination at the plethora of old weapons hanging on the walls and listening to Waterford musicians melody your soul right out of your body. Go!

How sweet the moonlight sleeps upon this bank!

Here we will sit, and let the sounds of music

Creep in our ears; soft stillness, and the night

Become the touches of sweet harmony.

SHAKESPEARE

FESTIVALS

The **Waterford International Festival of Light Opera,** begun more than twenty years ago, takes place during two weeks in mid-September. This is a huge phantasmagoric event (fringe festivals take up any slack) featuring amateur companies from all over the U. K. competing in performances of operetta or light musicals. Every pub in the city has special musical offerings during this time, as do the large hotels. Advance booking is necessary, but tickets are reasonably priced—generally from £3–£10. Call 051/75911, 75437 for ticket information.

The *Fleadh Cheoil na Mumhan* is a traditional festival held during three days in mid-July. Included are set competitions, *ceili mor,* open-air dancing, street sessions, and a general celebration feeling throughout the city. Most events are free, but call the Theatre Royal for complete info., 051/74402.

Just west of Waterford, in the historic town of Lismore, you'll find the **Festival of Early Music,** which takes place in mid-June for three days. Held in various venues throughout the town (St. Mary's Abbey, Lismore Cathedral and St. Carthage's Church), this festival combines outdoor events (during the afternoon, the Galway Early Music Ensemble usually performs in the center of Lismore) with gloriously historic indoor settings, and presents the very best in early-music compositions. Side events include street music and dancing in pubs and on Main Street and the town mall, as well as a festival club where visitors can meet the musicians. While not as large as other festivals, Lismore's Early Music Festival is one of Ireland's most atmospheric and comprehensive events. Advance booking is necessary. Ticket prices range from £6 for individuals to £15 for an all-inclusive-ticket for admission to all concerts and the extensive program book. Contact the West Waterford Festival of Early Music, Heritage Centre, Lismore, County Waterford, Ireland; 058/54975. You can also buy tickets in person (they go on sale June 10) from the Heritage Centre and the Post Office in Lismore.

CORK

Don't be misled by Cork's size; for a relatively small city, it has plenty of music to offer, and it's not all of the paying variety either. From lunchtime concerts to evening events held in the city's many parks, Cork is a great find for those who like their melodies spontaneous and economical. Check with the tourist board for a list of free events, or call the Cork School of Music at 021/965583.

CONCERT HALLS

The **Cork Opera House** (Emmet Place, 021/270022) replaced the old opera house, which burned down in the 1950s. A modern opera house with excellent acoustics, it offers drama, musical comedies, opera, Gilbert and Sullivan, jazz and ballet. Tickets range from £5–£15, and advance booking is necessary for major productions.

The **Triskel Arts Centre** (Tobin St., 021/272022) stages musical events ranging from jazz to art rock to traditional. Productions here are generally of the contemporary bent. Tickets range from £4–£12.

Music appeals not to a class, but to humanity. It gives us not the real, but the ideal.

FRANZ LISZT

CLUBS AND DISCOS

The club scene here is divided into the young and leather-clad crowd, which frequents the more rock- and metal-oriented establishments and the over-twenty-five, smartly dressed folk who congregate in the city's discos and hotels. No matter which option you choose, be prepared for lots of smoke and very lively crowds. Also, Union Quay (opposite the south mall and River Lee) is a particularly hot spot for all kinds of music, including the kind that happens on the street.

Mangan's (16 Carey's Lane, 021/279168) tends toward the young and restless. Acts vary as do prices (expect to pay about £5 admission). Also in this category are **The Pav** (13 Carey's Lane, 021/276330), **Fast Eddy's** (21 Tuckey St., 021/272252), **The Lobby** (Union Quay, 021/311113), **De Lacey House** (Oliver Plunkett St., 021/270074), **Mojo's** (George's Quay, 021/311786) and **Donkey Ears** (Union Quay, 021/967241) where you'd better be dressing with attitude.

Gays and lesbians flock to **Sir Henry's** (Main St., 021/274391), and **Loafers** on Douglas St.

On the gentler side, there's **Zoe's** (16 Oliver Plunkett St., 021/270870) with weekend specials and very hip clientele, **Reardon's Mill** (Washington St., 021/271969), **Oscar's** (Coburg St., 021/501518) and **Roxanne's** (Savoy Centre, 021/274150). All of these charge admissions ranging from £4–£6.

Nancy Spain's (48 Barrack's St.) features blues and country on weekends. There's a £4–£6 cover, which includes a pretty good meal.

And finally, you should check with the hotels for changing programs of cabaret, jazz, and dinner-music events. Try **The Grand Parade Hotel** (54 Grand Parade, 021/274391), the **Silver Springs Hotel** (021/507533) and the **Metropole Hotel** (MacCurtain St., 021/308122), which also contains the most popular jazz venue in town, the **Metropole Tavern.**

| SPOTLIGHT ON | ANDY IRVINE |

If anyone doubts that music is a timeless and universal language, consider the career of Andy Irvine. A twentieth-century artist whose material ranges from Woody Guthrie to the centuries-old music of Ireland and from the music of Eastern Europe to modern compositions, Irvine is a singer, songwriter, and gifted musician with an audience that spans Europe and North America.

Where did Irvine come up with this international blend of musical genres? It started in the late '50s, when he was pursuing an acting career and happened upon the work of Woody Guthrie. Interest sparked, he promptly switched from classical guitar, which he'd been struggling to master along with the acting to folk-style guitar adding harmonica, mandolin, mandola, bouzouki and hurdy-gurdy along the way.

Irvine spent his apprentice years traveling with Ramblin' Jack Elliott and Derroll Adams, playing Dublin's emerging folk scene and honing his talents with trips abroad. In 1966 he formed Sweeney's Men with two other prominent Irishers. The band is still acknowledged as a pivotal force in Ireland's traditional musical renaissance. Irvine recorded two hit singles with Sweeney's Men before his curiosity led him east to the Balkans. When he returned to Ireland eighteen months later, his music had clearly been enriched by a newfound expertise with the rhythms and textures of Eastern European music.

In 1972 Irvine founded Planxty with, among others, the musical giant Christy Moore. One of the most influential groups ever to emerge from Ireland's traditional scene, Planxty soon gained an international following, fueled by superb live performances and a sweep of recorded hits.

Upon the group's disbanding, Irvine, ever the internationalist, tried yet another musical collective—Mosaic—with members from Ireland, Denmark, Holland and Hungary. After one very successful European tour, the band was forced into retirement because of scheduling difficulties.

Patrick Street evolved from Irvine's 1986 tour of the States. The highly successful and internationally renowned "occasional band" has so far made four albums and toured the U. S. annually since 1987—a schedule that sometimes leads Irvine to speculate about the difference between touring in the U. S. and touring in the U. K. "Here you have folk clubs which tend to be upper rooms in pubs," he says. "But back home, you just have the Pub! And the Irish pub is still very much a social center. People don't just stand around facing the telly or the one-arm bandit. They come to talk and drink!"

In the last few years, Irvine has recorded two albums apart from Patrick Street, one an album of Bulgarian and Macedonian music called *East Wind;* the other, his long-awaited solo album *Rude Awakening,* which incorporates traditional Irish music (much of it from Northern Ireland), Irvine's own contemporary songs and Balkan instrumentals.

PUBS AND TRADITIONAL MUSIC

Cork has some of the best pubs in Ireland—many of them on Union Quay. Sessions, however, are sporadic, and you should always call first to make sure something's going on. Like pubs in the rest of Ireland, Cork's rarely charge for music, and if they do, it's usually £1–£2.

Try **An Spailpán F mac** (29 South Main St., 021/277949), which has music sessions every night except Monday and Saturday (on Saturday, they do more contemporary music—sometimes blues, sometimes country). **Canagan's** (24 George's Quay, 021/966240) might initially turn you off, as it's dark and dingy and frequented by seamier sorts. But it has what many others don't—no crowds—and if you fancy listening to an ole Irish reel with honest-to-goodness natives, check this place out. **An Bodhrán** (42 Oliver Plunkett St., 021/274544) is probably the most popular place in town, with regular sessions most nights except Monday and **An Phoenix** (Union Quay, 021/964275) is famed for its authentic decor (read slightly shabby, but genuine).

FESTIVALS

The **Guiness Jazz Festival** is probably one of the most international events in Ireland. Held in October, this event draws top performers (Ella Fitzgerald, Joe Williams, Sonny Rollins) who play along with local and U. K. cats. A host of venues are involved, and most clubs, pubs and hotels present concurrent events. Book early. Tickets (free–£15) sell out way in advance. Contact the Cork Jazz Festival, Metropole Hotel, MacCurtain St., Cork, Ireland; 021/508122.

Summer Revels takes place during August when everybody's ready for some all-out reveling. Held in various venues throughout the town (but mostly in the Cork Opera House), this festival features music, dance, comedy, vaudeville and spontaneous art forms. Tickets range from £6–£16. Contact the box office of the Opera House at 021/270022.

The **Cork International Choral and Folk Dance Festival** features competitive choirs and folk-dance teams from all over the world. Held at the beginning of May, this event spreads itself out over many venues; tickets are generally available, but call as early as you can. Contact City Hall at 021/312296.

Plato says that a change in the songs of musicians can change the state of the commonwealths.

CICERO

COUNTY KERRY

County Kerry is known as "The Kingdom," and a kingdom it surely is, with its surrounding green mountains and blue lakes, its glens and loughs and the coastline of Dingle Bay, its fishing villages, mountains, woods and—above all—its rolling green country. And so it is that you'll find here a royal dose of music of all genres and decibels and enthusiasms. At the top of the list, naturally, is the ever-present traditional-music scene. Locals, in fact, will tell you that there are more musicians here than in any other county in Ireland. A few days in Killarney, the capital city, alone, and you'll for sure be takin' that as God's gospel truth.

CONCERT HALLS

The **Arus Padraig Hall** (Lewis Rd., 064/33516) presents traditional Irish dances during the summer. Dates, times and frequency of presentation vary, so call first. If you can possibly catch one of these performances, do. This is one of Ireland's genuine venues.

The **Siamsa Tire Theatre** (Godfrey Place, Tralee, 066/23055) is Ireland's national folk theater presenting various musical events as well as a regular schedule of *siamsas,* whose goal it is to transport you back to those nostalgic days before fax machines when people used to sit around the fire and play music and sing songs. And to hear the many who have participated over the years, they succeed admirably. Whirlwinds of song, dance and music, these fantastic siamsas are known throughout Ireland as well as in the rest of the international tourist community for their ability to recreate the spirit of zest and camaraderie that existed in less technologically advanced times. Don't miss this! Held from June through September, tickets are £6 for adults and £5 for children.

✪ TEST YOUR MUSICAL I.Q.

Match the following Gaelic words—all culled from standard Irish tunes—to their English counterparts:

1. *nocht*	a) harvest
2. *waesome*	b) might
3. *dowie*	c) know
4. *dee*	d) own
5. *fae*	e) then
6. *hairst*	f) mournful
7. *syne*	g) nothing
8. *micht*	h) woeful
9. *ken*	i) die
10. *ain*	j) from
11. *kye*	k) cattle
12. *hairm*	l) go
13. *fower*	m) child
14. *byres*	n) four
15. *gang*	o) harm
16. *bairn*	p) cowhouse

(Answers on page 304.)

CLUBS AND DISCOS

Most of Kerry's nightlife happens in its pubs. There are, however, a few places where those of a more contemporary bent can go. Killarney's many hotels offer Irish cabaret sessions throughout the summer. Included are **Dunloe Castle** (Beaufort, 064/44111), the **International** (Kenmare Pl., 064/31816), the **Killarney Great Southern** (Station Rd., 064/31262), and **The Gleneagle Hotel** (Killarney, 064/31870), which has a changing roster of musical offerings. Wednesday is dinner, cabaret, and dance and Friday and Saturday in its **Wings Night Club,** you have a good chance of hearing at least disco—maybe even rock. The price of admission to all the above ranges from £5–£15, which usually includes dinner.

Revelles (in the East End Hotel, Killarney, 064/32522) also houses a disco. Over-nineteen crowd only; no jeans. **The Fáilte Bar** (College St., Killarney 064/33404) is a popular pub with an irregular schedule of pretty good rock. **Picasso's** (10 College St., Killarney, 064/31329) has good food and a resident jazz pianist in the evenings. And for country-and-western fans, there's **Fiddler's Green Inn** (Cork Rd., Killarney, 064/33388).

Outside Killarney, check out **Flamingo's Bar & Restaurant** in Abbeyfeale, which has Saturday night disco for £4 and Sunday night rock for £5. The **Tropic Nite Club** in the **Banana Beach Hotel,** Tralee, offers disco Saturday and Sunday nights and Sunday afternoons. **Club Berliners** in **Horan's Hotel** in Tralee has rock Friday and Sunday and free cabaret Tuesday, Wednesday, and Saturday. **Spiral's Nite Club** in **The Brandon Hotel** in Tralee has disco dancing Wednesday, Friday, and Sunday.

The **Central Hotel** (Main St., Ballybunion) offers live ballad and country music every night for a £4 admission. The **Atlantic Hotel** in Ballybunion features disco every night and special live acts on Saturdays.

PUBS AND TRADITIONAL MUSIC

Most of Kerry's pubs are crammed with tourists and proprietors do whatever they need to do to lure even more people through the door. That doesn't mean the charm's not there—just that you'll have to share it with hordes of other people. But the effort is worthwhile, if only because the music sessions are usually wonderful and include polkas, slides, jigs and reels.

One of the best is **McElligott's Bar** (Ardfert, 066/34444) with its resident crew of musicians and dark, smoke-painted atmosphere. Also try **O'Flaherty's Bar** (Ardfert, 066/34138), which also has a beer garden. **Laurel's** (Main St., Killarney, 064/31149), **Danny Mann Inn** (97 New St., Killarney, 064/31640), **Dunloe Lodge** (Punkett St., Killarney, 064/32502) and **Scruffy's** (College St., Killarney, 064/31038) are all very popular—read crowded. Good music sessions, though.

One not-to-be-missed pub is **Dan O'Connell's** (Knocknagree [NW Cork], 064/56238) where disciples of the great fiddler Padraig O'Keefe have been delighting the crowds for decades.

Others to try include **The Dingle Pub** (Dingle, 066/51370), **Sheehan's Bar** (Knocknagree, 064/56143); the **An Tochar Bar** (Kilmoyley, 066/33088), where you have a good chance of encountering locals including grandmothers and winos; and the **Ballybunion Golf Hotel** (Ballybunion, 068/27111), which is sometimes graced by one of the town's famous residents—the prolific composer and piper Liam O'Sullivan.

MUSICAL MOMENTS   *Who Really Discovered America?*

The question has been asked for centuries: was it Columbus in 1492 or Leif Ericsson in the year 1000? *Or* was it an Irishman in the year 500?

According to Irish legend, St. Brendan, the Abbot of Clonfert, set sail with a band of fellow missionaries aboard a skin-covered boat, or *currach,* to discover the "Land promised to the saints." Was that America? Many early explorers believed it was; many of the places mentioned in the Brendan legend appear in some of the ancient charts that guided explorers over the western horizon.

St. Brendan's voyage lasted seven years, and its story was related some years afterward in one of the world's earliest books, *The Voyage of St. Brendan the Abbot.* Tim Severin, a scholar in the history of exploration, found a curious element of truth in the ancient book—an element that set him to researching all the references he could find on ancient Irish voyages and St. Brendan.

Ultimately, he decided to test the legend and embarked on what he describes as a piece of experimental archaeology. He built a currach in the ancient way, named the boat *Brendan*, and on May 17, 1976, set sail from Brandon Creek, County Kerry, on the first leg of a journey to Newfoundland. The resulting voyage, documented by Severin in a book, remains one of the most extraordinary and fascinating historical reconstructions ever attempted.

When Shaun Davey, the young Irish composer, read the book, his imagination was completely captured by Severin's courage and determination. With the author's permission, he used the narrative account of the journey as the basis for a series of orchestral pieces for Uillean pipes. He called it *The Brendan Suite*, after *The Brendan Voyage*, the title of Severin's book.

The suite is a musical narrative of the voyage, divided into ten sections, each representing an adventure on the boat. Starting in a small harbor in Kerry, the suite (with the Uillean pipes representing the boat) follows the journey through the Faroes, to the Cliffs of Mykines, to Iceland and finally to Newfoundland.

The Brendan Suite has been performed in Kilkenny; Galway; Derry; at the Queen's Festival in Belfast; in London at the Royal Festival Hall (where the composer included a special guest part for guitar virtuoso John Williams) and at the Royal Albert Hall. Outside the U. K. the suite has been on the bill in Canada with the Quebec Symphony Orchestra; in Rennes and Lorient, France; in Sydney, Australia; in Munich, Germany; and in New York where it was recorded for broadcast by National Public Radio.

Liam O'Flynn plays the Uillean pipes in the recorded performance of *The Brendan Suite* (on Tara Records). One of the world's greatest pipers, O'Flynn is recognized in his native Ireland as the unrivaled successor to the late, great Seamus Ennis, who bequeathed his favorite ex-pupil, O'Flynn, his set of pipes.

Liam O'Flynn

Shaun Davey, the composer of *The Brendan Suite,* has reached the stage in his career at which, in addition to theatrical commissions, he is also in great demand for concert commissions. *The Brendan Suite* is one of these and by his own description has been the high point of his professional life so far.

Bailey's Corner in Tralee (066/26230) is known for its magnificent music sessions, as is **Ceolann,** located in the village of Lixnaw, between Tralee and Listowel (066/32323).

FESTIVALS

The most riotous festival (certainly in all of Ireland, maybe even in all the world) is **Puck's Fair,** which takes place during three let-it-all-hang-loose days in August. The pubs stay open for the *entire* event—seventy-two hours straight! Musicians, singers and dancers perform; venues are indoors and out and wherever else anybody can think of cramming an event. If you only have time to attend one festival while in Ireland, this would be a strong contender. For info, contact the Killarney Tourist Board, Town Hall, Main St., Killarney, Ireland; 064/31633.

Listowel Writer's Week is held during late May or early June in the town of Listowel, north of Tralee. Contrary to the image conveyed by its name, this is a multi-arts festival with musicians, dancers, singers and ongoing pub events enhancing the drama, poetry and fiction sessions. For information, contact Secretary, Listowel Writer's Week, POB 147, Listowel, County Kerry, Ireland; 068/21074.

Pan-Celtic Week features plenty of music, song and dance as Kerry welcomes back its Celtic ancestors—Scots, Welsh, Bretons and Basques—to celebrate the diversity of its heritage. People come from all over the U. K., and advance reservations are necessary for the main events. The event is held in April or May at various venues. Contact the Killarney Tourist Board at 064/31633.

The Rose of Tralee International Festival is, in theory, a beauty contest, as women come from all over the world to compete for the honor of becoming the next "Rose of Tralee" (remember the Rose of Tralee sung by tenor John McCormack: "she was lovely and fair, like a rose of the summer, Yet it was not her beauty alone that won me, O no it was the truth in her eyes ever dawning, that made me love Mary, the Rose of Tralee"). But it's a lot more than a beauty contest. Fireworks, street festivals, concerts, band recitals, traditional music and cabaret are included—whatever can fit into five days at the end of August. This festival is very large—over ninety thousand people attended in 1993. Tickets to most events are free, but if you're going to a concert or a big-name performance, expect to pay around £8. Contact the Festival of Kerry, 5 Lower Castle St., Tralee, County Kerry, Ireland; 066/21322.

SPOTLIGHT ON JOHN MCCORMACK: THE GREATEST IRISH TENOR

John McCormack (1884–1945) was perhaps the most famous tenor in Irish history. His popularity as a concert artist was almost unrivaled and enabled him to amass a lifetime fortune of over one million dollars. McCormack commanded a light, clear voice and sang with perfect diction as well as with great vocal finesse. He sang with equal eloquence both airs of the 1700s and Irish ballads.

McCormack began his career at the age of eighteen by winning a gold medal at the National Irish Festival in Dublin. In 1907 he made his operatic debut, performing in *Cavalleria Rusticana* at London's Covent Garden. He appeared at the Manhattan Opera House in *La Traviata* in 1909. He also sang with the Chicago and Boston opera companies and the Metropolitan Opera Company. In 1911 he toured Australia with Nellie Melba doing Italian opera.

McCormack abandoned opera in 1913 in favor of concerts. Although born in Athlone, Ireland, he became a U. S. citizen in 1917. In his later years he returned to live in a small village near Dublin and died there on September 16, 1945.

COUNTIES GALWAY AND CLARE

If you've been traveling a while through Ireland and concluded that you must surely, by this point, have experienced all there is to see and hear of Irish music, think again. The country's west coast—specifically counties Galway and Clare—is *the* capital of Irish music, the place where old and young come together in a lifelong love affair with all things musical and where—regardless of jobs and closing times and quality of voice—the music is all.

Music on Ireland's west coast—especially on the Connemara coast—is not so much about instruments as about songs, which are sung in the *seán nos* style, without accompaniment, heavily frilled and in Irish. This is the land of Willie Clancy, the great Irish piper; Gus O'Connor, the Doolin innkeeper; and Micho Russell, the tin whistler who, until his death in 1994, played nightly in the simple centuries-old style he'd learned over sixty years before. This is the land of festivals—big sprawling events lasting endless days and nights during which it seems everybody has a song and the streets are awash with revelers. This is also where you'll find the rocky promontories of Irish-speaking Connemara where music is a way of life and each family has its own performers and set performances. Don't be surprised if, as you're negotiating the winding roads of Connemara's coastline, you see men, women and children sitting out in front of stone houses singing and dancing in the middle of the day.

This is also the home of Doolin which—if the west coast were ever to elect a musical capital—would surely be it. A small village with few sidewalks and even fewer pretensions, Doolin's claim to fame—outside of its gentle beauty—is its sheer love of all things musical. Irish music reeks from every square inch here—whether in a pub, a street corner or a quiet country lane. If you have only one side trip to make on your tour of major places, this tiny gem should be it.

Ultimately, what it all comes down to is that you should not come to the west coast if the music you're seeking is rock or disco or a quiet jazz piano in a mauve lounge where people gaze into each other's eyes and murmur sweet nothings. If you come here—and you must come here if you're serious about music—you're coming for the ebullience of the music—for the trance of the melodies and the euphoria of the crowd at being so near "the voice of the heavens."

All that having been said, however, remember that "legal" closing times are 11:30 p.m. in summer, 11 p.m. in winter, although most hotels go until dawn and late-night clubs stay open (legally or illegally) until the music does down.

CONCERT HALLS

Even when it comes to concert halls, Western Ireland's venues deal mainly in traditional Irish fare. **The Arts Centre** (47 Dominick St. and 23 Nun's Island, Galway; no phone inquiries) offers a changing year-round program of theater, music, literature and visual arts. The musical events range from opera to traditional music and siamsas. Ticket prices range from £4–£15.

A lunchtime performance

The Druid Theatre Company (Chapel Lane, Galway, 091/68617) stages traditional and contemporary performances at lunchtime and in the evening. Tickets range from £5–£20, and schedules change frequently. The Irish-language theater, **Siamsa na Gaillimhe–Taibhdhearc Theatre** (Middle St., Galway, 091/63600, 755479, 62024) offers Irish music, singing, dancing and folk drama performed by a resident company of eighteen talented, energetic virtuosos who mime so expertly that it makes no difference whether or not you know the language. Performances are Monday through Friday at 8:45 p.m. from July through August. Tickets range from £3–£12.

SPOTLIGHT ON   RITA CONNOLLY

Some think of Rita Connolly solely as the interpreter of *Granuaile*, the symphonic work composed for her by Shaun Davey. Others associate her primarily with traditional music. All agree, however, that Rita Connolly is one of the great treasures of Irish music. An immensely gifted and evocative singer, Rita has performed before enthusiastic audiences in the U. S., France, Germany and England. Her most recent album, *Rita Connolly*, includes songs from the blues, soul, reggae, country and rock traditions and shows off a voice that copes beautifully with whatever it undertakes to tackle.

Rita Connolly

CLUBS AND DISCOS

While there are few *real* clubs in Galway and Clare, most of the hotels offer late-night entertainment. In Salthill there's **Murray's Piano Bar** in the **Hotel Salthill** (Center of the Promenade, Galway, 091/22448, 22711) offering varied entertainment nightly at 9:30. The **Atlanta Hotel** (Dominick St., Galway, 091/62241) also has a varied program—mostly jazz and easy listening. Ditto for the **Imperial Hotel** (Eyre Square, Galway, 091/63033) and the **American Hotel** (Eyre Square, Galway, 091/61300).

The **Skeffington Arms Hotel** (Eyre Square, Galway, 091/63173, 4, 5) has traditional music on Thursdays and Sunday nights and disco in the nightclub on weekends. The **Galway Ryan Hotel** (Dublin Rd., Galway, 091/753181) has entertainment nightly in the lounge during the summer season. **Bentley's** (Eyre Square, Galway, 091/755093) has two levels—rock downstairs, disco upstairs. The music on both levels is generic and soft. Whole meals are under £10, and the crowd is a blend of age groups drawn to this heavily advertised, standard-issue venue.

The **Blue Note** (3 William St. West, Galway, 091/589081) was named for the jazz record label, which gives you a good idea of its musical preference. The club attracts a twenty-something crowd and is casual and groovy with low light and an enclosed porch. The cover is £2–£3.

Sally Long's (Upper Abbey Gate St., Galway, 091/65756) has rock and heavy metal on Thursday and even heavier rock on weekends. There's a biker and young rocker crowd enjoying the pool table, pinball and biker photos. But—surprise of surprises—the crowd is as gentle as a lamb. Admission is £2.

Central Park Nightclub in **Brannagan's Restaurant** (36 Upper Abbeygate St., Galway, 091/65974) offers house and funk on weekends, country and western on Wednesday. Admission ranges from £3–£5. The club attracts a casual, mixed (twenties and thirties) crowd.

PUBS AND TRADITIONAL MUSIC

Let's begin the tour with the best first, the three big Doolin pubs that give the village its reputation as a place to have great "craic" (fun). The first is **Gus O'Connor's** (Doolin, Clare, 065/74168), a legendary pub run by a legendary family (one of the better legends is that Dylan Thomas married an O'Connor). Established in 1832, the family scion now at the helm is Sean O'Connor, who requires very little prodding to launch into a hysterical/historical overview of both Doolin and the O'Connor dynasty. Worth a trip purely for the array of artifacts crammed into its four walls (lobster pots hang from the ceiling, bicycles decorate the walls), O'Connor's is a must for music lovers. The music here is so much a part of the place that, until his death in February 1994, Micho Russell, the great Irish whistler, could still be seen playing in the same corner he'd occupied for over sixty years. O'Connor's attracts hordes of tourists; fewer in the afternoons when the place tends to fill with locals—but there's no music then.

The second in the triumverate is **MacDermott's** (Doolin, 065/74328) with its green-and-white walls, low wooden ceilings and atmosphere to spare. Also started in the 1800s, MacDermott's draws a more local crowd than O'Connor's and sponsors traditional music sessions from 9:30 p.m.–11:30 p.m. nightly.

SPOTLIGHT ON   GUS O'CONNOR

"I was literally born into this pub which has been owned by the O'Connors since 1832. Originally the landlords were McNamaras, and despite the legend going around that Dylan Thomas married an O'Connor, it was really a McNamara who married that great man.

"There are six of us here now: me, my wife, Doll, and our four kids, Sean, Noel, Susan and Terry. Sean pretty much runs the place, and doing a nice job of it too.

"What amazes me the most nowadays is how popular Irish music has become around the world. It wasn't always that way—it wasn't that way even in 1957 when tourism started picking up and we started to get a feel for how Ireland was being seen in other places. I guess a lot of the change has to do with how many of us moved out over the years and the fact that, wherever we go, we spread our melodies. But a lot of the emigrants are starting to return—especially the Americans. And when they get here, they love a good Irish session as much as anybody. The piping, the flutes, the concertina, whistles, accordian—they love it all!"

Gus O'Connor's Doolin pub

McGanus (Doolin, 065/74133) is possibly the least touristy of the three pubs. Not, however, for lack of either atmosphere or great musical sessions. In some ways, in fact, this is the best of the three with lively, friendly crowds, good food (try the veggie special for £4) and spontaneous music.

SPOTLIGHT ON | SHARON SHANNON

Sharon Shannon's version of traditional Irish music wears a broad grin and a hat set at a rakish angle. Hers is a unique achievement in a musical field long known for its serious intellectualism: almost singlehandedly, this twenty-four-year-old fiddle and accordian player has brought down to earth this mystical music called "Irish trad" and made it something to have fun by and with. In just five short years, Shannon has achieved what many once regarded as impossible: making Irish traditional accordian playing appeal to pop and rock audiences without losing contact with her roots.

Her involvement with traditional music began—where else—at home with her family. "My parents got us all started," she explains.

"They were really interested in music—they're set dancers themselves. There's four of us in the family—my brother Gary, my older sister Majella, myself and my younger sister Mary.

"We were," she says definitely, "*mad* for music. My parents and all the neighbors were very encouraging. Then there was a man called Frank Custy whose daughter, Mary, is a very fine fiddle player, who was a great music teacher. He used to run ceilidhs in Toonagh—that's a village near where my parents come from—and every Friday night we used all go over there. 'Twas the thing we most looked forward to all week."

Was her decision to play music full-time thought out—or did she just happen into it? "Well, I didn't *decide,*" she confesses. "I never knew what I wanted to do for a living. Even when I was going to school I was doing gigs, and when I finished with school I realized that I was able to get by with just the gigs. I really enjoyed it."

This off-the-cuff modesty obscures the fact that from an early age Shannon displayed an extraordinary musical talent and that by the age of ten she was playing tin whistle with top local musicians. While still in her teens, well-known British director Jim Sheridan invited Shannon to produce the music for the Druid Theatre's acclaimed touring production of Brendan Behan's *The Hostage*. She later joined the traditional group Arcady and in 1989, while recording her debut album in Kinarva, County Galway, she came to the attention of Mike Scott, the head of the prestigious Waterboys, who asked her to join his heavily traditionally influenced band. Shannon accepted and for the next eighteen months, toured with Scott and his merry band, eventually recording the album *Room to Room* with them. In 1991 the Waterboys split, and Shannon decided to get back to finishing her own album, which ultimately became *Sharon Shannon*.

In 1992 Shannon contributed two instrumental tunes to a compilation album titled *A Woman's Heart* (also featuring trad musical stars Frances Black, Maura O'Connell, Dolores Keane, Eleanor McEvoy and Mary Black), which quickly became the biggest-selling album of the year.

In December of that same year the shy young accordianist was honored when Gay Byrne, the host of the extremely popular *Late Late Show* on British TV, devoted a two-hour music special to her, featuring practically all the musicians she had ever played with in her short career. From that moment until now, life for Sharon Shannon has been a nonstop series of headliners and record-breaking tours.

Although she is first and foremost a player of Irish dance tunes, part of Shannon's appeal is her exploration of a wide variety of Celtic and other ethnic music. Only a handful of her repertoire is made up of old-fashioned traditional Irish tunes. Much of the rest is a survey of world music, including pieces from Quebec, Portugal, the American South, Cape Breton Island and Scotland.

The biggest key to Shannon's popularity is her playing. Although a more-than-respected fiddler, she is an extraordinary button accordianist. Still in her early twenties, she has become a celebrated musician with her own distinctive and highly influential sound. All over Ireland, young accordian players are busily copying her patented single-note triplets and retuning their instruments to approximate the clean, concertinalike tone she gets from her pint-sized Castagnari "box."

Fiddlers, flute players and other instrumentalists have also fallen under Shannon's spell; her swinging rhythms and distinctive repertoire are increasingly infiltrating Irish music sessions from Sligo to San Francisco.

Moving back to Galway, there's **The Forster Bar** (Forster St., Galway, 091/64924, 68293) where you can hear music and participate in sing-alongs every Friday and Saturday. **The Lisheen Bar** (5 Bridge St., Galway, 091/63804) has traditional music seven nights a week including a Sunday morning session (music here is equal to religion). **O'Flaherty's** (15 Eyre Square in the Great Southern Hotel, Galway, 091/22672) has carvery lunches (meat carved off the bone), a salad bar and great traditional music Thursday to Saturday.

The **Hotel Sacre Coeur** (Salthill, Galway, 091/23355) has sing-alongs nightly in July and August. And **The Hole in the Wall** (Eyre St., Galway, 091/65593) has a nice, authentic decor—a thatched roof out front, hanging plants and old wood—but its taped traditional music is often too loud. Sometimes the music is live, though. Check. **Paddy's** (Eyre St., Galway, 091/62240) specializes in American and Irish country music seven nights a week. Though its touristy and a little tacky, where else are you going to get this type of musical specialty? **Taaffe's Bar** (19 Shop St., Galway, 091/62905) has traditional music seven nights a week and a very casual, over-thirty crowd. Sessions go from 9:30 p.m.–11:30 p.m.

FESTIVALS

The biggie in the area is the **Galway Arts Festival,** which runs for twelve days in mid-July. Now in its eighteenth year, this hugely popular event features theater, street spectacles, music, film, exhibitions and children's events. Many of the shows take place in marquees and other temporary venues throughout the city. The festival includes more than three hundred fifty performers and events. Advance reservations are necessary for the more important venues. Contact Fergal McGrath, Festival Coordinator, Galway Arts Festival, 6 Upper Dominick St., Galway, Ireland; 091/63800.

SPOTLIGHT ON PATRICK BALL: MASTER HARPIST

For many years, the Celtic harp with its unique resonance and clear, bell-like sound, was an important part of Celtic life, especially in Ireland and in France's Celtic province, Brittany. The harp originated a thousand years ago in ancient Ireland, and shone through the age of the bards, bringing hope during long years of occupation and oppression.

But the Celtic harp is a challenging instrument to play well, and nearly two centuries ago, the wire-strung Celtic harp was abandoned in favor of the easier-to-play, more subdued gut-strung, "neo-Irish" harp. The few harps that *did* survive did so as museum pieces, and the incredibly large and varied Celtic-harp repertoire began to sink into obscurity. But for Patrick Ball, it was unthinkable to let that sweet voice fall silent.

Following in the Irish tradition, Ball is not only a harpist, but a gifted storyteller. He has recorded traditional songs from Ireland,

Scotland, Wales, the Isle of Man, Brittany, Belgium and England and even contemporary works written in traditional style for Celtic harp.

In keeping with his regard for historical accuracy, Ball plays a harp strung with brass wires, which he picks with his fingernails in the old style. In contrast to the nylon strings used by most current harpers, these metal strings produce a distinctive crystalline sound.

Patrick Ball insists that he didn't set out to become a harp player, but chose Celtic harp as a way to accompany the folk tales he told. He majored in history at the University of California with an eye toward following the family profession of law. But, somewhere along the way, he got sidetracked and wound up as the groundskeeper at a crafts school in Tennessee's Blue Ridge Mountains. There he fell in love with the colorful folklore and dialect of the Appalachian people.

Back in California, Ball fell in love again—this time with a Celtic harp he saw at a renaissance faire. For a time he took lessons, but eventually came to rely on self-teaching. He has made a particular study of the tunes of Turlough O'Carolan, the eighteenth-century blind harper who traveled the Irish countryside composing tunes for the modest and great, who, in turn, provided him with shelter and clothing.

Ball returns to Ireland often to research material for his concerts and constantly strives to blend the music and stories into a seamless performance. His latest recording, *Fiona,* is something of a departure for him, as only one O'Carolan piece is included. The rest of the material is traditional Irish, Scottish and Breton tunes. For the first time, Ball has used Uillean pipe, pennywhistle (played by Tim Britton) and fiddle (played by Kevin Carr) accompaniment. He is currently at work on a long-requested album of stories.

The International Pan-Celtic Festival takes place in Galway in mid-April, and serves as a kind of reunion for Celts from all over the U. K. Music, song, and dance. Contact Marie at 091/68876. The **Oyster Festival** *(Aras Fáilte)* is a great big splash of an event featuring—besides Galway oysters—music and song in the "Oyster Trail Pubs," which are just about all the pubs in Galway. The idea is that you go from one to the other, eating, merrymaking and washing it all down with a hefty dose of Guinness. The Oyster Festival takes place in mid-September when the oysters are at their best. Contact Ann Flanagan, Galway Oyster Festival, Galway, Ireland; 091/27282, 22066, 63081.

The **Salthill Festival** takes place in early July and lasts for eight days. This is a family festival of free open-air concerts and children's activities. Performers range from country and western to traditional to soft rock. If you want to experience a true local event, catch this one. For more info, call the festival office at 091/28700. The *Fleadh Mor* is an open-air festival of music and dance that takes place during one weekend in early July. An Irish-language event, this Galway County fair draws people from all over the U. K. Previous performers have ranged from Bob Dylan to Elvis Costello to Altan. Tickets are available at HMV outlets, or call 1550/122344.

The **Busking Festival** comes to Galway in July or August filling the city with street performers of all stripes. If you think there couldn't be any more street musicians than you already see on Galway's streets at other times of the year, visit the city during this festival. It's terrific fun and all free. Contact the Galway City Tourist Information at 091/63081. The *Fleadh Nua* is a late-May festival of music and dance in Ennis, County Clare, which pretty much takes over the town for its duration. Featured are Irish musicians, dancers, and singers—both local and from other counties. Contact Minnie Baker, Fleadh Nua Office, Crusheen, County Clare, Ireland; 065/27115.

The **Clifden Community Arts Week** is celebrated the last week in September and encompasses arts from photography to modern dance to tin whistling. Set in a gorgeous little niche of a village in the Connemara countryside, this festival seems to draw a goodly percentage of cream-of-the-crop performers. Various venues are involved and the whole town participates in the planning and execution of the festival, which results in a fine blend of local color and professional performances. Contact Brendan Flynn, Clifden Community School, Clifden, County Galway, Ireland; 095/21184.

SPOTLIGHT ON   ALTAN

"Let's cut to the chase: Altan is the best traditional band now active on either side of the Atlantic." Earle Hitchner, writing in *The Irish Voice*, echoes critics throughout Europe and America in praising the

Irish sextet. The group is clearly one of Ireland's most critically acclaimed and commercially successful traditional bands.

Individually, the members of Altan are masters of their respective instruments. Collectively, they are considered one of the most exciting groups in contemporary traditional music, combining technical brilliance with emotional depth. Altan features the angelic voice of Mairead Ni Mhaonaigh, singing in both her native Gaelic and in English; the blistering duo-fiddle attack of Mairead and Ciaran Tourish; and the sensitive flute playing of Frankie Kennedy—all backed by one of the best traditional rhythm sections in the business—Ciaran Curran on bouzouki and Danny Sproule on guitar. The newest Altan member is the young accordian player, Dermot Byrne, who is already marked as one of Ireland's top players.

The source and inspiration for most of Altan's music is firmly based in the tradition of Donegal in the northwest corner of Ireland. Donegal's history evolves from a people isolated by political borders and with a history of emigration, mostly to Scotland.

The music is comprised of jigs, reels, polkas and hornpipes as in the rest of Ireland, but the Donegal style borrows from the Scottish tradition and makes it its own. Nowadays, the rhythmic drive of Scottish Highlands and Strathspey are played alongside mazurkas (tunes of Polish origin, still being danced to in Donegal), along with a myriad of unusual pieces that were played by older musicians and passed on to the younger generations. Six members of that younger generation are in Altan, and they do an exceptionally fine job of preserving that music.

MISCELLANEOUS

Although there are a few music-tour operators in Ireland, we recommend **Green Music Tours** for its comprehensive knowledge and sheer love of Irish traditional music—especially that of western Ireland. The approach here is a holistic one which, in this case, means that a variety of influences are incorporated into your music education. This is not just about going places and listening to music; it's about understanding the variety of factors that affect the music's origin and appeal—the history of western Ireland's countryside for example, and how it affects the culture and sound of the music. Typical features of a Green tour are lectures (the culture of the saisán in Irish music and the bringing together of different people to form a spontaneous musical moment); visits to music, dancing and singing *saisán*; the opportunity to learn a dance or a song; and meetings with *saisán* musicians. One incomparable feature of this company is that they deal with small groups (no more than fourteen) only. "You could fit 50 people on a bus," says owner Bill Green (a Clare fiddler himself), "but it's too big, too impersonal. You can't form a relationship with the people, and if you can't form a relationship, then you're not really getting them involved in the music—they might as well be sitting in a classroom somewhere, learning from a book." Prices run about £80 per week without accommodations although Green can arrange accommodations to fit various budgets. Contact Green Music Tours, 66 Finian Park, Shannon, County Clare, Ireland; 061/360858.

The **Willie Clancy Summer School** (*Scoil Samhraidh*) is one of the most prestigious events in all of Ireland. Founded by followers of

---

FLASHBACK | **IRISH MUSIC AND A TRIP TO COUNTY CLARE**

Americans who come to Ireland generally accept that "Wild Irish Rose" and "Molly Malone" are *it* musically. They don't know anything else. Once you get there, though, and hear the real stuff, you realize how deluded you've been. The tin whistle—God, how I love that!

One thing I learned on my trip was that Irish folklore is where Irish traditional music comes from—the songs are stories, and the more they're sung, the more you develop stories behind the songs, and the whole thing takes on a kind of snowball effect.

The Chieftains were the ones who introduced me to Irish music. Once I heard them, I knew I'd been missing out on a lot musically. That's what spurred me to make that trip in the first place. Wow, what a turn-on it was when I realized I could walk into most pubs and hear Irish music that was generally better than any I'd heard on tape back home.

JOHN, BROOKLYN

Clancy, the great Irish piper, the school is held in Milltown Malbay in County Clare during eight days in early July. All types of musicians, but particularly pipers, come together to take part in classes on such things as set dancing, traditional singing, fiddle classes and button accordian classes. The week includes a musical tribute at Willie Clancy's grave and a series of recitals ending with a piping recital featuring pipers selected by members of the national piping federation. While you have little or no chance of getting in unless you're really accomplished in some aspect of music, you can hang out in Milltown Malbay, a beautiful coastal village south of Doolin, during this time and take advantage of the resident musicians who, in their off hours, head for the pubs to talk, drink and jam. This is *the* event in Milltown Malbay—the whole town focuses on the music.

If you've come to western Ireland and fallen in love with the music (and who *wouldn't?*), then you should think about visiting one or more of the area's many music stores so you can sample (and maybe even take home) the sounds of the local musicians.

One particularly good store is Doolin's **Traditional Music Shop** (065/74407) where proprietors Noirin and Harry Hamilton (Harry is originally from Vermont) will be glad to show you their stock of local music not generally available elsewhere. You can sample the music here and, if you have time, peruse one of their many books of musical history to find out something about the music's background. The store itself is worth seeing—in the 1850s it was a casting shop, and it still maintains that old-time, simple-laborer feel.

You might also want to take in a musical instrument store, the better to see and touch the instruments that make the glorious sound you've been hearing all around town (the voices, you'll have to simulate yourself). One good one is **Roundstone Musical Instruments** (I. D. A. Craft Centre, Roundstone, Connemara; 095/35808), which specializes in genuine goatskin and beech bodhrans. Also in stock are two-part "pocket whistles," rolled and tapered tin whistles, ebony flutes, music books, bodhran videos, harps and any other traditional Irish instrument you can think of. The shop stays open seven days a week from 9 a.m. to 7 p.m.

FESTIVALS IN NEIGHBORING COUNTIES

The **Castlebar Blues Festival** takes place during one weekend in early June in County Mayo. Fifteen bands play in various pubs and clubs in Castlebar during this well-attended event. For more info, contact Pat Jennings, festival coordinator at 094/23111.

Also in County Mayo is the *Ceol na Mart,* traditional nights of Irish music, song and dance followed by ceile more. It takes place in the Castlecourt Hotel in Westport every Wednesday night at 9 during August. Call Mrs. P. Kelly at 098/25205. The **Westport Street Festival** (County Mayo) is forty days of free street concerts, street theater, sporting and children's events. It runs from mid-July to late August. Contact Dermot Langen at 098/35178.

County Wicklow piper, with his pint

The **Boyle Arts Festival** (County Roscommon) is a major exhibition of contemporary Irish art, musical concerts, jazz and traditional Irish evenings held during twelve days in late July and early August. Venues range from the King House, a magnificent Palladian-style building, which has recently been restored, to Maloney's Bar on Patrick Street, to the Church of Ireland with its breathtaking acoustics. Tickets (free–£20) go on sale in mid-July and advance booking is essential. Contact the Festival Office, Heran's, St. Patrick St., Boyle, Ireland; 079/63085.

SPOTLIGHT ON   TURLOUGH O'CAROLAN

Turlough (Terence) O'Carolan (1670–1738) was one of the last Irish harper-composers and the only one whose songs survive in both words and music in any significant number.

O'Carolan was born in 1670 near Nobber in County Meath, Ireland, and in 1684 the family moved to Ballyfarnon in County Roscommon, where O'Carolan's father found a job in the iron foundry of Henry MacDermott Roe. MacDermott Roe's wife was responsible for O'Carolan's early education, but when he went blind from smallpox at the age of eighteen, she apprenticed him to a harper and maintained him for three years. When his apprenticeship was complete, she provided him with money, a guide and a horse.

As an itinerant harper, O'Carolan traveled widely in Ireland, enjoying a considerable reputation as an extraordinary songwriter and composer of extemporaneous verse, eventually emerging as one of the most famous of the Irish bards.

By the time he died in 1738, he had composed over two hundred songs, of which about one hundred were published in the 1700s. An edition of his verse was brought out in 1916, and his most famous interpreter today is Patrick Ball, whose goal is to record all of O'Carolan's later works.

During ten days in late July and early August, County Roscommon plays host to the **O'Carolan Harp and Traditional Music Festival.** Held in the small, impeccably groomed town of

Keadue, this is a festival of harp recitals, music, dance and ceilidhs. The culminating event is a harp competition, which carries a hefty cash prize. Advance booking is necessary—especially for the competition. Tickets range from £5–£14. Contact Padraic Noone at 078/ 47204.

SLIGO

Sligo is the capital of Yeats country—it's where the noted poet wrote many of his most famous odes and where you'll find his grave four miles north of town in Drumcliff. It's also a happening place musically, especially in the summer when students of all ages gather at Yeats's summer school and the town's eighty-odd pubs and discos fill to overflowing with music lovers of all ages and persuasions. Here in the northwest, the genre is flutes and fiddles, and on any given night you'll find some of Ireland's best saisán fiddlers twanging away in the pubs in and around Sligo.

Most of the action takes place in pubs and discos. One place you might want to try for larger-venue performances is the **Hawk's Well Theatre** (Temple St., 071/61518, 61526), which is used mainly for theater but sometimes presents a variety of musical events, among them, *seo cheoil,* evenings of traditional Irish music, dance, and storytelling sponsored by Comhaltas Ceoltoiri Eireann, Ireland's premier cultural association. Seo cheoil are generally offered every Monday in July and at various other times. Call for information. Ticket prices go from £5–up.

SPOTLIGHT ON ENYA: A CATHEDRAL OF SOUND

Born in Donegal County, one of the last bastions of the Gaelic language in Ireland, Enya's grandfather was a schoolteacher from the tiny island of Tory. She changed her given name, Eithne Ni Bhraonain, to Enya, the name of a local Tory goddess.

Enya started by playing assorted keyboards and singing on Clannad's fifth album, *Crann Ull.* But it wasn't until the 1982 album, *Fuaim,* that the youngest sister of Gweedore's most famous musical family got proper billing as a full member of the group.

Enya (seated left) and Clannad

By that time, tensions between Enya and the rest of the Clannad clan were beginning to build. Clannad wanted a new manager, David Kavanaugh, but Enya was quite happy with the old Dublin team of Nicky Ryan and his wife, Roma. So she left and changed her name to Enya. And the rest is the stuff of legend.

With her 1988 debut album, *Watermark,* the music of Enya was discovered by a worldwide audience. The LP sold a phenomenal four million copies, while its stunning single, "Orinoco Flow/Sail Away" went to number one in nearly every country with a musical chart. The album's extraordinary success catapulted Enya into the ranks of world-class artists overnight. Music from *Watermark* was eventually heard in the hit films *L.A. Story* and *Green Card,* and it suddenly seemed that Enya was everyone's favorite new artist.

The development of her albums begins as Enya writes melodies with arranging help from Nicky Ryan, her manager. The music goes next to Roma Ryan, who pens the lyrics in English and works with Enya to decide which songs will be translated into Gaelic and which will be performed in English. Then the exacting work of recording commences.

Because Enya and Nicky insist on recording all vocals live to capture subtle nuances not possible through electronic enhancement, the intricate harmonies require untold hours in the studio, with Enya singing up to two hundred separate vocal parts. Small wonder then, that her most recent album, *Shepherd Moons,* took over eighteen months of studio time to perfect.

But it was worth the wait. *Shepherd Moons,* like all of Enya's work, takes us to faraway places and reminds us that music—heartfelt and hearth-warmed—really can make the world, and our lives in it, better, more beautiful and, for at least the moment, peaceful.

CLUBS AND DISCOS

TD's (Union St., 071/61431) has rock on Thursdays and Saturdays, karaoke on Fridays and more traditional music Mondays, Wednesdays and Sundays—morning and night. The cover charge ranges from £1–£4, and the crowd tends toward youth, leather and volume. **The Adelaide** (Wine St. car park, 071/71113) has various rock bands Thursdays through Sundays (although Sundays are sometimes reserved for local folk bands). The crowd is stylish.

Murray's Bar on Connolly St. and **Club 2A Void** in the Clarence Hotel on Wine St. rock harder than most—the music ranges from indie to rap to alternative, from garage to ambient to raunch. Covers range from free to £4, and attitude is definitely necessary. Older folks (over thirty) might appreciate the **Blue Lagoon** (Riverside, 071/45407), which features both the **Oasis Nite Club** and the **Equinox Nite Club,** better—both specialize in light rock, jazz, piano bar and dancing to live acts.

The Limit (Wine St., 071/71113) rocks to hits of the '70s and '80s. No jeans or sneakers allowed. Ditto for the **Golf Links Hotel** (Strandhill, 071/68114). And finally, there's **Bonne Chere** (High St., 071/42014), which ranges from R&B to light rock—all of it for dancing.

PUBS AND TRADITIONAL MUSIC

Here's where Sligo really shines, with five traditional music spots for every disco. One of the oldest and the most famous is—like every other thing in town—named after the area's most famous historical citizen. **The Yeats Tavern** (Drumcliffe, 071/63117, 63668) offers great traditional music and not bad food either.

Another oldie is **Hargadon's** (O'Connell St., 071/70933), which features in addition to unbeatable jam sessions, mahogany counters, walls filled with memorabilia and a cast of old-codger residents who will talk your ear off about what constitutes good music. The **Pier Head House** (Mullaghmore, 071/66171) has an ever-changing roster of musical performers—some of them Irish traditional, others Irish country (bearing only a slight resemblance to American country). **Coragh Dtown** (Skreen, 071/66067) also has a schedule that blends Irish and country. **Harley's Inn** (Maugheraboy, 071/62973) offers Irish music Friday through Monday.

The **Orchard Inn** (Carney, 071/63116) is known for its outrageous jam sessions with musicians pouring from the floor lugging their instruments and an attitude that says "let's go for it."

Other spots to try include **Killoran's** (Tubbercurry, 071/85111, 85679), **McLynn's** (Market St., 071/42088), **Cissie Mac's** (Cashelgarron, 071/63323) and **The Railway Bar** (Lord Edward St., 071/62259—where you'll probably get Declan on the phone to tell you more than you want to know about performers and times).

FESTIVALS

The largest and most inclusive is the **Sligo Arts Festival** held in late September for ten days of musical bliss. All kinds of music are featured—classical, rock, jazz, traditional and dance. Street musicians add to the general mayhem, and it goes without saying that the city's pubs throng with musicians. Advance booking is necessary for the popular acts. Call the festival office at 071/69802.

Two smaller festivals are the **Summer Festival** in July, which includes a national fiddling competition that is not to be missed and the **South Sligo Traditional Music Festival,** which also takes place in July in Tubbercurry (south of Sligo). For information on either festival, contact the Sligo Tourist Board at 071/61201.

✪ Test Your Musical I.Q.

Match the Gaelic names for these instruments with their English counterparts:

1. *fidil*
2. *piopai*
3. *stoc*
4. *sturgan*
5. *octtedach*

6. *clairseach*

a) eight-string instrument
b) horn
c) short trumpet
d) Celtic harp
e) string instrument played with a bow
f) bagpipe

✪ ANSWERS TO TEST YOUR MUSICAL I.Q.

Page 277

1 g.,   2 h.,   3 f.,   4 i.,   5 j.,   6 a.,   7 e.,   8 b.,   9 c.,
10 d.,   11 k.,   12 o.,   13 n.,   14 p.,   15 l.,   16 m.

Page 304

1 e.,   2 f.,   3 c.,   4 b.,   5 a.,   6 d.,

Northern Ireland

Northern Ireland

Including   Belfast, Londonderry, and County Antrim

What you need to know about Northern Ireland is that it's a beauti-ful country with friendly people and a goodly number of musical goings-on. Yes, there was trouble then, and yes, there may be trouble again, but for now it seems, peace is the order of the day *"It's about time,"* reads a common bumper sticker, and about time it is. For twenty-five years Northern Ireland was, to all intents and purposes, engaged in Civil War. Shootings and bombings in which innocent bystanders were killed, were the order of the day. By conservative estimates, there were, at times, over eight thousand armed British soldiers loose throughout the country. In 1993 alone, more than 250 residents were killed and close to 2,000 wounded as Catholics and Protestants continued their two-decades-long conflict. But last year's political agreement between the Irish Republican Army (IRA) and the British government, brokered by the Clinton administration, has seen what appears to be the end of the violence.

By conservative estimates, there have at times been over eight thousand armed soldiers loose in Northern Ireland, and a lot of good it did those poor people. In 1993 more than two hundred fifty residents were killed and close to two thousand were wounded as Catholics and Protestants continued their two-decades-long conflict.

Amazingly, through it all, the arts scene in Belfast continued to flourish—some even refer to the current cultural climate as a "renais-sance." The city has a number of music halls, umpteen clubs and dis-cos and what seems like thousands of pubs which, in deference to "the troubles," have generally closed at 11 p.m. While the entertain-ment roster in other cities may be somewhat slim, the country has no dearth of festivals with which to take its mind off the political turmoil.

MUSICAL MOMENTS   Peace Together: Fighting Violence in Northern Ireland

Sometimes musicians come together on projects that benefit causes far from both their range of experience and their homeland. Other times, though, they zero in on problems close to home. In June of 1992, Peace Together was founded to make an album featuring a phenomenal collection of superstars performing songs related to the violence in Northern Ireland. Inspired by two Irish musicians, Ali McMordie (from Stiff Little Fingers) and Robert Hamilton (of The Fat Lady Sings), the Peace Together project was a call to end the troubles in Northern Ireland by highlighting the effect of war on young people there and across the globe.

Ali McMordie was inspired to organize the Peace Together Trust by his own upbringing in Belfast under street-violent conditions that he says "no young person should have to endure." He felt that the project would "get people talking about the situation" and that through the music, there could come about some sort of "solidarity."

While the organizing talents of McMordie and Hamilton were crucial to the project's realization, it was the extraordinary musical talent that turned the project's album into the hugely successful effort it was. The album's opener, "Be Still" combined the talents of Peter Gabriel, Sinead O'Connor, Fergal Sharkey (of the Undertones) and Nanci Griffith. Other highlights included "Satellite of Love" performed by U2 and Lou Reed, two songs penned by Elvis Costello—"Peace in Our Time" performed by Carter and the Unstoppable Sex Machine and "Oliver's Army" performed by Blur—and "Religious Persuasion" performed by Billy Bragg, Andy White and Sinead O'Connor.

As a result of all this combined effort, Peace Together became a project of major significance. Hundreds of thousands of dollars were raised to benefit the Peace Together Trust Fund, which continues to support cross-community cultural activities for the young people of Northern Ireland.

Peace Together—Sharkey, Gabriel, O'Connor

BELFAST

Northern Ireland's capital city is home to more than one-third of the area's population. Long known as an industrial center, the city has, in the last decade, gone through a reassessment of its potential, with a marked increase in commercial investment in its downtown sections and a corresponding increase in the number of related pubs, restaurants and discos.

Despite what you may have read about Belfast in the past, this historic city is definitely worth a trip—especially since it's only a two-hour train ride from Dublin and a wonderful base for exploring the surrounding hills. And while you're there, be sure to check out as many musical venues as you can. Regardless of its many troubles—or maybe because of them—the people of Belfast are anything but slackers when it comes to supporting a thriving music scene. Just remember, *orange* is the color to wear here—not green—although with the new peace, even fashion choices may change.

CONCERT HALLS

Classical music is alive and well in Belfast with four major halls devoted to its promotion. The largest is **Ulster Hall** (Bedford St., 0232/323900), home of the Ulster Orchestra. The hall, however, sponsors musical productions of many types—from rock to large-scale choral and symphonic works. Ticket prices range from £5–£15, and good seats for popular performances are usually sold out way in advance.

SPOTLIGHT ON   THE ULSTER ORCHESTRA

The Ulster Orchestra was formed in 1966 and expanded to symphony size in 1981. It includes among its many regular activities a winter concert series in Ulster Hall, Belfast, concerts throughout Northern Ireland and an annual visit to Dublin. It also plays a major role in the Belfast Festival at Queens, accompanies Opera Northern Ireland and hosts the summer Proms season in Belfast.

The orchestra has appeared on several occasions at the Henry Woods Proms at the Royal Albert Hall, London, as well as touring abroad. It also plays an important educational role giving many concerts in schools throughout the Province and, in addition to its extensive broadcasting commitments to BBC Television and Radio, maintains an ambitious recording program with Chandos Records.

The **Grand Opera House** (Great Victoria St., 0232/241919) is a recently—and lavishly—refurbished turn-of-the-century Victorian theater that offers a wide variety of entertainment options from international opera and ballet companies to major popular entertainers. There are generally no performances in late July and early August, but check just in case.

Queen's University Concert Hall (0232/245133) also offers a wide variety of performers as well as serving as the home of the Belfast Festival (see festival listings) for which advance booking is definitely necessary. Ticket prices range widely (from £4–£20).

King's Hall (Lisburn Rd., 0232/665225) serves mainly as a venue for concerts by superstars such as Van Morrison and Sinead O'Connor. Book early. The **Lyric Theatre** (Ridgeway St., 0232/381081) offers live entertainment ranging from musicals to dance. And the Arts Theatre (Botanic Ave., 0232/324936) offers popular productions, many of them musicals of the "Cats" variety.

One final venue: **St. George's Church** (High St., 0232/231275) sponsors an ongoing concert program (generally on Tuesday, Thursday, Saturday and Sunday). Tickets go on sale one month before each performance, and prices generally range from £4–£13.

CLUBS AND DISCOS

Belfast's nightlife changes more frequently than most other cities, so you should call ahead to make sure your destination hasn't become a new shopping center. The club scene is generally casual—lots of black leather and silver studs—and if you're averse to being in smoke-filled places, you might just want to settle for a nice walk along the water instead. Remember: there's an 11 p.m. curfew (this may change as peace becomes the norm), which means you have to be in the door by then. After that, closing times vary, but Belfast is not one of the world's late-night capitals.

The Duke of York (Commercial St. off Lower Donegall St., 0232/241062) is on two levels, both with live bands (including reggae) on Friday and Saturday. This is a very popular, very crowded place. Admission: around £4. **Brewsters** (71 Main St., Ballyclare [just north of Belfast], 0960/322475) has a late bar every Thursday, Friday, and Saturday night. The music tends toward rock and R&B. The admission is between £3–£4.

The Deer's Head Emporium (facing Castlecourt, 0232/239163) has a late bar and free admission. Music ranges from rock to soul to heavy metal. The **Ivanhoe Inn** (556 Saintfield Rd., Carryduff, 0232/812240) offers jazz on Wednesday and soft rock on Saturday in the lounge. There's no cover downstairs, and £2.50 to get into the upstairs club, which features '60s and '70s disco. This place attracts a slightly older crowd than most (over twenty-four).

Frame's Bar and Restaurant (beside the Belfast Telegraph, 0232/244855) has special food promotions (a three-course meal for £12 including a bottle of wine, £18 Thursday, Friday and Saturday) and music and a late bar Wednesday–Sunday. The music varies from rock to jazz to lite. **Empire Bar** (42 Botanic Ave., 0232/228110) is a huge place with a sporadic music schedule. When there *is* music, it's sometimes jazz, sometimes rock and metal. Each type seems to draw its own audience; the former, a yuppie briefcase crowd, the latter, young slackers.

SPOTLIGHT ON THERAPY?

"We all need struggle," says Therapy?'s lead singer and guitarist, Andy Cairns. "If the world was peaceful and calm and everybody loved each other it wouldn't be a very interesting place to live, would it?" To Cairns, struggle is mother's milk. Whether he's asserting that "all people are shite" (on the ferocious opening track of the group's new album, *Troublegum*) or admitting "the world is fucked and so am I" (on *Troublegum's* infectious riff-rocker "Stop It You're Killing Me") Cairns's unique world view—call it slapstick nihilism—comes through with bilious glee.

With the advent of the group's most recent album, the term "struggle" takes on a whole new meaning. Once again, Therapy? has reinvented its sound—gone are the shrieks and growls and gnashing power tools of past efforts. This time, the Irish trio kicks off much of the postindustrial shrouding that has defined them in the past and gives full focus to the ominously churning power at their core.

"We just got really bored with sampling," explains bassist Michael McKeegan. "We didn't feel we had to hide behind samples and constant chord changes anymore. I think it's partially a matter of increased confidence and partially not wanting to be one of those bands that puts out the same record year after year."

McKeegan needn't worry. In the six years since Therapy?'s first gigs around its Belfast hometown earned raves for the intoxicating distillation of hardcore's energy and pop's melodiousness,

McKeegan, Cairns and drummer and vocalist Fyfe Ewing have seldom repeated a step in their intricate dance on the grave of rock convention. *Troublegum* continues this assault on stagnancy, firing fourteen territory-defining rounds. With its swipes at religion, and psychotic travelogues into the heads of, among others, serial killer Jeffrey Dahmer, *Troublegum's* innards remain as soiled and twisted as Therapy?'s boosters have come to expect. Because, as Andy Cairns insists, success isn't about to spoil these rock hunters.

PUBS AND TRADITIONAL MUSIC

Pubs are very popular with Belfastians of all ages. Many have music saisáns, and the music is of the spare variety that generally typifies Northern Ireland—fiddles and flutes and no extra notes—very unlike the hip-hoppy, jubilant melodies of the rest of the British Isles. A few of the best pubs to try are **The Errigle Inn** (Ormeau Rd., 0232/641410), which has nightly saisáns upstairs; **Liverpool Bar** (Donegall Quay, 0232/324769), which prides itself—if you hadn't guessed by its name—on presenting a veddy English front. The music is good, though; **Kelly's Cellars** (30 Bank St., 0232/324835), which offers blues, folk and occasional traditional *saisáns* on weekend nights; **Pat's Bar** (Prince's Dock St., 0232/744524), a very atmospheric dockside pub with great music *saisáns* (check for times and dates); and **Madden's** (Smithfield, 0232/244114), which has a wide variety of ales and set music *saisáns* on Friday, Saturday and Sunday.

MUSIC WITH DINNER

Dining and dancing is a very popular form of entertainment in Belfast. In some places the music ranges from lite to jazz to big band, but others have what is called "carvery dances," which means music of a more traditional variety.

Tudor Lodge (0232/777017, 777623) has a type of dining/dancing plans (appetizer plus main course, including music for £5; just music for £2; or a larger meal and music for £7). Call to find out who's performing—you might want to avoid "sing along with Bobby Stinton—organist, vocalist, guitarist and cabaret artist," one of their regulars. Otherwise, this is a pretty good place.

The **Homestead Inn** (Drumbo, 0232/826273) has dinner dances on Saturday nights for £12.95. The music is '60s, '70s and best of the rest, which means lite. **The Royal Ascot** (Carryduff, 0232/812127) has a resident DJ on Saturday and live entertainment otherwise. Food and music are £11.50. This is an over-twenty-one, "smart dress" facility.

Passion, whether great or not, must never be expressed in an exaggerated manner, and music—even in the most harrowing moment—ought never to offend the ear, but should always remain music, which desires to give pleasure.

WOLFGANG AMADEUS MOZART

FESTIVALS

The biggest and best is the **Belfast Festival at Queen's**, which shares billing with the Edinburgh Festival as one of the two largest festivals in Great Britain. First presented in the '60s, the festival is now a mega-event with many arts (music, drama and film) and a distinct emphasis on music. Although classical music is favored, you'll also find a wide variety of jazz and folk performers. The setting is mainly the beautiful Victorian campus of Queen's University, but other locations are utilized as well, including the Grand Opera House, Ulster Hall and the Lyric Theatre. Advance booking is a must for this three-week event in November. For information and tickets, contact the Festival House, 8 Malone Rd., Belfast, BT9 5BN, Northern Ireland; 0232/667687).

SPOTLIGHT ON   JAMES GALWAY

James Galway is regarded as both a supreme interpreter of the classical flute repertoire and a consummate entertainer whose appeal crosses all musical boundaries. His virtuoso playing has placed him at the forefront of the classical-music world, while his lively sense of humor and ebullient character have made him popular with a vast and diverse audience. Through his extensive touring, his nearly fifty best-selling albums, his frequent television appearances and his holiday specials, Galway has endeared himself to millions of people.

Born in Belfast, Galway began playing the pennywhistle as a small child before switching to the flute. After playing for fewer than two years, he won top prize in three categories at a local flute competition and decided that this new instrument was to be his life. He continued his studies at the Royal College of Music, the Guildhall School in London and the Paris Conservatory.

Galway began his career as an orchestral flute player with the Wind Band of the Royal Shakespeare Theatre at Stratford-Upon-Avon. Subsequent posts at the Sadler's Wells Opera and the Royal Opera Covent Garden led to positions with the BBC Symphony Orchestra (playing piccolo) and with the London Symphony and the Royal Philharmonic in which he was principal flute. In 1969 Galway was appointed principal flute of the prestigious Berlin Philharmonic. In 1975 he set out on his own as a soloist. Within one year he had played one hundred twenty concerts, including appearances with all four of London's major orchestras.

Since then, he has circled the globe many times, keeping his artistry fresh with a healthy mixture of recitals, concerto appearances, chamber-music engagements, popular-music concerts and master classes. In addition to his regular performances of the standard classical repertoire, he often features contemporary music on his program and commissions a new flute concerto each season. He has also received Record of the Year awards from both *Billboard* and *Cash Box* magazines, as well as platinum and gold albums.

The **Belfast Music Festival** takes place during two weeks in late February through early March and includes declamation speech, drama, and music. This festival has been held every year since 1911 and is a real window into Belfast's everyday life; the **Early Music Festival** held in mid-March for two weeks features performances of thirteenth- and fourteenth-century pieces—many on original instruments.

The **St. Patrick's Day Celebration** includes parades, pilgrimages, street music, indoor music performances and a never-ending host of events. The events are held, naturally, on March 17. The **Belfast Civic Festival** takes place during the first two weeks of May and features concerts, competitions, tours and exhibitions. The Lord Mayor's Show (May 7) fills the city's streets with colorful floats and bands.

The **Jazz and Blues Festival** features international stars and many well-known jazz and blues players from England and Ireland. Venues are in both Belfast and Holywood; festival dates are generally in mid-June. This is a three-day event. The **Belfast Folk Festival** consists of poetry and dancing, in addition to music. Visiting artists and musicians enliven the local folk scene. Advance booking is generally necessary. The festival takes place during the second week of August.

Just north of Belfast on the Belfast Lough's northern shore is Carrickfergus Castle which, in summer, hosts an ongoing series of medieval banquets and crafts fairs. The banquets are multicourse meals accompanied by traditional music. They range in price from £10–£15. Call 096/035-1273 for more information.

Information for the following of Belfast's many festivals can be obtained by contacting the Tourist Information Centre, 59 North St., Belfast, BT1 1NB, Northern Ireland; 0232/246609.

LONDONDERRY

Known simply as "Derry," Londonderry is really two cities divided by twenty-foot-high, seventeenth-century walls. Inside the walls, all is cultural richness and historical beauty—Georgian and Victorian architecture, cobbled streets, the 1633 Gothic cathedral of St. Columb, ancient pubs. Outside the walls are also plenty of historical sites. The Guildhall, looking much like its counterpart in London, is there as well as a tiny crafts village tucked in behind the O'Doherty Tower. But there's more to this locale. You'll see factories, low-income slums, barbed wire and the remains of hundreds of years of violence.

And yet, Londonderry may well be one of Great Britain's most underrated towns. Not only is it one of the fastest-growing cities in the north, but it has a cultural life that is largely unparalleled. In the words of St. Columb, "The angels of God sang in the glades of Derry and every leaf held its angel."

CONCERT HALLS

Londonderry has a very strong musical tradition, and as you roam through the streets, you're likely to see musicians everywhere. The **Guildhall** (Shipquay Pl., 0504/365151) is the city's major entertainment venue. From opera to chamber music to jazz concerts to performances by the Ulster Orchestra, you'll find it all here. Tickets range from £4–£14 and, since this is *the* place to go, advance booking is necessary.

POP QUIZ 19

Who, born Helen Porter Mitchell in Australia of Scottish parents, was one of the three greatest opera stars of the nineteenth century?

ANSWER: Dame Nellie Melba

Other possibilities include **The Orchard Gallery** (Orchard St., 0504/269675), which hosts occasional musical events at, among other places, St. Columb's Hall; and **Magee College of the University of Ulster** (north of the city, 0504/265621). You might also want to check out **Long Tower Church** on Bishop St., which offers occasional musical programs.

CLUBS, PUBS AND TRADITIONAL MUSIC

Derry's informal nightlife is very limited. Because it's a college town, however, you'll always find a spirit of revelry if you look hard enough. Beware: closing time is 11 p.m. Residents of Derry may get rowdier and drunker than you might be used to, and walking in unfamiliar areas late at night (especially outside the walls) may not be the wisest thing. But the long years of "siege mentality" may also have thrown a positive light on the entertainment: when people feel oppressed, it usually draws them together in ways not possible in, for example, laid-back southern California. Ponder that as you check out the

MUSICAL MOMENTS   *"Danny Boy"*

One of the best known of the old tunes and the one most closely associated with the American-Irish experience is "Danny Boy," which was originally titled "Londonderry Air" (or "Air from County Derry"). Hailed by the English composer Sir Hubert Parry as the most beautiful melody ever written, the song was first collected and published in 1855 without title or words, and the identity of the composer has never really been ascertained. By the 1870s, the tune had acquired two different sets of lyrics—one, "My Gentle Harp" by Thomas Moore, the other, "Would God I Were the Tender Apple Blossom" by Katherine Hinkson. In 1913 Fred Weatherly recreated it as "Danny Boy," the version that became an overnight hit both in Ireland and among the one-million-strong Irish-American community.

Danny Boy

Oh Danny Boy, the pipes, the pipes are calling
From glen to glen, and down the mountainside,
The summer's gone, and all the roses falling,
It's you, it's you must go, and I must bide.
But come ye back when summer's in the meadow,
Or when the valley's hushed and white with snow,
It's I'll be here in sunshine or in shadow,
Oh Danny Boy, oh Danny Boy, I love you so!
But when ye come, and all the flow'rs are dying,
If I am dead, as dead I well may be,
Ye'll come and find the place where I am lying,
And kneel and say an Ave there for me;
And I shall hear, though soft you tread above me,
And all my grave will warmer, sweeter be,
For you will bend and tell me that you love me,
And I shall sleep in peace until you come to me.

following suggestions. One more thing: Derry bars are very fond of what they call "quiz evenings" where local teams pit their intelligence quotients against each other. These are great fun to watch, and who knows—you might get to chime in.

Dungloe Bar (Waterloo St., 0504/267716) has traditional music and atmosphere to spare. **Gweedore Bar** (Waterloo St., 0504/263513) has both resident gigs and informal sessions. **Castle Bar** (Waterloo St., 0504/263118) has good food and the old-fashioned looks of a quiet country bar. Check out the very good informal sessions. **Phoenix Bar** (Park Ave., Rosemount, 0504/268978) is a good place to go when you feel like big, young crowds and expansive conversation against a backdrop of regular fiddlers who will have you singing along before you know it.

The Derby (63 Great James St., 0504/361635) is pretty low-key, in both food and music. Try this spot when you need to relax. **The Clarendon Bar** (44 Strand Rd., 0504/263705) offers traditional Irish music several nights a week. The **Everglades Hotel** (Prehen Rd., 0504/467222) has live piano music nightly from 9 p.m.–11 p.m.

SPOTLIGHT ON VAN MORRISON

Van Morrison doesn't give interviews. He can be (and usually is) downright obnoxious when asked to sit for a standard question-and-answer routine. He articulates through his music—a collective body of work that spans almost thirty years, dozens of albums and a lifetime's worth of extraordinary vision.

Morrison was born in Belfast on August 31, 1945. His early work blended a variety of musical genres: skiffle, blues, R&B, jazz, bluegrass—you name it, Van did it.

In 1967 after eight years of seven-day-a-week gigging, Warner president Joe Smith recognized Morrison's genius and signed him to a contract. The result was *Astral Weeks*—one of the phenomenal albums of all time and a milestone in contemporary rock music. The eight tracks breathe with life—both life remembered and life lived. What's difficult to imagine is that Van was only twenty-two when he recorded the LP.

Throughout his career, Morrison has been known as much for his artistry as for the prodigiousness of his output. His early albums include *Moondance* (1969); *Van Morrison: His Band and the Street Choir* (1970); *Tupelo Honey* (1971), the cover of which shows Morrison with his wife, Janet Plant, on a farm in California's Marin County; the bluesy *St. Domenic's Preview* (1972); *Hard Nose the Highway* (1973); the live album *It's Too Late To Stop Now* (1974); and *A Period of Transition* (1977), which is a collaboration between Morrison and Dr. John.

A later LP, *No Guru, No Method, No Teacher* arrived in the summer of 1986, and once again Van Morrison was hailed as a musician of enormous stature and ability. What distinguished this work from others was its use of classical arrangements in which instruments such as cor angalis, classical guitar, oboe, grand piano and strings contoured the vocals to provide a chamber-music effect. On top of this, *No Guru* retained the traditional Irish flavor that has come to be associated with Morrison's later albums. Two more recent albums, *Enlightenment* and *Too Long in Exile* were critical and popular successes.

While the two most significant elements of Morrison's success have always been his voice, with its proximity to the sound of a saxophone, and his ability to excel in a variety of musical genres, he is most revered as a jazz composer—skilled in his craft and a perfectionist who, like John Coltrane and Miles Davis, reserves the right to control his image.

And control his image he does. Throughout his career, Morrison has found the interview situation a difficult one to handle and rarely, if ever, opens out his character this way. But a look at the contents of *No Guru* or any of his other autobiographical albums offers all anyone needs to know about this man who has so consistently proven his musical genius.

FESTIVALS

Derry boasts one of the most enjoyable events in all the British Isles—the **Busking Festival,** held late in August and attracting some of the most unusual street musicians you've ever seen—everything from skateboarding mimes juggling candelabras as they jump over five garbage pails to dwarf tap dancers tapping to the music of Fats

Waller. Cash prizes are offered to the top participants. For more information, contact the Londonderry Tourist Information Center at 8 Bishop St., 0504/267824.

POP QUIZ 20

Which '60s folk rocker is the father of actress Ione Skye?

ANSWER: Donovan

The **Lughnasa Festival** is a street- and river-based summer festival held early in August, which marks the traditional quarterly feast of the Irish year with music, theater, street performers and games. Contact the tourist bureau at 0504/267824. The **Fourth of July Festival** commemorates—are you ready for this—American Independance Day. This is a popular music festival featuring jazz, cajun and bluegrass, as well as outdoor street performances.

Octoberfest is Londonderry's time to celebrate dance, film, theater, literature, jazz and folk music and just about any other art form they can drum up. The entire city gets involved in this one, which continues for the entire month of October; it's a great time to party. Also in October is the **Pub Corporation Comedy Festival,** which takes place in some of the city's most picturesque pubs. Musicians provide the break between comedy acts.

COUNTY ANTRIM

The lunar landscape of the Giant's Causeway, lurking below the gaunt sea wall where the land ends, must have struck wonder into the hearts of the ancient Irish. Like them, Thackeray was very impressed by the strangeness of this place. "When the world was moulded and fashioned out of formless chaos, this must have been the bit over—a remnant of chaos," he wrote after his initial visit. What you'll probably be doing a lot of when you're here is walking, which is why you'll appreciate all the more a good pub and a great informal *saisán* of the enthusiastic music for which the people of County Antrim are known.

A few pubs you might try are **The Crosskeys Inn** (33 Grange St., off the main Randalstown-Portglenoe Rd., 0648/50694), which has multiple ongoing *saisáns* (sometimes as many as four bands play at once). The atmosphere is great, especially on a chilly night when the fire's going.

Joe McCullum's (23 Mill St., Cushendell) has lively traditional nights on Thursdays and Saturdays, which feature fiddlers from all over the county. The **Dunluce Centre** (0265/834444) is a virtual entertainment complex in Portrush, which offers ongoing, if sporadic, musical performances.

FESTIVALS

Antrim's **Oul' Lammas Fair** is Ireland's oldest traditional fair (chartered in 1606) and includes horse and sheep sales, hundreds of street stalls, homemade toffee known as "yellow man," edible seaweed called "dulse" and more music than you'll know what to do with. In the old days, it lasted a week, and there was plenty of matchmaking, as well as horse trading. Today, the fun is packed into two hectic days at the end of August. The event takes place in Ballycastle. For info, call 0232/333000. The **Fleadh Amhr n agus Rince** is a traditional festival of song and dance. It takes place at Ballycastle in mid-June for three days.

> *If I had to live my life again, I would have made it a rule to*
>
> *read some poetry and listen to some music at least once every*
>
> *week, for perhaps the part of my brain now atrophied would*
>
> *then have been kept active through use.*
>
> CHARLES DARWIN

The **Feis na nGleann** is a traditional Irish competition of dancing, music, poetry, crafts and sports. This feis originated in the last century and is a great opportunity for visitors to see sports like hurling, camogie and other Gaelic games. It happens in late June for three days in Carey, Ballycastle. The **Festival of Twentieth Century Music,** also in Ballycastle, is a biennial event held in April featuring both local and international performers and composers.

THE REST OF NORTHERN IRELAND

The best source of information for events throughout Northern Ireland, including prices and ticket availability, is the Tourist Information Centre at 0232/246609.

COUNTY DOWN

As with all other parts of Ireland, County Down goes a little crazy on March 17, the feast of St. Patrick. **St. Patrick's Week** here includes an important pilgrimage to the Slemish Mountains (1,437 ft.) where Patrick, the boy slave, was said to have herded swine for his master Miluic. The celebration also includes musical and other events in and around Downpatrick where Patrick established Ireland's first monastery. The **Fiddler's Green Folk Festival** is a five-day festival which takes place in Rostrevor in the first week of August and attracts international singers and musicians to this small town in the foothills of the Mourne Mountains.

COUNTY FERMANAGH

The **Fiddle Stone Festival** draws musicians from all over Ireland to the pretty lakeside village of Belleek (west of Belfast) to play in honor of various and sundry eighteenth-century fiddlers. It takes place during the last week of June and the first week of July.

COUNTY ARMAGH

The *Ulster Fleadh Cheoil* is a major traditional festival that attracts the best performers and dancers from all over the U. K. This is part of **Armagh Together**, which takes place during the third week of July for three days. The **International Mummer's Festival** is a week-long cavalcade of folk dance, music and "rhyming." It happens in mid-January.

| SPOTLIGHT ON | TOMMY MAKEM: THE BARD OF ARMAGH |

When you go to one of Tommy Makem's concerts, expect to be hurled headlong into a roaring good time before you know what hit you. He is a weaver of magical evenings on records, concert tours or in his own Tommy Makem's Irish Pavillion in New York City.

Armed with his banjo, his tin whistle, his sense of poetry and stagecraft, his bottomless store of songs and, most of all, his baritone voice, Tommy Makem has been redefining Irish music for more than thirty years.

A rare thing is Tommy Makem: singer, storyteller, actor and songwriter. He has written hundreds of songs, and many of them, such as the classic "Four Green Fields," "Gentle Annie," "The Rambles of Spring," "The Boys of Killybegs" and "Farewell to Carlingford," are standards in the repertoire of folk singers around the world.

Some of Makem's songs hark back to the bad old days of the Irish experience, but most of them bring Irish and Irish-Americans into a new vision of themselves as vibrant, creative people who do things, instead of having things done to them. The message in the songs of Tommy Makem is that it's a grand thing, indeed, to be a Gael.

As the son of the legendary song collector and folk singer Sarah Makem, he grew up surrounded by songs going back to the earliest mists of Irish history. The tunes he learned at his mother's knee in Keady, County Armagh, were the foundations for his dizzying rise to international stardom with the Clancy Brothers, as a duet act with Liam Clancy and, of course, as a brilliant solo performer.

By the time he was seventeen, Tommy Makem had taken to the stage and was the star performer with the Keady Dramatic Society. He won acting awards at drama festivals all over Ireland and any number of invitations to turn professional, most notably with Old Vic, England's famous classical theater ensemble. If that weren't enough, young Makem was also the lead singer with the Clippertones Show Band, whistle player with the local ceili band, lead baritone in his church choir and a piper in the local pipe band.

But like many young Irishmen and Irishwomen through the centuries, Makem saw that the future lay in America, and so he emigrated in 1956. He settled in Dover, New Hampshire, a mill town that served as a magnet for many of Keady's young who could find no work at home in Northern Ireland.

In 1961 Makem went to Rhode Island for an event that would change the course of his life. He appeared in the Newport Folk Festival, where he and Joan Baez were honored as the most promising newcomers on the folk music scene.

After that, Makem was as much in demand as a singer as an actor. Together with the Clancy Brothers, he played to packed houses around the world, from Carnegie Hall in New York to London's Royal Albert Theatre, Boston's Symphony Hall, and the soaring Sydney Opera House. The Clancy Brothers and Tommy Makem became the four most famous Irishmen in the world in a phenomenon that resembled Beatlemania in its intensity.

Makem left the Clancys in 1969 to establish a solo singing career. He immediately sold out the Felt Forum in New York's Madison Square Garden, and went on to three sold-out concerts at Carnegie Hall, three sold-out tours of Australia and many highly successful concert tours in Ireland and Great Britain.

Incredibly, Makem found time between concerts to do two television series for Scottish television; a series for BBC in Belfast; a series for Ulster Television; a nationally syndicated series for CHCH-TV in Hamilton, Ontario, which ran fifty-two weeks for four years; a network series for CBC from Vancouver, B. C.; and several one-hour specials for Radio Telefis Eireann in Dublin.

In April 1987 Makem was honored with a gold medal from the Eire Society of Boston for his contributions to Irish culture, and *Irish America* magazine named him one of the top one hundred Irish-Americans. The hyphen is appropriate, for Tommy Makem has distinguished himself as both the Bard of Armagh and one of the finest folk singers on the American scene.

Index

Notes

Notes

Notes

Notes

Notes

Notes

Notes

Notes

Notes

Notes

Notes

TRAVEL AND CULTURE BOOKS

"World at Its Best" Travel Series
Britain, France, Germany, Hawaii,
Holland, Hong Kong, Italy, Spain,
Switzerland, London, New York, Paris,
Washington, D.C., San Francisco

**Passport's Travel Guides and
References**
IHT Guides to Business Travel in Asia &
Europe
Only in New York
Mystery Reader's Walking Guides:
London, England, New York, Chicago
Chicago's Best-Kept Secrets
London's Best-Kept Secrets
New York's Best-Kept Secrets
The Japan Encyclopedia
Japan Today!
Japan at Night
Japan Made Easy
Discovering Cultural Japan
Living in Mexico
The Hispanic Way
Guide to Ethnic Chicago
Guide to Ethnic London
Guide to Ethnic New York
Guide to Ethnic Montreal
Passport's Trip Planner & Travel Diary
Chinese Etiquette and Ethics in Business
Korean Etiquette and Ethics in Business
Japanese Etiquette and Ethics in Business
How to Do Business with the Japanese
Japanese Cultural Encounters
The Japanese

Passport's Regional Guides of France
Auvergne, Provence, Loire Valley,
Dordogne & Lot, Languedoc,
Brittany, South West France,
Normandy & North West France,
Paris, Rhône Valley & Savoy, France
for the Gourmet Traveler

**Passport's Regional Guides of
Indonesia**
New Guinea, Java, Borneo, Bali, East of
Bali, Sumatra, Spice Islands, Sulawesi,
Exploring the Islands of Indonesia

Up-Close Guides
Paris, London, Manhattan, Amsterdam,
Rome

Passport's "Ticket To..." Series
Italy, Germany, France, Spain

**Passport's Guides: Asia, Africa, Latin
America, Europe, Middle East**
Japan, Korea, Malaysia, Singapore, Bali,
Burma, Australia, New Zealand, Egypt,
Kenya, Philippines, Portugal, Moscow,
St. Petersburg, The Georgian Republic,
Mexico, Vietnam, Iran, Berlin, Turkey

Passport's China Guides
All China, Beijing, Fujian, Guilin,
Hangzhou & Zhejiang, Hong Kong,
Macau, Nanjing & Jiangsu, Shanghai,
The Silk Road, Taiwan, Tibet, Xi'an,
The Yangzi River, Yunnan

Passport's India Guides
All India; Bombay & Goa; Dehli, Agra &
Jaipur; Burma; Pakistan; Kathmandu
Valley; Bhutan; Museums of India; Hill
Stations of India

Passport's Thai Guides
Bangkok, Phuket, Chiang Mai, Koh Sumi

On Your Own Series
Brazil, Israel

"Everything Under the Sun" Series
Spain, Barcelona, Toledo, Seville,
Marbella, Cordoba, Granada, Madrid,
Salamanca, Palma de Majorca

Passport's Travel Paks
Britain, France, Italy, Germany, Spain

Exploring Rural Europe Series
England & Wales, France, Greece,
Ireland, Italy, Spain, Austria, Germany,
Scotland, Ireland by Bicycle

Regional Guides of Italy
Florence & Tuscany, Naples &
Campania, Umbria, the Marches &
San Marino

Passport Maps
Europe, Britain, France, Italy, Holland,
Belgium & Luxembourg, Scandinavia,
Spain & Portugal, Switzerland, Austria
&the Alps

Passport's Trip Planners & Guides
California, France, Greece, Italy

PASSPORT BOOKS
a division of *NTC Publishing Group.*
Lincolnwood Illinois U.S.A.